MAY CONTAIN
TRACES
OF MAGIC

By Tom Holt

Expecting Someone Taller
Who's Afraid of Beowulf?
Flying Dutch
Ye Gods!
Overtime
Here Comes the Sun
Grailblazers
Faust Among Equals
Odds and Gods
Djinn Rummy
My Hero
Paint Your Dragon
Open Sesame
Wish You Were Here
Only Human
Snow White and the Seven Samurai
Valhalla
Nothing But Blue Skies
Falling Sideways
Little People
The Portable Door
In Your Dreams
Earth, Air, Fire and Custard
You Don't Have to be Evil to Work Here, But It Helps
Someone Like Me
Barking
The Better Mousetrap
May Contain Traces of Magic

Dead Funny: Omnibus 1
Mightier Than the Sword: Omnibus 2
The Divine Comedies: Omnibus 3
For Two Nights Only: Omnibus 4
Tall Stories: Omnibus 5
Saints and Sinners: Omnibus 6
Fishy Wishes: Omnibus 7

The Walled Orchard
Alexander at the World's End
Olympiad
A Song for Nero
Meadowland

I, Margaret

Lucia Triumphant
Lucia in Wartime

TOM HOLT

MAY CONTAIN TRACES OF MAGIC

orbit

www.orbitbooks.net
www.tom-holt.com

ORBIT

First published in Great Britain in 2009 by Orbit

Copyright © 2009 by The One Reluctant Lemming Co. Ltd

The moral right of the author has been asserted.

A CIP catalogue record for this book
is available from the British Library.

ISBN 978-1-84149-505-7

Typeset in Plantin by M Rules
Printed and bound in Great Britain by
Clay Ltd, St Ives plcs

Papers used by Orbit are natural, renewable and recyclable
products sourced from well-managed forests and certified
in accordance with the rules of the Forest Stewardship Council.

Mixed Sources
Product group from well-managed
forests and other controlled sources
www.fsc.org Cert no. SGS-COC-004081
© 1996 Forest Stewardship Council

FSC

Orbit
An imprint of
Little, Brown Book Group
100 Victoria Embankment
London EC4Y 0DY

An Hachette UK Company
www.hachette.co.uk

www.orbitbooks.net

To my father; who carried the bag with humour.
And to all salesmen everywhere.

CHAPTER ONE

He was losing her, he could tell. The polite smile was still there, but the eyes were glazing over, the mind was drifting away. Right, he thought.

'Or there's the new BB27Ks,' he said, increasing the volume just a trifle. 'I think they'd do really well for you. Ever since we brought them out, it's been phenomenal.'

He'd got her back, just for a moment. 'I read about them,' she said; just enough enthusiasm to dirty a microscope slide, but that was something like a ninety per cent improvement. 'How are they going?'

'Brilliant,' he said, 'absolutely brilliant. Doing very nicely. Everywhere I go, people keep telling me they're just flying off the shelves.'

Immediately, he knew he'd said the wrong thing; her mouth tightened, her eyes narrowed a little. No idea why. 'In fact, we're doing a special . . .' he started to say, but a flicker of movement behind her head snagged his attention and he dried up. On the top row of the shelf unit facing him, a cardboard box had just sprouted wings.

Sod it, he thought. The NM66.

'Um,' he said, as the box stretched, preened its light grey feathers and made a soft cheeping noise. The shopkeeper looked round, swore and grabbed at it, but it was too late. The box spread its wings, hopped off the shelf and glided lazily, just out of reach of the shopkeeper's flailing hands, over their heads, out through the open door into the street.

She looked at him.

'We're working on that,' he said sheepishly. 'Bit of a snarl-up with quality control, but they promise me the next batch . . .'

'Fifteen of them,' she said bitterly. 'In just one week.'

'It's the mating season,' he mumbled. 'But they've completely redesigned the DNA sequence, and that'll sort it, no problem. Meanwhile, if you'll just do us a returns note for the, um, escaped stock, we'll get that straightened out for you, and . . .'

He ran out of words. The expression on her face was quite clear: forget it, don't bother, save your breath. But that wasn't his way. He sucked in a little air, and said brightly, 'So, shall I put you down for three dozen of the BB27K, for starters? We're offering special display materials, dumpbins, special promotional . . .'

'No, thanks,' she said.

Oh, he thought. Right, fine. 'Well, I guess that's about it for today, then. Thanks ever so much for seeing me, and I'll be back again first week in June. Meanwhile, if there's anything I can help you with . . .'

It was like pouring water into sand. He was used to it, but that didn't make it fun. And it'd be nice, just once, if he got a chance to end a sentence with something other than three dots. He smiled, closed the lid of his briefcase, thanked her once again for her time and left the shop.

It was raining outside, needless to say, as though tears for the miserable fate of all salesmen everywhere were rolling down heaven's face. One of these days, he thought, I'll get a proper job, in an office, and I won't have to do this any more. One of these days.

He looked up, and saw the stray NM66 perched on top of a nearby traffic light. Stupid bloody things, he thought as the box, now distinctly damp, cooed mildly at him; not enough sense to stay out of the rain, it'll get all soggy and fall to bits if it's not careful.

He walked back to his car, which winked its indicators at him as he thumbed the plastic key thing. At least someone's pleased to see me, he thought.

Before he drove off, he filled in the order form. That didn't take long. No BB27Ks, no GP19s, he'd been stone-cold certain he'd be able to shift a couple of outers of YJ42s but no dice. Just a couple of trays of AA1s and the inevitable repeat order for DW6 . . .

That made him frown, as it always did. DW6: one of the firm's biggest sellers, but in seven years he'd yet to meet anybody who knew what the stupid stuff was actually *for*. It was, by any criteria, the weirdest, most totally improbable concept he'd come across (and in this business, that was saying a lot). None of the reps knew what it was supposed to do, the buyers hadn't got a clue, the shop managers and sales assistants didn't know; but *the customers bought it*, by the bucketful, by the skipload, so—

Never mind, he told himself firmly as he switched on the SatNav and waited for it to warm up. A mystery it might be, but at least he could shift it; three hearty cheers for small mercies. There were some months (and this might well prove to be one of them, the way things were going) when the only thing that stood between him and an excitingly challenging change in career direction was DW6.

Even so.

SatNav flickered into brightly backlit life, and he touched the nail of his index finger to the screen. The colours swirled, and it said—

(It said; *she* said –)

– SatNav said, 'Your route is being calculated; please wait,' and for a moment he forgot about snotty shop managers and flying cardboard boxes and his monthly target and perversely inexplicable megaselling DW6, because there was something about its voice, her voice, that was so wonderfully soothing and reassuring; like she understood him, like she cared—

He frowned. They'd warned him about that, of course. He glanced at the little screen, as the picture swung wildly through the x axis and settled itself. Straight on out of town until he hit the main A666, then take the second exit. Fine.

Not much traffic at this time of day. He'd warned them about the NM66, of course, told them till he was blue in the face and would they listen? Fat chance. He'd told them that it was just a matter of time before an escaped pair started breeding, and then the brown stuff'd hit the swiftly whirring blades all right: tabloid headlines, billion-dollar lawsuits, the boing-boing noise of rolling heads in the deep-pile-carpeted corridors of corporate power. He sighed. They lived in a world of their own in Kettering.

He turned the radio on, but it was some phone-in, so he fished about in the glove compartment for a CD. Now there (he thought, as he scrabbled one-handed through the plastic cases) was another bloody mystery, because a third of the stuff in there was garbage he'd never have bought in a million years, a third he couldn't even recognise, and of the remaining third that he was prepared to acknowledge as his own, the one thing he actually wanted to find was always missing. White Stripes; no, not today. Very Best of James Blunt – contradiction in terms. He looked up just in time to avoid smashing into the back of a lorry, and grabbed something at random.

It turned out to be a home-made job, no label or writing on it, so presumably one of Karen's compilation CDs – no idea how they came to end up in his glove compartment; another mystery. He stuck it in anyway, and it turned out not to be too bad after all, though of course he had to keep the volume right down so he could hear SatNav—

'After three hundred yards,' SatNav said, 'turn left.'

He realised he was smiling, and frowned instead. So what, she had, *it* had a nice voice: bright, warm, friendly, ever so slightly sexy but— All right, so *what*? Obviously they'd chosen a voice that was carefully designed to appeal to the tired, stressed-out male driver, and they were good at their jobs, and they'd succeeded. There was absolutely nothing wrong with that, nothing odd or sinister or strange about it, and if he'd rather listen to her – it – than to the Proclaimers or the miserable sods on the radio, that was perfectly all right, nothing whatsoever to worry about. Even so, he turned the CD player up just a little bit, and self-consciously tapped out the beat on the steering wheel with his fingers.

I worry too much, he thought; and when there's too much or too little to worry about, I worry about worrying. Maybe I should be worried about that, too. Or maybe I should just get a bloody grip, and concentrate on getting through the next call without screwing up too monumentally badly.

'At the next junction,' SatNav said, 'turn left.'

'What? Oh, yes,' he muttered, and dabbed at the indicator stalk. 'Thanks.'

'You're welcome.'

Now then, he thought. Next call was Stetchkin & Sons: old-established family firm, conservative, the archetypal no-call-for-that-round-here outfit, which meant he was going to have to come up with something pretty stunningly amazing if he was going to offload any BB27Ks on them. He rehearsed the standard pitch in his mind. No chance. Come on, he told himself reproachfully, you're a salesman, you can do this—

'I can,' he said aloud, like they'd told him to on his Innovation & Assertiveness Awareness Day (complete waste of time, except for the spring rolls at lunchtime). 'I can. There's no such word as can't.'

It sounded even sillier than usual, and he grinned. Yes, he thought, but just for the hell of it, like it's some kind of bet I'm having with myself; if only to see the look on old Mr Stetchkin's face when he realises he's just placed an order for three dozen of something he didn't know he wanted. I *can* do this—

'Yes,' he said. 'Can't I, SatNav?'

'Of course you can.'

He frowned, changed down to overtake a cyclist, and said, 'Yes, well, it's easy for you to say. You've never met old Mr Stetchkin.'

'Tell me about him.'

He grinned, and turned off the CD player. 'Oh God, where do I begin? Right, then, for a start he's seventy if he's a day, bald with little bits of white fluff over his ears like cotton wool, stupid little tufty white beard—'

'He sounds rather sweet, actually.'

Bitter laugh. 'I don't think so,' he said. 'He's one of those miserable, nit-picking types, never satisfied, nothing's ever right, won't ever listen to what you've got to say, reckons he knows it all, you really wouldn't—'

'After three hundred yards,' SatNav interrupted, 'turn right. And perhaps,' she went on, 'if he's been in the business for a long time and he's still going, maybe he does know it all. Or at least quite a lot of it.'

He was going to laugh derisively, but he didn't. 'It's a good business, Stetchkins,' he said thoughtfully. 'They've always done well, even in the recession. There's not many that can say that.'

'Now turn right,' SatNav said. 'So perhaps Mr Stetchkin's got good reason to think he knows it all.'

'Maybe.'

'I'd have thought someone like that would be quite proud of his experience.'

He frowned. 'Go on.'

'Oh, I was just thinking, after all those years in the trade, he must have heard every pitch there is, over and over again, till he's sick of hearing them all. People trying really hard to sell him things, I mean.'

'I suppose so,' he said. 'But that's not helping me, is it?'

'After six hundred yards, take the second exit. If I was Mr Stetchkin,' SatNav said, 'I wouldn't want some young rep coming into my shop and trying to shove some new product up my nose, telling me how wonderful it is. No, if there's a new line I might be interested in, I'd want to look at it carefully, see if it's any good and make my own decision. Don't you think?'

'Fine,' he replied huffily. 'That's me out of a job, then.'

'Not at all. Your job is to bring the merchandise to the customers' attention.'

'That's one way of looking at it,' he said sarcastically. 'Only I wouldn't last very long if all I . . .'

'Take the second exit.'

'What? Oh, shit, right.'

'Personally,' SatNav went on, 'if it was me, I'd start off just taking down the reorders, let him do all the talking to begin with, and then I'd say something like—'

'Like?'

'I'm thinking, please wait. Something like, "I don't know if you've got a moment, Mr Stetchkin, but I'd quite like your opinion of this new line we're bringing out"; and then you hand it to him and take a step back, and don't say anything until he's finished looking at it—'

'That's not bad,' Mr Stetchkin said.

Oink, he thought. 'You think it's OK?' he said.

Mr Stetchkin nodded. 'It's quite good,' he said. 'Neat. Well thought out. Good value for money.'

He frowned, like she'd told him to, and tried to sound slightly worried. 'You don't think the packaging's a bit, well, loud—?'

Mr Stetchkin shook his head. 'No, not really. Nice bright colours, catches the eye.'

'But isn't it a bit on the dear side? For what it is, I mean.'

Mr Stetchkin thought about that for a moment. 'I don't think so,' he said. 'Customers know they get what they pay for. If it was any cheaper, it'd send the wrong message. You wouldn't expect to get anything like this worth having for nine ninety-nine.'

'That's true,' he said, as though reluctantly conceding the point. 'And you think the way it folds up at the back is all right?

I was a little concerned people might think it's a bit, well, fiddly.'

Mr Stetchkin gave him a patronising smile. 'Hardly,' he said. 'Look, I can do it with one hand, see?' And he folded it up easily, as though he'd been practising for a week. 'No, I have to say, I really like this – What did you say the code was?'

He made a show of looking at his book. 'BB27K,' he said.

'Yes, thank you.' Mr Stetchkin handed him back the sample, and nodded. 'I'll take ten dozen.'

'I *think* we may be able to – Just let me check.' He looked back at the book and saw that it was upside down. Luckily, Mr Stetchkin hadn't noticed. 'Yes, we can let you have ten dozen, just about. Usual rate?'

Mr Stetchkin nodded again, and for a moment the shop seemed to flicker, because Mr Stetchkin *always* screwed you to the floor over discounts. 'Now then,' Mr Stetchkin went on, 'I'd like another six dozen of the DW6, and this time, tell them I don't want to find any of them with the seals broken, I think I may have mentioned this before—'

'It was amazing,' he said. 'Ten dozen. He took ten dozen, and—'

'At the end of the road, turn left.'

'Yes, I *know*, I've been here before. Now all I've got to do is shift three dozen more and I've made my target, and I'm pretty sure I can get rid of two dozen on the Valmet brothers, which just leaves one, and I'm home free.'

'That's marvellous. I knew you could do it.'

He was grinning again. But, he thought, why the hell not? Nobody else would've said that to him. 'I reckon we've done a good day's work today,' he said. 'You and me.'

No reply; but that was fair enough, it was a straight stretch of road. He sat back in his seat and tapped the wheel a few times, beating out the rhythm from one of the tracks he'd played earlier; catchy tune, he wondered who it was by.

'Excuse me.'

'Mm?'

'Only,' she said, 'I was wondering.'

'Yes?'

'This BB—'

'BB27K?'

'That's it, yes. Only . . .' Brief hesitation, like she was about to take a slight liberty. 'What is it? I mean, what does it actually do?'

He smiled. 'It's the latest thing,' he said. 'Kettering's mad about it, really pushing it. Hence the bloody enormous target.'

'Yes, but—'

His smile widened. 'It's a portable folding parking space,' he said. 'It comes in a little plastic wallet, and you take it out and unfold it and lay it down on the road, and it expands into a space big enough to take anything up to a small minibus. When you're ready to leave, you just pick it up and put it away and off you go. Even works on double yellows. I'm going to see if I can nick one for myself, it'll make my life so much—'

'That's a really good idea,' she said.

'Invented by Professor Cornelius Van Spee of Leiden,' he recited, 'a by-product of research into—'

'Wasn't he the one who went mad and tried to blow up the planet?'

He shrugged. 'Search me,' he replied. 'I just sell them. Or try to,' he added. 'And, thanks to you . . .'

'Not at all,' she said. 'You were the one who made the sale. I just—'

'Should I be turning right here?'

'What? Oh, yes, sorry.'

'No problem,' he said, turning the wheel. 'And then it's right at the crossroads, isn't it?'

'Yes. I mean, at the end of the road, turn right. Sorry.'

'That's OK.' He slid the gear lever into fourth. 'What were you telling me just now about Professor Van Spee?'

'Well,' SatNav replied, 'if he's the one I'm thinking of, he tried to create a pocket universe. There was a lot of trouble about it, at the time.'

He frowned. 'That's no big deal,' he said. 'I mean, we do those: the JH88C. Get away from it all in a world of your own for only two-nine-nine ninety-nine. We sell a lot of them.'

'Yes,' she said. 'But this one actually *worked.*'

'Ah.' He thought for a moment, then said, 'Hang on, though. The JH88C works. Any rate, I've never had any sent back, so they must be all right.'

Slight pause; then she said, 'The JH88C creates an interdimensional bubble capable of supporting one adult human for up to forty-eight hours at a time, while the inbuilt matter/energy transfiguration unit allows limited holographic imaging for a strictly limited range of pre-programmed fantasy activities. Van Spee's version was permanent, and you could do anything you liked in there.'

'Really?' He raised his eyebrows. 'Cool.'

'Cool,' she agreed, 'except that it did all sorts of horrible things to the real world. But he didn't care about that. Not a nice man.'

'Obviously.' He thought for a moment, then said, 'You know a lot about it—'

'For a SatNav, you mean?' She didn't say it nastily or anything, but he got the message. 'I don't just do quickest-way-from-A-to-B, you know.'

'That's for sure,' he said. 'You know, I went to this launch meeting about the JH88C, and they told us all about it and the points we should be stressing to customers and all that, but they didn't say anything about interdimensional bubbles or blowing up planets.'

'Didn't want to overload you with stuff you didn't need to know, presumably.'

'I guess so.' Pause; thought. 'But *you* know—'

'After six hundred yards, take the first exit.'

So he did; and a sociopath in a Daf sixteen-wheeler tried to carve him up on the inside, which provoked him into the use of intemperate language, and after that he'd forgotten what they'd been talking about; and soon afterwards they turned into Frobisher Way, and she said, 'You have now arrived at your destination,' and he parked the car and went in to the office.

'Oh, it's you,' said Julie on reception. 'You're late.'

'Am I?'

She nodded. 'He's waiting for you,' she said. 'In the small interview room.'

'Ah,' he said. 'Lucky me.'

As he trudged slowly through the industrial Axminster, he ran through a short list of possibilities. Get rid of the most unlikely ones first: he's pleased with me, he wants to give me a pay rise, he wants to promote me. Yes indeed; and the pig now boarding at gate number six is the 17:09 scheduled flight to Mogadishu. Rather more probable: he's pissed off at me, he's really pissed off at me, he's really seriously pissed off at me—

He knocked on the door, waited for the familiar grunt, and went in. At the far end of the room, his huge pink face reflected in the highly polished table top, sat Mr Burnoz, area manager; not a pleasant sight, but not so bad if you're expecting it. Opposite him was some scraggy kid in glasses.

'You wanted to see me, Mr—'

'Come in, sit down.' Mr Burnoz turned his head and smiled at the scraggy kid. Female, he noted, more than a passing resemblance to a weasel. 'Angela, I'd like you to meet Chris Popham, one of our sales reps. Chris, this is Angela –' some surname he didn't catch '– who's joining us for a month as part of her degree course.' Burnoz smiled hugely, as if he was trying to catch the sun in his teeth. 'Angela's taking advantage of our sponsored graduate-intake programme. Ultimately we're hoping she'll be joining us at Kettering, meanwhile we're giving her this opportunity to get some front-line hands-on experience in basic marketing.'

A chill sensation, like a column of frozen ants climbing up his leg. 'That's great,' Chris said through a fixed smile. 'How do I—?'

'We thought it'd be a really good idea if Angela sat in with you while you do your rounds for the next six weeks,' said Mr Burnoz, cheerful as a game-show host, oblivious as an ice-breaker grinding through permafrost. 'You can show her what it's really like in the trenches, so to speak, the raw, bloody cut and thrust of modern marketing. Not something you can get a feel of from books or sitting in front of a computer screen, I'm sure you'll agree. I know Angela's really looking forward to it.'

In which case, Chris thought, never under any circumstances play poker with this child for money, since she clearly guards her emotions like a dragon on a pile of gold.

'Absolutely,' he heard himself croak. 'Great idea.'

'Splendid,' said Mr Burnoz, as the scraggy kid shifted her head a fraction to the left and gave him a look that would've separated paint. 'In that case, why don't you pick her up outside the building here at, what, let's say six-fifteen tomorrow morning, and you can take it from there.'

Chris hoped he'd managed not to let the pain show in his face. 'All right, then,' he said. 'I'll look forward to it.'

The raw, bloody cut and thrust of modern marketing. That was, he told himself as he slouched back across the pure-wool tundra, one way of describing it. But offloading a trainee – and not just a trainee: a graduate trainee, a graduate bloody trainee who hadn't even graduated yet, a *kid* – on him was a refinement of cruelty he wouldn't have thought anybody, even Mr Burnoz, was capable of. It was heartless, it was vicious, savage, inhuman and unnatural; furthermore, he was at least ninety-nine-point-nine-eight per cent sure that Mr Burnoz hadn't meant it that way. Far from it. Somebody – Kettering, presumably – had sent Mr Burnoz a memo saying *offload this skinny kid on one of your reps*, and Mr Burnoz had chosen him at random, or because he'd seen his name on a report or an expenses claim at some point recently, and had recalled it when faced with the chore of placing the trainee . . . Arguably, that was worse. Which would you rather be: the martyr on the lonely gallows, or the hedgehog squashed flat by the artic whose driver hadn't even seen you?

Back into reception, where Julie – she was married, and every time she mentioned her husband Chris couldn't help thinking of those birds in Africa who live by picking shreds of meat out of the jaws of crocodiles – handed him a sheaf of yellow While You Were Out notes, which he stuffed into his briefcase without looking at them. A *trainee*, he muttered to himself as he splashed through puddles in the car park, a sodding *kid*. And six-fifteen in the bloody morning.

He'd started the car and let in the clutch before he remembered; and then he felt a little better. Today was Wednesday, Karen's evening class, which meant . . . He smiled, eased the car into gently purring motion, and drove gracefully home, stopping to let other people go at junctions.

There was a note on the kitchen table: *no food*. Chris acknowledged it with a slight nod. Sometimes, though rarely, Karen cooked. He didn't hold it against her; he guessed it was something she felt she had to do now and again, and it was probably just as well that she got it out of her system, rather than bottling it up and getting some sort of a complex. Nonetheless, in their house the definition of good food was like the proverbial definition of good news. He'd get a burger instead, or a kebab. Things were looking up.

Chris changed quickly, lynching his suit on a wire hanger and pulling on a pair of jeans, transferred his wallet, phone and keys to his civilian jacket, checked the mercifully mute answering machine and lunged back out again, walking quickly without actually running, as if escaping from a PoW camp. A glance at his watch told him he was cutting it fine, for which he had Mr Burnoz and the skinny teenager to thank. As he turned the corner by the pillar box, he realised that he was rehearsing an opening line in his head. He wondered about that, just briefly, but so-whatted away the tender shoots of guilt. My evening off, he told himself. I deserve it.

She'd got there first; she always did. She'd bagged a table – not too close to the door, the bar or the toilets – and bought the drinks. She always did it, and he'd never once commented on it. Furthermore, she always smiled when she saw him. He couldn't think of anybody else who did that.

(But that's OK, Chris told himself, his inner voice just a touch nervous inside his head. That's the difference between a permanent might-as-well-be-married girlfriend and a, well, a *friend*. A friend is someone who likes you.)

'Sorry I'm late,' he said, dropping into his seat. 'Held up at the office. Don't ask. No,' he added, as his fingers closed around the cool, damp body of the glass, 'Ask. I need to whine at somebody.'

'Fine,' she said. 'Whine away.'

So he whined: Mr Burnoz (she knew all about him by now), the trainee, six-fifteen in the morning. She nodded at just the right times, precisely the right tempo and degree of spinal flex, the murmurs and tongue-clicks interpolated at exactly the right moments. All fake, of course; but somehow, that didn't spoil it. Quite the reverse, in fact. Chris knew perfectly well that if her boss called her in and assigned her a trainee to babysit for six weeks, she'd accept the assignment as an interesting and worth-while challenge, and by the time the six weeks were up the trainee would scuttle back to college with a renewed sense of purpose, and quite likely they'd send each other Christmas cards for the rest of their lives. So of course she didn't understand why he was ranting about the bitter injustice of it all, but nevertheless she was pretending to, and that was really very kind—

'Anyway,' he said (rant over; and yes, he felt a whole lot better now), 'that's quite enough of that.'

'Yes,' she replied, with a very slight nod of her head. 'So, how's Karen? I haven't heard from her for ages.'

'Oh, same as usual.' He was frowning, for some reason. 'Still doing the evening classes. And working late.'

She absorbed the information without any show of opinion. It was a special talent of hers. 'She always was a busy bee,' she added. 'I remember her in our A-level year—'

'You can't talk,' Chris felt constrained to point out. 'You were worse.'

She nodded. 'Still am,' she said. 'All work and no play makes Jill a senior executive officer and deputy head of department. Of course,' she added, 'it helps if you enjoy what you do.'

He frowned a little. 'Quite,' he said. 'Killed anything interesting lately?'

'As a matter of fact, yes. We had a level-three infestation just outside Faversham, and it was my turn. Bloody Robinson tried to gazump me, but I insisted. Two of them,' she went on, fiddling with the rim of her glass. 'A nesting pair.'

In spite of himself Chris was impressed. 'They're supposed to be particularly nasty, aren't they?'

Nod. 'We eventually got them cornered in the toilets of a sort of Happy Eater place – me, Derek and old George Ruffer – he's supposed to be semi-retired now but he still turns out when we're short-staffed. They had to cone off two lanes of the motorway. Got them in the end, though.'

'Rather you than me,' Chris said, with genuine feeling. 'I really don't know how you can do that,' he went on. 'I mean, quite apart from the danger. I just can't get my head around how you go about it. Mentally, I mean. You wake up, coffee and cereal, what shall I wear to work today, seat on the train if you're lucky, and then, ten minutes after you've clocked in you're out there with a suitcase full of weapons fighting the forces of primeval darkness. I don't think I could face it, really.'

Jill shrugged. 'It's interesting,' she said. 'Also useful, you've got to admit.'

'Dirty job but someone's got to do it?' Chris pulled a face. 'Come on,' he said, 'that's not the real reason.'

'Very true.' She smiled. 'The real reason is, if I stick at it for another three years—'

'And manage not to get killed or horribly mauled—'

'Yes, quite. If I stick at it three more years, I'm practically guaranteed the next junior secretaryship when one crops up, which otherwise I wouldn't have a hope in hell of being considered for until I'm at least forty. And after that—'

Chris pulled another face, and Jill laughed again. 'Well, I'm sorry, that's just how I am,' she said. 'I like being ambitious, it keeps things interesting. I know it doesn't suit you, and that's fine. I guess I'm just not a rut person. And if it means having to kill a few demons now and again, there's worse ways of making a living. Accountancy. Insurance. Anything with children.'

'Or selling,' he said. 'Now there's a dead-end career if you like.'

'Quite.' Jill grinned. 'Look at you, for example. Seven years of devoted service, and they land you with a trainee. Give me a nice, straightforward demon any time.'

Chris realised he was scowling, but made no effort to stop. 'Ah well,' he said. 'I didn't go to university, so what can I expect?'

She didn't react; she never did. But Chris felt something click into place between them, separating them, and (as always) wished he hadn't said it. Meanwhile, she was looking at him, and he could read the message as clearly as though she had a ticker-tape machine on her forehead. *It's not just because she's a trainee*, he read, *it's because she's a graduate trainee. Can't forgive her for that, can you?* He shrugged, and she knew him well enough to accept it as a retraction, a reset to zero, as though the U-word hadn't been said out loud that evening.

'Changing the subject,' he said briskly (and a slight glow in Jill's eyes meant she approved), 'there's something I've been meaning to ask you, since you know all about the business and everything.'

'I do,' she said. 'Go on.'

So he told her all about the DW6 mystery; but he hadn't got very far when she stopped him.

'How do you mean,' Jill said, looking uncharacteristically blank, 'powdered water?'

Chris looked at her. 'You're kidding me, right?'

But she wasn't, because she didn't do that sort of thing. He paused, while the world went all to pieces and slowly re-formed around him. 'Are you seriously telling me you've never heard of—?'

Jill frowned. 'Come to that,' she replied, 'are you seriously telling me there's such a thing as powdered water?'

'Apparently.' Chris shrugged. 'At least, it's this sort of very fine grey powder, like a kind of mixture of talc and soot. It comes in a plastic tub with a kidproof lid, you can have the one-kilo size or the five-hundred—'

'Powdered *water*?'

'That's what it says on the label,' he replied, ever so slightly defensively. 'Mind you, I've never actually seen it in action, so to speak. But—'

Jill was focusing on him. He knew that look. It was lucky she didn't wear glasses, or she'd burn holes in things. 'It's a gag thing, surely. Like pet rocks and bottled LA smog, novelty Christmas gifts for sad people.'

Chris shook his head. 'I don't think so,' he replied. 'We don't do stuff like that.'

Now Jill raised her eyebrows; not a good sign. Two gym mistresses and a maths teacher had needed counselling, back in Year Ten. 'Does it say on it how you're supposed to use it? I mean, are there instructions on the tub?'

Another headshake. 'All it says is, *instant powdered water, just add . . .*'

Pause. She was thinking. 'Just add?'

'And then three dots,' he told her. 'Just add dot dot dot. Oh, and there's a lot of legal stuff: *for use as a water substitute only, may contain traces of—*'

'Just add.' Jill's thoughtful frown had escalated into a scowl. 'That's silly,' she said.

'Yes.' His turn to frown. 'Really, haven't you heard of it? I thought you knew all about – well, trade stuff. Magic artefacts and their properties. Didn't you do a—?'

'A course, yes,' Jill said. 'In my second year at Lough-borough. And yes, we did everything, you name it, from mandrake roots to elixirs of eternal youth.' A thought struck her; Chris could see the ripples of impact in the lines appearing on her forehead. 'Is it a fairly recent thing?' she asked. 'Only I suppose it could be a recent invention, hence not covered in the course.'

Shrug. 'Don't think so,' he replied. 'I get the impression from customers that they've been ordering it from us for years.'

'Powdered water, for crying out loud.' Now he'd done it; a question to which Jill didn't know the answer. She hated those. 'And you've no idea what the people who buy it use it for?'

'That's what I wanted to ask you.' Now he was starting to feel guilty. She took things seriously. Something like this could spoil her whole day. 'I wish I hadn't asked you now. Only I was sure you'd—'

'No, that's fine.' She sounded like she was having trouble remembering he was there. 'I'll ask around at work,' she said, making an effort to break free of the mystery. 'Someone's bound to have . . . And you sell a lot of this stuff?'

'Hundreds of kilos,' Chris replied. 'One of our best lines. Most of the places I go've got a standing order.'

'Oh. Oh well. As soon as I've found out about it, I'll tell you. Just add,' Jill repeated, the frown coming back and changing her face into one he hardly recognised. 'Just add what, though? And why bother? I mean, it's not as though water's all that hard to come by in this country. For export, yes, I could see the point. But when all you've got to do is turn on a tap—'

This could go on all night, Chris realised, and it wasn't the way he wanted to spend his evening off. If he wanted tension and one-sided conversations, he could talk to Karen— 'Anyway,' he said, a little louder than he'd meant to, 'how's everything with you? Apart from work, I mean,' he added quickly.

'What? Oh, fine.'

'Heard from any of the others lately?'

He was on firm ground there. Jill had taken on herself the duty of collating and distributing detailed updates on everybody in their year, and needless to say, she did it very well. 'Paul's still with the BBC, of course, he's producing gardening programmes now. Amelia's transferred from the Tank Corps to

Signals. Sara got deported from Bolivia for raising awareness about something or other; she's being very smug about that. Colin's still on the run, there was a sighting in Leeds about six weeks ago, they assume he's trying to leave the country on a false passport—'

Fine. Ten minutes or so later, the difficulty had evaporated, though Chris knew it hadn't really gone away. Rather, Jill had filed and stored it, and sooner or later an answer would be forthcoming. He noted with approval that at no point had she said, 'Well, why the hell don't *you* ask someone, it's your stupid firm that makes the stupid stuff,' or words to that effect. She understood perfectly why that simply wasn't an option; though of course, if she was a sales rep for JWW Retail, it'd have been the first thing she'd have done. As for that cursory *What? Oh, fine*, he was prepared to take it at face value; not because he wasn't interested. Quite the opposite. One of these days, he'd get an answer to that question that he knew he wasn't going to like. The longer that particular experience could be postponed, the better.

They chatted aimlessly for a while after that, and Chris managed to keep the conversation away from any more danger areas, though it was touch and go a few times; the nastiest moment was when Jill started complaining about how she'd been putting on weight again (and, since she'd raised the subject, it was perfectly true; but he knew it didn't signify, since she had one of those Stock Exchange metabolisms – massive gains one week, huge losses the next – and so long as she kept two sets of clothes, one in size zero and the other in extra-large, he couldn't see how it could possibly matter to a rational human being . . . In the event, he deflected her away from all that by asking her about the demon-hunting business; it wasn't something he liked being told about, but it was better than a detailed analysis of her latest diet.

'We really need to find out how they're getting through,' Jill was saying. 'Until we know a lot more about that, it's really just guesswork and how quickly we can react once an infestation's been reported to us. There's theories, of course, but none of them seem to hold up once you try applying them in practice. For example, there was this article in *New Thaumaturgical Quarterly* about quantum fluctuations in the Earth's metadimensional field—'

'Is that right?' Chris said hopelessly. 'I didn't even know we had a—'

'Which,' Jill ground on, 'may give rise to anomalous cross-field events which the demons could've evolved to exploit, sort of like cracks, or bubbles. But it's all a bit vague and theoretical, if you ask me. I still prefer the hypothesis put forward by Kanamoto and Van Spee in 1846, which seeks to explain demon incursions in terms of artificially induced Otherspace interfaces, presupposing a negatively charged ionic curtain existing somewhere in the D6 void—'

In other words, white noise, which Chris had long since learned to tune out; it was soothing, when you were sitting in a pleasant pub holding a full glass, and basically he just liked hearing the sound of her voice: eager, earnest, clever, friendly, safe; not asking him to understand, let alone agree or form an opinion. It wasn't like when Karen talked at him, when there was always a very real threat that there'd be a test afterwards, or a sudden silence which he was supposed to fill with exactly the right form of sympathetic reassurance. Most of all, he liked being talked at by Jill because she never ever talked about Us; though the downside of that was that there wasn't an Us for them to talk about. But, he felt sure, even if there had been (if only –), she'd never have dreamed of talking about it. He couldn't imagine her doing such a thing. To the best of his knowledge, in all the years he'd known her she'd never been half of any kind of an Us. She belonged to too many people, he supposed, too many friends all relying on her to listen and understand. A greater Us, of which she was the coordinator and historian. For a moment he felt a stab of jealousy, but it didn't take long for it to pass.

Closing time swooped down too soon; Chris said goodnight

and walked home. It was only as he unlocked the door, shoving the thing he'd been carrying in his right hand under his arm so he could get out his keys, that he realised he'd picked up her bag by mistake. Ever since he'd known Jill, she'd always had a carrier bag; Tesco or Safeway in the early days, upgraded to M&S once she left school and started earning; these days, now that she was affluent and successful, it'd be something black or burgundy with gold lettering on it, but still a plastic carrier, her trade mark. What she carried in her carriers had always been something of a mystery, since she packed her vital instruments – purse, phone, glamour-repair kit and the like – in a conventional handbag, usually of great elegance and splendour. But she also had the knack of frustrating curiosity without even seeming to try; the carrier always came to rest between her feet, or wedged between her thigh and the side of the chair, safe from surreptitious investigation. But not, apparently, this time.

Chris paused, standing in the hall by the cheap Ikea phone table, and tried to reconstruct the sequence of events. Jill had stood up; the carrier had been in her hand, but she'd rested it on the table while she'd put on her coat; he'd picked it up to give it to her, but then she'd dropped her handbag, and by the time she'd retrieved that they'd been talking about something – Izzy Bowden's divorce, he recalled – and then someone had nearly barged into them and they'd been preoccupied with taking evasive action; and they'd walked out of the pub together, and *he'd still been holding the carrier—*

Chris went into the kitchen and sat down. A square of spilt milk on the worktop told him that Karen was home – she had an unfortunate tendency to attack cardboard milk cartons with wild enthusiasm and knives, which meant milk went everywhere when she poured – but he couldn't hear her crashing about and she hadn't called out when he opened the door, so presumably she'd already gone to bed. He put the carrier bag down on the kitchen table and looked at it, torn apart by opposing forces of extraordinary power.

On the one hand: anybody who took advantage of an honest mistake to go snooping about in other people's private carrier bags was obviously lower than a basement, and even the thought of doing such a thing made Chris shudder. The honourable course of action would be to seal the top with parcel tape and quickly leave a message on her answerphone to say he'd got it. On the other hand—

As the debate raged inside him, Chris examined the outside of the bag. It was dark navy blue, with *Shotwell & Hogue* written on it in curly gold italics. He knew them, of course. They were on his patch; good customers, in fact they'd taken a dozen BB27Ks purely on his unsupported recommendation. Somehow, that tipped the balance (he had absolutely no idea why). Feeling like someone robbing his child's piggy bank to get money for drugs, he gently opened the bag and peered inside.

Something of an anticlimax. Inside the bag Chris saw a paperback book (something by Alan Titchmarsh entirely unrelated to gardening), a packet of plain digestive biscuits, a baseball cap with the letters DS on the front and a pair of black patent shoes. He frowned, feeling let down and betrayed as well as guilty. It was a bit much, he felt, to have sold his soul and forfeited his honour for this collection of old tat.

The phone rang. Chris let go of the bag and lunged back into the hall, to shut the stupid thing up before it woke Karen.

'Chris?' It was Jill.

He scowled. 'Yes, I've got it,' he said. 'Your blasted bag. And before you ask,' he added, 'no, I haven't looked inside it. It must've been when you were putting on your coat, I suppose I—'

'That's OK,' Jill said; and it wasn't just his imagination, she did sound relieved. 'I was just worried I'd left it in the pub, that's all. Look, is there any chance you can drop it round at my place on your way tomorrow morning? Only—'

'Sorry,' Chris said, 'not really. I've got to pick up that bloody trainee at six-fifteen, remember. Which reminds me,' he added. 'Must remember to set the alarm.'

'You could leave it in the porch,' Jill said. 'Or ring the bell and I'll pop down.'

Chris felt his eyebrow hitch. 'At half past five in the morning?'

'I'll be up, I expect,' she replied, in a voice he couldn't immediately analyse. A pause; then, 'It's just that strictly speaking we're not supposed to take confidential stuff out of the office, and the new manager gets quite stressy about that sort of thing. I don't want to give him an excuse to have a go at me.'

'Fine, no problem,' Chris replied, as he thought: Confidential stuff? Would that be the top secret paperback or the For-Your-Feet-Only slingbacks? 'I'll drop it off, then.'

'Thanks.' Again, the relief. 'Just ring the bell, don't wait for me. Sorry to have bothered you.'

As Chris returned to the kitchen to pick up the bag and put it in the hall where he wouldn't forget it, the criminal urge came back. After all, Jill wouldn't know if he took just one more peek, and somehow the fact that she'd lied (confidential stuff, mustn't leave the office; yeah, right) made it seem tantalisingly easy. This time, though, he fought it back, and that made him feel rather proud – she'd lied, he'd resisted temptation, so he'd managed to fight his way back to the moral high ground, which is always nice. He turned off the lights and went to bed.

The blue Shotwell & Hogue carrier bag waited until it was quite safe – the humans were making loud respiratory noises, indicating deep sleep – then stirred, its thin plastic fabric shivering like the shell of a hatching egg. If anybody had been there to see, he'd have had a frustrating time of it, because as the bag shivered it sucked in darkness from the surrounding shadows, a useful trick well known to its kind. When it felt dark enough to be safe, it shook itself like a dog and stood up, the plastic stretching and moulding itself into a new shape: humanoid but short, bow-legged, crouching. It took a step forward, leaving the cap, the shoes, the book and the empty biscuit wrapper (it had been peckish) lying on the carpet. Treading carefully, it stepped over them and walked silently through the hall into the kitchen, following the human's scent trail. It found nothing of great interest there, though it did pause to lap up the few drops of spilt milk, and went on into the sitting room, where it rubbed itself against the television screen, happily absorbing the static electricity, pulled out the plug and licked the brass prongs. A few sights and smells there, but nothing it could really use; the good stuff had faded, dried up so that it tasted dusty and bitter, all the nourishment desiccated out of it. A pity: if it had been there a week earlier it could've had a feast. It yawned and stretched; then, taking extra care not to make a sound, it gently nudged open the bedroom door and peered round it, to stare at the two humans asleep in the dark.

CHAPTER TWO

There were two women on his shoulders, one beautiful and nice, one ugly and nasty, and as he approached the end of the road, they were both yelling at him: turn left, urged the nice one, turn right, said the nasty one, and he wished they'd both shut up so he could *think*. And the junction was getting closer and closer, but instead of slowing down he was speeding up, towards the brick wall, so unless he decided which way to turn *right now*, he was going to crash and die—

The noise wasn't screaming brakes after all; it was the alarm clock. He shot out a hand, knocked it over, groped, grabbed it, erupted out of bed and ran, his thumb still searching for the stupid little button that turned the stupid thing off . . .

Safely into the kitchen, and Chris was fairly sure that he'd made it without waking Karen up. She was, he supposed, a nice enough person really, but if her sleep was disturbed she turned into a monstrous clawed snarling thing, and stayed that way the rest of the day. He flopped down in a chair, put the clock on the table and caught his breath. Then, very carefully, he sneaked back into the bedroom and got his clothes.

A quarter past five in the fucking morning. Chris didn't have time for breakfast, or even to boil a kettle, but his mouth was sticky and foul and he desperately needed caffeine in some form; he caught sight of the coffee pot, picked it up and felt a certain amount of liquid shifting around inside it. Last night's coffee, cold and full of grounds. He put the spout to his mouth, tilted the pot and glugged thrice. Disgusting, but better than nothing. I am not a morning person, Chris admitted to himself as he tried to remember how to tie shoelaces. On the other hand, this isn't the morning, it's the middle of the fucking night. Therefore, I am in my element, on the top of my form, one hundred per cent functional and ready for anything. Right, then, let's go.

The car purred into life with a tickle of the key, revoltingly happy, like a dog being taken for a walk. Chris had remembered the stupid carrier bag, or at least tripped over it in the hall (he remembered how he'd violated it last night; in the brain-bleaching banality of early morning, he wondered why the hell it had seemed like such a big deal) and set his course accordingly.

Jill lived in one of those interesting old industrial buildings converted into flats, right at the very top; she'd told him about it once, and it had turned out to be rather less interesting than he'd first thought. There was a glass-and-steel porch with a buzzer-box. He pressed her number, put the carrier down, and—

Someone had eaten the biscuits. Chris frowned.

Was I drunk last night? he wondered. Couldn't remember; which argued that he had been, but the absence of hangover proved conclusively that he hadn't. Karen, then. It was possible, she'd been known to get up in the middle of the night and eat things.

Embarrassing, but too late to do anything about it now. Chris glanced at his watch; running late, needless to say. He really didn't want to concede the moral high ground to the thin trainee by keeping her waiting. He hopped back into the car and put his foot down.

She was there when he pulled in, the only living creature in the car park. He opened the door, and she got in.

'Sorry I'm late,' he said, 'only I had to—'

''Salright.'

Ah, he thought, yet another one who won't let me finish a sentence. Just what I needed, really.

She was red-haired and pale, with a nose and chin that looked as though they'd just emerged from a pencil sharpener, and she seemed to be huddling inside her clothes as though trying to minimise the contact between the hated fabric and her skin. Not that Chris could blame her; ten to one her mother had chosen the suit for her (first impressions are so important, dear; if that was how it had been, Mummy had succeeded beyond her wildest dreams, though someone should have told her that not all impressions are good). It made the girl look like a prisoner of war, captured in some particularly bloody engagement between two opposing armies of chartered accountants. Well, Chris thought, fine: she doesn't want to be here, I don't want her here; in a reasonably logical world, we'd do a deal. I'd drop her off wherever she wanted to go, we'd both pretend she'd done the rounds with me, and both of us would have a marginally less excruciating day. But it doesn't work like that, does it?

'So,' he said cheerfully.

The trainee was staring through the windscreen at some indefinite distant point.

'So,' he repeated. 'You're Angela.'

She didn't look round, but maybe her mouth tightened just a little.

'I'm Chris,' he ground on.

'Hello.'

'And you're doing the graduate-intake initiative.'

''Sright.'

They tell you, practically from the cradle, that Man is a social animal, loneliness is a truly terrible thing, and humans can really only be happy in the company of their fellow creatures. Shocking, the way they're allowed to lie to you like that. 'That's where the firm pays for your college tuition and stuff, and in return you come and work for us afterwards.'

'Mm.'

Well, Chris thought, at least she's not one of those terrible gabby females who won't ever shut up. Indeed. Quite the bloody opposite. 'Well,' he said, 'I guess I'd better fill you in on what we're going to be doing today. First we'll be calling on Cotterells, they're what we call a typical mum-and-dad independent; there's quite a lot of them still, though the big foreign multiples are just starting to get established over here, Zauberwerke and Boutiques de Magie and Sorcery Source; but they're still only, what, fifteen per cent of the overall sector as a whole—'

'I know all that,' Angela said, each word an effort, like digging coal. 'I'm doing my dissertation on the structure of the magical retail trade, so you don't need to tell me.'

A very faint emphasis on the 'you'. Well, that was fine, too. 'A dissertation,' Chris replied. 'Fancy. That must be a lot of hard work.'

'Mm.'

OK, Chris said to himself, let's not talk. Let's sit here in stony silence, me driving, you hating the whole of Creation. He drove, therefore, for a quarter of an hour, allowing his mind to drift. Bloody Burnoz, he thought, lumbering me like this. And what's it going to be like at the shops? Fat chance I'll have to do any selling with this millstone round my neck. How am I supposed to do my job with—?

He realised he didn't have the faintest idea where he was. Silly: he drove these roads for a living, he knew every alley, lane and byway – except this one, he admitted. Must've taken a wrong turn somewhere.

Um, Chris thought.

Under normal circumstances (in which, of course, this wouldn't have happened to begin with) he'd just flip on SatNav and she'd have him out of there and back on the straight and narrow in a minute or two. For some reason, though, he really didn't want to use SatNav while the miserable girl was in the car; as if she wouldn't understand, as if it'd somehow be inappropriate, like snogging in the office. He looked in the mirror, then straight ahead, just in case he'd missed some obvious landmark he could triangulate by. No such luck.

'Um,' he said. 'You wouldn't mind just getting that map off the back seat, would you?'

Angela turned her head and looked at him. 'Why don't you use your GPS?'

It was a moment before Chris realised what she was talking about. 'Oh, that,' he said. 'Bust. Doesn't work. Been meaning to get a new one.'

(Forgive me, he thought; but it was switched off, and couldn't absolve him.)

'All right.' She stretched past him and got the map. 'But I'm rubbish at map-reading.'

A truthful girl, whatever her other faults. If she'd been Columbus's navigator on the *Santa Maria*, the world's leading superpower in the twenty-first century would probably have been Australia. Eventually, after a misguided tour of half the lanes-with-grass-growing-up-the-middle in the Midlands, they floundered out onto a dual carriageway that he knew, unfortunately going the wrong way. But it only took ten minutes to get to a junction where they could turn round, and that left them a mere forty-five minutes behind schedule—

'Do you get lost a lot?' she asked.

'No,' Chris replied.

Thanks to some dangerously reckless driving (Angela didn't approve of speeding, Chris could tell) they reached Cotterells an hour after they should've arrived. Not good; Mandy the manageress was a nice girl, but heavily into punctuality.

'This is Angela,' Chris said – he found he still couldn't remember her surname – 'she's going round with me for a few weeks, learning the ropes.'

Mandy the manageress smiled at her, and he could practically feel the goodwill bounce off and shatter. Great start. It was as though all the friendliness and rapport he'd built up here

over the last few years had been hoovered up into a great black
bag. Mandy was distinctly chilly as he tried in vain to interest
her in the new range of bottled dreams, and the portable parking spaces went down like a lead balloon. Even the DW6 order
was down by a dozen on last time (yes, but what do they *do*
with it?) and he wasn't offered a cup of tea, which was definitely a first.

Curiously, when they got back in the car and set off for the
next call the girl seemed marginally happier. At least, the sharp
edge of her frown blurred just a little, and after ten minutes she
spoke without being spoken to first.

'You didn't have much luck there,' she said.

'No.'

'I don't think that woman likes you very much.'

'Mandy?' Chris frowned. 'Oh, she's all right. We get on
pretty well, usually.'

Pause; then, 'I expect it's really important, getting on well
with the customers.'

'It helps,' he said. 'I mean, obviously there's going to be
some who just don't want to know, but basically we're all in the
same business. If they want stuff to sell to their customers,
they've got to get it from somewhere, and our range just happens to be one of the best in the trade. Got to believe in what
you're selling,' he went on, 'because if you don't, they pick up
on it really quickly, and then it's forget it. Believe in the stock
and try and be nice to people, that's really all there is to it.'

Angela shrugged, as if to imply that the other one was fes-
tooned with little tinkly silver bells. 'I don't think I'd be any
good at this,' she said. 'I don't get on well with people.'

No, Chris thought, you don't. 'It's a knack,' he said. 'You
learn it, along with the other tricks of the trade. Mind you, it
helps if you like the sound of your own voice.'

'I don't,' she said. 'I think my voice sounds horrible.'

Two things we agree about; at this rate, we could be friends.
'So, you aren't planning on going into the marketing side,
then?'

Angela shook her head. 'Research and development,' she said. 'I've got extremely advanced magical abilities, or at least that's what they told me when I went for my interview. They seemed very keen to have me,' she added mournfully. 'Specially when I told them about my uncle.'

'In the trade, is he?'

She nodded. 'Professor of Applied Effective Magic at UCLA,' she said. 'And his father was head of demonology for Leclerq Freres in São Paulo, so it sort of runs in the family.'

'Sounds like it,' Chris replied, trying really hard not to sound in any way jealous or resentful. 'Of course,' he went on, 'my grandad was in the trade too.'

'Oh yes?'

He nodded. 'Senior chargehand at JWW Industrial by the time he retired. Spent most of his working life in the genie-bottling plant. Very responsible job, you can imagine.'

Angela didn't say anything, and on balance Chris approved of her decision. Not a lot to be said, really. But the silence got on his nerves after a bit, so he said, 'Research and development generally, or is there anything in particular you're—?'

'Well,' she said, 'in my second year I did quite a bit on trans-migration of energy – you know, spontaneous generation of morphogenic fields, subatomic disruption, ionic interface re-sequencing, all pretty basic stuff but potentially quite interesting if you look at it from the standpoint of effective metanormal transmutation, and my tutor's currently working in theoretical cross-dimensional transmigration, which of course would change everything if he can make it work, so I think I'd quite like to be in on that, if it comes to anything. I mean, the practi-cal applications in the construction and entertainment sectors alone would be pretty exciting, not to mention the possibility of finally bridging the effective/practical dichotomy—'

Chris tuned out. It was depressing; she made it sound like *science*, and surely the whole point of what they did in the trade was that it wasn't science, it was *better*. All that stuff about energy and atoms and ions; it sort of took the magic out of it, somehow. At any rate, she seemed happy enough babbling on about it, and she clearly hadn't noticed how what she was saying was affecting him. That or she didn't care. All in all, he was in a thoroughly bad mood when they rolled up outside Domestic & Commercial Magic for their next call.

'Just let me do the talking, all right?' he said (which, he'd have been the first to admit, was like telling the Pacific Ocean not to catch fire). 'This lot – well, I'm not saying they're difficult exactly, more sort of cautious. Don't particularly like reps. But I can handle them, so—'

Angela nodded, and Chris led the way into the shop.

It was the smell, more than anything: a strong but delicate scent of violets and roses, combined with just a hint of woodsmoke. A civilian would've taken no notice, or made a mental note to ask the shopkeeper where they got their potpourri from. But Chris was no civilian, and he'd come across that smell before.

'Get out,' he said. 'Back the way you came. Don't look at anything. *Do it.*'

Pitch the tone of voice just right, and even graduate trainees will do as they're told. Anglea backed out of the shop; Chris really, really wanted to follow her, but he couldn't, not without looking, just in case there were survivors. Not that there'd be much he could do for them—

Slowly he turned his head, and for a moment he wondered if he'd lost it completely and made all that fuss over nothing. No blood, severed limbs, giblet-splatters on the walls; the shop-fittings untrashed, the stockroom door still squarely on its hinges. But the shelves behind the counter were bare, and he knew without having to look further that there was nobody else in the shop. Nobody human.

But why? he asked himself. *Not that they need a reason—*

One of the things that made Chris uncomfortable about what Jill did for a living was the heroism element. She never called it that, of course, pulled a face at him if he ever used the word, but that didn't mean it wasn't appropriate; and he had this thing about heroes. Didn't hold with them. They made him nervous, mostly because he simply couldn't fathom what made them do all that stuff. Why anybody with more brains than a teaspoon would willingly advance into danger, when they could perfectly well run away, he couldn't begin to understand. Altruism, to save others, to make a difference; the thrill, the adrenalin rush, the only time you feel really alive is when you're staring Death in the tonsils; he'd heard all the justifications loads of times, from some of the best heroes in the business. Made no difference. He still didn't understand.

He was, therefore, both surprised and extremely unhappy with himself for taking a couple of very tentative steps forward, away from the door, towards the counter. Out of my tiny little mind, he told himself, why the hell am I doing this? And the only answer he got was: Please hold, we'll get back to you as soon as we've figured it out for ourselves. In the years and decades and centuries and millennia it took for him to cross the seven yards separating the door from the counter, Chris tried to remember everything he'd ever learned about Domestic & Commercial Magic Ltd that might conceivably be relevant. Didn't take long; they were an average, run-of-the-mill small chain operation, consisting of five shops in the west and south Midlands, stocking an unambitious range of general merchandise for the commercial, manufacturing, construction and entertainment & media sectors, with small but active niche markets in spatio-temporal design and archaic enchanted weaponry—

Oh, Chris thought. Three guesses what they came for, then.

He'd reached the counter. Very slowly, he leaned across, to see if there was anything— There was. He had to look twice before he could make a positive identification. Looking back the second time was the most unpleasant task he'd ever set himself, and he wasn't getting paid for it or earning brownie points or anything.

Poor Mr Newsome. Not his favourite shop manager, by any stretch of the imagination. He had an infuriating habit of whistling softly under his breath while you were trying to pitch him a new line; he never took more than four dozen of anything (except DW6, of course), and he was a terror for sending back anything that had the slightest mark or crease on it. Over the years Chris had got the impression from the two girls who worked there that Newsome was a bit of a martinet, inclined to snarl and whine about sixty-five-minute lunch hours and incoming personal calls on the company's phone lines. Nearly everybody who'd ever met him compared him, appearance and personality, to Captain Mainwaring (but without, according to Veronica from Zauberwerke, the wit, charm and sex appeal). Not, then, the most endearing man who ever lived. Even so.

Whatever it was that had done for him had aimed for outright decapitation. Probably it had underestimated the density and tenacity of Mr Newsome's unusually thick neck. Consequently, it had managed to tear through the left-side skin, flesh, tendons and blood vessels and had cracked open the spinal column, but that was as far as it had managed to get. As a result, Mr Newsome's head lay tilted to one side, as if it was a removable component that had got stuck. Apart from that, he looked fine – suit neat, shirt hardly stained at all, shoes still bright-shiny polished, nicely manicured hands limp and relaxed at his sides. In an ideal world, you'd be able to fix him by unscrewing the damaged components and slotting in new ones. But the world isn't ideal, and even magic has its limitations. Poor Mr Newsome.

Oh well, Chris thought; I knew I recognised that smell, and I was right. Clever old me. Now do something really clever, and get yourself out of here in one piece.

From the counter to the door, seven yards, seven ordinary paces, seven small steps for a man. No way in hell was he going to turn his back on the counter. He started to move; and, more to keep his mind occupied and off the thing behind the counter he couldn't see, he looked around him, at the otherwise perfectly normal shop that just happened not to have anything on its shelves right now—

Correction: he'd missed something. In the middle of the top shelf, perfectly still and facing him, was the ugliest garden gnome he'd ever set eyes on in his life. Odd, Chris thought; that's the sort of thing you'd expect to see in a garden centre rather than a magical-goods shop. Not that anybody, not even the disturbed people who buy garden gnomes, would ever part with money for *that*—

The gnome winked at him.

Not supposed to do that.

The gnome winked at him again, and grinned. And, now he came to think of it, that wasn't a gnome, it was something quite other; and the long, flat shiny thing that it was holding in its palpably-not-gnome's hands wasn't a fishing rod, either. Oh, he thought. Well, it was a pretty lousy excuse for a life, but it'll be over any minute now, and then maybe I can be something else.

The thing that demonstrably wasn't a gnome was looking at Chris, head tilted just a little on one side; considering him, quite calmly, weighing up the necessary expenditure of effort against the likely rewards and benefits. He kept perfectly still while the un-gnome was thinking, just in case any action on his part, any slight movement, say, or funny little squeaking noise he might make should affect the creature's judgement. It took its time, and he had a nasty feeling that his left foot, frozen in the act of taking a step back, was starting to go to sleep. He was wondering just how long he could keep it up, in fact, when the creature (not a gnome; quite sure about that) shook its disproportionately large head an inch or so from side to side, and its lips moved, shaping the words *no, not today.*

As Chris put his weight on his numb left foot, he wobbled, and that made the creature twitch; like a wolf, he thought, instinctively programmed to react to movements of prey species that were suggestive of weakness or panic. But he kept going, and it didn't move, though its eyes were still fixed on him, downloading information at a tremendous rate, every detail of his body weight and mass, likely speed, agility, defensive and evasive capabilities. As his shoulders drew level with the frame of the open door he saw it yawn. Then he spun round and ran.

Angela was standing by the car, for crying out loud. 'Get in,' Chris howled, lunging for the door handle, his other hand scrabbling in his pocket for his keys.

'What's going on?' she said. 'Has something—?'

'*Get in the fucking car.*'

Tone of voice, you see. Only, he knew it wasn't something he'd be able to do in cold blood, so to speak. It needed that extra incentive.

Chris didn't actually look to see if Angela was safely inside, or if she'd fastened her seat belt. He twisted the key, felt a stab or pure joy as the engine fired, and jabbed his elbow down on the locking pin to lock all the doors. A quick glance back towards the shop door, then a fluent wrench at the gear lever, and his left foot stamped down on the clutch—

'Aren't we going to make the call, then?' Angela said.

Chris reversed fast and without looking, felt the back end of the car bash into something, stuck the gearstick into first and floored the pedal; round the corner, thirty seconds at maximum burn up the main road, then into the first lay-by he came to. He didn't make a totally wonderful job of stopping; in fact, he rammed the car's nose into a hedge and stalled the engine. Then he wound down his window, stuck his head out of it and –

'Are you feeling all right?' Angela asked.

– Threw up with prodigious force; which was, he felt, about as much answer as her question merited.

'Fine,' he croaked, wiping his mouth. 'Never fucking better. And you?'

Now she was looking at him as though he had two heads. 'What's the matter?' she said. 'There's something wrong, isn't there?'

'You might say that.' His hands were shaking so badly he couldn't even get his phone out of his pocket. 'Here,' he snapped, 'make yourself useful. Ring this number.'

With surprising meekness, Angela took out her phone, flipped up the lid, and waited. Chris couldn't remember the number, of course. It was stored in his phone, along with all the other useful data.

'Call the office,' he said, his voice flat as he gave her the number. 'Ask Julie on reception to get you the number for Felixstowe. She'll know what that means,' he added quickly, as her lips parted. 'Then dial that number and hand me the phone, OK?'

He'd never actually spoken to Felixstowe before, and when a cool, brisk female voice came on the line and asked him which service he required, his mind went blank, and he sat frozen for several seconds while the phone squeaked 'Hello?' at him, until the girl poked him hard in the ribs, and he pulled himself together with a snap.

'Demon control,' Chris said.

'Putting you through,' said the cool voice, and a moment later, a man was asking him where he was, how many, what subspecies—

'I don't know, do I?' Chris snapped. 'Lesser greater spotted Ibbotson's fucking warbler. It was smallish and sort of grey, it was sitting on a shelf in a shop and it winked at me. All right?'

The man told him there was no need to shout (which was, Chris strongly felt, simply not true) and started asking him for his name, date of birth, address, occupation, work and home phone numbers, e-mail address—

He gave it, then doubletook and said, 'What do you need my e-mail address for?'

'We're compiling a database,' the man replied, 'as part of our ongoing e-technology initiative. Would you like to receive our monthly newsletter?'

Quite some time later, the man told him to stay put and a dedicated incident-management team would be along at some point to sort it all out. 'Thank you for calling Demon Control Services,' he concluded. 'Should you require further assistance, access our website at doubleyoudoubleyou . . .'

'Here,' the girl pointed out, 'that's my phone. Don't do that, you'll break it.'

'Sorry,' Chris said, and handed it back.

She put it away. 'They didn't seem very helpful,' she said. He shrugged.

'Government,' he replied. 'Anyway, they'll take it from here. None of our business any more. We just stay put and wait for them, and everything'll be just fine,' he added, glancing to make sure that the car doors were locked. Not, he reflected, that a little bit of glass and pressed steel sheet would slow up one of *them* for very long.

'Back there.' Angela's voice was quieter and a little bit higher. 'Was it really a—?'

'Yes,' Chris said.

'Oh.' Not scared, though; he'd assumed it was fear, but it wasn't. He couldn't actually decide what it was. 'What had it done?'

'Killed the manager,' he replied. 'Which is unusual,' he added, more thinking aloud than communicating, 'because they aren't usually that violent. I've got a friend in the agency, and she's told me a bit about them. They don't usually attack unless they have to, it uses up a lot of energy and they're very – efficient.' He frowned. 'I don't think it was hungry, the body was just lying there, hadn't really been touched. Also, it had cleared off all the shelves, like it was looking for something. My guess is, it was there to get weapons. It's a line DCM specialise in, and the one I saw was holding something like a great big knife; sort of turning it over in its hands and looking at it, the way you do when you've just bought something.' Chris shivered. 'Anyway, like I said, not our problem. I'd better phone in and explain, get Julie to ring round the shops, tell them we've been held up.'

They arrived much sooner than he'd expected: a fleet of white vans, a couple of marked police cars, and suddenly he was being talked at by half a dozen people at once, all of them asking the same things, none of them appearing to listen to a word he said. They took no notice of the girl; she sat still and quiet for a long time, then got out a book and began to read.

'It was shortish, sort of a grey colour, with a big head,' Chris said, for the sixth or seventh time, 'and it just sat there on the shelf, grinning at me.'

The man frowned, as if that made no sense at all. 'Do you know if it was armed? Had it got a weapon of any kind?'

'Yes, I told that other man just now, it had a big sort of knife thing, I think it stole it from the shop—'

'Do you think the weapon might have come from the shop? They're listed as specialising in enchanted arms and armour.'

Chris sighed. 'You know what, it's a distinct possibility, now you come to mention it. Never would have occurred to me, but—'

The man was tapping something into a laptop resting on the car roof. 'You'd better give me your full name, address, date of birth—'

It occurred to Chris that unless he did something, this might very well continue for the rest of his life. 'Just out of interest,' he said, 'do you know someone called Jill Ettin-Smith? She works in your department, and—'

The man looked up from his screen. 'You know Jill?'

He nodded. 'We were at school together.'

'Oh.' The man snapped his laptop shut. 'Oh, right. Actually, she should be along any minute.'

'Really? Small world.'

'Not really. She's the head of this department.'

Chris was surprised, and impressed. Jill talked about work a lot, sure, but very little (now he came to think about it) about what she actually did there; whether she was important or not, stuff like that. Part of him felt slightly ashamed at being surprised. The rest of him couldn't quite come to terms with someone who'd copied off him in maths at age twelve being put in charge of anything.

He didn't see her, though. They stopped asking him questions, piled back into their vans and drove away, and he

assumed she must've gone straight to the shop, which was fair
enough (though surely there was very little chance that *it* would
still be there, after all this time). And it stood to reason, it was
a serious business and she was a professional, not to mention a
head of department, serious management, she wouldn't have
time to stop off and pass the time of day with an old school
friend, even though he'd obviously just had the shock of his life
and could've done with the reassurance of a familiar face—

'Right,' Chris said, rather loudly, 'that's that, we'd better get
on and do some work, especially since we probably won't be
getting any orders from DCM any time soon. Pity, I was pretty
sure I'd be able to get shot of three dozen TR77Bs on them.'

The girl gave him a look that'd have annoyed him under
other circumstances, but after all the fuss and aggravation she
was the least of his problems. He asked her for the map and
pretended to study it while he pulled himself together.

'Now then,' he said, 'Sedgely's.'

Not the first time he'd come across that smell.

The first time, many years ago but still crisp and sharp in his
mind, lodged there like shrapnel from some old war; no bother
most days, but gradually moving inwards, always gently pressing on the nerve. The stupid thing was, he should have missed
it; he had no business being in there when it happened, he was
breaking about a dozen school rules, and for what? Just some
stupid dare.

It had all been Benny's fault; Chris had told them all, the
headmaster, the girl's parents, the men from the government.
Benny had dared him to spend the whole lunch break hiding in
a cubicle of the girls' toilets – why this was important to Benny,
he had no idea and it hadn't occurred to him to ask. Foot soldiers don't ask the field marshal what he wants the stupid hill
for. He'd been given his orders, and that was that.

The first twenty minutes had been really rather dull. He'd
heard cubicle doors closing, the occasional whoosh of plumbing, nothing particularly titillating or suggestive of the hidden
mysteries of biological otherness. He'd been wishing he'd

brought his maths homework to be getting on with when he heard voices he recognised, and froze. Karen Hitchins was asking Jill Ettin-Smith if she could borrow her RE notes. He didn't really give a damn about Karen Hitchins's opinion of him, but Jill was another matter entirely. She had the knack of being disappointed in people; the look that said, I thought you were different. Worse than detention. Chris concentrated on keeping perfectly still and breathing very quietly.

A third voice; well, they always go around in threes, don't they? He couldn't make out who it was, so he consulted his mental database of school political alliances. Karen and Jill used to go around with Amelia Morris, but earlier that term Amelia had defected to the cool gang, and Ellie Kranz had been co-opted to replace her. Five would get you one, there-fore, that the third voice was that of Ellie, about whom he knew nothing and cared less—

Then the smell. Because it was all flowery and sweet, Chris had assumed it was some kind of toiletry or cosmetic; from its intensity, he guessed someone had just spilt the bottle. The conversation stopped abruptly – he'd felt a cramp of fear in his stomach; had they seen the toes of his palpably masculine shoes through the gap under the door? And then the scream.

Some years later, when he'd moved in with Karen Hitchins, he'd tried to ask her what she'd seen, what had actually hap-pened, but she'd pretended she hadn't heard the question, and he knew better than to mention the subject ever again. Jill had only told him what she'd told the government people: a demon had appeared out of nowhere, killed poor Ellie, ripped her head off her shoulders and vanished, taking the head with it – And afterwards, when his parents collected him from the school, and he'd worked so hard to find the words to tell them: Jill Ettin-Smith said it was a demon, like from Hell, and I know it sounds stupid but I believe her, I think demons must be real. And they'd looked at each other, and then at him, and his dad had said, we believe you, son, we know they're real, listen—

– Which was how Chris had come to learn about the reality of magic, the existence of sorcerers and demons, and what Grandpa had really done for a living, and how these things ran in families, and for all they knew he might have it too. Which had turned out to be the case; though, according to the government people who did the tests, he was little better than borderline, no real chance of him ever being able to practise professionally, even if he went to university and did the degree course; certainly no scholarship, which he'd have to have, since you couldn't get a student loan for thaumaturgical studies. And that was that, which was why he now carried the bag for JWW Retail, as close as he'd ever get to the real thing—

Maybe because Chris was still in shock and therefore not really trying, he managed to shift a phenomenal amount of stuff off on Sedgely's, including four dozen BB27Ks with display materials and a dumpbin. He thanked them automatically, wrote the order up in the book and drifted back to the car.

'Might as well stop for lunch now,' he heard himself say. 'There's a pub on our way to Milford & Shale's, miserable place but it means we won't have to go out of our way. All right by you?'

'OK.'

Miserable, as it turned out, was putting it mildly. The landlord made them feel about as welcome as a notifiable disease, the food took half an hour to arrive and even the pub cat wouldn't touch the sausages. That, as far as Chris was concerned, was just fine. It wasn't really a happy day, and anything nice or fun would've seemed faintly grotesque.

'I don't know the exact figures,' he was saying, replying to the girl's question. 'There's more of them about than you'd think, but not enough to be a real problem. We keep the lid on it pretty well, which is why you don't see anything about them on the telly. Actually, an attack's generally quite good for business. We sell quite a few demon-related products: early warning alarms, liquid demon-repellant, pepper sprays—'

'Pepper sprays?'

Chris nodded. 'Didn't you know, they're an endangered species? Though not nearly endangered enough, if you ask me. Still, there it is. You and I can't go around knocking them off, it's got to be done by trained authorised personnel. So, yes, pepper sprays. They tell me nothing pisses a demon off quite as thoroughly as a face full of pepper, but that's the law.'

'Oh,' Angela said. 'That's stupid.'

He shrugged. 'Not up to me,' he said. 'Also, to be fair, they're bloody hard to kill. Friend of mine works for the department – you know, those comedians we met back there – and apparently you need very specialised kit, not the sort of thing that fits neatly in your handbag or jacket pocket. Anyhow,' he added, as she started to ask another question, 'let's not talk about it any more, if you don't mind. All right?'

She shrugged too but he could see that she wasn't happy. 'If you like,' she said.

'Thanks. So,' Chris went on, taking a deep breath, 'apart from that, how are you finding it?'

'What?'

'The business. The thrill of the open road, the challenge of hand-to-hand marketing. About what you'd expected?'

Another shrug. 'More or less,' Angela said. 'Though really it's not about, well, magic, is it? You might as well be selling envelopes or toilet rolls.'

'Yes,' Chris said. 'Except I wouldn't be, because all that stuff's done by technology now, electronic point of sale reordering and centralised buying. But this is an old-fashioned business, so they still need reps. Which is just as well for me, really.'

'I suppose.' Angela looked away, then down at her finger-nails, which were bitten short. 'Anyway, I get the general idea. You go round the shops and try and get them to buy stuff. That's about it, isn't it?'

'Broadly speaking.' Chris offered a corner of his fried-bread crust to the cat; it stared at him, yowled and ran away. 'Still, it's as close to the interesting stuff as I'll ever get. Not like you, with your high-powered research.'

'Actually, it's mostly pretty boring,' Angela replied. 'I mean, when I was a kid I thought it'd be all invisibility cloaks and turning people into frogs, but it's not like that. Really, the only difference between what I'm doing and ordinary physics and chemistry is that there's a little chip of Knowing Stone inside my calculator instead of silicon, so it doesn't need batteries.'

Chris nodded. 'We sell those,' he said. 'They're not very reliable, though. Drop them or leave them out in the sun and they're knackered.'

All in all, a long, fraught day. Karen was out when Chris got home, so he defrosted a pizza and sat down in front of the telly. Nothing on the news about the grisly murder of a shop-keeper in the West Midlands, so maybe he'd imagined it after all.

He was halfway through his pizza when the phone rang. 'Chris?'

There was an edge to her voice, but he could understand that. 'Hi, Jill. How did you get on with the—?'

'Did you open my carrier bag before you gave it back?'

He jumped, as though the phone had bitten his ear. 'What? No, of course—'

'There was a sealed packet of biscuits in there and now there's just a wrapper.'

So the day hadn't finished with him quite yet. 'Was there?' 'Yes.'

Chris hesitated. 'I guess Karen must've eaten them. I left the bag on the kitchen table. She must've wandered down in the night and—'

'They were plain digestives. She hates plain digestives.'

'Does she?'

'Yes.' Less than friendly *tsk* noise. 'I know that for a fact, Chris, she was my best friend at school, remember?'

And he, Karen's long-term significant other, hadn't got a clue what sort of biscuits she did and didn't like (but Jill, he happened to know, adored chocolate hobnobs). 'Is that right?' he said. 'I never—'

'Which means,' Jill continued grimly, 'she wouldn't have eaten them. But somebody did.'

He really wasn't in the mood for anything like this. 'Look, for crying out loud, Jill, I'll buy you another damn packet of biscuits, all right? But for the record, I didn't eat—'

'I don't care about the biscuits, I want to know if you looked in the bag. Well, I know you did,' she went on (had he ever heard her this angry before? Not as far as he could remember), 'what I need to know is exactly what you did.'

This is silly, Chris thought. Jill and her stupid bloody carrier bags. 'All right,' he said, 'I may have just glanced inside it quickly, as I was putting it down on the—'

'You just looked. You didn't take anything out.'

'No.'

'You mean, no apart from the biscuits.'

From silly to annoying; evolution in action. 'I didn't touch the fucking biscuits. I don't like plain digestives either. Just as soon eat plywood. And no, I didn't touch anything in the stupid bag, all right?'

Silence at the other end. Anybody else and he'd have construed it as sulking, only Jill never sulked. Mind you, Jill never freaked out about anything as trivial as biscuit theft, either. But when she spoke again, her voice was different. Not less agitated, but clearer in her mind, maybe. 'All right,' she said, 'if you're absolutely sure.'

'Yes.'

'Fine. That's all I needed to know.' Pause. 'You haven't got a cat or a dog or anything like that, have you?'

'You know we haven't, Jill, because of Karen's asthma.'

'Yes, of course. Mice? Rats?'

'No.'

And this time – well, not relief, but the lowering of tension that

comes with a mystery solved, even if the solution is unpalatable.
'So, you really have no idea what could've eaten the biscuits?'

'No.' As Chris said it, he frowned, and the question formed
in his mind; so, if it wasn't Karen, who the hell *did* eat the—?

'OK. Thanks for clearing that up.' But I didn't, he thought;
there's been something weird going on, and I can't account for
it. 'Sorry if I came across a bit nasty – I didn't mean to bite
your head off.'

Pause. Freudian slip, if that was the term he was looking for.
At any rate, it could be taken as a perfectly valid explanation for
Jill stressing out like that. 'Talking of which,' he said, his voice
a little higher and falsely cheerful, 'did you find the – well, the
thingummy that did in poor Mr Newsome?'

'No.' Definitely not happy about that. 'By the time we got
there, the trail had gone cold. We even tried scrying in water,
but it knew what it was doing, covered its tracks very well.'
Long pause, then: 'Is Karen there?'

'No, she's out.'

'When you see her, maybe it'd be better not to talk about it,'
Jill said, sounding much more like herself. 'Because of – well,
you know, what happened. I happen to know it's a very sore
subject with her, she can get a bit extreme about it, and if she
gets the idea there's one on the loose out there, it could mess
her up a bit. So, keep quiet about it, will you?'

'Sure,' Chris replied without thinking, mostly relieved
because Jill was back to normal. 'And there's no reason why the
subject should come up, we're not exactly a had-a-nice-day-at-
the-office-dear kind of household.' He hesitated for a moment,
then said, 'Look, about your biscuits, I'll get you another—'

'Forget about it,' Jill replied, and she sounded quite normal.
'Actually, your poltergeist or whatever it was probably did me
a favour, I really can't afford to go stuffing my face with biscuits
unless I want to end up looking like a small whale.'

End of conversation. Chris put the phone down, then
looked at it for a few seconds, as though he suspected it of
playing games with him. Yes, all right, post-traumatic stress

syndrome or whatever the medical term was, maybe Jill was a little bit off her head tonight because of what she'd seen at the shop. But that still left the problem of what had munched its way through an entire packet of digestive biscuits, and the more he thought about that, the stranger it became. Furthermore, now he came to think of it, the unidentified muncher had eaten all the biccies and then put the wrapper back in the bag. Karen wouldn't have done that, she'd have binned it, no doubt breathing a heavy sigh as she did so because it was non-recyclable, and it'd have had to have been a fairly sophisticated mouse—

Under other circumstances, if he'd had a problem like that, he'd have phoned Jill; who'd either have explained it away in ten seconds flat, or told him not to be so stupid as to worry about it. Option not available. Chris sat down with his half a cold pizza on his lap, and tried to rationalise it, but his mind kept slipping off it, as though it had been waxed.

Karen got home just after ten; in a foul mood, overtired and overwrought. There'd been a screw-up at work, she explained, and she'd had to stay on and sort it all out in time for the meeting tomorrow. Chris didn't ask for details and she didn't offer them. He heard her slamming cabinet doors in the bathroom as he closed his eyes and went to sleep.

He had the dream again. Not that he minded. It was a nice dream, his favourite.

He was in the car, somewhere in Staffordshire, although the view through the window was of mountains, their sides covered in an endless sea of pine trees, shimmering faintly grey in the summer heat. Sitting beside him, she'd just said, 'At the end of the road, turn left,' though the road went on, straight as an arrow, as far as the eye could see.

'The road is very long,' he said. He talked like that, in the dream.

'You will know when the time comes to turn left,' she replied.

'How will I know?'

'I will be here to tell you.'

He didn't look round. 'I am glad you will be here with me when the turning comes,' he said.

'I am always with you,' she said, and he could feel the warmth of her radiance, and the edges of his vision blurred golden from the light that shone from her, and he passed a signpost that said *Stoke on Trent 455 miles.*

Oh good, he thought; because when he saw that sign it meant it was the point in the dream where he was allowed to ask one question and still be able to remember the answer when he woke up. It was amazing, the sort of stuff she knew about, and she'd never been wrong yet.

'SatNav,' he said, 'who ate the biscuits?'

Silence for a while, and then she said, 'The one who is to come ate the biscuits, Chris.'

Oh, he thought. Never wrong yet; but there were some nights when she came over all cryptic, which was only to be expected when you considered that she was just his problem-solving subconscious mind, sublimated into the form of the only entity in the world he really trusted.

'I do not know who that is,' he said. It was all right to admit stuff like that, in the dream. In real life, of course, women expect you to be bloody telepathic.

'When the time comes, you will know,' she said. 'After six hundred and fifty-four miles, prepare to turn left.'

Oh no you don't, he thought; so he asked, 'Who is the one who is to come, SatNav?'

'The one who is to come will unite the children who fell,' she replied. 'The one who is to come will lead them along the road they have to travel, taking the third exit at the next round-about. But you will not remember that when you wake up, because it is still hidden.'

Oh well, he thought, fair enough. 'Why did the one who is to come steal Jill's biscuits, SatNav?' he persevered, and in front of him the road narrowed, hedges closing in around him like the fingers of a grasping hand.

'I do not know,' she replied. 'Presumably the one who is to come happens to like plain digestives, though personally I prefer Maryland chocolate-chip cookies.'

For some reason a great surge of joy swept through him as she said that, and he was about to tell her that he liked them too when Karen wriggled, made a noise like a pig and dragged all the bedclothes over to her side, waking him up.

CHAPTER THREE

'It's not really our sort of thing,' the manager said, after a long silence. 'No, sorry, I don't see our customers going for that,' she added, as the tiny genie hovered a few inches above the spout of its lamp, its minuscule fingers dabbing at the keypad of its mobile phone. 'I mean, it doesn't really *do* anything, does it?'

Very true, Chris thought. 'You get three wishes,' he said cheerfully.

The manager shook her head. 'Not much good for anything, though, are they? Can't do this, not allowed to do that—'

'Terms and conditions apply,' he conceded reluctantly. 'But it's very attractively priced, and you can add the upgrade packs, which give you extra wishes, so—'

'No,' she said firmly. 'No, we already do the Imadjinnation range from Zauberwerke, they're much better, you get six wishes as standard and they can actually *do* stuff. All yours does is sit there on its little cloud, saying, "That option is not available with this product." Sorry, but I'll pass on that one, thanks all the same. What else have you got?'

'Ah,' Chris said. 'Now I know you're going to love this.' He opened the sample case and took out the book. '*The Book of All*

Human Knowledge, new edition. Always been a strong seller, and now all new with additional—'

'No.' She cut him off. 'Sorry, we had two dozen of them last year, and when the customers got them home and opened them, all the pages were blank. Very embarrassing for us, having to explain—'

She had a point there, too. Even with the all-new operating system (which he told her about, but she clearly wasn't impressed) the *Book* was severely limited by the fact that it only told you what you *really* needed to know, not what you wanted, or what you *thought* you needed. If you tried to override the system – by, for example, thinking *this isn't what I wanted to find out about, why hasn't the stupid thing got an index?* – the *Book* tended to freeze, its pages blank apart from a tiny little black hourglass constantly revolving on the copyright page, just below the ISBN number.

Chris moved on. 'Instaglamour cream,' he said, holding up a small glass jar. 'Apply sparingly last thing at night, and in the morning you're irresistibly beautiful; no-quibble guarantee, lasts up to nine hours, very sensibly priced at—'

'We stock the Superglamor-Me from Michigan Magical,' she said wearily. 'Lasts longer, doesn't fade in direct sunlight. I'm surprised you're still bothering with that stuff.'

He explained that the Instaglamour came in four handy sizes, whereas Superglamor-Me only came in three, and it was the glamour cream of choice of international supermodels such as Ariana Vetterli and—

'Who?'

'She's not so well-known over here,' Chris admitted. 'Very big in Monaco, though, and she won't use anything else. We provide a range of promotional—'

'Nah. And the same goes for the Silvertongue syrup,' she added. 'Doesn't work. After all,' she went on, a trifle unnecessarily in his opinion, 'if it worked, you'd be using it and I'd be buying your stuff.'

'There's an ethical code,' he replied weakly. 'We're not allowed—'

'Is that it, then?' she said, giving him that never-really-expected-anything-from-*you* look that he'd grown so tired of over the years. 'Only I've got the Kawaguchiya rep coming in at twelve-thirty – I'm taking him to lunch.'

Chris managed a smile, somehow or other. 'That's about it for this month,' he said. 'Apart, of course, from our very latest new line, which I've been saving till last because I just know it's going to blow your socks off. The JWW BB27K—'

'Oh, that.' She grinned. 'Heard all about it from Susie at the Telford branch. She had a customer, she bought one and parked her car in it, came back half an hour later and the car'd gone. Vanished. Called out the AA, finally got the supernatural breakdown service, the bloke told her it'd fallen through the fabric of space/time into a pocket reality and it'd cost nine hundred quid plus VAT to get it out again. And it was only a cruddy old Fiesta, so it wasn't worth it. No, you can keep them, I'm not having them in my shop.'

There was, of course, a perfectly rational explanation in that case, and if the customer had read the instructions properly and checked for ley lines, like the booklet said, it wouldn't have happened. But he didn't bother telling her. Waste of breath. 'Well,' Chris said, 'if you change your mind you've got my number. So, shall we just run through the repeat orders?'

She nodded. 'Just the DW6,' she said. 'I think we'll up that from nine dozen to twelve, just in case we get a sudden run. Your delivery people are so slow—'

Just for a moment he was tempted to ask, but he didn't. 'Right-oh,' he said. 'Twelve dozen dried waters, what else can I—?'

'That's all,' she said. 'See you next month, then.'

It could've been worse, he told himself as he walked back to the car. Could've had that bloody trainee with me. Small mercies.

(Angela the trainee had called in sick; or at least, her mother, who happened to be a personal friend of Mr Burnoz – would've been nice if Angela had thought to mention that – had rung him at home to say her daughter had come back a nervous wreck and what was that stupid Chris person thinking of, taking her where there could be demons, it was just a wonder she hadn't been killed or horribly mutilated, and she was really upset about it . . . Sometimes small mercies are very small indeed, and come with a side salad of aggravation.)

But at least, without her there, he could use the SatNav—

Chris stopped dead, his hand on the car door handle. *Why* would he want to use the SatNav when he could find his way from Kettles to Black Country Esoterica blindfold on a dark night in the fog? He let go of the handle as though there might be something infectious on it, and took a step back, nearly treading on the foot of a passing stranger.

There was that problem. He'd been warned about it, at the sales conference when they'd launched the product: the JWW Queenie (Quasi-Intelligent Navigational Instrument, Queenie; for which some genius in marketing had been paid good money) was the state of the art, a million per cent more accurate and reliable than the Stone Age non-magic version that ran on some kind of radio signal beamed off an American military satellite, but there was a problem. No bother if a few simple precautions were observed, and they'd tweaked the bugs enough to get it to comply with the latest EU regs, but—

Actually, Chris thought it was more than a little problem, and when they'd told him he could have one he hadn't been keen. I know my way round my own patch, thank you very much, he'd told them, I certainly don't need a bloody con-demned soul imprisoned in a little plastic box with a set of OS maps to tell me how to get from Wolverhampton to Stafford without going through Birmingham city centre.

It's fine, they told him, the wards and containment spells are absolutely watertight and foolproof, there's absolutely no way the bugger's getting out of there, you've just got to be a tiny bit careful, that's all. Asked to define 'careful' in this context, how-ever, they'd gone ever so slightly vague – treat it with respect, don't play with it, use a bit of common sense, and other well-meaning but useless advice. Chris had driven for a month like a lorry driver hauling nitroglycerine until Ben Jarrow, who had the south-eastern patch, finally told him what all the fuss was about. Yes, the unit was powered by a living entity, usually a sprite, dryad, water nymph or salamander; invariably, one that had committed some crime against the laws of its community and been given a life sentence. But that was fine, since the wards really did work, otherwise the standards commission would never have signed off on it. The only danger lay in getting – well, Ben had said, looking a little strange, in getting attached to it. What, caught up in the wiring or something? No, Ben said patiently, getting fond of it. Talking to it. Maybe starting to believe it was talking back, having a conversation. But the risk wasn't worth worrying about, he'd continued, because who in his right mind would start talking to a navigational aid? Only someone who was a bit not quite right in the head, or a really sad bugger – And in any case, he'd added, if you do start to feel like you're getting caught, all you've got to do is turn the radio on, or play a CD, and the spell's broken. Simple as that.

You never think it'll be you. You always reckon you're too smart, and then it's too late; you're hooked, caught, in the shit, and everybody's giving you sad, sympathetic looks that really mean *told you so*. So easily done. But, Chris told himself, as he nerved himself to touch the car door again, it's all right, I caught it in time, I'll be sensible from now on and it'll all be fine.

So he climbed in and sat perfectly still for a moment or so; then he leaned across and reached for the radio. For a split second, his fingers brushed the SatNav's little rectangular screen, and he felt a sudden urge to press the button; bad, he thought, very bad, and stretched past it until he felt the radio knob click into place. Safe. There, see? Nothing to it, really.

The radio. The Jeremy Vine show; the daily current affairs phone-in spot. He put up with it for ten minutes, then turned it off, reflecting that if the spirit of the SatNav really was a nasty piece of work suffering eternal damnation for its sins, the only real difference between SatNav and the radio was that

Jeremy was getting paid. After that he drove in silence for a bit; then, more through absent-mindedness than anything else, he turned on the CD player.

That tune again. It really was rather catchy, though Chris couldn't remember a note of it after it had finished – a point in its favour, since there's nothing worse than having a song rattling around in your head all day. Distracting, though; which meant the diversion on the outskirts of Walsall took him completely by surprise, and before he could react he'd been swept away by the currents of the traffic and was heading at considerable speed in the wrong direction.

Sod it, Chris thought, because the country he was being swirled along through was some way off his customary route, and he didn't know offhand how you got back onto the main dual carriageway, which in any event was closed for resurfacing. Just as well, he told himself, that I've got my little friend here. He pressed the button, frowned – something at the back of his mind; no, gone – and waited for—

'Hello, Chris,' she said.

'Hi. Look, I'm trying to get to—'

'Walsall,' she said, 'but you missed the diversion. Not to worry. Your route is being calculated – please wait.'

So he waited; and while she was thinking about it, he said, 'You missed a bit of excitement yesterday.'

'Poor Mr Newsome. It must've been terrible, finding him like that.'

'Well, it wasn't much fun,' Chris replied. 'Standing there with that thing sat there looking at me . . .'

'I think you were very brave,' she said. 'Most people would've panicked.'

'It wasn't like that, actually,' he replied. 'It's a funny thing, but when something like that happens – I don't know, maybe it's the survival instinct suddenly cutting in and taking charge, but I knew exactly what I had to do: keep still and quiet, no sudden movements, get out of there nice and slowly and don't break eye contact. Mind you,' he added, 'it helped a lot that it'd already had its dinner. I got the impression it simply couldn't be bothered with me.'

'It's true,' she said. 'They don't tend to attack unless they're hungry or something upsets or annoys them. Most of them, anyway. There are some who kill for the sheer pleasure of it.'

'Ah well,' Chris said, suddenly anxious to change the subject. 'You figured out where we are yet?'

'At the next roundabout, take the third exit.' Pause; then, 'Your apprentice isn't with you today.'

Apprentice, he thought; as in *The Sorcerer's*. Nice thought. 'No, I think she was suffering from a bit of the old delayed shock,' he said. 'Handled it pretty well at the time, I thought, but I guess it must've got to her later, after she got home.' He overtook a slow tractor, then said, 'What do you make of her, then?'

'Quiet,' she said. 'Reserved, a little shy. Perhaps not very keen to be here. And young, of course.'

Chris nodded. 'Stroppy,' he said. 'Loads of attitude. Apparently her mum's an old friend of Dave Burnoz's, which explains how I got stuck with her.'

'Rather an honour, don't you think?' she said. 'To choose you to look after his protégée, rather than one of the others.'

'Nah,' he said, though secretly he was rather taken with the idea. 'It's just that I'm the rep for this area and she lives locally. Also, it's a rotten job, so naturally it comes my way.'

'You're too hard on yourself,' she said soothingly. 'I think Mr Burnoz chose you because you're a good salesman.'

'And because she lives on my patch.'

'That too.'

Chris drove on for a while; she'd got him back on course, on schedule too, so there was no need to rush. It was turning out fine, so he wound the window down a little and savoured the feel of the warm air on his face. Next stop was the Magic Shack – you never knew what sort of business you'd do there, could be a substantial order, could be nothing. He made a resolution to be positive. He was going to sell them lots and lots of stuff, including (at this point it was necessary to suspend reasonable disbelief) at least four dozen BB27Ks. He had a good feeling about it.

In the event, entirely justified. *Five* dozen BB27Ks, with special promotional material; also two dozen bottomless purses, a gross of Instaglamour cream, two pocket universes and his entire car stock of anti-demon talismans. In fact, the only line he wasn't able to interest them in was DW6—

('We've been meaning to ask you,' said the eager, bespectacled young assistant manager. 'This is probably a very silly question, but what's it actually *for*?' So, no sale there—)

The only slight flaw in an otherwise extremely pleasant call was a return: one NK77B, rejected by a customer as not fit for purpose—

'But how did she know it's not working?' Chris asked.

The assistant manager looked at him. 'She tried it. It didn't work. It's quite simple, really.'

Normally he wouldn't have bothered arguing the toss, but today he decided to give it a go, just for the hell of it. 'But it's such a subjective thing, isn't it?' he said, smiling insidiously. 'I mean, a mirror of desire, shows you what you really want. What did she actually see in it?'

The assistant manager grinned. 'She saw herself looking into a mirror of desire that worked properly,' he replied.

'Oh.'

So Chris had taken it back, all neatly packed away in its carton, and thrown it on the back seat along with all the other junk that had come to rest there over the years. Annoying, but not his fault. He started the engine and drove away.

He hadn't gone far when he hit the diversion again, but not to worry; he leant across and pressed SatNav's on switch. Nothing happened.

He swore, jerking the wheel, and the car swerved alarmingly. He pulled himself together, straightened up, made himself concentrate on the road. Chill, Chris told himself, it's just something broken, that's all. But that didn't work, because it wasn't an it, it was a she, a living creature shut up in a plastic box. Warm day; maybe the poor thing was suffocating in there. Anxiously he scanned the road ahead, and was enormously relieved to see a lay-by, not far off. He pulled in, switched off the engine, unbuckled his seat belt and leaned forward—

– And, in doing so, happened to glance in his rear-view mirror. He froze. In the mirror, grinning at him, was a demon.

Being incapable of movement and therefore having nothing better to do with his time, Chris looked at it. Its skin was grey, the colour of builder's mortar, more like elephant hide than anything you'd expect to find on a human. Its body was about the size of a ten-year-old child's, but its head was bigger than his own, hairless, with round lidless eyes that were perfectly black. The teeth in its thin, very wide mouth were all about an inch long, thin and slightly curved, ending in needle points. It had a tiny snout rather than a nose, and its ears were pointed, just like Mr Spock's. It was bony but with well-defined muscles, its elbows grotesquely pointed, its hands broad and inhumanly flat, with long, slim, five-jointed fingers tipped with claws, like a cat's. And it was grinning; well, of course it was. With those teeth, if it closed its mouth it'd do itself an injury.

Well, Chris thought, here we go, just like poor Mr Newsome. He wondered if it would hurt, if there was an afterlife, and if so was there a Nice Place and a Very Bad Place, and was the Nice Place as he'd always imagined it, a bit like the hotel in the Malverns where they had the annual sales conference. He didn't waste time speculating about the Very Bad Place, because as far as he was concerned he'd been there already, leaving at age seventeen with six GCSEs.

'Hello?' he whispered.

The demon made a very soft hissing noise, like a gas fire before you light it, and slowly extended its right arm. Chris closed his eyes, kept them screwed tight shut until he felt something brush against his cheek, and smelt that smell again. He yelped and squirmed up against the car door, his eyes opening by reflex; and he saw the demon's arm, reaching carefully over his shoulder and touching the SatNav's power button with the point of its index claw.

'Your route is being calculated, please – oh.'

For a split second, Chris felt an urge to grab the demon's wrist and pull it away, keep its filthy claws off her – But he didn't, and the demon withdrew its arm, winked at him, kicked open the nearside back door and scampered out.

'Twice in two days,' the government man said. 'They must like you.'

Not, Chris felt, a tactful thing to say, and if that was an example of his taxes at work he had a good mind to vote for the other lot next time round. No suitably pithy comeback occurred to him, so he gave the government man a nasty look instead. In the distance, from where he was sitting on the verge he watched the men in Day-Glo yellow jackets coning off the road, while sniffer dogs of a breed he'd never seen before and hoped never to see again were snuffling up and down the tarmac.

'Look,' he said feebly, 'I've told you everything I can remember, can I go now? Only—'

'No chance,' the man replied scornfully. 'Forensic's going to want to pull this car apart down to the sub-atomic level, so unless you fancy a long walk you aren't going anywhere.'

'Oh,' Chris said. 'I was hoping to scrounge a lift—'

Now he'd offended the government man. 'Sorry, but we've got a job to do here. We're not a taxi service. Now, we'll be needing your clothes.'

'What? You must be—'

'For analysis,' the government man explained briskly. 'DNA traces, maybe flakes of skin or traces of spit, if we're really lucky. Don't know if they'll want to shave all your hair off, it depends on what we find on the clothes and the car, but don't go touching it unless you absolutely have to or you could disturb the evidence.'

The government man went away, and Chris sat perfectly still for a quarter of an hour, as if his patch of grass was the only safe place left in the whole world. Then a familiar voice said his name, and he looked up.

'I got here as quickly as I could,' Jill said, sitting down beside him and opening her carrier bag. She wasn't wearing Day-Glo yellow like the others: a plain dark M&S business suit and white blouse; very grown up, he couldn't help thinking. 'Here, have a mini Swiss roll – you must be starving.'

Chris took one from her but made a real mess of taking off the foil wrapping. She took it back and did it for him.

'Are they really going to shave my hair off?' he asked.

She grinned. 'Bless them,' she said. 'They're so thorough. It's all right, I'll have a word with them.'

'And my clothes? Only this is my good suit, and—'

'I'll make sure they don't shred it,' Jill said. 'So,' she went on, 'now you know what I do at work. Fun, isn't it?'

Chris shuddered. 'And you actually – well, kill them?'

She nodded. 'Actually, it's not so bad once you get used to it. It's a bit like picking up your dog's mess in a plastic bag: you try not to think about what you're actually doing, and then it's no big deal.'

'I've never had a dog.'

She smiled. 'I know,' she said. 'Probably for that very reason. Have another Swiss roll, keep your blood sugar up.'

Pause; then, 'Do you think you'll be able to find it?' Chris asked with his mouth full.

Jill shrugged. 'Depends on the dogs, mostly. Trouble is, they can be pretty cunning about masking their scent. We've got helicopters out with ultra-blue thaumaturgical sensors, but they only really work at night – daylight blurs the image too much. The foot patrols might get lucky, I suppose, but I'm not holding my breath. So,' she went on, 'tell me what happened.'

So he told her – the truth, whole and nothing but – right up to the moment where the demon had reached past him with its arm. For some reason, he left that bit out—

'And then it winked at me, kicked the door open and scarpered,' he concluded. 'And that's all, really. Doesn't sound much, when you're telling someone else.'

'On the contrary,' Jill replied seriously, 'you've given me at least half a dozen good strong leads, which'll be very helpful. For example, the pointed ears. That's a dead giveaway.'

'Is it?'

'Oh yes.' Profound nod. 'Means it's a quaerens – that's Latin for someone who looks for things, a searcher. Reconnaissance and special forces, essentially. If it'd been basic rank-and-file infantry, it'd have had rounded ears with long, pendulous lobes, while the engineer and technical grades have ears that stick out sideways, and the sappers haven't got ears at all. The five finger-joints mean it was probably a mature specimen – the juveniles don't grow the fifth joint till they're at least seven hundred years old. Actually you're privileged, if you care to look at it that way: the quaerens grade's pretty rare. Some of the guys in the department have been in the business thirty years and never seen one.'

'Bloody hell, Jill,' Chris growled. 'You make it sound like birdwatching.'

She laughed. 'Some of them are bit like that,' she sort-of-whispered back, 'they've got copies of the *Observer Book of British Demons* that they carry with them wherever they go, and whenever they come across a grade or a subspecies they haven't seen before, they tick them off the list and boast about it for days in the canteen. All a bit sad, really, but I guess it's their way of keeping motivated. At least they don't have the dead ones stuffed and mounted any more, like they used to when I joined the department.'

She was being deliberately chatty; long practice at putting witnesses at their ease? Somehow Chris didn't like that. He was supposed to be her friend, damn it, not a witness. But then, he'd always reckoned that with Jill, work came first. And at least she wasn't threatening to shave off all his hair. He licked melted chocolate off his fingers.

'What's got me puzzled,' she said, 'is the way it just *left*—'

'Without killing me first, you mean?'

Jill frowned, as though he'd said something in bad taste. 'Well, bluntly, yes,' she said. 'The thing about demons is, they never waste energy.'

'What, they insulate their lofts and stuff?'

She recognised that as flippancy and ignored it. 'Demons have the most amazing metabolisms,' she went on. 'Absolutely incredible rate of cellular regeneration, which is why you can cut off a hand or a foot and twenty minutes later it'll have grown back, good as new. If only we could crack the science behind it we could do the most amazing things with human medicine, but for some reason the demons aren't terribly keen on cooperating with our researchers.' Bleak grin. 'Anyway, it's good from their point of view, makes them practically impossible to kill without magic, but it means they use up a hell of a lot of energy; so they eat masses but that's awkward for them considering *what* they eat, they can't go around slaughtering people every time they get a fit of the nibbles or they'd pose a real threat to human society and it'd turn into open war. They've got more sense; they know that if they keep their attacks down to a minimum we'll keep covering it up to stop the public at large finding out that they exist – can't have that, obviously, there'd be mass hysteria. So,' she went on, after a pause for breath, 'they've learned to conserve their energy. Like, you've seen lions at the zoo, right? All they do is lie around sleeping all day, because when they hunt – assuming they're not in zoos, I mean when they're in the wild – they burn off about a million calories a second, so when they're not hunting, they just flop. Same with demons, only more so, of course. I mean, just the effort of projecting themselves out of their native dimension and into the material world is enough to drain their batteries, which is why you only see them when they're actively on the warpath, so to speak. Which is why,' she went on, 'I can't really figure out why your one went to all the trouble of materialising in your car, and then just smiled nicely at you and buggered off.'

'I see,' Chris replied. He was starting to shake now. Delayed reaction, presumably.

'Lucky for you, of course,' Jill added, 'but a mystery. Now the one you saw yesterday, that was classic post-attack lethargy. It'd worn itself out killing the shop person, it simply couldn't be bothered with you. That's when they're at their most vulnerable, actually, just after feeding. Their batteries are flat after the kill, and until they've digested some food – they digest really quickly, but it still takes time – they're basically too weak to move, and their defences are low, too, which makes killing them that much easier.' A thought struck her, and she looked sideways at him; not one of her usual repertoire of looks. 'The one yesterday,' she said. 'Pointed ears?'

Chris tried to remember. 'No,' he said. 'More sort of knobbly, like stone muffins.'

'Ah.' She nodded. 'Just occurred to me, it might've been the same one, tracking you. They do that sometimes,' she added blithely. 'Just seem to fixate on a particular human, follow him around for a bit before they strike. We've got no idea why they do that.'

'Oh,' he said. 'I wish you hadn't told me that.'

Jill laughed, as though he'd made a joke. 'No,' she went on, 'there must've been something that stopped it attacking you, something that either drained its energy or put it off, made you seem unappetising, as it were. Something you had with you in the car, perhaps.'

Chris pursed his lips. 'Such as?'

'Well, there's all sorts of things we believe they don't like. Same as vampires and garlic, only it's a bit subtler than that, different things repel different demons. For example—'

'Hang on,' he interrupted, 'we sell stuff like that. LY42V, Evil-Off anti-demon talismans. Very good line, we do a lot of them, especially around the Walsall area—'

Jill giggled. 'Sorry,' she said, 'but they're a bit of a standing joke in the department.'

'Oh.' Chris scowled. 'They don't work, then.'

'Well, yes and no,' she replied. 'Actually they're a pretty effective defence against female Grade 6 servitor demons – that's basically cooks, laundry and clerical staff, which to be honest with you aren't that much of a problem since they almost never show up in the material world, unless they're really hungry and desperate. So essentially your talisman things are a bit like an umbrella one inch square, keeps off some of the rain but not most of it. Though,' she went on, 'I suppose if you had a lot of them, twenty or thirty—'

'Car stock,' he said excitedly. 'It's one of the lines where I carry a couple of dozen in the car, so if a customer needs stock in a hurry I can supply them on the spot.'

'Ah.' Jill looked interested. 'In which case—'

'Except,' he said suddenly remembering, 'I sold the whole lot to Paul at the Magic Shack this morning, just before it happened. So it couldn't have been that, could it?'

Sigh. 'Not really, no. Oh well,' she said, 'if it wasn't that, it must've been something else. We'll check out everything you've got in the car – don't look at me like that, it's not my fault. I'll see if I can arrange a car you can borrow till we've finished with yours, how'd that be?'

'Thanks,' Chris said, a trifle grudgingly. 'But all my samples—'

'Sorry.' Jill shook her head. 'Get them back to you as soon as possible. Meanwhile, I'd say you've got an ironclad excuse for taking the rest of the day off. Now that can't be bad, can it?'

She had a point there, to be sure. 'You couldn't possibly ring my boss, could you?' Chris said. 'Tell him it's a matter of national security and all that. Otherwise he'll be on at me for skiving.'

'No trouble,' Jill replied, with a grin. 'In fact, I could say we'll be needing you on call for the next twenty-four hours so you can't possibly go back to work till after the weekend. All right?'

Chris nodded solemnly. 'I always knew you'd come in useful for something one of these days,' he replied.

★

The car she got for him was a big black BMW, with cruise
control, a radio like something from NASA and (Chris discovered joyfully as he scrabbled about in the boot) one of
those magnetic sirens you can slap on the roof, like in the cop
shows. He couldn't quite bring himself to use it, though, and
when he tried to turn on the radio an extremely snotty voice
asked him for his security access code, and said some really
quite hurtful things when he said he hadn't got one. The
cruise control had him zooming down the motorway at a hundred and ten miles an hour, until he finally managed to turn
the bloody thing off.

The clothes were an improvement, too. Jill had coerced one
of the Day-Glo men into lending him some in return for his
own, which had been sealed in plastic bags, tagged and packed
in a massive steel lead-lined trunk. The replacements fitted
better than his own, and the polo shirt had a little goblin
embroidered on the pocket, over a crest and the letters DS.
Chris had an idea he'd seen it before somewhere; a bit later, he
remembered that some of Jill's stuff had the same logo, so it
was probably some kind of designer something. He speculated
briefly about neglecting to give it back when his own clothes
were returned, but accepted fatalistically that he wouldn't get
away with it.

The rest of the day was his own; strange and unfamiliar concept. He couldn't remember offhand when he'd last had a day
of his very own. Days belonged to work, apart from holidays
and weekends, which belonged to Karen and were spent shopping for and assembling flat-pack chipboard furniture and
visiting her loathsome relatives. The best part of half a day all
to himself, to spend as he chose; with the added bonus of
needle-sharp designer clothes and a big fast black car filled
with the government's petrol. It was almost as though God
had given him a gift voucher for his birthday.

Yes, Chris thought, as he drove, but what am I going to do
with it? Go home? No way – I can go home any time. All right,
then, I can drive somewhere, which is what I do all day every

day for work. Or I can drive home, park the car and spend the afternoon in a pub . . .

(Cautionary tale widely repeated by the JWW Retail reps; about a customer who bought a JWW Sheer Genieus djinn-in-a-bottle. Three days later he lurched back into the shop looking haggard and miserable, demanding his money back. Why, asked the girl behind the till, what's wrong with it? Bloody thing told me I could have three wishes, the customer replied, and I've spent the last three days trying to decide, and there's *absolutely nothing I want*. Except (the customer added) my money back—)

He pulled in at a Little Chef, ordered the Alabama Sunrise jacket potato and chips, and stared out of the window for a while, watching the cars queuing for petrol. The terror had worn off, but there was still a residual ache, like a bruise, where it had been. Demons, he thought; there really are such things as demons, they're out there wandering around, invisible, and they *eat* people. Not the most cheerful of thoughts.

The Alabama Sunrise arrived: medium-sized industrial potato with a bit of cheese melted in it, and a few bits of leaf scattered round the edge, plus a small mountain of chips. Chris stabbed the fork against the potato's dense hide and felt the tines bend.

Then a thought struck him, so dreadful that he nearly choked. *SatNav!*

Strip the car down to the sub-atomic level, the Day-Glo jerk had said. Even if he'd been exaggerating somewhat, it was more or less inevitable that they'd stick a screwdriver into her casing and prise her open; and then what? Would she survive? How did this imprisoning thing work, anyway? Could they take her out, peer about inside the casing for very small demons, then put her back again, good as new? Somehow he doubted that. Not government thinking. Their attitude was likely to be more along the lines of smash it open with a hammer, zap anything inside, chuck the remains in the skip and if they want to try claiming compensation for damaged property, bloody good luck to them.

No way, he said to himself; got to save her before it's too late. With an effort he elbowed a path through the panic in his mind and tried to think what to do. Jill, of course; she was the boss, she could stop them. And she would, he knew, provided he gave her a half-sensible reason—

'Excuse me,' said the waitress, 'but do you know you're eating your tie?'

Which was perfectly true. 'Sorry,' Chris said, once he'd fished it out of his mouth. 'I was miles away. You see, the government's taken my SatNav, because of the demon, and they're going to kill her unless I stop them—'

Hearing it out loud, together with the stuffed expression on the waitress's face, had a sobering effect on him; a bit like jumping into a nice hot bath, only to find that someone forgot to turn on the immersion heater. 'Only joking,' he said cheerfully. 'Can I have some more coffee, please?'

Probably, Chris told himself (the waitress was looking back at him over her shoulder, presumably in case she was called on to be a witness at some point in the future), it was just as well. In the back of his mind he could hear Ben Jarrow's soft, bleating voice: can sometimes be a bit of an unhealthy influence, you'd do well to be on the lookout for warning signs. Could it really be happening to him? he wondered; not a comfortable thought. But now it seemed like the Day-Glo crowd had solved the problem for him: no more SatNav, no more unhealthy influence. He'd miss her, of course, but if he really was falling under the spell of some kind of malign power . . . Not that he could bring himself to believe it, but presumably that was how all the victims felt. In which case, he owed Jill and her brightly coloured staff a vote of thanks. Which would be worse, he speculated, being possessed by a dark spirit or eaten by a demon? Both, he decided.

The more Chris thought about it, the dodgier his recent behaviour seemed to be. Now he came to think of it, he'd actually talked to the horrible machine; worse still, it had talked back to him. Funny how he hadn't really remembered it before. It had been like a dream, a wispy vague memory that seeps away as you wake up, and half an hour later you can't recall a single detail. That, surely, was suspicious in itself, implying that the critter in the plastic box was deliberately covering its tracks by doing things to his memory.

The thought made him shudder so much that he spilt coffee on his knee. Now, though, it was as though the spell had shattered, and he could hear himself talking, *chatting* with the thing, asking its advice about how to handle the difficult shop managers, moaning to it about the trainee. Even by the fairly relaxed standards of the retail sorcery trade, that was pretty odd behaviour, a man his age with an imaginary friend. More than that: an imaginary friend with a criminal record, currently doing life for some particularly nasty crime. And maybe – this one made him wince so hard that he nearly knocked over the table – maybe SatNav had something to do with the fact that he couldn't seem to go more than five miles these days without tripping over demons. After all, if she was a criminal (murder? necromancy?) there was at least a possibility that she was plotting her escape with the demons – while you're ripping him limb from limb, if you could possibly see your way to cracking open my plastic box, I could just slip away in the confusion and everybody'll assume I got broken by accident, and they won't come after me—

No, even now that the spell was broken Chris couldn't make himself credit that. Except, of course, that the last thing the demon did before kicking open the door and bolting had been to lean across him and do something with SatNav's controls. At the time he'd been sure it had switched her off, but maybe he'd got that wrong. He cursed himself for being too chicken to tell Jill about that. It was going to be embarrassing when he spoke to her next and filled in the missing details, which he now knew he had a duty to do since it could possibly explain everything. And, even more important, there was something that SatNav herself had said, he was convinced of it, though he couldn't actually bring to mind what the exact words had been.

He gobbled down the rest of his chips, paid the bill and

hurried back to the car. Quick check to make sure there weren't any demons hiding under the road atlas on the back seat, and he set off for home. But with a detour: he stopped off at Enchanted Worlds in Nuneaton, where he was fairly sure they quite liked him, and asked to see a copy of *The Book Of All Human Knowledge*.

'It's a random quality-control check,' he said, and he could see they were impressed. 'We've been getting reports of defective stock, so naturally—'

'We haven't had any problems,' the girl said. 'Well, apart from the thickies who don't read the instructions, but that's the public for you, we just tell them to—'

Chris gave her a big buttery smile and waffled for a minute or so about proactive customer support being the backbone of inclusive retailing, and she brought him a copy of the *Book*. He thanked her and asked if he could take it through into the staffroom for a few minutes. No problem, she said. She even made him a coffee.

The *Book*, as so many customers had pointed out, had no index; no need for one, since the *Book* knew better than you did what you really needed to know. But, for professional-grade users, there was a hidden way in: you folded back the corner of the copyright page, and a menu dropped down. Press *show hidden* with your thumbnail, and you got a list of options, including *Index*—

Chris scrolled down to *demons*, selected that, scrolled down further to *killing* and prodded the word with the pad of his index finger. The page went blank, apart from the universally loathed little black hourglass, then filled with print.

*Because they are **multilocated** in several different dimensions simultaneously, demons are notoriously difficult to kill; furthermore, their highly advanced and adaptive **metabolisms** allow them to recover almost instantaneously from exceptionally severe wounds, and their skins are impregnated with **armour charms**. Magic of some sort is almost always* *necessary, but nearly all the known spells, charms, curses and incantations are species-specific, making positive identification (see **appendix 12**) an essential preliminary exercise; unfortunately, the speed and ferocity of demon attacks generally leaves little time for considered identification, and demon-killing is generally regarded as an exercise best left to highly trained professionals who can recognise instantly which species and **grade** they are confronting, and select their combat strategy accordingly. The only 'one-size-fits-all' approach recognised by most competent authorities is physical cutting with either a **living sword** (of which only seven are known to exist) or a **pantacopt**, in the unlikely event that such an article is available at the time—*

Chris frowned, and touched *pantacopt* with his finger. The page cleared, the revolting little hourglass twirled, and then a small box appeared asking him for his user name and password. But that was all right; he knew the universal key.

He cleared his throat. 'Seven nine seven one A-square standard,' he said. The box vanished, and was replaced by—

Sorry, your attempt to access restricted information was unsuccessful. This may be because—
– you mumbled
– you have a cold
– you have a strong regional accent or other speech impediment
– you have recently undergone dental treatment and your mouth is still anaesthetised
Please rectify the problem and try again

Chris said something vulgar and indicative of a limited vocabulary. It was an open secret that several of the other reps had spent their own money on the Kawaguchiya NZ3000 *Open Book*, which didn't have all this interactive shit but did have an index. He cleared his throat again, sat up straight and did his best Alec Guinness impersonation, and this time got—

*The **pantacopt** is a magical weapon of exceptional power, capable of cutting through practically anything; furthermore, anything severed by one cannot be repaired, rejoined or revived, even by the most extreme magic. Resembling a long thin sheet of metal foil, it operates by disrupting the severed object in all known **dimensions** and **timeframes** (making it impossible for the severed object to be taken back through time) while simultaneously cauterising the cut edges with **transfiguration spells** that transform them into mutually repellent elements, such as **fire** and **water**). Possession of **pantacopts** is illegal in most jurisdictions; in consequence, they are often magically disguised as everyday mundane objects, such as—*

He closed the book with a snap. Oh, he thought.

Back at the office Chris had a desk. On his first day in the job he'd gone through the drawers, the way you do, and one of the bits of stray useless junk he'd found in there was a tapemeasure; something he hadn't got but would soon be needing, since Karen wanted new carpet in the bathroom. So he'd slipped it in his pocket and promptly forgotten all about it, until the next day, when Julie from reception came crashing in asking if he'd seen a tapemeasure anywhere. Rather than confess that he'd stolen it, which would have been embarrassing, he'd said no, but Julie had insisted on turning the whole room upside down looking for it, and when the search proved futile she gave him ever such a funny look and went off in a foul mood. Later, when carpet day arrived, Karen had already gone out and bought a tapemeasure, and the stolen one had ended up in the kitchen drawer where hammers, screwdrivers and other DIY-related hardware went to hide; and he had no reason to believe it wasn't still there.

Unlikely, of course. Probably it was just the office tapemeasure, and Julie had been all pissy about not finding it because Julie was all pissy about everything. Even so.

'Was it all right?' the girl asked him as he emerged from the staffroom.

Chris shook his head. 'I'll give you a returns note,' he said, stowing the book in his jacket pocket. 'Mind you send it in with the next invoice. Any other problems, while I'm here?'

He drove straight home and hurried into the kitchen. It was there, buried under a dense seam of Rawlplugs, little metal things and bits of wooden dowel left over from various flat-pack assembly sessions. He picked it up nervously (*exceptional power, capable of cutting through practically anything*) and put it down gently on the worktop. Just a tapemeasure, yellow, with the name of a big DIY chain printed on it; except, he noticed for the first time, the name was spelt wrong—

Chris knew about that: the fundamental law of physical metamorphosis, by which any object magically transformed into something else will always have one slight flaw or mistake in it – a piano with one too many keys, a nine-legged spider, or anything produced by Microsoft . So, whatever the hell it was, it hadn't been a tapemeasure originally. Which proved nothing; could just as easily be that someone in the office, needing to measure something and being too idle to go round the building looking for the tapemeasure, had magicked a box file or a stapler. That was far more likely—

He stared at it. A magical weapon of exceptional power; sounded really cool on the page, but maybe not so cool if you had one lying on the table in front of you, lethal, illegal and almost certainly very dangerous to use. On the other hand, if he really was being followed about by demons, it'd be reassuring to think that he had some sort of an edge—

Ouch; no pun intended. He looked around for something expendable, and assembled a carrot, a pencil and (for the hell of it) a heavy glass floral paperweight that Karen had been given as a leaving present by her enemies at her previous job, and which had so far resisted all efforts to smash or chip it. The carrot and the pencil he set up trestle-fashion, their ends perched on the rims of coffee mugs. Couldn't do that with the paperweight, so he rested it on the tiled floor.

'Here goes,' Chris said aloud, nestled his thumb against the small chrome tab that stuck out of the body of the tapemeasure, and pulled.

It looked just like a tapemeasure: yellow steel strip, with numbers printed on it. This is silly, he thought; I bet it's exactly what it looks like, a thing for measuring things with. In which case, argued his malicious inner voice, you can whack the carrot with it and nothing will happen, and then you can get a grip on yourself, forget all this dark magic stuff, and—

He didn't think he'd actually touched the carrot with the edge of the steel tape, just brought it very close; but the carrot halved, and the two pieces fell on to the worktop with a gentle thud. He froze, too scared to move; oh shit, he thought, it's real, it works, now what the hell do I do? For one thing, how do you get the tape back inside the plastic case without strimming off all your fingers?

Chris tried the pencil, which subdivided instantly. He was holding the tapemeasure at arm's length now, his head craned back and away, and he thought, what kind of dangerously irresponsible lunatic would disguise something like this as a tapemeasure and then leave it lying about in a desk? And then he remembered the way the demon had grinned at him, and the feel of its arm brushing against him as it leaned forward; he relaxed just enough to move, and addressed the paperweight, squaring up to it the way he'd seen samurai do in films. Then, very carefully, he nudged the glass with the edge—

Fuck, he thought; and then, Karen's going to kill me when she sees this. The tapemeasure hadn't just gone through the paperweight (the halves of which had rolled away across the floor) but the tile as well, which had cracked in two. Thanks to the handy numbers printed on the side, he knew precisely how deep it had gone: nine inches, and he'd barely touched it.

He drew it slowly out of the crack in the tile. There was the usual button on the side of the casing – press it forward and the tape would snap back into the handle. He didn't fancy trying that, for some reason, but (maybe it was because he was nervous, which made him grip too hard and press the button accidentally) it did it anyway. There was a cracking noise, he felt the recoil as the chrome stop slammed against the plastic case, and – well, there it was, lying in the palm of his hand, a simple, inoffensive tapemeasure. He could almost have convinced himself that none of it had happened – if it hadn't been for the carrot, the pencil, the paperweight and the bloody great big crack in the kitchen tile, which Karen would notice the moment she set foot through the front door, and she was going to be so mad at him—

Glue, Chris thought desperately; or Polyfilla and some of her make-up stuff, to make it the same colour as the tile. It was a good idea, by his standards, and it should have worked, except that nothing he tried would make the Polyfilla stay in the crack. He even tried looking up mending enchanted cracks in the *Book*, but all he got was an error message and please try again later; and when he tried again, what he got was—

. . . *Operates by disrupting the severed object in all known* **dimensions** *and* **timeframes** *while simultaneously cauterising the cut edges with* **transfiguration spells** *that transform them into mutually repellent elements.*

Told you so.

CHAPTER FOUR

Needless to say, Chris didn't tell Karen about the panta-copt, or the demons. He said he'd accidentally knocked the paperweight onto the floor, and it had busted the tile and broken in two. She sulked about it all evening, then swept off to bed like a diplomat walking out of peace negotiations. It disturbed him to discover how little he cared.

He was pretty tired too, but he didn't want to go into the bedroom while there was any chance that she'd still be awake, so he settled down in the armchair with *The Book of All Human Knowledge*. For some reason, the stupid thing kept wanting him to read about Gandhi, but he really wasn't in the mood, so he used his master key and looked up satellite navigation systems, magical—

*... Operated by a captive spirit, typically a **nymph**, **sprite** or **genius loci**, although entities as diverse as **angels** and **demons** have been successfully used; generally, however, the spirit is a convicted criminal, condemned to life imprisonment in its native jurisdiction, which means that navigation spirits are usually only sourced from communities with whom the equipment manufacturers have made suitable arrangements. The spirit is kept restrained inside the apparatus by a variety*

of **containment charms;** *equipment offered for sale inside the EU must carry enchantments rated to Level 9 or above under the terms of EU Directive 5567442/91B. Although considered safe for everyday use, these devices carry an undeniable element of risk. There have been authenticated cases of* **malign influence** *and* **possession,** *especially where the equipment is in daily use, and the user is particularly vulnerable, weak-willed, impressionable, of below average intelligence or starved of affection—*

(Yup, Chris thought, that's me; five out of five.)

In cases where **possession** *has become complete, very little can be done to save the victim, who is usually confined in secure quarantined accommodation so as to prevent him from becoming a danger to himself and others. If the victim realises his predicament early enough, however, the* **possession** *process can easily be interrupted – simple distractions such as the playing of music or radio broadcasts are often sufficient – and in most cases the victim will make a full recovery without unduly distressing withdrawal symptoms. Danger signs to watch out for include engaging the apparatus in conversation—*

Oh, he thought. More or less what Ben had told him, and if it was in the *Book* it had to be true. Although there wasn't much there that he hadn't already known, reading it had left him feeling shaken and upset; he closed the *Book* and switched on the telly, but he had to keep the volume so low, in order not to wake Karen, that he couldn't follow the plot, and soon gave up. He'd decided it was safe to go to bed when the phone rang.

'Sorry to call so late.' Jill's voice. 'I'm not disturbing you, am I?'

'Just a second.' He'd bought an extra-long flex for the phone so that he could take it into the kitchen if anybody rang after curfew. 'That's better. OK, fire away.'

'I was thinking,' she said. 'About your demon. Are you absolutely positive you haven't left something out? Only I just can't account for why it didn't attack.'

Chris almost told her; about how the demon had reached past him and touched the SatNav button. Things were different now, he could see that. Before, the captive spirit's enchantment had made him want to protect it; now he knew the awful truth, so why shouldn't he tell Jill? Sure, she'd probably lecture him about being vulnerable, weak-willed, impressionable, of below average intelligence and starved of affection, but he could handle that – he'd never had a high enough opinion of himself to be upset by the truth. Telling her would be the sensible thing to do. But he didn't.

'You're really, really sure?'

'Yes, for crying out loud.'

'Oh,' Jill said, 'right. In that case, it's a mystery. Look, about the car, and Norman's clothes . . .'

You had to hand it to Jill when it came to making arrangements. She'd spoken to Mr Burnoz personally – he'd sounded very impressed when he found out who he was talking to – and of course Chris mustn't dream of coming back to work until after the weekend. Gerald from the department would call round in the morning to bring back his car and pick up the BMW and the designer clothes, and there'd be a statement for him to sign; just routine, nothing heavy.

'Oh, and one last thing,' she said, sounding rather too much like Lieutenant Colombo for Chris's liking. 'That packet of biscuits.'

'What pack—'

'In my carrier bag, you remember. Don't suppose you've had any further thoughts about that, have you?'

'No.'

'Only . . .' Hesitation; very unlike her. 'Only, that's another mystery, and I hate them. Oh well, never mind. See you Tuesday, as usual?'

Fine, Chris thought, as he put the phone down and carried

it back into the hall, but that wasn't what she'd started to say. *Only*, he'd be prepared to bet money on it, had been the preamble to an explanation of why the stupid biscuits mattered so much, and she'd started and then changed her mind. Why? Because she didn't trust him? Out of the question, after all these years; except, of course, that he'd been lying to her, and he had a nasty suspicion that she knew it. For two pins he'd have called her back and told her about the demon and SatNav. But he didn't.

Something was bugging him, and he couldn't quite reach it; something that someone had said, some very little thing, perhaps the way it had been said rather than the words themselves. Chris got undressed and went to bed, but he couldn't stop rummaging around in his mind; until, quite suddenly—

He saw it, as clearly as if his eyes were open; the demon's long, thin arm seen in the rear-view mirror, coming at him, going past, brushing his cheek (only how could he have seen it? He'd had his eyes shut at the time. Maybe this wasn't his memory—) and the clawed finger reaching out to touch; and then the voice of the SatNav—

'Your route is being calculated, please – oh.'

The last bit: of course. At the time, he'd assumed it was just perfectly normal surprise, but it hadn't been, had it? Not 'oh' short for 'Oh my God, what's happening?' because the inflections were all wrong. Surprise, yes, but too mild to be any sentient creature's reaction to waking up and finding a demon leering at you. Rather, it was, 'Oh, it's you, what're you doing here?', implying—

– Implying, Chris thought, his stomach lurching, that she recognised it. She'd met it before, knew its name, if demons had names; knew where it should have been, hence the surprise to find that it wasn't.

He opened his eyes. Faint orange glow from the street lamp outside, bleeding through a crack between the curtains. Once your eyes had got used to it, you could make out shapes, the door, the fitted wardrobes from Homebase, Karen's dressing table. That was why the demon hadn't attacked him, because of SatNav—

No, that didn't work either. It had appeared – if he'd understood what Jill had told him, it took them a lot of effort to do that, moving from one dimension to another or something *Star Trek*-sounding like that – and it had grinned at him, and then it had switched on SatNav, *and then it had left*. SatNav had recognised it, sure, but it hadn't stopped to talk to her or anything like that. Grin, reach out, press button, bugger off. Still didn't make any sense; in fact, it was even more bewildering than it had been.

Jill must've guessed, Chris thought; she must've known there was something weird going on, hence the phone call. Well, obviously he was going to have to tell her now, because there was no way he'd be able to keep something as crazy as that bottled up inside his head. He felt as though someone had stuck a hose in his ear and turned on the tap.

He had one of those luminous-dial watches; three a.m., so even Jill would be asleep, and he couldn't phone her till morning. But the pressure kept building, until he couldn't bear to lie still; he slid out of bed, crept into the living room, quietly closed the door and turned on the light.

The *Book*, he thought; tells you what you really need to know. Chris didn't really believe that, just a sales pitch for the buyers, but it was all he could think of, and he had to do something. He pulled the *Book* towards him across the table, opened it in the middle, and saw—

*Gandhi; Mohandas Karamchand Gandhi, born 2 October 1869, Porbandar, India. Best known for his policy of **non-violent resistance** to British colonial rule, leading to independence in—*

For crying out loud, Chris thought, and went back to bed.

★

He was tied to a rock on the summit of a cloud-capped mountain, and around him soared four vultures, bare-necked, broad-winged, screaming as they swooped at his face, talons extended, veering away a fraction of a second before making contact. At each swoop he flinched, but they judged the distance exactly; he could feel the slipstream, but the anticipated impact and tearing of flesh never came.

One of the vultures was Karen. 'It's your turn to put the rubbish out,' she screamed. 'You broke the tile in the kitchen and you never *talk* to me any more.' He wasn't all that bothered about her. The second vulture was Jill, and she was shrieking, 'You lied to me, you *did* eat my biscuits, I'm going to shave off all your hair and tell them you were hiding in the girls' toilets.' He was sad to think that she didn't like him any more, but he recognised it was his own silly fault for violating her private, personal plastic bag, so fair enough. The third vulture was Angela the trainee, and although she swooped and wheeled like the others, he could see that her heart wasn't in it and she was bored and it was just stupid, flying around in circles like this, but her mother was making her do it and it was all so bitterly unfair. The fourth vulture was Julie on reception, same as usual.

But then (and this had never happened before) a fifth vulture joined the flock, a huge black silhouette with an enormous wingspan; not a vulture, a – what's the word? – condor, like on the nature programmes; it didn't have a face, but as it rushed towards him – and he knew it wasn't going to turn away at the last moment like the others did, it was going to strike, and take half his face away with it – he heard it call out, 'Your immediate future is being calculated, please wait . . .'

He woke up; and the voice wasn't that of a giant condor, it was the phone ringing. Beside him, Karen snarled ominously in her sleep, so he slid out of bed and tiptoed at the double into the hall.

'Sorry to call so early,' Jill said, 'but I thought you ought to know. Your SatNav.'

Chris frowned. 'What about it?'

'It's escaped.'

Three, maybe four times in Chris's life when he'd gone from three-quarters asleep to very wide awake in under a sixtieth of a second: once when Karen's parents had come home much earlier than expected, once when he'd started to drop off at the wheel on the M5; none of them had been much fun, and this time was no different. 'What the hell do you mean, es—?'

'They just called me,' Jill said. 'They prised open the casing, and it was empty. Nothing there.'

Chris opened and shut his mouth a few times, goldfish fashion, then said; 'But that can't happen, can it? I mean, there's all those spells and—'

'Well, apparently it has,' Jill said calmly. 'And, strictly between ourselves, it's not the first time.'

'Oh.'

'Most of the previous cases were on the early models,' she went on, 'before they beefed up the defences, but there was one in Denmark just last year, a Kawaguchiya RoadImp. Killed six people before they managed to catch up with it.'

'Oh.'

'The thing is,' Jill went on, 'in nearly all the recorded incidents, the first thing the escaped thingy did was make a beeline for its owner. In fact, they think that's what prompts them to break out: they get sort of fixated on the person they navigate for. Kind of like having a crush on someone, but also wanting to tear them limb from limb. Well, if they were well-balanced and normal, they wouldn't have been banged up in a plastic box to start with.'

'Oh,' Chris said, this time with extra feeling. 'And you think—'

'There's no need to panic,' Jill said chirpily. 'Your car was in the secure compound all the time, we've got loads of wards and stuff, it's highly unlikely it'll be able to get off site. But I thought I ought to warn you, just in case.'

'Um,' he said. 'I mean, right, thanks for telling me.' Pause; then, 'If it does, you know, show up here, what should I—?'

'Phone me,' she said, 'or the hotline, if I'm not here. You've got my mobile number, haven't you?'

'Is that all? I mean, is there anything I can do while I'm waiting for you to get here?'

'Tackle it yourself, you mean?' Disapproval in her voice. 'I really wouldn't advise that. Leave it to us, all right?' Jill paused, then added, 'It all seems to be happening to you at the moment, doesn't it?'

'Yes.'

'Odd, that.'

'Yes.'

Another pause. 'And you're absolutely sure there's nothing you aren't telling me?'

It was the perfect opportunity; and it was so obviously the sensible thing to do, because it was quite clear she suspected something, so Chris had nothing to gain by keeping quiet; and if the horrible monster from inside SatNav really was on the loose and out to hunt him down, surely it was only common sense to tell Jill so she could help protect him. But he said, 'Look, you keep asking me that. If there was anything at all, I'd tell you, right?'

'Yes, of course you would, I'm sorry. It's just such a coincidence, that's all. Mind you, we do have a couple of lines we're following up; like, for example, there's some thing, some object you've inadvertently got hold of, and it's drawing them.'

He liked the sound of that. 'Really? That happens, does it?'

'It's not unknown. Could be some powerful magical artefact that they're keen to get their hands on, for example. Or maybe it's something they've made into a sanctuary – that's where they take some everyday thing and create a transdimensional bubble where they can hole up and rest; you know, a bit like a—'

'Pocket universe,' Chris interrupted breathlessly. 'I know all about them, we sell them. I've got a dozen in my car boot right now. Or at least, you've got them,' he added quickly. 'And, bloody hell, what about the BB27Ks? Could they hide in one of them?'

'I don't know. What's a BB27K?'

'Portable parking space. Look, I'm no expert, but I think it works more or less the same way as the pocket universes, some dimension thing. And I carry loads of them as car stock, I've been trying to get rid of them all month, but you can't hardly give the things away.'

'It's possible,' Jill said sceptically. 'Though I wouldn't have thought—'

'There was that woman,' Chris went on. 'One of the managers told me about her. Parked her car in a BB27K and it fell through a hole into a completely different reality. Sounds just like what you were talking about, and they wouldn't have to adapt it or anything – it'd be perfect.'

'All right,' she said, 'we'll check them out, just in case. I suppose it could be something like that – I mean, there doesn't seem to be any other rational explanation.'

After she'd rung off, Chris crept back into the bedroom and fished the tapemeasure out of his pocket. *Phone me. Leave it to us.* Yes, right; and while he was holding and pressing 1 and listening to the 'Four Seasons', the ravening monster would be tearing off his head, just like poor Mr Newsome's.

Well; he was a realist. So most likely the monster would get him, even if he did try and make a fight of it; that, or he'd cut off his own leg trying to get the tapemeasure out in a hurry. But at least he'd have stood a chance, if only very briefly. Better that his last moments on Earth should be characterised by futile valour than spent trying to explain about escaped fiends to someone in a call centre in Mumbai. Not much better, but still.

Chris made himself a cup of coffee (black, no sugar; more suitable, he felt, for a warrior than his usual milky-sweet slop) and went through into the living room, trying to remember what he was supposed to be doing today. Karen had given him his orders for the weekend – something about stripping off wallpaper – but demons and fugitive monsters had driven them from his mind. He shuddered. Right now, if he was lost in a dark wood and a fiery angel appeared to him and gave him the choice between a life of heroism, adventure, selfless sacrifice and eternal glory on the one hand, and DIY and visiting Karen's relatives on the other, his only question would be whether there'd be time to nip into Focus on the way over to Cousin Brenda's. But that's the bummer with life. You don't get to make the important choices at a convenient time.

So true. Admittedly he'd chosen to hide in the girls' toilets (seemed like a good idea), but without knowing what the consequences of the act would be. At that crucial moment, when a fiery angel would've been a tremendous help rather than a health and safety issue, he'd been on his own, with nothing but the puerile blandishments of Benny Pickering to inform his decision. If only—

Someone was ringing the doorbell. The postman, Chris told himself, or the Argos courier or the Avon lady; well, if they insisted on ringing at seven o'clock on a Saturday morning, they'd have to put up with the spectacle of him in his pyjamas. He lumbered into the hall and opened the door.

'Oh,' he said.

Hadn't meant it to sound like that; but that was how it sounded, and he had an idea that there were very few people on the planet more capable of distinguishing subtle, if unintentional, nuances of disappointment and irritation.

'Hello,' said Angela the trainee. 'I'm disturbing you, aren't I?'

One of the reasons why the truth is so unpopular is that it can be so bloody inconvenient. 'No,' he therefore said, 'not a bit, come in. Only, please keep your voice down, my, um, partner's still asleep.'

A crash from the kitchen gave him the lie in his teeth. 'Actually,' Chris said, 'if you wouldn't mind just waiting there a second, I'd better just tell her you're here. She might be—'

He tailed off. She was thinking *walking about without any clothes on*, whereas he hadn't said *a bit snotty otherwise* just in case she overheard. He three-quarters closed the door in Angela's face and limped into the kitchen.

'Oh,' Karen said, 'you're up.'

He nodded. 'Look,' he said quickly, trying to sound ever so everyday about it, like he habitually interviewed work colleagues early on Saturday mornings in his pyjamas. 'It's a real nuisance, but someone from work's just turned up, must be important or—'

She shrugged, as if to say that nothing he did could revolt or disappoint her any more. 'Fine,' she said. 'You'd better take him through into the lounge. Of course, the place is a complete disgusting tip, but he'll just have to put up with it.'

Chris neglected to point out the basic flaw in her assumptions. Angela always muttered, so with any luck Karen wouldn't hear her and realise she was a she. He wasn't quite sure why it mattered, but his instincts, finely honed as those of a small vulnerable forest creature, told him it probably did. 'Right,' he said. 'I'll—'

'And if he wants coffee it'll have to be that crappy instant muck you bought, because there isn't anything else.'

'OK. That's fine.'

Not a chance in hell that Angela would accept a coffee from him, in any case. She'd regard it as fraternising with the enemy, the sort of thing women had their hair cut off for after the liberation of Paris. For the record, he was desperate for a coffee, but he'd just have to wait.

Chris nipped back into the hall and opened the door. Angela was still there, looking awkward and unwanted at him. 'Sorry about that,' he said with a slightly crazed smile. 'Come on through.'

'You're still in your pyjamas,' she said.

'Yes,' he replied. 'Can I get you anything? Coffee?'

She gave him a look, as though he'd just demanded her first-born child. 'No, thanks,' she said. 'Look, I know I'm messing up your weekend, but Mr Burnoz said I had to come over. I'd have rung first, but I didn't want to disturb you.'

The logic of the young. Quite possibly his mind had worked that way once, though he couldn't remember any specific instances. 'It's no bother,' he said. 'So, what's—?'

She was huddled in the armchair, looking down at her hands. 'Mr Burnoz said he's being hassled by the demon-control authorities,' she said. 'Apparently they rang him at home – they need us both for questioning, about that poor man at the shop. He told them he'd had a call from them earlier saying you were a nervous wreck and suffering from post-traumatic stress, and they said they didn't know anything about that; so he called my mother and said he wanted me to go round to your place first thing in the morning, and then we could both go to their office and answer their questions; only if you were really at death's door, I was to call him back and he'd explain to them.' She looked up and frowned at him. 'He said something about "the second incident", whatever that means. Do you know what he meant?'

Chris nodded. 'One of them got into my car yesterday,' he said.

Her eyes became very large and round. 'What, a—?'

'Yes.'

'That's awful. What did it do?'

He shrugged, the self-effacing hero. 'I looked in my mirror and there it was, on the back seat. Then it grinned at me, kicked the door open and jumped out. And that was all, basically.'

'But that's—' She'd been about to say *that's really unusual* or something of the sort. 'Bad enough,' she said. 'Did they catch it?'

'Not yet,' Chris replied. 'They asked me loads of questions and took my car for forensic tests. They think it might have been hiding in something I was carrying; a sanctuary,' he added, remembering the technical term Jill had used. 'Something like a BB—'

'You know a lot about it,' Angela said.

It was practically an accusation. 'Picked up quite a bit from them while they were interviewing me,' he said. 'Listen, give me ten minutes to get dressed, and then I suppose we'd better be getting along, if it's so urgent.'

When he got back, he found Karen in the living room with her. Angela was looking at something terribly interesting on the carpet, while Karen was mauling a cushion with her fingers. She looked up as he came into the room and said, 'How long are you going to be? Only we're supposed to be at Molly and Clive's by one, and you were going to make a start on the bathroom.'

On the other hand, Chris thought, getting dragged out by the government on a Saturday morning had its bright side. And it was his civic duty, of course. 'I don't know,' he said. 'Could just be a couple of hours, could be all day. I'll phone when—'

'Doesn't matter,' Karen snapped. 'I'll just have to tell Molly you're ill. Again,' she added. 'But you've got to get that bathroom started – I've got the carpet on order.'

(And he couldn't help thinking: when did it all change? Because at school, and just afterwards, it was Karen who chased after me; she laughed at my jokes and smiled a lot, and once she came to a football match with me. I still love her, of course, but something changed. At which point, in some remote siding on a rural branch-line of his mind, a train of thought gradually shuffled into movement.)

'Was that your wife?' Angela asked when they were outside, walking to where he'd left the car.

'Yes,' Chris answered, because he couldn't face explaining. 'You mustn't mind her, she's been under a lot of pressure at work lately, makes her a bit—'

'Is she in the business too?'

He nodded. 'She's in the mineral rights department at Donder and Busch. Scrying for natural gas deposits under the North Sea, mostly. Of course, they do it all from aerial photographs.'

'It's a big firm, isn't it?'

'Quite big, yes. She's assistant head of section,' he added, trying to make it sound like he was boasting. She didn't seem interested.

'We did scrying at uni,' Angela said. 'I was rubbish at it. It must be boring, doing that all day.'

'I don't think she does much actual scrying these days. More sort of managerial.' Shouts at people, in other words. 'Hence the pressure.'

'Ah.'

There was the black BMW, property of Her Majesty's government. It'd have been so nice if he could've hung on to it just a little bit longer, but Jill's people would be coming to collect it that evening. Or, come to think of it, they'd probably take it off him when he got to their offices, and give him the bus fare home. Life can be so—

'What's DS stand for?'

Chris's mind went blank; then he realised he must have put yesterday's shirt on, the polo shirt he'd got from Jill's bloke. 'I don't know,' he said. 'Designer Shirt, probably. Or somebody's name.' He was about to say it wasn't his shirt, but he didn't. Maybe he thought it wasn't worth mentioning.

'And that's not your car, is it?'

'No. It's one they lent me while—'

He stopped. There was something wrong with the car. He lunged closer, and saw that the window had been forced open and the interior was a mess. The seats (the beautiful plush German luxury seats, a tantalising hint of a world of opulence and ease that he knew he could never attain) had been ripped up, the plastic dashboard panels were cracked and distorted where somebody had tried to prise them off, and the glove compartment door was hanging loose by one mangled hinge.

'Fuck,' Chris said.

She frowned. 'It's a bit scruffy,' she said. 'Was it like that when you got it?'

He stuck his head through the open window and looked

more closely. Further desecrations: the footwell mats had been ripped out and shredded, the padded headrests had been slit open, the ashtrays had been torn out, and the attackers had put a lot of effort and ingenuity into trying to get the radio, though somehow or other it had held out and beaten the siege, like Malta, though paying a dreadful price for its resistance. It was enough to break your heart.

'Oh,' Angela was saying. 'Someone's tried to break into it.'

Chris wasn't interested in anything she might have to say. The ghastly thought had just struck him that, since it had been in his possession at the time, he might be liable for the repairs.

'Bastards,' he mumbled. 'Bastard bloody kids, just look at what they've—'

'I don't think it was kids,' Angela said quietly. 'Look.'

She was pointing at the murdered seats, and she had a point. It wasn't just random slashes; there were five long, straight, parallel lacerations in the shape of a capital I. Someone with an excessively vivid imagination might well attribute them to a powerful long-fingered hand, tipped with very sharp claws.

'I think they were looking for something,' she said.

Oh, Chris thought. 'You reckon?' he said, and noted that his voice was higher and squeakier than usual. 'I suppose so, yes. Wasting their time, of course, that's the stupid thing. Apart from the radio, there wasn't anything in there worth nicking.'

'How do you know?' Angela said thoughtfully. 'You said it's not your car. For all you know, there might've been something hidden in it.'

Suddenly, having to pay for the damage no longer seemed the worst thing Chris could imagine. The claw marks; and the strength it must've taken to crack the dash like that, even if they'd been using a jemmy, and he had an idea they hadn't.

'I suppose I'd better call the demon-control people,' he said wearily. 'If it was a – well, one of *them* that did this, they'll want to do all their forensic stuff on it. We'd better not touch anything. Last thing I need is another bollocking.'

'But we're supposed to go straight to their office,' Angela objected. 'Mr Burnoz said it's really urgent.'

She was starting to get on Chris's nerves. 'Fine,' he said. 'And exactly how do you suggest we get there? We can't drive this wreck. Even if it's still running after what's been done to it, we'll smudge all the pawprints and stuff.'

'That's all right,' she said. 'We'll go in my car. It's parked just round the corner.'

It hadn't occurred to him to wonder how she'd got there; as far as he was concerned, she was just a pest who sprouted up out of the ground to torment him. 'Your car,' he repeated.

'Yes. Look, why don't you phone the demon people to come and see to this car, and then we'll drive over to their place in mine.'

There was a flaw in her reasoning, but Chris was too shocked and preoccupied to bother isolating it. 'Yes, all right,' he said distractedly. 'We'll do that, then. Where did you say your—?'

He'd been expecting something ancient and beat-up and studenty; but her car turned out to be an almost new shiny red Suzuki jeep, the interior clean, tidy and smelling discreetly of air freshener. Her mother's, he rationalised, borrowed for the morning.

'Do you know how to get there?' Chris asked as he put on his seat belt. 'I don't.'

Angela flipped open the glove compartment and pulled out a map, printed off a computer. 'I got it off Google,' she said. 'I've marked the route in yellow felt tip.'

Well, he thought. Clearly they do teach them something at university, besides how to carry their liquor and stuff newspaper into the pockets of pool tables so as to play for free. 'I'll map-read,' he offered.

She started the engine. 'All right.'

'Right.' He studied the map, turned it the right way up, and found where they were. 'OK, carry on to the end of this road and turn right.'

Naturally that made him think about SatNav, which in turn reminded him of what Jill had told him. Hang on, he thought; what if it wasn't a demon that trashed the Beemer? After all, demons don't have a monopoly on claws and sharp pointed teeth. The SatNav entity had broken out of the government labs, and Jill had as good as told him it might come looking for him. So, what if it had been SatNav – disturbed, psychotic and lovesick – who'd junked the car, searching for clues that'd lead her to him? Chris thought about that. It was a motive; maybe not a very good one, but surely rather more plausible than a mystery demon he'd never met getting fixated on him.

'Well?'

'Well what?'

'Which way now?'

'Sorry,' he mumbled, and checked. 'Yes, fine, got it. At the roundabout, take the third – no, forget that – take the fourth exit.'

'There isn't any roundabout,' Angela pointed out. 'Just a junction. Do I go left here or right?'

'Course there's a— No, sorry, hang on,' Chris added, peering at the map. 'That's the flyover, not the railway bridge. OK, turn left here, then carry straight on till you get to the—' Truth was, he'd never been much good at maps. In fact, if mapreading was an event at the 2012 Olympics, the only way he'd make the national team would be if there was a mass outbreak of the Black Death around Christmas 2011. It was a skill he hadn't needed lately, of course, because he'd had his own personal navigator, perched on the dashboard, always ready with the answers. He was going to miss her, he realised. Then he pictured the BMW's shredded seats, and those long, steady sweeping cuts.

'I don't think this is the right way,' Angela said.

'No, we're bang on course, there's the railway line, look, so—'

'That's the canal, not the railway line.'

So it was. 'All right,' Chris said, trying to make it seem like he was indulging her in some trivial whim. 'Take the next right, then immediately left—'

'I'd rather not,' she said. 'This is a car, not a narrow boat.'

She had a point there. 'Sorry, make that left, then immediately right, which ought to bring us out onto the B6603—'

Ten minutes later, Chris gave up. 'Just pull over as soon as you can,' he said wearily, 'and you have a look at the stupid thing. I can't make any sense of it. I mean, it just doesn't seem to bear any relation to what's actually there on the ground, if you follow me.'

She looked at him. 'Don't be silly,' she said. 'It's a map.'

Which was entirely true. But, according to the map, the canal was over *there*, not right in front of them, because there were the gasworks, there was the railway, you didn't have to be bloody Lewis and Clark to figure it out; in which case, the map was *deliberately lying to him*—

Chris pulled himself together with a snap. It was, of course, possible that the Ordnance Survey was part of a vast murky conspiracy to drive him out of his mind, but he was inclined to doubt it, all things considered.

'We're going to be so late,' Angela said mournfully. 'We were supposed to go over there right away, Mr Burnoz said.'

Hardly what he needed to hear, lost in the urban jungle. 'Fine,' he said. 'Soon as you can pull over, we'll look at the map and find out where we are.'

Pulling over, however, wasn't that easy; not on a dual carriageway with lorries surging around them like a school of giant dolphins; and every minute was taking them further in the wrong direction. Then he saw a signpost: they were only half a mile from the Ettingate Retail Park, one of those out-of-town shopping developments; two dozen megastores and, it went without saying, ample parking facilities. 'Next left,' he ordered gratefully.

The main cark park was huge, about twice the size of medieval London. It was also full. They'd driven round it twice before Chris noticed a single solitary space, far out on the eastern spiral arm. 'There,' he said urgently, pointing. 'Quick, before some other bugger—'

Angela might have been female, but she could park; secretly and grudgingly, Chris was impressed. Maybe it'd be too much to expect her to be able to read maps as well, but he doubted she could make a worse job of it than he'd just done. She backed in – dead level, equidistant from the white lines on either side, a small miracle of offhand precision – put on the handbrake and killed the engine.

'Now,' Chris said, pointing at the map, 'if we're here, then that must be the main A6674—' Suddenly everything went dark, like an eclipse. He looked up, but Angela wasn't in the driver's seat any more. It was light inside the car, but it was as though someone had pasted black crêpe paper on all the windows. He swore and tried to open his door; the lock operated, but the door was jammed and wouldn't move, as though he'd parked too close to the garage wall. It was also getting very, very cold. Not right, he told himself, this is something bad, quite probably not in Kansas any more, and he hadn't got the faintest idea what he should do about it.

The car began to rock gently from side to side. Chris tried the door handle again, and yelped with pain as his fingers touched it: burning hot, presumably a hint. He whimpered, but a small part of his mind was telling him, *where there's a hint, there's a hinter. If someone's trying to tell you something, then this is deliberate, not just some random natural disaster.* Fair point, but he wasn't reassured. Quite the reverse, in fact.

'Hello?' he said, in a funny little quavery voice. 'Who's there? Excuse me.'

The car stopped rocking, which was good, because the movement was doing things to his bladder. But that wasn't all. Everything around him, the car door, the dashboard, the roof, was gradually beginning to *fade*; the colour was leaching out of them, making them look like pencil outlines that hadn't been coloured in yet. He stared at the gear lever and realised he could see through it. Also, there was a distinctive smell that he was fairly sure he recognised. Not good at all.

Chris held up his hand and looked at it; at rather than through, which was something. At this rate, though, pretty soon the car was going to evaporate completely. He wriggled, realised he was still wearing his seat belt, tried to press the release button and squealed with terror as his thumb passed straight through it without touching anything; the belt, however, still held him firmly in the seat, which continued to bear his weight even though it was now little more than a water-colour smudge. He jerked his head round to stare at the back window, but there was nothing to see, just black.

The car went on fading, and Chris imagined what it'd be like once it had gone completely, leaving him sitting in a box full of nothing, with empty black walls. Somehow he didn't fancy that at all. He'd always been a bit nervous about confined spaces, even at the best of times, of which this wasn't one. The hell with this, he told himself, got to get out of here. Even the darkness outside the absence-of-windows had to be better than this. But the seat belt, though now to all intents and purposes invisible, wouldn't let him go – he could feel it even though he couldn't see it, and he really wished he had a knife or a pair of scissors—

Hang on, Chris thought, I can do better than that. The tapemeasure, the pantacopt: it could cut through anything, so the *Book* had said. Seat-belt webbing, invisible car doors, maybe it could even slice a way through the solid black darkness outside. Worth a try, at any rate. He dug his fingers into his pocket, but it was empty, and with a pang of deep sorrow he remembered: earlier that morning, he'd fished the tapemeasure out of his jacket pocket, just after Jill had rung and he'd been getting himself into a state about being stalked by the SatNav monster. What he couldn't remember was putting it back again. In which case, it was still at home, in his dressing-gown pocket, maybe, or sitting on the table in the kitchen. Marvellous, he thought. Just the fucking job.

The light inside the car, or the space where the car had been, was beginning to fade, and suddenly Chris thought hang on, I know what's happening, I must be dead; no, listen, it all fits, that's why Angela suddenly vanished, and why I can't move, also the sudden cold and everything fading away. So stupid of me not to have realised before: I died. Heart attack, or a stroke, or maybe there was a demon hiding in the back somewhere, and when we stopped the car it jumped me and pulled my head off. He caught himself adding, *so that's all right, then*; because it would be all right, wouldn't it? There was nothing bad or scary about death when you stopped and thought about it; it's perfectly natural, happens to us all, and once you're dead it's over, and nothing bad can ever happen to you again. Compared to the other alternative explanations – the weirdness, the implications of the world outside turning black and the car just melting away – it was positively reassuring—

'No, you're not,' said a voice.

Chris jumped in his seat, as far as the invisible seat belt would let him.

'You're not dead,' the voice said. 'You should be so lucky.'

It wasn't a nice voice; it was high and thin and scratchy, not a human voice, though he noted that it spoke flawless received-pronunciation English, accentless, like a Radio 4 announcer. It wasn't a voice that came out on the air expelled from lungs past vocal cords, regulated by the movement of lips; it was a synthesised voice, a talking thing, and he was hearing it with his mind rather than his ears.

'Keep perfectly still,' the voice said. 'We'll get to you as soon as it stabilises.'

As soon as what does what? The feeling of calm, even euphoria, that had spread over Chris when he'd thought he'd died had dissipated like damp off a windscreen when you turn on the blower. Instead he felt bitterly cold and totally vulnerable, as though all his skin had fallen off and he was just one great big open wound. Also, it'd be very nice if he could get to a toilet very soon.

'Won't take long,' the voice said, and if it was trying to sound soothing it was making a real hash of it. 'Then you're coming with us.'

'I'd rather not,' Chris said aloud, which made the voice laugh so much that his head shook.

'Not up to you,' the voice said. 'Right, that's about it.'

There was nothing left of the car, or the seat he'd been sitting on. He was sitting on nothing at all; he couldn't feel it, even, but he was sitting rather than lying, because his back was bent and his knees were at right angles to his spine. He couldn't feel the seat belt either, but something, some force was operating on his chest, keeping him from moving.

'Now I'll give you three guesses,' the voice said, 'and you've got to tell me what I am. Ready?'

Chris tried to open his mouth, but it wouldn't.

'Something beginning,' said the voice, 'with D.'

Death? he thought hopefully.

'No. Second guess?'

Something that pins you to a chair and tortures you. Dentist?

'Warmer, but no.'

Oh, he thought.

'Yes.'

So, Chris thought, this is it, then. This time I'm really in the shit.

'No. Being in shit really isn't that bad. It's squishy and smelly, but you survive. Your living soul isn't ripped out of your body and shredded into mush. We recommend that you select a more pertinent metaphor.'

At the end of all things, after fear and panic and false hope and despair, comes irritation, and an unwillingness to be mucked around with by someone who thinks he's really smart. What do you want? Chris thought. Get it over with and then please go away. I really don't like you very much.

'All right,' said the voice. 'Just tell me where she is, and then I'll kill you. Can't say fairer than that.'

Where she is? I don't understand.

Inside his mind, a tongue clicked impatiently; probably scaly and forked, but to him it wasn't scary, just annoying. I don't know who you mean, he thought.

'Loyalty,' said the voice. 'Courage. Heroism, even. It says in here that you don't believe in heroism.'

In here?

'In your mind.'

Well, it's perfectly true, I don't.

'Well, then. Tell us where she is, and then it'll all be over.'

And then Chris thought, hold on; if you can read my mind, why are you asking me questions?

He was briefly aware of a feeling of discomfort; not his own. 'There's bits we can't reach,' the voice said, 'not unless you open them for us. Which you're strongly advised to do, by the way, because the bits of your mind we can reach include – well, let's see, this bit here. Wonder what happens if I do *that*?'

It was a kind of pain Chris had never felt before, bearing the same relation to the worst pain he'd ever felt that concentrated orange juice straight from the bottle bears to the diluted stuff you actually drink. It wasn't localised anywhere, like toothache or a crushed toe; it was everywhere, in everything.

'So that's what it does,' said the voice. 'Fancy that.'

The curious thing about it, though, was that although it was agonising and excruciating and turned his brain to mush, it didn't *really* hurt because—

'And if you think that was bad,' he heard the voice say.

– Because he didn't believe in it; because it wasn't real, precisely because it wasn't in any one place, it didn't relate to anything; it was virtual pain, and he was feeling it not because he was suffering genuine physical damage but because some evil little grey bugger was prodding a nerve centre in his brain with a pointy fingernail.

You really don't need to do that, Chris thought irritably. If I knew who you were on about, I'd tell you.

'You know perfectly well,' said the voice.

No, I *don't*, he snapped back, and you're too busy being cruel and merciless and all that rubbish to tell me, which is just *stupid*. The trouble with you is, you enjoy your work too much.

More pain, much more intense, but Chris ignored it and thought, you can do that till the cows come home but it's not going to get you anywhere. But if you'll just tell me—

No reply, just more pain; and he thought, oh for crying out loud. It was, he reflected, a bit like those long, dreary rows with Karen, where she wouldn't tell him what the matter was, he was supposed to figure it out, or guess, or use telepathy; and it was bad enough when she did it, but he was prepared to put up with it from her because she was his girlfriend, and apparently that was part of the deal. But the owner of the voice had no such claim on him, so he was rapidly running out of patience—

The pain stopped, but not because the owner of the voice wanted it to. 'Oh,' it said; and then, 'How are you doing that?'

I can't be bothered with it, Chris thought back. Now, will you answer the question?

'You know perfectly well—'

No, I don't, he thought; and then he realised, you can't say the name, right? It's some stupid rule. You can't say the name unless I say it first.

'Something like that,' the voice replied grumpily. 'But you do know, you're just being difficult.'

Chris was feeling very tired and fed up now. All right, he decided, let's think. So he thought; and somehow he knew he'd gone into the part of his mind where the demon couldn't get in, and it was so nice to get away from it for a moment, not because of the pain or the fear but because the demon was so obnoxiously boring and stupid. Now then, he thought, what was the question? Ah yes. Where is she?

He scanned the list of possibilities: females of his acquaintance who'd disappeared. It wasn't a long list; just one, in fact. Angela the trainee, who'd been sitting next to him and had then just vanished . . .

Hello, he thought, I'm back.

'Well?'

I think I know who you're on about, Chris thought, but I'm afraid the answer's still the same. I don't know.

'Yes, you *do*,' the voice screamed at him; rather childishly, in his opinion. 'She was with you, in the car – her smell was all over the seat.'

Yes, that's right, he thought wearily, she was with me but now she's gone, you can see that for yourself. She just vanished, and I haven't got a clue where she's gone to. Surely you can tell if I'm lying to you or not. Well?

A long pause. Then the voice said, 'Shit.'

So you agree. I'm telling the truth.

'Looks like it,' the voice conceded unhappily.

Right, then, Chris thought briskly, in that case, you'd better get on and kill me, hadn't you? Come to that, you might even let me go.

Silence; then, just as he was starting to wonder, the voice laughed and said, 'Nice try.' At which point, all that calm, stoical acceptance that had purged him of the fear of death sizzled away like milk on a hot stove, and terror came flooding back, and Chris discovered that, after all, he really, *really* didn't want to die, especially not if there was even the remotest chance that it'd hurt. He launched himself at the invisible seat belt, which bounced him sharply back against the invisible seat, so he tried to wriggle sideways, and found he couldn't do that either; and he couldn't hear the voice any more, and that was all the confirmation he needed, because anybody could see that demons aren't the sort of creatures who talk to their food—

But there was another voice, one that Chris recognised. 'Get away from him,' she shouted, and he heard the demon hiss; not with his mind but with his ears. Then a noise just like a butcher cleaving through a thick joint of beef, and a scream, not human, and the *ting* of one metal object glancing off another. Then another scream, as much rage as pain, and the sound of a woman grunting with effort; and then the light came on.

It was like when Karen suddenly switched on the bedside lamp, when she'd woken up in the middle of the night and needed to read for a bit before she could get back to sleep. The sudden glare was like a slap on the face, and Chris instinctively turned his head away from it. When he looked back, he saw her; the most beautiful creature he'd ever seen. Not just film-star or supermodel beautiful; they are, after all, only human. The point being, she obviously wasn't. In fact (he rationalised later) she didn't actually look all that much like a human female; or rather, she looked like the original, of which human beings are cheap knock-off copies you buy on market stalls. Human skin doesn't glow, and neither does human hair shimmer; it's too thick and stiff and hard, though you don't notice it until you get a chance to take a good close look at the real thing.

She was dressed in some sort of silvery thing that was either scales or feathers or, somehow or other, both. She was leaning forward with both hands on the grip of a sword (except it wasn't; where the blade should have been there was just a long thin black line, so thin it barely made three dimensions) and the light he was staring at her by came, he realised, from her skin and hair and that funny silvery dress; it defined the shape where the car had been, but there was nothing contained in that space besides the two of them and a moderate helping of air.

'It's you,' Chris heard himself say. 'I recognised your voice.'

She turned her head to face him, and her eyes were as bright as a welder's arc, burning half-moons across his retina as her head moved. 'I don't think so,' she said.

'Yes, it is, it's you,' he insisted. 'You're her. You're SatNav.'

The eyes flared; he raised his hand to shield himself from them, but it did no good. He could still see them through his own palm.

'Oh shut up,' she said, and she swung the sword up and brought it swishing down, straight at him. Chris opened his mouth to scream, but nothing came out, and he felt the unseen seat belt give way. Without it to restrain him he rolled forward out of the invisible seat, and as he fell towards the solid black ground the light faded; not to pitch black but to a gloomy sort of twilight, because that was how dim and feeble ordinary daylight was in comparison.

He sat up. He was sitting on the tarmac of a parking space in the Ettingate Retail Park car park, in between an old red Volvo and a silver Peugeot, and there was a thin smear of blood seeping through his shirt front from a shallow graze, roughly where a seat belt would normally have crossed his chest.

CHAPTER FIVE

'And you're sure it was her,' Jill said, for the fifth time. 'You're *sure*.'

'Absolutely,' Chris replied, stifling a yawn. 'I'd know her voice anywhere. It's been telling me where to go for the last five months.'

Jill's office wasn't a bit like he'd imagined. He'd had this mental picture of something out of an American cop show, the 14th Precinct or whatever: open-plan bustle, men in shirt-sleeves, phones ringing, a Brownian commotion of activity. But no. It was small – the building used to be an ordinary mid-Victorian house, Jill had told him, and her bit of it had been a boiler room – and cluttered, with filing cabinets jostling round her desk like gawpers at an accident scene. There were piles of green, blue and beige folders all over her desk, the windowsill and the floor. She had a computer and a phone, a stapler and a Darth Vader coffee mug, and in one corner there was an umbrella stand, crammed with weapons. He'd been trying not to stare at them ever since she'd brought him in.

'Sorry,' Jill said, 'but I'd like to go through the sequence of events just one more time. I'm sure I must be missing something.'

(There was an axe, for example, and a sledgehammer, two

short spears and a variety of different swords – straight and curved, long, short, thick and thin – and a big slashy sort of thing with very peculiar lettering on the blade, and something that looked like a saw on a stick—)

'We got lost,' Chris said wearily. 'I got us lost, I'm not much good at maps—'

'That's strange,' she interrupted. 'In your line of work, I mean. I'd have thought you must've got quite good at reading maps. You haven't always had a—'

Delicacy of feeling, he assumed, made her tail off before actually saying the S-word. 'I managed,' he replied. 'And after a bit, you keep going to the same places, you know the way, you don't need a map.'

Jill's eyebrow raised a little. 'That's another thing,' she said. 'You've got your set rounds, right? And, like you say, you know how to get to them, you could probably find your way around your routes with your eyes shut. So why did you need to use the—?'

He broke eye contact and didn't reply.

'It's all right,' she said nicely. 'You aren't the first person it's happened to, you know. And it's important that we understand exactly how close the – well, the link between you and it was. You see, the closer the link, the worse the obsession is, if they get loose. If you only used it, say, once a month, it'd be hard for it to find you. But if you used it every day—'

She looked at Chris as she said it. He nodded.

'If you used it every day,' Jill repeated, 'it sort of gets tuned in to you, and it can home in on you really easily. Which I guess explains how she found you.'

Chris grinned sadly. 'My own stupid fault, in other words.'

'You can see it like that if you want to,' she replied. 'I don't. Personally I think they can be very dangerous things, and there ought to be strict controls on how they're sold. But,' she added, with a shrug, 'the people who matter don't agree with me, or at least not yet, so there we go. Anyway, I'm sorry, I interrupted. Go on with what you were saying.'

So he went through it yet again, while Jill made them both a coffee with the kettle perched on a crag of folders: the car park, Angela's sudden disappearance, the demon, the threats, the pain, where is she, all that—

'And it was just about to kill me,' Chris said, 'when she turned up.'

(There was a photo of Jill's mum and dad on the desk, buried among the paperwork like miners trapped in a cave-in. He barely recognised them, because of the dust on the glass.)

'It does seem like a bit of a coincidence,' Jill said, not for the very first time.

He shrugged. 'Yes,' he said, 'it does, rather. Anyway, I couldn't see what was going on, but I'm pretty sure she fought the demon, because it screamed a lot, didn't sound like it was having a very nice time, and when the lights came on it wasn't there any more, and she was looking a bit puffed, leaning on the sword thing she had with her. A bit,' he couldn't help adding, 'like that one you've got there. Look – wedged in between the meat cleaver and the polo mallet.'

Jill smiled indulgently. 'You mean the estoc,' she said. 'And the meat cleaver's a bardische, and that's not a polo mallet, it's a martel. You use it for hammering stakes into the hearts of vampires.'

'Oh.'

'Quite,' she said. 'Serves you right for asking. Actually,' she added, 'now you mention it, that's quite interesting, if what it had really was an estoc.'

'What's an—?'

'Very specialised,' she replied. 'Quite rare, too. The blade is a single hair from the head of a fallen angel.'

'Oh.'

'Really, it is,' Jill said, with a grin. 'No kidding. It's given like a really, really heavy relaxing treatment, to keep it straight, and it'll cut through pretty much anything.'

'Like a pantacopt,' Chris said, without thinking.

She gave him ever such a funny look. 'A bit like a pantacopt,' she replied. 'Only not as good, obviously.' She paused. 'You're pretty well informed, aren't you?'

'Ah well,' Chris replied, trying to sound flippant, and failing. 'Magic artefacts are my business, so I know a lot of—'

'Not one of JWW Retail's biggest-volume lines, though, are they? Or if they are, we really ought to know about it.'

'I read about them in some book, OK?' He could feel the conversation starting to seize up, like an unlubricated engine. 'Stuck in my mind for some reason. They reminded me of light sabres, in *Star Wars*.'

'What in what?'

Chris frowned. 'It's a film,' he said.

'Oh.' Jill shrugged. 'Anyway,' she said, 'if the entity from your SatNav really has managed to get hold of an estoc, that's not good at all. I'm starting to wonder if it stole it from here, before it broke out. We'll have to do an inventory.'

'Glad you're taking it seriously,' he said. 'Bearing in mind it was me she tried to chop up with the bloody thing.'

'Quite.' Jill leaned back a little in her chair. She was starting to get a bit of a double chin, he noticed, and her face was a bit rounder than it used to be. 'About that. You say it attacked you.'

Chris nodded. 'Oh yes,' he said. 'After she'd chased off the demon.' He paused, then said, 'I guess it was my fault. You see, I recognised her voice, when she yelled something at the demon, and I told her so. I said "I know who you are" or something like that. She said no, I must be wrong, but I insisted, and then she slashed at me with the sword thing. Luckily she missed me but cut the seat belt, and I fell forward and – well, there I was in the car park. But it was me insisting I knew who she was that made her go for me, I'm sure of it.'

Jill nodded. 'You were very lucky,' she said. 'All the way through, in fact. Actually, it's amazing you're still here.'

'That's nice to know,' Chris growled; then, 'Look, what exactly *did* happen to me? You've been asking all these questions, but you haven't told me anything, and I think I've got a right—'

'Fair enough,' Jill said. 'All right, this is what we think happened. Most of it's just speculation, mind, we don't actually know, but the theory is that you were lured there deliberately by the demons, because they think you know something.'

Chris scowled. 'They should've talked to Miss Hickey, then,' he said. 'She always reckoned I didn't know anything.'

'I don't think they're interested in GCSE-level geography,' Jill replied. 'We do know that it wasn't your trainee that called at your flat. We checked; her mother said she was in her room all morning, working on a research project for her degree course, so she never left the house. What you saw was probably a demon under a glamour.'

'Oh.'

'No reason why you should've suspected anything,' Jill said. 'It's fairly basic technology, and just the sort of thing demons are good at. Also, we checked with your Mr Burnoz and it was the first he'd heard of any of it; so it's definitely looking like a set-up, and they wanted you in that car park at that particular time.'

'I see,' Chris said. 'Why there?'

'Geometaphysical fault line runs slap bang though the middle of the Ettingate Retail Park,' she told him. 'Been known about for centuries, but when we told the local planning authority they just weren't interested. We think the demons chose it because the fault makes it easier to shift a material object – you, for example – out of our dimension into theirs. That and the portable parking space.'

'What, they used a BB27—'

'Probably stolen from your car,' Jill said, with a commiserating smile. 'It's well known that they can cause dimensional-interface ruptures. They'll have kept the space empty while they were waiting for you to arrive with some kind of illusion, so the shoppers would've thought the space was taken. The demon pretending to be Angela simply parked the car on top of it and – swoosh, there you go.'

'Hang on, though,' Chris said. 'We were lost, I got us lost. So how did they know I'd drive us to exactly that—?'

Another smile. 'The map was jinxed,' she said. 'Again, fairly elementary stuff. It made you go there. So there's one positive thing to come out of all of this. You're not nearly as rubbish at map-reading as you thought you were.'

Chris sighed. 'Sort of makes it all seem worthwhile, really.'

'Quite.' Jill laughed. She had, he remembered, always laughed at his jokes. 'So the real mystery is,' she went on, 'what it is that they think you know, and they're so desperate to find out. It must be something really important to them, because all this, the planning, the set-up, it's a hell of a lot of trouble for them to go to; really expensive, in terms of energy expended in our dimension, I mean.'

Chris nodded. 'You told me all about that,' he said.

'Which brings us back to the question,' Jill went on, with a sigh. 'Who's this *she* they're so dead keen to find?'

'I've been thinking about that,' he said. 'SatNav – the, um, entity inside my SatNav; she's a she.'

Jill frowned. 'So am I,' she said. 'Actually, so are a lot of people.'

'Yes, but maybe she's involved in all this.' Chris hesitated; but surely it couldn't do any harm now, not after SatNav had tried to kill him – 'There was one thing I didn't tell you, about the other demon. The one yesterday.'

Her eyes gleamed. 'I thought so,' she said. 'Well?'

So he told her; how, just before it left the car, the demon had reached past him and turned SatNav on with its claw. 'And that's all,' he concluded lamely. 'I didn't tell you at first because I didn't think it was important—'

'Fibber.'

'All right.' Chris held up a hand in front of his face. 'You're right. I was afraid that if I told you, your people would take her away and break her open or something. I didn't want anything to happen to her.' He raised both hands and spread his fingers: surrender. 'You know why, don't you?'

Compassion; compassion in victory, which isn't quite the same thing. 'Like I said,' Jill replied, 'you aren't the first, I don't suppose you'll be the last, and I'm not going to pass judgement. And you've told me now, which is the main thing. And yes,' she added, 'I do think it's significant. Not absolutely sure why, but I have a feeling about it. Like, it may just answer the really big question that's been bugging both of us: why you?'

Chris tried to think, but – 'All right, then. Why me?'

'Simply because the thing happened to be banged up in your SatNav,' she said. 'If that's what they're after. It's just a hypothesis at this stage,' she added quickly. 'Barely that, even. Still, half a hypothesis is marginally better than a complete and utter clue deficiency. All right,' she said, 'I think that's everything for now.' She glanced at her watch. 'Lunchtime,' she said. 'I reckon the least the government can do is buy you a pint and a sandwich after screwing up your Saturday. Or would you rather get on home?'

Be back by one, Karen had said. Well, no chance of that now. What a pity. 'On expenses?' he queried.

'Your taxes at work,' Jill replied. 'Tell you what: a pint, a sandwich *and* a packet of crisps. We can always make up the budget deficiency by firing a few clerical officers. And,' she added, 'I promise not to say a word about demons or malevolent SatNav entities or geometaphysical rifts. Deal?'

Jill kept her promise. Instead, they talked about old friends from school, all of whose lives turned out to be either vastly better or immeasurably worse than his own. That left Chris fifty per cent depressed and fifty per cent obnoxiously smug, and two pints at lunchtime added a haze of gentle anaesthesia. She paid for his taxi home.

The bathroom, he remembered; he was supposed to start stripping off the old wallpaper. The cheerful part of him thought *why not*, and the miserable part thought *might as well*, so he went into the kitchen to assemble the necessary arsenal.

There on the table was the pantacopt-tapemeasure. Bloody stupid thing to leave lying about, he told himself sternly; what if Karen had found it and started playing with it? She could've turned herself into salami before she'd realised there was something wrong. He took it into the bedroom and hid it under the bed, out of harm's way.

How to strip off wallpaper. First, you get it wet with the stuff from the bottle. This makes it soggy, and then you scrape at it with the scraper. Chris had never been any good at it, but it hadn't mattered when he was young, because one of grandad's friends from the factory came round and did it by magic in ten minutes flat. He'd taken the trouble to learn the magic words, but he couldn't make them work. Hence the bottle of stuff, and the scraper.

Half an hour of picking and worrying away at it, and he'd cleared a space the size of a wine-bottle label. He wasn't sure when Karen'd be back, but he was conscious of the need to get a move on. He dabbed on more of the stuff and scraped harder, with the result that he snapped the scraper blade, cut his thumb, jumped back in alarm and knocked over the stuff bottle, spilling the remaining contents into the sink.

At least it hadn't gone all over the carpet tiles. Still, it was a pretty close approximation to a disaster, and for a while Chris stood there feeling sad, unable to think of anything he could do about it. Then a thought struck him.

It was sheer desperation; but – well, the *Book* had said they cut *anything*. He retrieved the tapemeasure, ran out nine inches of blade and (bending it slightly so it lay flush against the wall) stroked the half-soggy wallpaper with it.

Instant success: it came away like shaving foam under a new razor blade. He tried it again. His next sweep cleaned off three square feet, leaving the plastered wall smooth and unmarked. At this rate – his inner accountant was totalling up the brownie points, and the result was staggering. If only he could contrive to get the whole job finished by the time she got back – not implausible, at the rate the tapemeasure was going – not only would he be forgiven for not being home in time to go social-ising, but there'd be enough change left over to pay for at least one, maybe two further mistakes. Right, he thought.

The blade made a gentle hissing noise as it snowploughed through the paper, and the lack of stuff from the bottle didn't seem to make any difference at all; magic, he assumed. How nice it must be, he thought, ever so slightly resentfully, to be able to do proper magic, like this, all the time: magic to wash up and hoover, dust, scour ovens, wash cars. How useful; how convenient. Instead, all he got was demons and geometaphys-ical rifts, action-adventure stuff which scared him rigid and interfered with his chances of making his monthly target. Even the stuff he sold to the shops – well, it wasn't action-adventure, but a lot of it was just toys, junk, no practical application in the real world. Now, if only JWW Retail could come up with a line of genuinely useful consumer and household items—

There was, Chris noticed, something written on the wall, under the archaeological strata of wallpaper layers. He could make out the top halves of a row of letters, big block capitals in blue chalk. Mildly intrigued, he scraped down a little further until he could read them:

DANGER

He frowned. Gas main? Electricity cable? Nice of whoever it was to mention it, but a little more information would have been helpful. He scraped a little further.

YOU ARE IN TERRIBLE DANGER

All right, he thought, but please be more specific; *do not drill here*, or something like that. Also, terrible danger? As in bringing the whole wall down, or frying himself to a crisp? He scraped down, and got:

TRUST NO ONE

He stood back and scratched his head. A practical-joking painter and decorator with a flair for melodrama. 'You included,' he said aloud; then, with a shrug, scraped a bit more.

EXCEPT ME, OBVIOUSLY

Um, he thought. Well; a practical-joking painter and decorator with a flair for melodrama and delusions of humour might have guessed what a normal person's reaction might be. He was getting close to the bottom of the wall now, and had to stoop to scrape the next patch:

THE DEMONS ARE HUNTING YOU. THEY WILL

Oh shit, Chris thought.

Let's see, he said to himself. We've been here, what, four years; we redid the bathroom when we moved in, but we were in a hurry, so we just papered over what was already there; and there's three, no, four layers; so that's our layer and three more. Which means this lot's been here a long time, and there isn't any way of writing *through* waterproof vinyl wallpaper. In which case, this message can't be for me, can it? Well?

He read it again:

THE DEMONS ARE HUNTING YOU. THEY WILL

They will what? He got on his hands and knees and scraped right down to the skirting board:

CONTINUED ON NEXT WALL

Fine. He went into the kitchen and fetched the folding steps, and started scraping at the top of the right-hand wall.

HUNT YOU DOWN UNTIL THEY FIND YOU. THEY HAVE ALREADY

He slipped on the top rung of the steps, dropped the tapemeasure and grabbed at the wall with his left hand to steady himself. Then he looked down and saw, with a resigned wretched feeling, that the tapemeasure had sliced the doors off the bathroom cabinet. Marvellous, he thought. If I wasn't in terrible danger before, I am now.

TRIED ONCE. NEXT TIME I WILL NOT BE THERE TO SAVE YOU. THE ONE WHO IS TO COME MUST BE PROTECTED AT ALL COSTS. ONLY YOU CAN

Oh for crying out loud, the telephone. Chris hopped off the ladder, carefully laid the tapemeasure on the floor, and scampered through into the hall.

'There's been a development.' Jill's voice, sounding rattled. 'It's really weird, I can't—'

Not *now*, he thought. 'Look, Jill, could I call you back? Only I'm sort of up to my eyes right at this very moment.'

'It's back.'

All right, then. 'What's back?'

'The entity,' she said. 'It's back inside your SatNav. We went to do a low-level demiurge scan on the casing, and it's definitely in there.'

'Oh,' he said. 'That's good, isn't it?'

'Sort of.' Definite hesitation in her voice. 'Only, the thing is, it's sort of barricaded itself in, and we can't open it up. God only knows how it's doing it, some kind of really powerful Gatekeeper or Portcullis charm, the energy drain must be off the scale, but it's managing it somehow.'

He thought for a bit, then said, 'Hardly surprising, though, is it? I mean, she must know that if you can crack the casing open, you're going to do nasty things to her, for escaping. Not,' he added quickly, 'that I've got any sympathy, I'm just saying. It's basic survival instinct, surely.'

'I suppose,' Jill replied. 'It's still crazy, though. For one thing, if it managed to get loose why in heaven's name would it want to come back? It's like an escaped convict breaking back into prison. Doesn't make sense.'

She had a point, as always. 'Even so,' he said. 'She's back under lock and key, so all's well that ends well.'

'It's not as simple as that. In the first place, how did it get out? Second, how did it get back in again and why? Third, how's it managing to keep us out, and how come a fairly low-grade entity like that's generating that kind of power?'

That jogged Chris's memory. 'Talking of which,' he said, 'I meant to ask you. What *is* she, exactly? I mean, you just keep saying *the entity*. Is she a demon, or what?'

Jill sounded shocked. 'Oh no, nothing like that. Something pretty innocuous; well, relatively. They can all be bloody dangerous if you aren't careful. No, it's just a plain ordinary dryad, no big deal, or so you'd have thought.'

'Fine. What the hell's a dryad?'

'Oh, right. It's a nature spirit or genius loci, almost exclusively associated with forests. They live in trees and protect them from enemies. Basically, just an elf.'

'Elf?'

'Yes.'

For a moment, the word made no sense. 'Like, Santa's little helpers, that sort of thing?'

'No,' Jill snapped impatiently. 'Tell you what, look it up. There's a very helpful guide to species recognition and characteristics on our website, doubleyoudoubleyoudoubleyou dot delendisunt, all one word, dot gov dot uk forward slash entities. All you need to know in one handy easy-to-access reference. All right?'

'Just a tick, this pencil's not very – what was that word, delen—?'

She spelt it out for him. 'Got that? Fine. Look, sorry but I've got to dash. Just thought you'd like to know. One less thing to worry about – well, for you, anyhow.'

An elf, Chris thought as he put the phone down, she's an elf.

He tried to picture an elf in his mind, but the image that presented itself didn't seem quite right, and he had a feeling he was probably getting 'elf' muddled up with 'smurf'. Anyway, it didn't matter. If she was safely back in her casing, it was, as Jill had said, one less thing to stress out about.

Talking of which—

Back into the bathroom, grab the tapemeasure, up the ladder, scrape, and—

YOU'RE BACK, THEN. GOOD OF YOU TO SPARE THE TIME

He sighed. 'I'm sorry,' he said aloud. 'Now, you'd got as far as "only you can—"'

ONLY YOU CAN BRING THE ONE THAT IS TO COME ACROSS THE INTERFACE

His arm was starting to get ever so tired. 'Is that right?' he said. 'What interface?'

Scrape, scrape, scrape; and—

WHO WERE YOU TALKING TO, ANYHOW?

Chris scowled, 'Just an old school friend, if it's any of your business. Look—'

The tapemeasure slipped out of his hand and slid down the wall, taking a great swathe of paper with it. Nice trick, he couldn't help but concede.

YOU MUST SET FREE THE ONE WHO IS CURSED, RESCUE THE ONE THAT IS TO COME FROM THOSE THAT ARE HIDDEN AND END THE WAR AMONG THE CHILDREN OF THE DARK. IF YOU FAIL, YOU WILL DIE AND THE HUMAN RACE WI

'Hang on,' he panted, moving the stepladder. 'OK, the human race wi—'

LL PERISH. EVERYTHING DEPENDS ON YOU

His right hand was starting to go numb. He rested it for thirty seconds, then scraped some more:

I WILL HELP YOU, AS I HAVE ALWAYS DONE. HOWEVER, SINCE

The tapemeasure slipped out of his hand again. This time, luckily, it missed the fixtures and fittings and flumped down on the floor. He snatched it up, and—

YOU MISSED A BIT

He blinked, then looked up. Sure enough, there was a little patch of paper that had escaped the blade. He flicked it off, then went back to where he'd got to.

Nothing there.

He did the rest of the wall. Nothing. Just plain, uninscribed plaster as far as the eye could see.

By the time Karen got home he'd done the whole of the bathroom, every last square centimetre. Also, he'd been over the whole lot with sandpaper and a wire brush; to get off any loose plaster, he explained, and make sure there was a firm sur-face for the new paper to stick to. She did manage to find fault with some dark smeary marks, like badly erased chalk, but her heart clearly wasn't in it, and she barely sulked at all about him not being back by one as he'd promised.

That night, Chris didn't sleep at all well. A dream kept going round in his head, repeating like a loop.

There was the demon, edging towards him; in the dream it was light in the box formed by the faded car, and he could see it clearly. It crawled on all fours as far as his feet, then looked up at him with fiery orange eyes, and whimpered, 'Help me, please.' As it said the words, a shadow fell across it, so he couldn't see it any more; and then an egg the size of a rugby ball split open, and SatNav jumped out, golden and shining, and said, 'Leave her alone, she's just a baby,' and then popped back into the egg, whose shell flew back into place like a rewound film. Then he stood up, and the egg was in his pocket, and it was saying, 'At the end of the world, turn right.' And then Jill popped up out of nowhere, grabbed him by the hair and laid the blade of a tapemeasure across his throat, at which point he woke up.

Being awake wasn't much better; he had that extra-creepy feeling he hadn't experienced since he was a small child, that there was something in the room, watching him. As if that wasn't enough to be going on with, something was nagging away at his mind, and he couldn't pin it down; something to do with water polo, and websites. When he drifted off to sleep, the dream came back again, waking him up. And so on.

Chris spent Sunday hanging wallpaper, but no more messages came. Just after lunch, he got the *Book* out and looked up pantacopts; same entry as before, but he'd missed a bit where it said about the disorientating effect of handling such a powerful magical object if you weren't used to it. Delusions and hallucinations were common side effects, it said, and recommended the wearing of gloves, eye and ear protection and a surgical mask.

So maybe he'd imagined the whole thing; the writing on the wall, talking back to him. It was a comforting thought, and since he'd scrubbed away the chalk (if there'd ever been any to start with) he had no verifiable evidence; or, in other words, nothing to contradict the must've-imagined-it hypothesis. Magical radiation leaking out of the tapemeasure and driving him nuts; add to that the delayed shock of his meeting with the demon – or had he imagined that too? No, because Jill had been to the car park, and her instruments had picked up the burn of demonic body heat all over the place. So that had definitely happened, unfortunately.

The dream was waiting for him as soon as he went to bed, and the pattern repeated as before. He woke up for the third time just after three a.m., and thought the hell with this, I'll get up and make myself a cup of tea, and perhaps that'll disturb the cycle.

It was while the kettle was boiling that the mystery resolved itself; it sort of popped out, like a loose tooth. Where he'd been going wrong, of course, was water polo. Not water polo after all. What he should have been thinking about was polo shirts; to be precise, the one he'd been lent by the government man, with the letters DS on the pocket.

Quietly as a little mouse, so as not to wake Karen, he crept into the living room, turned on the computer and plugged in the phone jack. Doubleyoudoubleyoudoubleyou dot delendisunt (all one word)—

Eventually, the home page of the Department of Metaphysics shimmered onto the screen, and there, in the top left-hand corner, was their departmental logo; a hand clutching a badly drawn sword, and under it a scroll with the words *delendi sunt*—

Whatever that meant; but now at least he knew what DS stood for. Not that much of a mystery. Chris went back into the kitchen and made his cup of tea; then, since he wasn't feeling sleepy any more, he clicked on the links page to *Supernatural Entities of the British Isles* and scrolled down to *dryads*. He read what it had to say, but there wasn't really anything that Jill hadn't already told him, so he switched off and disconnected.

So she'd come home, had she? One less weirdness to worry about. Presumably they'd keep her there and find some way of breaking into the casing, and then dissect her or whatever you did with stroppy entities. He didn't feel terribly wonderful about that; but then, she'd tried to cut him open, hadn't she? In which case, serve her right.

From there, his thoughts strayed to the demon itself. Logically, he supposed, he ought to be in a right old state about that. His escape had, after all, been as narrow as a country lane; if SatNav hadn't turned up when she did and chased the demon away, he was fairly sure it'd have killed him, and it was still out there, and it had deliberately targeted him, going to all that trouble and effort. True, now it knew that he didn't have the information it wanted, so presumably now it would leave him alone, go and hassle someone else – he remembered poor Mr Newsome and winced – but even so, he couldn't help wondering: *where is she?* Odd question to ask. At the time, he'd been stone-cold certain he didn't know the answer, and it was on that presupposition that his belief that he was now safely out of it rested. But suppose he did have the answer, but without knowing it? Possible, since he hadn't got a clue who *she* was. He did know a fair number of women, after all, and one of them could be the person the demon was after; could be Jill, for example, or anybody – Karen, Angela the trainee (all this stuff had only started when she arrived in his life), Julie at the office, Karen's cousin Melanie, anybody at all. Until he could be absolutely certain that he didn't know the answer to the demon's question, it really wouldn't do to get complacent.

Well, fine; now he had something to worry himself sick about all over again, very well done indeed, but without knowing who *she* was, he had no way at all of either setting his mind at rest or confirming that he was squarely in the demon's cross-hairs. Naturally, he'd told Jill all about what the demon had asked; she'd just frowned, then shrugged, no suggestions or explanations, and she was the only person he could think of who might possibly know. So: dead end.

Chris picked up his teacup, and noticed it had left a ring on the cover of the *Book* –

The Book. Supremely advanced technology but a total dead loss commercially, because it told you what you *needed* to know, not what you *wanted* to know. Well, he thought; if ever there was a case of genuine, not to say desperate need, surely this was it. He shifted the cup to the table, rested the *Book* on his knees and opened it, as stated in the instructions, at random—

Gandhi; Mohandas Karamchand Gandhi, born 2 October 1869, Porbandar, India.

He used a word his mother wouldn't have liked, and closed the *Book*. No wonder they couldn't give the bloody things away. It crossed his mind that the demon was simply behind the times and not particularly well up in current affairs; but it had specifically said *she*, not *he*, so that ruled Gandhi out as the object of its search. He yawned, and went back to bed, and dreamed he was back at school and having to do the reading in assembly with no clothes on; which, compared to the dreams he'd been having lately, was practically a lullaby.

'I heard about what happened,' said Angela the trainee as they drove through the outskirts of Telford. 'It must've been terrible.'

She really did have a little Suzuki jeep, which showed the sort of attention to detail that demons were capable of, but they'd picked up on things like the *US Out Of Kiribati Now* sticker in the back window and the door compartment stuffed full of used tissues. You had to admire good fieldwork. He had to admit, though, the demon Angela had been a much better driver.

'Oh?' Chris said. 'Who told you?'

'The government people rang to find out where I was,' she explained. 'Mummy answered; she told them I'd been in my room all day. They told her.' She went to change up into third and got fifth instead. 'Sounds like you were really lucky.'

'I was,' he said. 'I'm pretty sure it'd have killed me if—'

He hesitated. Had the government people told her about SatNav's intervention? Probably not. An escaped SatNav entity was just the sort of thing they'd classify, on general principles. He considered telling her anyway, but decided against it. Too much background to explain, and he didn't feel like going into all that.

'I was going to ask you,' Angela said, as she swung out to overtake an ambling JCB. The brave little engine whinnied as she flogged it. 'How did you get away?'

'I don't know,' he replied. 'There was this strap thing holding me in, where the seat belt had been, and it suddenly sort of gave way, and I fell out, and there I was on the tarmac, back in the real world. Otherwise – well, doesn't bear thinking about, really.'

He'd hoped that would end the inquiry, but apparently not. 'That's odd,' she said. 'Because if they took you into their dimension, presumably they'd be using a level seven containment spell to keep you there, and that's what would've been holding you down, and something like that wouldn't just break of its own accord. I mean, either they must've released it or something else must've disrupted it, one or the other.'

'Is that right?' Chris said uneasily. 'Lucky for me, whatever it was.'

There was definitely something very different about Angela today. It wasn't just that she was chattier, friendlier, more relaxed, less sullen and withdrawn. The way she looked had changed, too. She looked – well: the difference between scrag end of lamb and words is that words are better unminced. She looked nicer. Lots nicer. All the sharp edges seemed to have gone from her face, there was a bit of colour in her cheeks, if he didn't know better he could've sworn she'd filled out a bit. The result wasn't bad, actually, though of course that was none of his business. Even so; he couldn't help glancing sideways, while she was busy not mashing a cyclist into the side of a parked van. Make-up? He couldn't see any, but he was no expert—

Make-up, he thought; we sell that. Instaglamour cream, available in four handy sizes. One of the few advantages that the JWW product had over its rivals, one which he kept on forgetting to mention when he was pitching it in the shops, was that it didn't just spruce up the way you looked, it improved your personality as well; your voice sounded nicer, people believed what you told them, your jokes were suddenly funny, you were generally more fun to be with – though of course you had to be careful not to overdo it, as Tony Blair had found out to his cost. Still, it worked, which was more than could be said of everything in the JWW range—

It was like the old hairspray commercial: was she or wasn't she? Hard to tell. If she was, it could only have been a little bit, a quick dab on each cheek and the tip of the nose, but that was what they recommended in the little leaflet; just a little to start with, or people would notice, and gradually work your way up. Or maybe she was just that much more relaxed, or something had happened to put her in a good mood, and without the spiky attitude he was seeing her as she really was. Maybe it was just because she was driving her own car rather than being driven in someone else's. Whatever; it meant that today promised to be slightly less wearing than Thursday, and that couldn't be bad.

'Is this the right road?' Angela asked. 'I don't know this area.'

Chris nodded. 'Straight on till you come to a T-junction.' For some reason, his voice faltered as he said it. 'Then left and immediately right.'

'Thanks.' She flicked hair away from her face. 'I've got a rubbish sense of direction. What I could do with is one of those SatNav things.'

The tone of voice so carefully pitched, but still not good enough; he felt as though someone was running a wire brush over the soles of his feet. 'They're all right,' he said. 'But it doesn't do to rely on them.'

'Really? I'd heard they were pretty good.'

'They can let you down,' he replied. 'You're better off with a map.'

(Not always true, he reflected, thinking of the jinxed map that had taken him to the Ettingate Retail Park. Basically, you couldn't trust *anything*; and then he remembered that a wall had recently told him that. And he'd been trying so hard not to think about it—)

They'd come to call on Mercian Magic, one of his better customers; whether or not the manageress fancied him, as some of the unkinder voices in the office had been heard to suggest, they always ordered in well on the new lines and, to do them justice, managed to get rid of them. Properly speaking, it wasn't the right day, but he'd phoned ahead and yes, they could see him at nine-forty; a nice easy call, he'd promised himself, to ease himself back into the swing.

As Chris got out, he felt his phone clunk against something in his jacket pocket: the tapemeasure, just to make him feel a tiny bit more secure. 'Tell you what,' he said, as they walked up to the shop door. 'I'll start off with the usual stuff, and then you can pitch them the new lines. If you feel like it, of course.'

He had no idea why he'd offered, but Angela squealed 'Ooh, yes please' before he could come up with a viable weaselling-out strategy, so that was that. 'Um, you do know about the—'

She nodded. 'I've been reading up on our product portfolio,' she said. 'Which one do you most want to shift?'

'BB27K,' he said immediately; no need to think about that.

She smiled. 'Well, if they want a testimonial, you can honestly say they work.'

Maybe I liked her better when she was sullen, Chris said to himself, and pushed open the door.

There was some man he didn't know behind the counter; a big, square man who looked like a builder. 'Hello,' he said. 'I'm here to see Christine.'

The man looked at him. 'Rep?'

'That's right. Chris Popham, JWW Retail, and this is my associate, Angela—' Screw it, he couldn't remember her surname. *This is my associate Angela* made her sound like a faded blonde in fishnets who passed him the top hat with the rabbit in it and got sawn in half. Still—

'Christine's left,' the man said, with just a hint of smugness. 'I'm the new manager. John Iconodule.'

'Ah.' Briefly disconcerted, but a good recovery. Chris held out his hand, which Mr Iconodule apparently failed to see. 'Pleased to—'

'You aren't down in the book,' Mr Iconodule said.

Chris smiled feebly. 'Well, it's not actually my usual day, but I did phone through—'

Mr Iconodule frowned, held up a hand as though commanding a dog to sit, scrabbled in a small sheaf of bits of paper, found one, smoothed it out and scowled at it.

'Ah, right,' he said. 'Stupid girl took the message, can't read her writing. So this is you, then.'

'Suppose it must be,' Chris said. It was supposed to be airy banter, but it came out sounding half-witted. 'Look, if it's not convenient, I can come back.'

'That'd be a bit pointless, since you're here,' Mr Iconodule said, raising an eyebrow. 'You'd better make it quick, though. I've got Zauberwerke coming in at ten.'

A good pitch is a thing of light and air, a gossamer-light touch on the customer's heart and mind. The tone is brisk but chatty, posited on the assumption that of course the customer wants as much of this excellent merchandise as the seller can spare him; fortunately, since he's a favoured client and a personal friend, he can usually be accommodated. Phrases like 'This is going to do really well for you' and 'I think this is exactly what you've been looking for' should dart out like white doves from the magician's hat, inspiring the client, making him feel good about his commercial judgement and breadth of vision. Businesslike, to be sure; but not so intense that the negotiations can't be put on hold for five minutes while conversation is made about the wife's back, the daughter's GCSE grades, the football, or the number of VAT inspectors required to change a light bulb.

This pitch wasn't like that. Chris could feel himself wallowing, like a car stuck in mud, and the harder he revved his charm, the more the wheels spun. Mr Iconodule wasn't interested in JWW's new, improved bottled dreams or the Haitian

Surprise melting wax (pins sold separately). All he wanted was another nine dozen of the DW6, and he kept glancing down at his watch.

Desperation time. 'In that case,' Chris said, 'my colleague would like it if you could spare her a minute of your time to hear about our new line in portable folding parking spaces. Angela?'

Such a difference. For the first thirty seconds, he was stunned; then furiously jealous; then he pulled himself together and started paying close attention, in the hope of learning how it was done. That didn't do him much good. Angela was brisk but chatty, rewriting the rules of engagement so that she was the one doing the customer a favour, businesslike but not intense, pausing for digressions on house prices, ice hockey and reality TV. When she finally released him, she'd got an order for eight dozen BB27Ks and helped him see the error of his ways about the bottled dreams, the melting wax and the Miracle Sprout padded insoles (guaranteed to leave a trail of spring flowers wherever you walk; may contain traces of chlorophyll).

'Is that the time?' she said. 'We'd better leave it there for now, then. Didn't you say you'd got Zauberwerke coming in at ten?'

Mr Iconodule gave her a slightly dazed look. 'Forgotten about him,' he mumbled. 'Sod it, yes. Not sure why I'm even bothering, they've never got anything worth having.'

(And Chris thought: that settles it. Instaglamour cream; which is unethical, and banned, and if she gets caught selling to the customers with it on it'll be me that gets the bollocking. On the other hand—)

'Thanks,' Angela said as they left the shop, 'that was fun. I can see how you get a sort of rush out of doing this.'

(There was a jar of it, he remembered, in his sample case. Just a tiny little smudge on the tip of his nose and the point of his chin; nobody'd ever know—)

She opened the car door for him, and he climbed in and

pulled down the seat belt, ready to clip it on. The feel of the webbing was unpleasantly familiar; the demons had copied that exactly, too. He could remember how it had buckled as he drove his fingernails into it –

'Where next?' Angela was saying; asking him for directions. You know, as in *At the end of the road, turn* – It took him a moment to get his mind back; it had strayed off, like a bad dog. 'Back onto the ring road,' he said, 'and then we want the B194 as far as—'

Chris was pretty sure what she'd done; the question was, why? Made no sense. There were all sorts of reasons why someone should want to daub on the Instaglamour. It could get you love, popularity, the trust of the electorate (though the discerning buyers in Hollywood, Westminster and DC tended to go for Zauberwerke's LikeMe; twenty per cent more effective and without the unfortunate dermatological side effects). It could make you adored, worshipped, revered. It could even shift BB27Ks, though of course you weren't supposed to do that.

But why should Angela the trainee put the stuff on just to spend a day doing the rounds with him? If she'd read the little booklet that came inside the box, she must have seen the Dire Warnings section: apply not more than once every ten days, remove with JWW GlamourOff within six hours, failure to observe safety precautions may result in lasting physical and spiritual damage or death, and that's if you're lucky. The natural assumption was that she wanted him to like her, or she was anxious to make a good impression on the customers, but neither of those would wash. After all, she was trainee management, graduate entry, being put through uni by the firm because they believed she was destined for greatness. She had no reason to be interested in anything here; she was just passing through, because she'd been ordered to, and it didn't matter whether anybody liked her or not, or whether she impressed some underachieving rep who'd never make it off the road and into management. As for – well, a personal, as opposed to a business motive, he was inclined to doubt that, in the same way that he was sceptical about the sun being a fiery chariot drawn by milk-white horses. In which case—

She was telling him about someone she'd met who'd actually met someone who knew Morrissey. He suppressed a frown. That was first-date chatter, and besides, she didn't seem to be giving her full attention to the traffic and other road users. In which case; for some reason Chris couldn't begin to guess at, he'd recently become special, an object of interest to a community he'd only vaguely heard of until they started popping up all round him, ripping off heads, hitching rides in his car, kidnapping him and asking him weird questions. Was it logical to assume that he was caught up simultaneously in more than one strange and inexplicable sequence of events? Not really.

But consider the facts. Angela the trainee had come into his life on the insistence of his boss, Mr Burnoz – crass, prosaic, insensitive, perhaps the most annoying man he'd ever met in his entire life – but nevertheless *safe*. He simply couldn't imagine him being mixed up with demons or even demon-hunting. Mr Burnoz was a simple man. He existed only to supervise the exchange of goods and money, and anything that didn't directly concern that process was as alien and irrelevant to him as a Rachmaninov piano concerto to a Trobriand fisherman. And – not just presumably, but as a matter of record – Mr Burnoz knew Angela, had known her some time as a friend of the family, probably given her a vague smile as she sulked at dinner parties; Mr Burnoz *proved that she existed*, that she was a real person with a family and a history, therefore not a demon-wrought illusion. By implication, he vouched for her, and although there were times when he'd gladly have fed Mr Burnoz to a tankful of piranhas, Chris was prepared to take his unspoken word on something like this.

Maybe he should ask Jill what she thought; but that didn't feel right, somehow. He could see the look on her face, the twitch of an eyebrow, the expression that said, *you know perfectly well why, and please bear in mind that Karen's my friend too* – and it wasn't like that, he was prepared to bet money on it, but that'd be the conclusion she would jump to, if only because it was a perfectly reasonable one – to an outsider who wasn't there to see for herself.

'And the scary coincidence is,' Angela was saying, 'that a friend of my dad's was at college with a girl who went out for a while with a man who used to work for the same company that did the lighting at a gig in Preston where the warm-up band had once—'

'Look out,' Chris yelled.

Poor road skills but top-notch reflexes; she dragged the wheel round, nearly crunching the jeep into the crash barrier but avoiding the oncoming lorry by at least a quarter of a millimetre. A horn dopplered away behind them; she straightened up and went on, '– Been on tour with Morrissey back in the nineties, well, when I say on tour, they did a couple of gigs with him in Scotland, I think, but even so, it just goes to show it's a pretty small world –'

Chris was forgetting to do something: to breathe. He gobbled a double ration of air, and made his hand let go of the seat belt. 'Is that right?' he whimpered. 'Like you say, it only—'

He forgot the rest of what he'd been going to say. He was staring down at his left hand, slowly unclenching from around the seat belt. A habit of his, purely unconscious, when he encountered lethal danger as a passenger on the road. He'd done it only yesterday, tearing a fingernail as he'd dug his nails into the canvas while the demon prowled round him. And again just now, when he'd grabbed a handful and squeezed—

But not dug his nails in, he was pretty sure about that. There hadn't been time, and his fingers were still sore from yesterday, so instinctively he'd squeezed instead of digging. A personal choice, and equally valid.

In which case, though – he glanced quickly across so make sure Angela wasn't looking, then down at the belt, to confirm. In which case, why were there nail marks, deep and crisp and even, scored into the webbing at precisely the point on the belt where he'd just grabbed it?

CHAPTER SIX

There were, of course, alternative explanations. For example: the demon who'd abducted Chris yesterday had borrowed Angela's car, while she was in her room doing her college assignment, and put it back again after the bungled kidnapping attempt was over. Piece of cake for a demon; but why bother? Any old car would've done, since he hadn't had a clue what she drove, or even if she had a car at all. All right, then, how about: she was a distinctly unnerving driver, and the nail marks weren't his; they'd been left there by a previous passenger. He liked that one a lot, but he didn't believe it.

On the other hand, did he really believe that Angela the trainee, vouched for by Mr Burnoz, hand-picked by JWW Retail as a future jewel in their corporate crown, was really in league with demons, and had helped them set him up? Harder to swallow than a razor blade. Also, the same objection held true: why use her car, he thought again, when any old banger off the street would've done just as well? Unless, of course, the jeep had been specially modified to do the necessary magic to get him into the demons' dimension. As a hypothesis, however, it was still thin enough to grace any catwalk in Paris; and even if he believed it, which he didn't, what (being realistic) was he proposing to do about it?

Well: one thing Chris quite definitely wasn't going to do was risk any sort of confrontation. Quite apart from the possibility that Angela had demon allies at her beck and call, accusing someone of being a cat's-paw for the forces of darkness would be quite excruciatingly embarrassing. How would he work it into the conversation? And what was he supposed to say when she looked at him and said, 'You *what*?'

No: a sensible, rational man would do what sensible, rational men are supposed to do when confronted with the raw face of evil; look the other way until it's gone, and then call a policeman. In this case, Jill. Either she'd tell him not to be so paranoid, in which case he could revert to the terrified-previous-passenger theory and think no more of it, or else Jill would send in the black helicopters and it'd be out of his hands and someone else's problem. Assuming, of course, that she wasn't leading him into another trap. Well: he could feel the casing of the tapemeasure, pressed by the seat against his hip. He felt slightly reassured, but not nearly enough.

'Here we are,' Angela was saying, 'Boisdark Road. That's the address, isn't it?'

Chris nodded. 'About halfway down on the right. I usually park on the petrol station forecourt; just opposite, look.'

Messrs Ackery & Slade, trading as Magical Mystery Tour: a hard sell at the best of times, but although they were notoriously reluctant to take more than one dozen of anything (except DW6, of course) he'd always got on well with Dennis and Frank. A plan of action started to take shape in his mind.

'Hi, Dennis.' Big smile. 'Look, can I use your phone? My battery's flat.'

No problem. He left Angela the trainee giving Dennis the BB27K spiel and darted into the stockroom. So far, so good.

So far and no further. The voice at the other end of the line was sorry, but Ms Ettin-Smith was out of the office for the rest of the day. Yes, they had her mobile number but they weren't authorised to disclose it. They would, of course, be overjoyed if he left a message for her and would pass it on as soon as she came in tomorrow morning; no, they couldn't pass on a message right now, as Ms Ettin-Smith had left strict instructions that she wasn't to be disturbed except in an emergency; no, they weren't prepared to accept his assurance that this was an emergency, and they'd be obliged if he wouldn't take that tone with them. So sorry. Have a nice day.

Chris hung up, feeling worried. Always the problem with policemen: never one around when you really need one. Ludicrous situation, he thought: there he was, doing the rounds with someone he had reason to suspect was in league with the Common Enemy of Man; a half-sensible human being would run a mile, hide, emigrate to somewhere comparatively safe, like Iraq or Afghanistan, instead of getting back in the car, the quite possibly enchanted car in which he'd very nearly been murdered less than twenty-four hours ago, and driving to Lichfield to sell yet more powdered water to the retail magic trade. Why? Because he was afraid that if he dropped everything and ran for it, he'd lose his job? Well, fine. A bit like refusing to leave a burning house because you haven't finished watering the plants.

I could do it, he thought; I could sneak out the back, get a bus into the town centre, find a travel agent, get myself booked on a flight to Switzerland (the only country in the world where magic doesn't work; nobody had ever managed to find out why, though it was generally reckoned that the banks had something to do with it), stay there until it's safe to come back—

He shrugged. It was entirely feasible, but he couldn't do it, purely and simply because there was the possibility that he was wrong, and he wasn't being stalked by demons, which meant he'd be making a whole lot of inconvenient and disruptive fuss over nothing, and then he'd feel really *silly*. Quite. And, no doubt, that was probably the way people's minds had worked when there'd been a chance of stopping Hitler or containing the spread of the Black Death. Which was just another way of saying that people tend to get what they deserve; true, but massively unhelpful.

'Did you make your call?' The round, bearded face of Frank Ackery was beaming at him from the edge of the stockroom door.

Chris nodded. 'Thanks,' he said.

Frank grinned. 'That assistant of yours,' he said. 'Bit keen, isn't she?'

You could say that. 'Sorry,' Chris said. 'Is she making a nuisance of herself?'

Shrug. 'She's sold Dennis two dozen of those parking spaces of yours, which I'd have thought was impossible, and now she's within an ace of talking him into five dozen pairs of winged sandals, even though we've got nine dozen of the Zauberwerke version on the shelf right behind your head, and you could grow potatoes in the dust.' Frank sighed. 'Fifteen years we've been in business together, I'd have sworn he was charmproof. She permanent, or what?'

Chris shook his head. 'Management trainee,' he replied. 'Just getting a few weeks' experience in the trenches.'

'Thank God for that,' Frank replied. 'The last thing this business needs is reps who actually sell us stuff.'

'Quite.'

That was the cheery badinage done with, but Frank didn't move; he was deciding whether to say something. 'I gather you've had an exciting time of it lately.'

'Who told you that?'

'My cousin Penny in Demon Control,' Frank replied. 'Like your shirt, by the way.'

The polo shirt, with DS on the pocket. 'Not mine,' Chris said. 'Borrowed it from—'

'She told me,' Frank went on, dropping his voice a little, 'that you've had a bit of aggravation from *them*.'

No need to ask who *they* were. 'Yes,' Chris said.

'Sorry to hear it,' Frank said gravely. 'Been there,' he added. 'Not nice. Did you ever know Billy Tomacek?'

'The name's vaguely familiar—'

Frank nodded. 'My best mate at school,' he said. 'Married my cousin Penny. The reason you recognise the name is, he was killed by demons about five years ago. The biggest bit of him they ever recovered fitted nicely on a microscope slide.'

'Oh.'

'You could say that, yes. Reason I bring it up is, before they killed him they'd been hassling him for weeks; turning up everywhere he went, that sort of thing. The first three times, he managed to give them the slip. He was a bright lad, Billy.'

'I see,' Chris said, his voice suddenly weak. 'What happened—?'

Frank was silent for a moment. 'We're still not exactly sure,' he said. 'He left a message on Penny's phone at work to say he'd got her message and he'd see her there; which didn't make any sense, because she hadn't called him. So they took his answering machine apart and found it stank of demons; one of them must've got inside it and left a false message from Penny telling him to meet her somewhere. And that's where they were waiting for him.' He shrugged. 'No idea why, of course. It's like they picked him at random. The only link was Penny working for the department, but that's a bit tenuous, obviously.'

Quite, Chris thought; as far-fetched as his best friend being the head of the demon-hunters. 'Coincidence?' he heard himself say.

'We just don't know. The only other thing he said in his last message was something about Gandhi, which makes no sense at all. Anyway, when Penny told me about your spot of bother, I thought, I know him, he comes in our shop, next time I see him I'll tell him to keep his head down. So,' Frank added. 'Think on.'

'Yes,' Chris said feebly. 'Right.'

'Also.' A marked hesitation this time. 'You might find you have a use for these.' Frank dipped his fingers into the top pocket of his jacket and fished out a pair of sunglasses. 'Here,' he said, 'try them.'

Chris frowned. 'But it's not very bright in here, Frank.'

'Try the fucking sunglasses, Chris.'

Put like that, how could he refuse? He took them, and noticed how heavy they felt, as though the frames were lead and the lenses inch-thick steel. He perched them on his nose. They hurt.

'Fine,' he said, in a suffering-gladly voice. 'So what's the big— Oh.'

Frank was still there, still standing exactly where he'd been a moment ago, but there was a difference. To be precise, he had something sitting on his shoulder. It wasn't a bird, but it had wings. It most definitely wasn't human, though it had hands and feet and a more-or-less round head. 'Frank,' Chris said quietly, 'what's that on your—?'

Frank smiled at him. 'My constant companion,' he replied, 'ever since Billy died. Other people have chips on their shoulders when they're pissed off about something. You might say this is taking it to the next level.'

'Frank—'

The thing, whatever it was, yawned, revealing three rows of upper-jaw teeth and four below. Eight eyes, and the lobes of its ears drooped like streamers. 'It's a Fury,' Frank said. 'Oh, there's loads of other names for them. It's a cross between a memory and an obligation, I guess you could say. Or an external conscience, maybe. Like I said, it came to live with me when Billy died, because he was my best friend and there wasn't anybody else. It'll stay there until I do something about his death; and, since I'm a coward, that means we're more or less stuck with each other. Actually, it's no bother; doesn't eat much, toilet-trained, you'd hardly know it was there; and nobody else can see it, of course. Not unless they're wearing the specs.'

Chris thought about that. 'Hardly any bother.'

Grin. 'It talks to me,' Frank said. 'When we're alone. Reminds me. Really very polite and reasonable, you couldn't accuse it of making a fuss. It just says things like *pity Billy couldn't be here to see that* or *that's a good one, just wait till you tell*

Billy, no, sorry, I forgot, you can't. The really bad thing is, you get used to it after a while. I feel a bit ashamed about that.'

The Fury stretched its wings, gently brushing Frank's cheek; it'd be like a brief itchy feeling, Chris supposed. Then it stuck its head under one wing and went to sleep.

'Anyway,' Frank said, 'that's the glasses for you. You'd be amazed what you can see with them on. Not a JWW product,' he added. 'Feinwerkhaus of Vienna, pre-War; haven't been made for years, so they're pretty rare now. I'll have them back when you've finished with them, but right now I reckon your need's greater than mine.'

The pain in Chris's nose was getting tiresome; he slipped the glasses off, and at once the Fury disappeared. 'Can they show up—'

'Demons?' Frank nodded. 'But not all the time, which is a bit of a bummer. As I'm sure you know, demons don't hang around this dimension any more than they can help. Once they come through, of course, they're pretty obvious – you don't need smart specs to see them. Otherwise, when they're on the other side of the line waiting to come through, the specs aren't a lot of use, except for one thing. You get a sort of shimmer effect, a bit like— Oh, sod it,' he said, as the phone started to ring. 'Hang on, I'd better get that. Don't go away.'

While Frank was talking – just a bunch of yeses and I sees – Chris examined the sunglasses a little more closely. The frames looked like plain orange plastic, but he could just make out, in tiny raised letters on the sides of the arms, the letters DS.

'Sorry about that,' Frank said, and his voice was distinctly strained. 'Anyway, there you go, hope they'll be of some use to you. I'd better get back to the shop now, if that's OK.'

'Hang on,' Chris said, 'what about the—?'

He was talking to an empty doorway. Odd, he thought, to break off like that just as he'd got to the useful bit. A sort of shimmer effect. Could mean anything.

Even so. Now he came to think of it, he had an idea he'd heard of something similar; not sunglasses, but a mirror, in which things were reflected as they truly were, not as they pretended to be. The same basic technology, presumably. In any event, he could see how they could come in very handy, and not just for identifying demons. Then he thought about the Fury, and it occurred to him that some things are best not seen.

He went back through into the shop. Frank was serving a customer – a refill for one of the old PP12N genie lamps, by the look of it – while Angela was showing off the new GF92 instant thunderstorm to a thoroughly dazed-looking Dennis Slade; wisely, she'd set it up inside an upturned goldfish bowl, and even from across the room he could see the lightning flashes piercing the inky black clouds. Frank won't like that, he thought. He'd bought fifteen of the old model last year, and even though the R&D people swore blind that they'd thoroughly debugged it and it was now possible to turn it off—

Chris realised he was still holding the sunglasses. Quickly he slipped them into his pocket, almost as if he was afraid Frank would change his mind and ask for them back. *Give them back? No chance.* The thought crossed his mind the way a rabbit darts across the road in front of you, just before you jump on the brakes and listen to your tyres lose half their value. Stupid, he thought. If Frank wants them back, of course he'd return them. He just hoped very much that he wouldn't.

The replacement genie was being difficult about going into the bottle; the customer was holding tightly onto the lamp, while Frank tried to squash the little swirling blue cloud down into the spout with the palm of his gloved hand. Clearly a generous man; he'd misjudged him all these years. But then, he thought, I'd never have guessed about his long-term companion unless I'd seen it for myself. Something like that must do strange and terrible things to you.

A sort of shimmer effect. He tried to picture it. No, too vague.

'Well, now.' He realised Dennis Slade was talking to him. 'I think that's everything. No, hang on, we haven't done the dried water. Better make it six dozen, we're down to our last carton. Been a hell of a run on it the last couple of weeks – if you hadn't been coming in today I'd have had to phone you. Can you talk to the warehouse, see if they can't hurry it up a bit?'

Chris wrote up the order in his book, deliberately taking his time, but Frank was still fully occupied with the genie; he'd managed to stuff it in head first, but its claws and tail appeared to have got stuck, like Winnie the Pooh in the rabbit hole, and Angela was giving Chris meaningful looks; come on, let's get out of here before they change their minds. Gandhi, he thought; and if that's a coincidence I'll eat my own head.

He couldn't stay in the shop any longer without drawing attention to himself, so he smiled, thanked Dennis Slade, asked him to get Frank to ring him about the thing they'd been talking about, and followed Angela back into the street—

'How about that, then?' Her face, no longer pointed like a weasel's but attractively heart-shaped, was glowing. 'Two dozen of the BB27Ks, five dozen MP66As, a whole palletful of the Multi-Function Megacurses and fifty instant thunderstorms.' She smiled at him and said, 'I can see why you like doing this job. It's a real buzz, isn't it?'

'Yes.'

'I've got to admit,' she rattled on, 'I think I nearly blew it with the Megacurses. I could feel I was pushing him where he didn't want to go, and he'd have taken twelve dozen just so I'd let him off the hook, but there was this little voice in my head saying, go on, you can do it, so I pressed him, and it was really close but I kept on and he gave in, and after that it was easy, I think I could've sold him anything by then. In the end I guess I was feeling sorry for him. After all,' she added sagely, 'got to remember, we're in this for the long term, the sustainable trading relationship. If we kid them into taking stuff they'll never be able to shift, we're shooting ourselves in the foot. We want them to trust us to know what they need better than they do.'

Angela got in the car and reached across to unlock the passenger door. Chris opened it, but didn't get in. Scared?

Well, naturally. But it wasn't the fear so much as the bewilderment. 'Hop in,' she ordered. 'It's MageWorld in Lichfield next, isn't it?'

Switzerland, he thought. Alps and banks and edelweiss and cowbells and men in leather trousers with feathers in their hats. Not in the EU, as far he could remember, so you'd need a visa, and very expensive, someone had told him, four quid for a beer and the cheese is all runny. Better, braver, to stay the course. He hopped in, as ordered, and put on his seat belt.

'I was thinking,' Angela said, as she ground the jeep into first gear and pulled away, testing the reflexes of an oncoming lorry, 'how'd it be if, instead of pushing the BB27Ks, we sort of try and make out they're really hard to get hold of – you know, demand much higher than anticipated – and say we're really sorry but we're having to ration them, no more than six dozen per customer? That'll make them scared they might miss out, and then we let them twist our arms and sell them eight—'

A sort of shimmer effect. Well, maybe he'd recognise it when he saw it. Chris took the sunglasses out of his pocket and folded back the arms.

'Mind if I borrow them?' Before he could answer, she'd snatched them out of his hand and shoved them onto her nose. 'Thanks,' she said. 'Bright sunlight when I'm driving gives me the most appalling headaches.'

For the record, it was overcast, dark and gloomy, ideal vampire street-party weather. He took a deep breath and said, 'Excuse me, but would you mind giving those back?'

She didn't seem to have heard him.'Usually I keep a pair in the glove box,' she said, 'but like a fool I didn't put them back last time, and now can I find them? These are pretty good, not too dark. I can't be doing with those polaroid things.'

'If you ask me, they're a bit heavy.'

'Really? Can't say I noticed. And we needn't just stick to the BB27Ks,' Angela went on. 'We can sort of drop hints there's a snarl-up with shipping or something, four or five lines in danger of running out, so panic-buy now while stocks last.'

She laughed attractively. 'I expect all this is really old stuff and I'm reinventing the wheel like mad, but—'

Chris tried to make a grab for the glasses, but she was too quick for him. She slapped away his hand so hard that he yelped. 'What're you *doing*?' she squealed, but he tried again. This time she swerved, whacked into the central crash barrier, bounced off it and ended up in the long grass at the side of the road. But she still had the glasses.

She took them off and closed her fist around them. 'That was pretty stupid,' she said. 'We could've been—'

'Who are you?' he said.

Angela turned her head and looked at him, and all the glamour was gone. Her face was thin and sharp again, her nose a beak, her mouth a two-dimensional line. 'Are you feeling all right?' she said.

'No. Answer the fucking question.'

A moment of perfect stillness and quiet; then she shrugged. 'Give you a clue,' she said. 'Nice shirt.'

'What? Oh, you mean—'

'Got one just like it,' she said, 'only in pale blue. Lieutenant Angela Schlager, Demon Control directorate.' She paused, then said, 'You're supposed to give me the password.'

For a moment Chris's mind went blank, then he realised: she doesn't know it's not my shirt. DS. He scrabbled in his memory, then said, 'Delendi sunt.'

She nodded briskly. 'That's the trouble with this organisation,' she said. 'Paranoia. Nobody talks to anybody else. I mean, it wouldn't have killed Dave Burnoz to tell me you're on the Job too.'

Without thinking, Chris said, 'Is he—?'

Angela laughed. 'There you go,' she said. 'Proves my point. You work for the creep – at least, that's your cover – and you don't even know he's on the bloody team. We're all so busy playing spies, we end up with a stupid situation like this. In fact, if you hadn't been wearing the logo I'd never have guessed, either. A bit bloody obvious, by the way,' she added.

'You know they're only supposed to be worn off duty, like the baseball caps.'

Baseball caps, Chris repeated to himself. Yes, of course an organisation like that would have baseball caps, and sweatshirts and sports bags and probably golf umbrellas too, all with the logo on. You were probably issued with them on compulsory paintball weekends.

'Sorry,' he said. 'About—'

She shrugged. 'My fault,' she replied. 'Should've guessed as soon as I saw the glasses.' She leaned across him, opened the glove compartment and produced an identical pair. 'Did you really think I was – you know?'

He nodded. 'Sorry about that, too,' he said.

'That's all right,' she said indulgently. 'So, what've you got?'

Ah. Then inspiration struck him, and he said, 'You first.'

That was OK, apparently. 'Well,' Angela said, 'I'm almost certain we've traced it to Nottingham, which means it's very likely that the first one you saw was just a scout, probably from a completely different faction and not really anything to do with our boy. Obviously, your run-in yesterday shows that they don't know any more than we do, which I guess is encouraging. It's the second one that's got us puzzled. We think—' She paused to look him in the eye. 'We think that that one was her.'

It took Chris a moment to remember how his mouth worked. Where is she? the demon had asked. 'You think so?'

Angela nodded. 'It all fits, doesn't it? Look, we know she's on the run and the other factions are after her. She needs a place to hide, but she desperately wants to be able to come back, as soon as it's reasonably safe. Where better to go to ground till the heat's off? I mean, nobody would think of look-ing for her there, and even if the other lot found her, they wouldn't be able to break in, at the very least she'd be protected as long as she sat tight. What do you think?'

I think I could quickly learn to love runny cheese and cow-bells. 'It's possible, certainly,' he said. 'But—'

'I know what you're going to say. You're going to argue that if you and I could figure that out, so could they, and so they didn't need to scoop you in yesterday. Well, maybe they're just thick, or maybe they don't talk to each other, just like us.' She shrugged. 'What's your take on all that? I mean, you're the one it all happened to, you actually saw her. Well?'

Chris thought of all the films, and the cop shows, and smiled gently as he said, 'Sorry, can't tell you that. At least, not till I've cleared it with Jill first.'

It was the only name he had to drop, but sometimes one is enough. Angela's eyes widened for a moment. 'You report directly to Colonel Ettin-Smith?'

He nodded; the stern, taciturn type. 'You've come across her, then.'

'She recruited me,' Angela replied, 'in my first term at Loughborough. Sorry,' she added, 'I hadn't realised you were special ops.'

Indulgent grin, setting a bewildered subordinate at her ease. 'It's like you said,' he told her, 'nobody talks to anybody else in this man's organisation.' (He was quite proud of 'this man's', though he couldn't remember offhand where he'd got it from. *M*A*S*H* or *The A-Team*, probably.) 'Anyhow,' he went on, 'now we've got that straight, tell me something.'

Eager nod. 'Sure.'

'Why the Instaglamour cream?'

'Oh,' Angela said. 'That.' She shook her head. 'Does it bother you? Only I can—'

'It's not that,' Chris said. 'I was just curious. You do know reps aren't allowed to use it.'

'Aren't they? Oh.'

He smiled. 'Don't worry about it,' he said. 'I expect Dennis and Frank'll just assume you have a naturally bubbly and outgoing personality.'

'Right.' She nodded. 'Actually, that's all it is. I mean, you've seen what I'm like without this muck all over my face. Bit of a handicap when you're trying to get people to tell you things. So yes, sometimes I use the cream. But I won't do it again, if it bothers you.'

'You carry on, if it helps you get the job done,' Chris said magnanimously. 'Right,' he went on, 'we'd better get a move on, or we'll be late for MageWorld. Don't want to blow our cover, do we?'

The rest of the day was fraught and rather weird, but a considerable improvement nevertheless. Now that Chris had revealed himself as a fellow demon-hunter, Angela seemed to regard him as not just a colleague but a friend, and started telling him her life story. He learned, for instance, that she'd sworn to devote her life to the cause when her best friend's cousin's boyfriend's mother's nephew had been attacked and horribly maimed by demons, so that when Jill arrived at Loughborough on a recruiting drive Angela had jumped at the chance. 'I've always wanted to do something that mattered,' she said. 'You know, to make the world a better place and stuff. Originally it was going to be either working with endangered tapirs in Borneo or raising consciousness about the plight of the exploited copra miners of Kiribati, but then I realised what my true mission in life was and, well, since then, I've never really looked back.'

A slice of luck, Chris couldn't help thinking, for the copra miners of Kiribati, but he was generous enough not to begrudge it to them. 'That's wonderful,' he said. 'To have a really genuine vocation, I mean.'

Angela did a no-big-deal shrug. 'You're the same, I bet,' she said. 'I mean, none of us are in this for the money or the pension scheme. How about you?'

He was too weary to make something up, so he gave her an edited version of what had happened in the girls' toilets at school. It went down well.

'So you've known Colonel Ettin-Smith for years,' Angela said. 'That must've been awesome. I mean, she's so committed.'

'I guess,' he replied. 'But you know what it's like with people you were at school with. Even when they're seventy and all high court judges and Cabinet ministers, you can't ever really bring yourself to believe they're grown-ups.'

'I didn't have any friends at school,' she replied solemnly. 'I hated them, and they all hated me.'

That he could believe. 'Oh well,' he said. 'All different now, I expect.'

'No, not really.' She overtook a cyclist; he watched the poor devil in the mirror as he battled to regain control. 'But I've got my work, and that's all that matters, isn't it?'

'Quite,' Chris said.

He had his work too, of course. Angela, however, continued to be an unethically-magically-enhanced asset, even managing to bounce Bernie Playce of Orion Sorcery into taking six dozen bottled genies and a whole case of blessings. Chris was pleased, but surprised; as far as he was concerned, the glamour had worn off as soon as he accused her of using it. Bernie, however, showed all the signs of a glamour victim – bulging eyes, glazed expression, difficulty with words with an S in them – so apparently it was working on him. Presumably an open accusation broke the spell; worth remembering. By the time she dropped him off outside his flat that evening, he'd sold more in a day than he usually managed in a good week.

There was a note from Karen on the kitchen table: emergency meeting at the office, didn't know when she'd be back. Chris scowled at it and threw it away. If she'd been home, he'd been going to tell her the whole story, just to get it out of his system – and, after all, she was in the business, considerably more knowledgeable and high-powered than he was, for all he knew she might have been able to come up with a sensible course of action. Instead, he phoned Jill and got her answering machine. He left a message: call me as soon as you can.

He microwaved a pizza, poured himself the last can of beer and switched on the telly, which offered him a choice between snooker, two soaps and a makeover show. He reckoned he'd suffered enough for one day, so he switched off and decided to play some music while he caught up on his ironing, which had been building up rather, to the point where it represented the domestic equivalent of Third World debt. For some reason he couldn't seem to find any of his usual comfort listening, just heaps of Karen's stuff, which tended to give him headaches. At the back of the drawer, however, he unearthed a CD he couldn't remember having seen before. It had an all-black sleeve, on which glowed the silver words *Now That's What I Call Really Bad Music 56*. Hm, he thought, and glanced at the list on the back. Nothing he'd ever heard of, but he was intrigued, and put it on.

As a professional salesman, Chris was impressed; here was an item of merchandise that really did deliver exactly what it promised on the box. But there's a sort of magic about extremely bad music, when you're in just the right kind of mood; you carry on listening in awed fascination to see if it can get any worse, and you're rarely disappointed. He stuck it for twenty-five minutes, and found he'd polished off six shirts, nine handkerchiefs, eight tea-towels and a couple of pillow-cases without even noticing. Charms to soothe, he thought; he took the disc out, jailed it securely in its box, and stuck it in his jacket pocket.

Jill rang back as he was putting the iron away.

'Angela Schlager,' she repeated. 'Yup, I know her all right.'

'Thin girl. Pointy face.'

'That's her. Looks a bit like she stole a magic ring five hundred years ago, and she's been guarding it in a cave under a mountain ever since. Keen, though. Maybe a bit too keen. Why?'

Chris explained, all except the polo-shirt bit; instead, he attributed his outing of her to intuition. It didn't sound right, but Jill didn't pick him up on it. 'It's going to be a bit awkward,' he went on. 'I mean, I'm stuck with her for weeks still. What if I say something and she realises I've been lying?'

'You'll feel really stupid,' Jill replied reasonably. 'Talking of which, why *did* you pretend to be one of us? It seems such an odd thing to do.'

Minus the polo shirt and Angela leaping to conclusions on the strength of it, the story did seem a bit dubious. 'Dunno, really,' he replied. 'I guess I wanted to find out what she knew.'

'Oh. Why?'

'In case it was something to do with all this horrible stuff that's been happening to me. Which it is, obviously.' He hesitated, then said, 'I don't suppose you can tell me—'

'You don't suppose exactly right. Sorry.'

'Ah well.' Chris tried to sound more disappointed than he actually was; really, though, he was more concerned with getting off the subject of why he'd pretended to be an undercover demon-hunter. 'Well, that's all I wanted to ask, really. Thanks.'

'No problem. Oh, by the way,' Jill added. 'We're finished with your car, so you can have it back. We'll drop it round first thing in the morning so you can use it for work.'

'Excellent,' he said. 'Not sure I could've taken another day of your esteemed colleague's driving. I mean, she did a fantastic job of taking my mind off being haunted by demons, but on balance I think the demons are less of a threat.'

Karen got home shortly after eleven, just as Chris was about to go to bed. He got as far as 'You'll never guess what happened—', but then she turned out the light and went straight to sleep.

When Chris opened the front door and saw his own car parked outside, he felt a lump in his throat that had nothing to do with porridge and stale bread. True, compared with the BMW or even the jeep it was just a tin can on wheels, but it was, in a very real sense, his home; more so than the flat could ever be. It was his main defensible space, where he could retreat and lock the doors on the world, and he'd missed it.

SatNav wasn't there, of course. There was just a smudge on the windscreen where her rubber sucker had been, and the knob was back in the lighter socket where her flex used to plug in. He reminded himself of how narrow his escape had been, and started the engine.

Angela wasn't pleased. 'I like driving,' she protested, when he told her they'd be using his car instead of the jeep. He pointed out that it wasn't fair on her to put all those extra miles on her personal vehicle, when the company supplied him with a car. She assured him that she wasn't bothered about that, but he insisted. His conscience, he said, wouldn't let him—

(Conscience; the Fury on Frank Ackery's shoulder. He shuddered. Angela said something about a nip in the air and turned the heater on.)

Maybe she was sulking about the car issue, or maybe she was thinking about something else; they drove in silence for a while, and then Chris asked if she minded if he had the radio on. 'You go ahead,' she replied, making it sound like he'd just declared war, and he thought: raw emotion, at this hour of the morning, just what I really need.

He stabbed the button with his finger and got music; rather nice, though he hadn't heard it before. He was just getting into it when Angela reached across and turned it off.

'I was listening to that,' he said.

She scowled at him. 'We need to talk,' she said.

Oh, he thought; because when women say 'We need to talk,' especially in that tone of voice, what they really mean is, 'You're going to listen, and it's going to take a very long time, and the subject isn't going to be Aston Villa's chances of avoiding relegation.'

'Fine,' he said. 'Fire away'; and then her phone rang.

One of the things about demons that unsettled Chris – a very small thing compared to the rest of it, but disturbing nonetheless: if there really are such things as demons, does that necessarily imply that there's such a thing as God? Or is that just a sign of intellectual laziness and a failure to understand the maths and the metaphysics? Well, he thought, as Angela yanked out her phone and snapped 'Yes?' at it, I can cut through all that stuff and say quite definitely that God exists and He's taken pity on me at last. Oh, and please, he added under his breath, please let it be her mother, and keep her on the phone till we get to Stafford.

(And it *was* her mother, and they were through Stafford and out the other side before Angela said her last 'Yes, I know, I'm sorry' and jammed the phone back in her pocket; and yes, it was a bit scary, but in the nicest possible way—)

'You were saying?' he said smoothly.

'What?'

'You wanted to talk to me about something.'

She gave him a foul look. 'Later,' she said. 'We're nearly there.'

'So we are. Well, never mind.'

Their first call was an old favourite of Chris's: Honest John's House of Spells, established 1956, an extraordinarily tall, thin shop squeezed in between a tyre-and-exhaust place and a sandwich bar, with stock piled up in heaps wherever you looked and a stuffed goblin on the counter instead of a cash register. Honest John had been Chris's first-ever customer. He was almost as tall and thin as his shop, with a greasy curtain of long grey hair, a matted beard like a vertical hearthrug and an eyepatch. The scuttlebutt in the trade was that John was actually the last of the old Norse gods, hiding out from the countless firms of lawyers who wanted to serve him with product-liability writs concerning the creation of the universe. Whatever; Chris had always got on well with Honest John, though he had a healthy respect for his pair of pet ravens.

'Morning,' said John. He gave Angela a long, hard stare, then frowned and moved a little to the left so he couldn't see her. 'I got a bone to pick with you.'

'Oh yes?'

'Those crystal balls,' John said. 'You can have them all back.'

'Oh,' Chris said. 'Don't they work?'

John grinned at him. 'They work just fine,' he said. 'You power them up, and the first thing you see is, *This product will cease to function twenty-four hours after the warranty expires.* I got them all packed up out the back, you can take them on with you when you go.'

'Fair enough,' Chris said. 'Oh, this is Angela, she's—'

John didn't seem to have heard him. 'Just as well you're here,' he said. 'I'm down to my last half-dozen dried waters. Got any in the car?'

Several times Angela tried to butt in, but John seemed incapable of seeing or hearing her. He placed a large order for curses, took a dozen BB27Ks to see how they'd go and insisted on being shown the TimeOut Instant Bank Holiday—

'It's pretty straightforward,' Chris explained. 'It looks just like an ordinary DVD, right. You stick it in any conventional DVD player, and hey presto, twenty-four hours of uninterrupted leisure time to spend as you wish. And it's outside of linear time, so it's ideal for lunchtimes, coffee breaks, any time when you're stressed out and really need a breather. Look, I'll show you.'

Three minutes or twenty-four hours later, John said, 'There's a towel over there, look, next to the card terminal.'

'Thanks,' Chris replied, rain dripping down his nose. 'You've got to admit, though, it's very realistic.'

'I'll think about it,' John replied, as Chris dried himself off. 'Now then, ever-filled purses, I was thinking about doing a buy one, get one free—'

A very good order indeed, and it took a long time, partly because John wanted Chris to demonstrate several other lines, partly because the ravens kept swooping down and trying to peck Angela's eyes out; and since John was refusing to acknowledge her existence, he couldn't be prevailed upon to call them off. In the end, she mumbled something about waiting in the car, and fled.

'That was a bit uncalled for, wasn't it?' Chris said, as the shop door closed behind her.

'What was?'

Oh well, he thought, and carried on writing out the order. When it was eventually finished, he asked if he could use John's bathroom.

John looked at him. 'You sure?'

'Well, yes. I mean, it's not quite desperate yet, but—'

Shrug. 'Second floor, first on your left. Password's *Götterdämmerung.*'

Hardly designed to inspire confidence; but it proved to be a perfectly ordinary shop toilet – narrow, faintly grubby, wisps of dusty cobweb festooning the pipes, cardboard boxes of stock blocking access to the facilities, brick dust in the sink, a bent coat-hanger in place of the more usual chain and the door wouldn't shut properly. Chris washed his hands in grey water, wiped them on the threadbare towel and reached out to put the seat back down—

Odd, he thought. Since he'd used it, about ten seconds ago, the lavatory had changed. Instead of a short drop and a disinfectant-blue meniscus, there was a tunnel, a bit like the London Underground stood on end. It was lit by flaming torches in holders driven into the wall at regular ten-yard intervals, blurring into a solid line of light in the far distance. He felt a surge of vertigo and straightened up quickly, grabbing the towel rail for support. Not a pretty sight, but by no means the strangest thing he'd ever seen in a shop toilet. He turned to leave and collided with Honest John, who was standing in the doorway.

John grinned at him. 'Now wash your hands,' he said.

'I already did,' Chris replied.

'Fine,' John said, and shoved him hard in the chest.

Chris lurched backwards, and the insides of his knees hit the rim of the toilet bowl and buckled. For a moment he seemed to hover, arguing the toss with gravity; then he toppled backwards through the hole in the toilet seat, which opened like a mouth to swallow him. His head caught the edge of the seat and he yelped, and then he was plummeting through empty air, a line of upside-down torches flashing past his eyes as he fell.

CHAPTER SEVEN

Be quiet, Chris's mother used to tell him, and don't make a fuss; and on the whole he'd done his best, no matter what life had thrown at him. When Danny Quinn had put a dead mouse in Miss Blake's desk and Chris had been given detention for it, when the assessment board had told him he hadn't got the gift, when Jill had given him the polite but comprehensive brush-off; when demons started popping up practically everywhere he went, he'd kept his face shut and his upper lip rigid and moved on. It was one of the few things he liked about himself: the calm, stoical acceptance, the refusal to break down and make an exhibition of himself.

But what the hell. As the air buffeted his face and the slipstream set him spinning, he opened his mouth, filled his lungs and yelled. Didn't do any good. Didn't even make him feel better. Like so many of the things your mother warns you against, when you actually get around to trying it you realise you haven't really been missing anything much through all those years of noble abstinence.

A flaming torch whizzed past his nose, scorching the very tip, but all he had left by way of lamentation was a rather low-key whimper. Hard to get all het up about a trivial burn when you're about to be mashed into pulp on gravity's anvil.

A second or so later, he banged his knuckles quite hard on something, probably a torch bracket, but did he complain about it? Certainly not.

He'd stopped. That puzzled him for a split second, until the pain in his arm and fingers clarified matters. When his hand had bashed into the torch bracket, he must instinctively have grabbed at it and, somehow or other, managed to close his hand around it and hang on. He was therefore dangling one-handed from the bracket, swaying slightly, with a hundred yards or so of tunnel above his head and rather more under his feet.

You could call it an improvement if you were so inclined, but as far as Chris was concerned it was just another imaginative way of experiencing pain before he died. Pretty hopeless, by any criteria. No way in hell he'd be able to climb out of there, and how long could he reasonably expect to maintain his grip? Ten seconds? Fifteen at the very most? Pointless. The sensible thing would be to let go, get it over with. Just relax those fingers and let it happen. No silly fuss.

His fingers stayed clamped tight shut. Well, fine, if they insisted on making a fatuous gesture. It really made no odds, after all. He sighed, and waited for his grip to fail. A handy opportunity, he decided, to have his life flash in front of his eyes while he was waiting. It was the only part of this experience that he felt any real enthusiasm for. The idea had always intrigued him; he'd often wondered which episodes in his life story the Great Editor would choose to montage for him – the most significant, naturally, but who was he to judge which moments had actually made all the difference? Maybe – too late now, of course, for it to be any use – the ultimate slide show would give him the hints he needed to make some sort of sense of a life that had always seemed while he was living it to be wildly and unnecessarily obscure—

No slide show. No smiling host with a big red book. No blinding flashes of clarity. Also, he couldn't help noticing, no grip failure. Either he was a hell of a lot stronger than he'd always thought, or something was going on.

Screw it, Chris thought, and tentatively flexed his fingers. They came apart quite easily, though they were painful and stiff, as though he'd been carrying a heavy supermarket bag. No contact whatsoever with the torch bracket, but he wasn't falling. Bloody odd, he thought, and looked down at his feet.

He was standing, he discovered, on a bird. A hummingbird? He was no ornithologist. One of those tiny, brightly coloured little buggers who can hold still in mid-air by flapping their tiny wings a million times a second. All he could see were the blurred wing-tips and the point of its beak, but there was no doubt about it; the little sweetheart was carrying his entire weight on its minuscule back, and apparently thinking nothing of it.

Not possible, that went without saying. Magic, then. That actually made him feel a lot better. A real hummingbird couldn't bear his weight for a split second, but who knew what a magic one might be capable of? Only one way to find out.

So he waited patiently, watching the bird's wings, and nothing happened.

Then he thought: forget about the bird for a moment, pretend you're standing on a ledge or something, and for crying out loud think of some way out of this. Easy to say, he thought back at himself, but this is about as bad a position as it's possible to be in, really the chances of me getting out alive are—

Not that bad, Chris thought suddenly, if someone were to stand at the top of the tunnel and let down a long, strong rope. I could tie it round me, and then all they'd have to do would be to pull me up. True, nobody knows I'm here except John, who pushed me down here in the first place, but that's all right. After all, I have my phone. All I have to do is phone – well, Jill, obviously, she can send helicopters and storm troopers, strong men with cranes, wenches with winches, and I'll be out of here like a cork out of a—

No signal.

For some reason, that upset him rather more than the falling stage of the proceedings had done; the hope, he reckoned, so much more painful than the terror or the despair. He started shivering, so much so that he lost his hold on the phone and dropped it. He watched it fall ever such a long way before it vanished into the darkness.

For two pins, he thought, I'd jump. But he didn't. Instead, he thought: all right, what else have I got? Quick rummage in his pockets. A CD case, containing *Now That's What I Call Really Bad Music 56*. A comb. A wallet. A pen. A screwed-up piece of tissue paper. A copy of *The Book of All Human Knowledge*—

Well now, Chris thought, what about that? A book guaranteed to tell you what you really need to know. Tiresome and irritating, yes, and about as user-friendly as a shark, but *guaranteed*, with the full authority of JWW Retail behind it. Compared with the next best alternative, which was standing on a hummingbird waiting for something to turn up, it did seem curiously attractive.

He glanced down to make sure the bird was still fluttering away – yes, fine – then opened the *Book* in the approved manner, at random. As was often the case, the words were blurry and illegible at first; if the information you needed was in any way abstruse or out of the ordinary, it took a while to search and assimilate. But he was a patient man. He gave the *Book* an encouraging smile, and tried not to think about the first signs of pins and needles in his right foot.

The print clarified, as he'd known it would. It read—

Downloading Updates; Please Wait

Ah, he thought.

There had been a fair few complaints about that; but, as Chris explained whenever a customer raised the issue, one of the *Book*'s main advantages over inferior rival publications was the support package; constant revision meant it was up to date literally to the minute, ensuring complete accuracy and guaranteed user satisfaction. True, from time to time you had to wait around for a bit, but that was a small price to pay for something you could trust absolutely.

Ten minutes later, the words dissolved and were replaced by—

Installing Updates: Installing 1 of 47
Estimated Time Remaining: 1 hour 40 minutes

Oh, he thought. Well, maybe if I just—

Interrupting Update Installation Will Result In Corrupt Data And Irreparable Damage

On the positive side, there was a little animated picture of a clown doing handstands, presumably to keep Chris from getting lonely while he waited. He watched it for twenty minutes, after which its charm seemed to fade a little, so he spent the remaining eighty minutes swearing at the *Book*'s designers. He was just getting into his stride when the text flickered again, and read:

Updates Installed Successfully
You Will Need To Restart Your Application

But all that proved to mean was closing the *Book* and opening it again; which got him—

Gandhi; Mohandas Karamchand Gandhi, born 2 October 1869, Porbandar, India. Best known for his policy of **non-violent resistance** *to British colonial rule, leading to independence in—*

What? Chris thought. No, really, please. Another time, sure, but not now. What I need to know is how to get off this bird and back up this vertical shaft without slipping, falling and going splat, so can we please try again? Please?

He closed the *Book*, then opened it.

Gandhi; Mohandas Karamchand Gandhi, born 2 October—

He'd never ground his teeth before – read about it, certainly, but never actually done it; wondered how you went about it, because it seemed such an odd way of expressing frustration and rage. In the event, it came quite naturally. Didn't help much, though. Never mind; he had the key. Fold back the corner of the copyright page, and a menu drops down. Press *show hidden* with your thumbnail, and you get a list of options, including *Index*. Keep it simple; he touched his nail to *Falling*, and waited:

Application blocked.

Beneath his feet, the hummingbird wobbled. Poor little bugger, he thought, he must be knackered. He pulled the menu back up and tried *Heights, great*. Then he had a go at *Down, problems associated with* and *Gravity, hostile* and even *Splat*; but each time, all he got was—

Application blocked.

The bird was definitely starting to slow down. Instead of a blur, its wing-tips were becoming visible. Chris tried just opening the *Book* at random, on the off chance that it had fixed itself. More fucking Gandhi. He whimpered. The shock was starting to wear off, like a local anaesthetic, and panic was slowly creeping in. Magic, yes, but magic is very real and it'll kill you given half the chance, and even an enchanted hummingbird couldn't stay flapping its wings for ever and ever. A nasty thought occurred to him; maybe the bird was a JWW Retail product. In which case, he was screwed—
When absolutely all else fails definitively, consult Help. Back to the index, apply quivering fingernail. He got—

For Help, shout 'Help!'

Oh, for crying out loud, he thought. 'Help!' he yelled. His voice dopplered away down the tunnel, the sound bending into strange and unnerving contortions. The page flickered, and read:

Help not required. Please make another application

'Yes, it fucking is,' he shouted at the *Book*. 'I'm going to die, you stupid object. Tell me how to get out of this, quickly.'
Flicker.

Incorrect application. See details?

'What? Oh, yes, all right.'

Your JWW Retail The Book Of All Human Knowledge *has been precisioneered to supply you with the data you need, when you need it. In order to provide you with the best service possible, your JWW Retail* The Book Of All Human Knowledge *applies **advanced filtering technology** to assess and determine your most urgent and pressing need. Where the JWW Retail* The Book Of All Human Knowledge*'s assessment is at variance with your own, rest assured that the product's **thaumaturgically™** controlled judgement is almost certainly superior to your own.*

Salesmen are like priests; they can only operate effectively if their faith is unshakeable. Once the thin, sharp blade of doubt penetrates the armour of unquestioning belief, it's time to book your place in the handcart, if possible specifying a seat facing away from the handles, for a trip to the bad place. Sure, the customers complained about the *Book*. They complained a lot. They said it was a useless piece of shit, only fit for regulating wobbly tables, they were insulting the intelligence of their clientele just by having it in the shop. But they said the same about everything, and they only did it in the hope of screwing Chris for bigger discounts, or out of the primitive tyre-kicking instinct that's so deeply rooted in us all. The thought that, just for once, they might have a point came as a very nasty blow, and almost made him fall off his hummingbird.

'Screw you,' he said, therefore. 'I'm about to die, I need *help*, not a bloody history lesson.'

Incorrect application. Your JWW Retail The Book Of All Human Knowledge *comes pre-loaded with Know Thyself 2.0, the latest in* **character assessment software**, *and has determined that you are a person of exceptional* **intelligence** *and* **resourcefulness**, *more than capable of dealing with the physical threat you are currently facing without the need for assistance from your JWW Retail* The Book Of All Human Knowledge. *Should you wish to be advised about the genuinely urgent danger you are presently in, please start a new application.*

He closed his eyes. 'Gandhi, right?'

Correct. Submitting application. Mohandas Karamchand Gandhi, born 2 October 1869, Porbandar, India. Best known—

Chris slammed the *Book* shut, toyed with the idea of dropping it down the shaft, realised he couldn't be bothered, and stuffed it back in his pocket. Story of my life, he thought; someone else always knows better. Wanted to do Art and Drama for GCSE, got told don't be stupid, what you want to do is Business Studies and Maths. Wanted to be a sorcerer; no, he didn't, he wanted to be a rep. Wanted to marry Jill; got Karen instead. No point in getting worked up about it at this late stage. Really, it was a question of perspective; as in, is there really any merit in getting upset about losing a life as lousy as mine? Well, no. Just a pity that the poor hummingbird should've been put to so much trouble for nothing.

Unless, of course (the thought hit him like a hammer) he'd been missing something. After all, the *Book* was a hundred per cent reliable and accurate. Guaranteed.

'Bird,' he said.

'Tweet.'

I'm going to feel such a twat if this works, he thought. 'Take me up.'

'Tweet.'

Chris felt the increase in wingbeat tempo through the soles of his shoes. By now, what with cramp and ankle fatigue, he was having trouble just standing still. As the bird started to rise, he felt himself wobble alarmingly, and had to wave his arms about to keep his balance. As the ascent continued, however, he got the hang of it and kept perfectly still. To keep his mind off what was happening, he thought: yes, but why did Honest John push me down an enchanted toilet in the first place? Furthermore, what's going to happen when I get to the top and he realises I'm back? Are we going to have to go through all this again, or should I do something brave and aggressive, like cut his head off with the tapemeasure?

He really didn't like the thought of that, and tried to talk himself into believing that it had all been an accident, or a misunderstanding; an ill-judged practical joke that had gone a bit further than it should have done. But he wasn't that persuasive. The bastard had definitely pushed him, and although it was true enough that it's a wise man that knows his own toilet, chances were that he'd done it with malice aforethought.

Chris considered the chances of being able to sneak out of the shop unnoticed, and put them at around four to one. The question was, however, did he want to creep away, as though he was the one who'd done something wrong, or was he prepared to stop being the universal victim and do something about it?

Well, no, in case Honest John thumped him and threw him back down the bog. Making a stand, drawing a line in the sand, fighting for your fundamental human rights are all very well if the circumstances are with you – if you've got a gun and the bad guy hasn't, for example, or if you're backed up by a large number of big, ferocious supporters. Otherwise, you're essentially encouraging the culture of violence and oppression by giving the thumper something to thump.

He was nearly there. As his eyes came level with the rim of the toilet seat, he whispered, 'Stop,' and the bird obligingly obeyed. He looked round, as far as his limited field of vision would let him. No Honest John, nothing at all except the toilet-roll holder and a partial view of a stack of cardboard boxes in the opposite corner. 'Up,' he said; and when the moment was right, he stepped off the bird onto the seat, slipped, fell forward and crashed into the pile of boxes.

They weren't hard or sharp-edged or anything, but as they collapsed around Chris they made a noise like a roll of thunder. He scrabbled about until he found his feet, thinking, It's a big shop, well, a tall shop, anyway, John's bound to be downstairs serving a customer, he won't have heard—

'Bloody hell,' said Honest John. 'You're back.'

He was standing in the doorway holding a big mug of coffee, and the look on his face was simply weary, a man having to deal with a tiresome nuisance that he thought he'd got sorted; and then he sighed. 'All right,' he said. 'Back you go,' and he went to put the mug down—

Later, when he was replaying the scene in his mind for the seventh or eighth time, Chris decided it was probably the sigh that did it, though he gave himself some credit for spotting the strategic moment, when John's gaze was off him and he was concentrating on putting the mug down without spilling it. Where the technique came from, he had no idea, since the last time he'd been in a fight had been when he was eleven, and he'd lost conclusively. He quite liked the hypothesis that there were invincibility charms woven into the polo shirt, but it was probably just beginner's luck. In any event, his kick landed inch-perfect, with a fair degree of weight behind it.

Honest John doubled up without a sound, sort of hung in the air for a moment, then collapsed sideways, like a stack of bean cans when you sideswipe it with your trolley. Chris stared down at him for over two seconds, and all he could think of was how very, very upset John was going to be when he recovered from the pain and got up again. It was that (he decided later) rather than righteous fury that prompted the course of action that followed.

He fumbled the tapemeasure out of his pocket, knelt down, pulled out fourteen inches of blade, brought it as close as he dared to the side of John's neck, and tried to think of what to say. It always came so easily in the movies, some Chandlerian wisecrack, but he couldn't help thinking how embarrassing it'd be if John suddenly jumped up and smacked him in the mouth while he was still in mid-aphorism. Anger would've been really useful, but he'd mislaid it at some point. He settled for 'Excuse me.'

John's eyes opened and tried to focus on him. 'Mm.'

'Sorry,' Chris said, before he could stop himself. 'Look, do you know what this is?'

'Pantacopt,' John mumbled. 'Put the fucking thing away before you do me an injury.'

'Sorry,' Chris repeated, 'but no, not until you've told me why you tried to—'

The difference between men of violence and ordinary people is that the former don't bluff and the latter do. No earthly use threatening to cut someone's head off, even if you're holding an extraordinarily powerful magic weapon a quarter-inch from their jugular vein, unless you're really prepared to do it. The man of violence always knows you haven't got the determination, which is why he has no trouble in taking the weapon away from you and turning it against you. Unless, of course, you're a complete butterfingers—

A moment of absolute silence; and then Chris thought, in a deep chamber of his mind where the panic couldn't get through: Hang on, shouldn't there be blood? And shouldn't the body be sort of twitching horribly about; automatic vestigial nerve activity and stuff?

The head lay perfectly still where it had fallen, but the lips parted, moved soundlessly for a second or two, then said, 'You clown.'

Later, he was mildly proud that his first, overwhelming reaction had been relief. 'Fucking hell, John,' the words came tumbling out, 'I thought I'd killed you. Are you—?'

'Immortal,' the head replied irritably; and then, 'I thought you knew that.'

'There's rumours in the trade, John, but I never really—'

'You *bastard*! You dangerous bloody lunatic.' The eyes rolled. 'For all you knew, you could've actually killed me.'

'It was an accident, John, really, I didn't mean—'

'Bloody hell.' The body shook a little, as though something was making a monumental effort to get it to move, but not quite managing it. 'You do realise what you've done, don't you? Fucking pantacopt wounds, you can't rejoin them. You knew that, you arsehole.'

'I really—'

'Which means,' John went on, ignoring him, 'that, since I'm immortal, I'm going to have to go around for the rest of eternity with my head stuck to my neck with bloody gaffer tape.'

'Oh.'

'Too bloody right, *oh*. You might want to think about that for a moment. No sudden movements. Think of all the things I won't be able to do, for fear of my head coming off and rolling across the floor. For ever and ever,' he added, with a wealth of feeling. 'And don't you dare say superglue, or I'll make you wish you'd never been born.'

'I'm really sorry, John,' Chris whimpered. 'Look, where do you keep the tape? I'll—' He paused. No sudden movements, John had said. And even a twelfth-dan martial arts master would have trouble beating someone to a pulp if he could only move really, really slowly in case his head fell off.

When your enemy is pathetically helpless, it's not so hard being tough. 'I'll get the tape for you, John,' Chris said (voice starting off a bit wobbly but firming up) 'if you'll tell me why you pushed me down the bog. Otherwise—'

'Fuck you, I'll get it myself.' The eyes closed, screwed up with effort. Nothing happened.

'Why did you push me down the toilet, John? Come on, it's a fair question.'

John's next remarks demonstrated a very limited vocabulary, but didn't constitute an acceptable answer. So Chris repeated the question.

'Like I'm about to tell you.'

Chris shrugged. 'No answer, no gaffer tape. Your choice.'

The scowl shifted emphasis a little, away from anger towards apprehension. 'I can't tell you,' John said. 'If I do, they'll—'

'They'll do what, John?' Inspiration. 'Something worse than – oh, I don't know, using a pantacopt to dice your stupid head like an onion? Even gaffer tape's got its limits, you know.'

'You wouldn't do that.' Scornful, but just the tiniest crack of doubt.

'I wouldn't want to,' Chris said. 'Like I wouldn't want to cut anybody's head off, even if they'd just shoved me down a toilet.' Maybe, just maybe, he was winning.

'How'd you get back up again, anyhow? I thought you didn't have the gift, so—'

'Maybe you were wrong.'

'You wouldn't do it.' But this time it was a self-negating statement. Just to press the advantage home, Chris picked the tapemeasure up off the floor and looked at the head with what he hoped was a sort of mental-geometry expression. 'I've got friends, you know,' John said. 'They'll come looking for you.'

'Would they be the ones who told you to flush me down the bog, John? Or were they a different lot of friends?'

'You don't scare me, you—'

'I feel really sorry for you,' Chris said. 'I mean, living through all eternity's got to be bad enough, but all eternity in *slices*—'

'All right,' John replied, and his tone of voice suggested that they weren't going to be friends any more. A part of Chris, small but real, mourned for the loss of a really stonking big order. 'I'll tell you what I know, and then you can bugger off and never come back. Right?'

'If that's what you want, John.'

Honest John sighed. 'It was demons,' he said. 'They told me if I didn't do it, they'd lock me up in a cave in the heart of a mountain. Satisfied?'

Chris didn't feel very good about that. An immortal wouldn't starve to death, or suffocate when all the air was used up. He'd just get very, very bored, waiting for the rain and the wind to erode the mountain away. 'I'm sorry,' he said; and this time he meant it. 'All right, can you tell me their names? What they looked like?'

Another sigh. 'Demons don't have names, fuckwit. In fact, they're allergic to them – I thought everybody knew that. And they looked like demons. That's it.' John sounded sincere enough.

'You're sure?'

'Yes. Like it says over the door,' the head added, and its lips twitched just a little bit. 'Honest John.'

Well, quite. 'All right,' Chris said. 'I'll fetch the gaffer tape.' He stood up, knees stiff after all that crouching, then paused and added, 'Where does the tunnel go to?'

'Not a clue. Why don't you go back down there and find out for yourself?'

Chris got the tape. It was a tricky job, supporting the head with one hand and applying the tape with the other; it got tangled, and he dropped the head a couple of times, which didn't improve John's temper. The result looked a bit like a Christmas present wrapped by a five-year-old.

'Now remember,' he said nervously, as he bit through the

tape and smoothed down the end, 'no sudden movements, or—'

Presumably, reattaching the head completed some circuit or other; John immediately came to life, sat up and made a grab for Chris's ankle. He missed, and the jerking motion was too much for the gaffer tape; John's head came unstuck just above the nape of the neck, toppled forward and fell off. 'Shi—' it said on the way down, and then the bump as it landed must've stunned it. Oh well, Chris thought, you do your best for people and this is how they thank you for it.

It was only then, as he went back downstairs into the main area of the shop, that it occurred to him to wonder what had become of Angela. No sign of her in the shop, and she wasn't waiting for him at the car. No surprise there; but where had she gone, and what had she done? More to the point, what had she refrained from doing? He thought about that. He'd nipped off to the toilet and hadn't come back. How long he'd been there he wasn't entirely sure, but at least a couple of hours, thanks to the *Book*. Too much to expect that she'd guessed something was wrong and rushed off to call for help; as witness the complete absence of SWAT teams, black helicopters from Jill's demon-hunters. The likeliest explanation was that John, having pushed Chris down the loo, had gone back and told her that her colleague had been suddenly called back to the office or some such implausible drivel, which she had naturally believed. At that very moment she was probably sitting on a train on her way home, thinking harsh thoughts about inconsiderate jerks who swan off and leave other people stranded. Yes, Chris thought, but wouldn't she have thought it was odd that he hadn't taken the car?

The car. He looked at it and felt a surge of passionate relief. Climb in, lock the door, start the engine and drive away, safe in his small steel sanctuary, where he'd face nothing more lethal than the homicidal antics of his fellow road users. There were times when he believed he was only truly happy in his car; alone, not being hassled by other people, with the seat adjusted just how he liked it, the radio to entertain him, the broad sweep of the open road offering him endless possibilities. True, it was a bit disturbing to listen to himself sounding like a sentimental version of Jeremy Clarkson, but he couldn't help the way he felt. Home is where the clutch is, and that was all there was to it.

Before he got in, he peered round inside, looking for demons. Silly, because how would he know if one was there? A bit like going down into the cellar with a torch looking for the future. He sat down, locked the doors, put on his seat belt and turned the key—

She was back.

Chris was so used to seeing her there, her black plastic casing fixed to the windscreen with a rubber sucker pad and a clamp, that it took him a moment to realise what he was looking at. But it was her all right. He recognised her screen, her controls, her little bit of black flex that connected her to the lighter socket. But – he scrabbled about in his memory, and was absolutely positive about it – she hadn't been there earlier, when they'd driven up here, when he'd parked the car before calling on Honest John.

Not good; not by any stretch of the imagination. She was supposed to be safely sealed away and under armed guard at Jill's headquarters, not snuggling up to his windscreen. Chris remembered what Jill had told him, about how they fixated on you and stalked you relentlessly, until they struck. Had it been she who'd suborned Honest John, and was she here to make sure her orders had been carried out, or to do the job properly herself? Buggered if he was going to hang around to find out. He yanked at the door handle, which broke off in his hand, just as the car pulled smoothly away from the kerb and joined the stream of traffic.

Maybe because he spent all his working life behind the wheel, Chris was a nervous passenger at the best of times. Being driven by Angela had been bad enough. Being driven by his car was rather more than he felt he deserved, for all his many and serious character defects. He grabbed the wheel, but it was like arm-wrestling a bodybuilder. The brake was frozen solid. He tried turning off the engine, but all he succeeded in doing was snapping the key off in the lock.

Been here before, he thought, as he stabbed in vain at the seat-belt release button. They were quite a long way from the Ettingate Retail Park; maybe the demons had another, handier portal. He tried screaming, but needless to say nobody could hear him. Calm down, he ordered himself; you got out alive last time, maybe you'll be lucky twice. Somehow, though, he wasn't convinced. Last time – last time, it hadn't been SatNav who kidnapped him; she'd come bursting in just as the demon was about to murder him, but it was the demon who'd done all the tedious groundwork, and the whole car thing was presumably the demon's MO of choice, not SatNav's. Well, he thought, maybe she's a copycat as well as everything else. Since there was absolutely nothing he could do about anything, it really didn't matter all that much.

The car swung out to overtake a school bus; Chris tried waving to attract their attention, his hands demonstrably not on the wheel, but the kids in the bus just waved back and made faces at him. He couldn't help wincing as the car zoomed past a speed camera. Seventeen years without so much as a speeding ticket, and now he'd die with four posthumous points on his licence.

The indicator stalk dipped and he heard the ticking. That made no sense. He knew this road, and there wasn't a turning for at least three miles. Only now there was, and they were leaving the dual carriageway, swirling round a loop, then back across the dual carriageway over a bridge that most definitely hadn't been there when he came this way a few hours ago. He tried to recall the local geography. There couldn't possibly be a road here, he told himself, because there was a town in the way, whereas the car was driving down a narrow lane with high hedges on either side. Nice, remote spot, he thought hysterically, where nobody'll hear me scream. Oh *God*—

And then: Hang on, though. Still got the pantacopt.

Chris didn't fancy any of the available options: either cut a hole he could jump through, or try and hack through a fuel line, maybe even the front axle. All very well in theory, but a bit too Indiana Jones for someone whose idea of vigorous exercise was getting up to change channels instead of using the remote. Cut a hole in what, for crying out loud? Door? Yes, fine, and then he'd roll out and smash his skull on the tarmac as he landed. Roof? Don't be ridiculous. And it was all very well thinking vaguely about fuel lines, but wouldn't that make the car blow up? Fine if you knew what you were doing, but definitely in the don't-try-this-at-home category for the absolute beginner.

There was a third option, of course: wait till we stop and the enemy comes to get you, and – well, he'd defeated Honest John, an immortal and quite possibly the Norse god of war – by accident, yes, fine, but if he could cause mayhem like that through mere clumsiness, what could he achieve if he was really trying? Cut his own leg off, probably.

The car was slowing down. Also, it was getting distinctly murky outside the window – impossible, since his watch said it was still only half past one. But the car turned on its head-lamps, twin light sabres slitting open the darkness. Conclusively, not in Staffordshire any more.

Oh well, Chris thought, there's always the fourth option: keep still, yowl unsuccessfully for mercy and, at some point, die. It had the advantage of simplicity and relative ease; no prior experience necessary. But it wouldn't come to that. Jill's people would turn up just in time and save him. They'd have been alerted by the snapshot taken by the speed camera. Number-plate recognition technology would pass the word down the wire to their central computer, they'd look at the photo, see that he wasn't driving the car as it shot past the camera at ninety miles an hour, and then, of course, they'd realise that something was wrong and scramble the black Hueys. They'd start from his last known location, split up, search in grid patterns using heat-sensitive detectors to track the car's exhaust trail, right up to the point where the car had left the main road and taken a turning that didn't actually exist, down a lane that wasn't really there—

So, no last-minute escape this time; no fluke swordstroke cutting him free instead of open, no load-bearing hummingbird to carry him away. The incompetence of the forces of darkness in the matter of disposing of their victims might be a staple of fiction, but it wasn't something you could rely on indefinitely. Sooner or later, by the law of averages, even dark lords and evil geniuses must occasionally luck out and kill someone—

The hummingbird. It was a sad commentary on how Chris's life had been lately that he hadn't given it a thought. Falling to his death, he'd landed on a hummingbird; well, doesn't everybody? Now he stopped to think about it, of course, it was weird, bizarre and extraordinary; it might also be taken as an indication that somebody up there was looking out for him, somebody who knew where he was and what kind of danger he'd be likely to find himself up against. Fine; he had absolutely no quarrel with that. But – again the depressing intrusion of weirdness into the normal everyday interplay of hope and despair – what sort of guardian angel, protecting you in your hour of need, sends you a two-inch bird, rather than a helicopter, say, or a winged horse, or a special-forces assault team? At the very least, a guardian angel for whom whimsy counted for more than efficiency or getting the job done. Just my luck, Chris thought bitterly. I have to get the comedian.

The car stopped. He looked up, and a flicker of light caught his eye. SatNav's screen was glowing its distinctive shade of sky blue. A sudden surge of anger filled him, and before he knew what he was doing he'd hauled the tapemeasure out of his pocket and pulled out eighteen inches of blade. Cuts through anything, the *Book* had said; did that include malign entities in plastic boxes? Well, if it could slice up Norse gods, he didn't see why not.

'You have arrived,' said her voice, 'at your destination.'

Why that should have been the last straw he couldn't have explained, but it was. With a growling noise he couldn't have reproduced in cold blood, he lashed out with the tape-measure.

Chris felt no resistance as the blade passed through the plastic; might as well have been waving it in the air, but the casing was suddenly in two halves, sagging desolately off the rubber sucker. He froze, wondering what the hell he'd just done. Had he killed it? As far as he could see, the box was empty: no wires, batteries, chips, circuit boards, just a vacant shell. No blood, either. He looked round, but nothing had changed. He was still in the car, in the dark, on a road where no road should have been. The only difference was, he'd just committed plasticide.

'Hello?' he said, his voice shaking. It had never occurred to him that he'd ever actually try and kill anybody, or even anything, no matter what the circumstances. He'd just wanted to teach the box a lesson, like bashing a recalcitrant photocopier. He wasn't the killing sort. He'd been known to feel searing pangs of guilt about throwing out the rubbish, haunted by the mental image of terrified milk cartons and pizza boxes chomped up in the dustcart's insatiable jaws. And SatNav – well, he knew all about her now, how she'd preyed on him and stalked him all that time, when he'd thought they were friends. But that didn't make it right—

Turn the radio on.

Her voice, in his head. A voice he'd know anywhere; a voice that told him what to do, and he did it – turn right, turn left, follow the course of the road; a voice he'd come to rely on, trust. Looked at another way, yet another bloody woman ordering him about, but this one had never lied to him, argued with him, made him feel about two inches tall, demanded that they talk about their relationship. All she'd ever done (apart from stalking him and abducting him in his own car) was see him right, through the very worst the Midlands road network could throw at him.

Turn the radio on. Please.

Ah, he thought. The magic word. Never could resist that.

Chris reached forward and hit the button, and it was as if someone or something gently deflected his fingertip away from the radio and towards the CD player. He felt the spring-loaded plunger engage, completing the circuit, and the radio's little screen lit up. *Now playing: Now That's What I Call Really Bad Music 56; Shake It Loose, by the Lizard-Headed Women.*

The intro alone showed that the track richly deserved its place in that particular compilation. You really want to listen to that? he thought, and her voice in his head replied, *yes.*

'Really?' he said aloud.

You don't like it?

'Well, it's—' He tried to think of something nice to say, like when Karen put her music on, back at the flat. He'd got quite good at it over the years, but this time his talent failed him. 'It's awful,' he said.

Yes. I think so too.

'Right,' Chris said. 'In that case, why do you—?'

He broke off. Her last words had been inside his head, but outside it too. He couldn't bring himself to turn his head, but he glanced up at the rear-view mirror. There was someone sitting in the passenger seat beside him. A girl, a beautiful girl with long dark hair, high cheekbones and pale green eyes. Practically the girl of his dreams.

'Hello,' she said, and smiled. 'Pleased to meet you.'

CHAPTER EIGHT

'Hello,' Chris replied.

'Thanks for driving me home,' she said. 'Would you like to come in for a coffee?'

Said the spider to the fly. He was still holding the tapemeasure.

'Sorry about the music,' she said. 'It's probably the worst song ever released, even including James Blunt. That's why I chose it, of course.'

Not making a great deal of sense, he thought, though he couldn't fault her taste in music. 'Who the hell are you?' he said, still not looking round.

'I'm SatNav,' she replied. 'As you know perfectly well. Look, if you're upset about me driving us here—'

Upset. Marvellous choice of words. 'Yes,' he said. 'And stay away from me.'

'You don't know where I've been?' It was the voice that did it, of course; either because it was pitched exactly right to dig down deep into the male libido, or because he was conditioned to do what it told him. Both. Whatever. He turned his head and looked at her.

'Do you trust me?' she said.

At last, a question he could answer. 'Yes,' he replied. 'But only as far as I could throw you.'

She smiled. 'That's far enough,' she said. 'Come on, I won't eat you.'

Or, Chris thought, I could try and make a fight of it. With this exceptionally powerful magical weapon, so powerful it's illegal, so sharp it cut Honest John's head off with one fumble. Even a novice like himself could probably put up a pretty good fight with a weapon like that, maybe chop off her arms or cut her in two right down the middle. Or he could put it away, now, before he did any more damage with it.

'Thanks for getting me out of there,' she said. 'You've got no idea what it's been like, cooped up in that thing.'

'Got you out,' he repeated; and then he remembered what Jill had told him, about the containment spells, and how the casing was a prison, absolutely secure, that nothing could break out of or into. Except, of course, a pantacopt.

'Oh,' he said. 'I see.'

'Come and have a coffee,' she said, with a smile he could really have done without. 'And I'll explain.'

The other magic word. Well, he thought. At the back of his mind was some fairy tale or other, where the wicked witch could only get you into her lair if you agreed to go; maybe she couldn't kill him if he stayed in the car, something like that. Supernatural rules of engagement were profoundly weird, so he understood, and as complex and Byzantine as tax statutes or EU directives. And Jill had warned him about her, and he trusted her—

'I sent the hummingbird,' she said. 'Does that make any difference?'

It was no good, he had to ask. 'Why a hum—?'

'I said I'd explain,' she replied. 'If you come with me. Milk, no sugar, right?'

There were lots of fairy stories and folk tales about gullible men who met unscheduled beautiful girls, of course; men who went to sleep in enchanted castles and woke up twenty years later on cold hillsides, or who were never seen again, always something nasty, never anything nice. On the other hand, real life had its moments too. There aren't any fairy tales where the handsome prince marries a girl he believes is a fairy princess, but she turns out to have a turn of phrase like a drill, an insatiable desire for soft furnishings and a constant need to talk about Us; and twenty years later, the prince is woken up by the alarm at six in the morning in a Sandersons-catalogue bedroom to go to a lousy boring job to pay the awesomely vast mortgage on the enchanted castle, and maybe, just maybe, it all comes down to the same thing in the end.

'You'll explain?' he said.

'Yes.'

'Actually, it's milk and one sugar,' Chris said. 'And have you got any biscuits? I missed lunch.'

Yes, but it actually was a castle.

It loomed at him out of the darkness as he closed the car door: a gatehouse with towers jutting out of a high wall, with a drawbridge and a portcullis and everything. It was like – he stopped dead in his tracks halfway across the drawbridge when he realised what it reminded him of – it was like the plastic castle he'd had when he was a kid, the one that had come in the boxed set with the knights on horseback, with the holes in their hands you could clip little plastic swords and lances into, until you lost them. Exactly like it, apart from being bigger and built, presumably, of stone. Or did all castles look the same? He hadn't paid attention in history, so he didn't know; maybe they were all built the same, like houses on an estate.

'This way,' she said.

I know, Chris thought, as they passed under the gatehouse arch; and it was silly, but he couldn't help looking up, just in case it was there, though of course it wouldn't be. But it was; in huge letters carved into the stone, weathered by centuries of frost and rain, partly obscured by moss and creeper, but so big it was still perfectly legible:

MADE IN HONG KONG

Ah, he thought, and he reached out to touch the wall, solid, cold and damp. Silly buggers, he thought.

The door was oak, studded with nail-heads the size of apples. It creaked as she pushed it open with a gentle shove. 'Make yourself at home,' she said. 'I'll put the kettle on.'

The door slammed shut behind him, and he knew without trying it that it wasn't going to open for him. Pity.

Make himself at home. Right. No need. It looked exactly as it had done when he'd left it that morning, right down to the cup he'd left on the table and the TV listings magazine on the floor next to the sofa. Which meant that either she'd lifted it straight out of his head or else she'd been there; neither of them exactly comfortable thoughts.

'I get it,' Chris said. 'An Englishman's home is his—'

She sighed. 'Don't tell me,' she said, 'it's one of those things that aren't supposed to be taken literally. Metaphors?'

He nodded. 'I imagine they're buggers if you're not used to them.'

'Quite. Where I come from, we say what we mean.'

He sat down; not in the armchair, where he usually sat. 'And where would that be?' he asked.

She perched on the edge of the table; slim, elegant, a vision. 'You don't know,' she said. 'I'd have thought *she*'d have told you. Your friend.'

'She said you were a—' Stupid word had slipped his mind. 'Sort of an elf who lives in trees.'

'Did she now.' Those perfect lips compressed into a line as thin as the blade of the tapemeasure. 'Fancy that.'

'It's not true, then? You're not a—'

'Dryad,' she replied, pulling a face, as though she was anxious to get the word out of her mouth as quickly as possible.

'Well, you aren't to know, I suppose. But for your information, dryads are six inches long and covered in knobbly grey bark, though not all of them have beards. No, I'm not one of them, thank you very much. I,' she said – very slight pause; melodrama – 'am a princess of the Fey.'

Not fair; just because he hadn't been to Loughborough. 'I'm sorry,' he said. 'I don't know what that means.'

'Oh.' Her eyes opened wide. 'Really?'

'Yes.'

'Oh, right. Well, in that case—' She broke off. 'Stay there. I'll be back in a minute.'

Didn't like the sound of that at all. 'What's the matter?'

'The kettle just boiled.'

Whoever the Fey were, they made good coffee. He said so, and she grinned.

'Beginner's luck, then,' she said. 'We don't use the stuff. In fact, we're allergic to it.'

'What, even decaf?'

She shook her head. 'What does coffee do? I mean, its most notable side effect?'

He had to think. 'Keeps you awake?'

'That's right.'

Broad, slightly patronising smile. 'That doesn't suit us at all,' she said. 'The Fey only exist in dreams, you see; on this side of the line, at any rate. We have our own place, on the far side. But we prefer it here. It's warmer. Also, over there we don't really *exist*; not like we do here.' The smile didn't fade. On the contrary, it froze. 'People use coffee to stay awake so they don't dream and we can't come through. You can see why we aren't keen on the stuff.'

Chris couldn't think of anything to say.

'Actually,' she went on, 'my particular subsection of the Fey have evolved past that. Well,' she qualified, '"evolved" implies progress; let's say we mutated, to fill an otherwise neglected ecological niche.'

She was still just as beautiful as she'd been a moment ago;

but now, as he looked at her, he couldn't help thinking about other images: things with too many legs and eyes, pincers, carapaces; things that moved very fast, and laid their eggs in their prey. 'Is that right?' he mumbled.

'You don't like the sound of that.' She was grinning. 'You think it's creepy.'

Quite. And crawly, for that matter. 'No,' he whimpered. 'I don't know the first—'

'My sect of the Fey,' she said, 'cross the line in music. Think about it,' she added, presumably reacting to the look on Chris's face. 'That's what music does, it takes you away from here and now to another place. In our case, literally. Instead of travelling through dreams, we ride the music into your head; and once we're through, we exist.'

It was as though someone had just turned on the light. Music; the CD player in the car. Every time he'd talked to her, had a conversation, it had been just after he'd played music; usually one of those compilation discs that seemed to breed in the glove compartment, none of which he could ever remember putting there. And just now, after the drive: *turn the radio on.* And she'd deflected his hand towards the CD player, and –

'Hang on,' he said. '*Now That's What I Call Really Bad Music 56?*'

She shrugged. 'Each of us has what you might call a master key, a piece of music that can get us through, no matter what.'

'"Shake It Loose", by the Lizard-Headed Women?'

'Well,' she said, a trifle defensively, 'it's go to be something that doesn't get played a lot, or it'd be like living in Piccadilly Circus, portals opening everywhere you look. I chose a song nobody in their right mind would play deliberately. Sorry,' she added with a dazzling smile, 'for any inconvenience.'

That's why I chose it, of course. Well, at least she was consistent. 'Jill said you're stalking me,' he said. 'She said it's happened before, with SatNavs. And you tried to kill me.'

'No, I didn't.'

'Yes, you did,' Chris shouted. 'When I was in that car in the

Ettingate Retail Park. You tried to kill me, but you cut the seat belt instead and I managed to get away.'

An oh-for-crying-out-loud look on her face; one he'd inspired in many people over the years, but never so intense. 'I was *rescuing* you, you halfwit,' she snapped. 'At great personal inconvenience, let me add; I had to arrange for "Shake It Loose" to be played on the Jeremy Vine show, and he never does requests, it was sheer luck one of the technicians happened to fall asleep at just the right moment, and a friend of mine managed to get into his dream. That's why I was a bit late,' she added. 'Sorry about that. But really, you shouldn't have got yourself into such a mess in the first place.'

Oh, Chris thought, it's all my fault; should've known, it always is. 'I don't believe you,' he said. 'Jill told me—'

'And if it comes to her word against mine,' she said coolly. 'I see.'

He was mildly startled by that. 'Well, yes,' he said. 'She's one of my oldest friends, we've known each other since we were kids, and she's never lied to me or—'

'And you're in love with her,' SatNav said, all matter-of-fact, as though she hadn't just said out loud what he'd been not-thinking for dear life for the last sixteen years. It caught him off guard, like a sudden kick to the balls from a lollipop lady on a level crossing, and he didn't interrupt as she continued: 'I know, it clouds your judgement, doesn't it? Just ask yourself this, though. *Has* she ever lied to you? Led you astray?'

No, Chris tried to say; but the word wouldn't come out of his mouth. It had launched itself when she said *lied*, but sort of bounced off *led you astray*; because there was one thing, one silly little thing – trivial, like Jill always having a plastic carrier bag, completely unimportant in the larger scale of things. But *led him astray*; she had a point there.

Jill was the world's worst navigator. Standing joke among all who knew her, endearing rather than infuriating, given that in all other respects she was so utterly competent. But stick her in a passenger seat and hand her a map, and you were practically assured of a long and interesting ride to places you'd never even heard of before. It was a miracle, they said, that she didn't starve to death through getting lost between her living room and her kitchen. Of course, nowadays, with satellite navigation and stuff, it really didn't matter, and naturally Jill had the latest state-of-the-art outfit on her dashboard, and the slight character flaw no longer mattered. But led him astray? Yes, loads of times. But that was silly, completely unimportant, nothing to do with trust and integrity and all those great big things. It *was*. Really.

'Not like me,' she said softly. 'You always know where you are with me.'

It was, Chris had to concede, a very eloquent appeal to someone who was always on the move. His life revolved, after all, around two questions: Where am I? What's the time? And no, she'd never led him astray; never lured him up a dirt track with grass growing up the middle or stranded him on a deserted airfield and told him he was in the centre of Wolverhampton, never tempted him to drive the wrong way down a one-way street or off the edge of a gap in the middle of an unfinished flyover; and when she told him he was four miles from his destination and he'd be arriving there in eight minutes, he could rely on that absolutely, a tiny island of reliability in the great ocean of doubt. Even so.

'What do you want from me, anyhow?' he said.

Her eyes glowed faintly. 'Your help,' she said. 'Please.'

That didn't sound right. 'Really?' he said. 'What could I possibly do that'd help you? I'm just a rep, and you're a— What did you just say you were?'

But there was an unmistakably self-satisfied look on her face, a unilateral declaration of victory, that told him she reckoned she'd won. 'A princess of the Fey,' she said. 'Are you ready for your explanation now, or would you like another coffee first?'

Where I come from (she said) is very different from here. Everything on this side of the line is so *solid*; it's like it's made up its mind what it's going to be, and that's all there is to it. It's not like that back home. Things change. Everything changes. Between pulling out a chair and sitting down on it, there's always the risk it might melt away, or turn into a bottomless pit, or a crocodile. Well, you know what it's like in dreams. The laws of logic and physics are different there. Oh, it's an exciting, challenging environment, but it can all be a bit fraught. Every time someone gets up to make a speech or a presentation, he discovers he can't remember his lines and he's got no clothes on, and you can't even walk down the street without being chased by wolves that look just like your old geography teacher. It's a miracle anything ever gets done at all, and as for the trains running on time, forget it.

I guess that's why we like it here; more as a place to visit than somewhere you'd actually want to live, but there's definitely an appeal in knowing that if something was a cement mixer two minutes ago, it'll most likely still be a cement mixer in five minutes' time. You've got clocks and watches that actually make sense, and as for maps— Don't get me started on maps. They're just so amazingly *cool*.

My lot – the music Fey – like I said, we're niche creatures. The other Fey don't like us very much. It's not right, they reckon, messing with this-side people when they're awake. It's sort of a religious issue, really. They say that if God had intended us to cross over in the daytime, He'd have given us a human race made up of shift workers and sleepwalkers. As you've probably guessed, we don't agree. We wanted to be able to get across any time we felt like it, and so we invented music.

Well, where did you think it came from? It's not something that occurs naturally, after all – it's completely artificial, like maths. We sort of bred it into human DNA, gradually, over the millennia; a little trapdoor inside every human head.

Parasites? That's a bit harsh. I think 'symbiotic' sounds nicer. Like the little birds who pick bits of meat out of crocodiles' teeth. After all, you get something in return. You get music. Not such a bad deal, is it? Especially since only one in a billion of you knows we even exist.

Anyway, that's us. We think we're harmless, inoffensive creatures who just wanna have fun. Your lot don't seem to see it that way. Admittedly, there have been times when our lot have gone too far. Only a few years ago, the queen of the orthodox Fey tried to invade your side of the line and exterminate the lot of you, which I'm prepared to admit was entirely uncalled for, and it's no thanks to us that she failed. But it cuts both ways. Your lot have done some pretty unpleasant stuff too. I mean, look at PCE—

Oh come *on*, you must've heard of—

Fine. PCE. Pandemonium Consumer Electronics, since you've clearly been living in a cave for the last twenty years. PCE was the pioneer in metaphysical variable state cybernetics, and you know how they did it? Right. They built a new generation of intelligent, intuitive, non-Boolean electronic gadgetry by trapping our people in dreamcatchers, mutilating them and using them to power their products. Computers, yes, but not just computers: dishwashers, DVD players, microwave ovens, air-conditioners, games consoles, you name it. Basically, it was slavery. They caught us, crippled one side of our brains so we couldn't ever get back to our side of the line, suspended us in stasis fields in sealed boxes – well, I'd rather not go into it, if that's all right with you. It's not something any of us like to dwell on. But it kind of explains why Queen Judy felt the lot of you needed wiping out, and why so many of us went along with it.

Anyway, that's all water under the bridge as far as I'm concerned, and yes, PCE doesn't do that stuff any more, though they're still in business; very much so. Who do you think made me?

'You?' Chris said. 'You mean you were—'

She smiled and shook her head. 'No way,' she said. 'After the Queen Judy business, our lot and your lot sat down round

180 • Tom Holt

a table and actually talked to each other for a change. PCE agreed to end the abductions and the brain surgery and the stasis fields, and in return we supply them with a certain specified quota of Fey every year. It's not perfect, but—'

'Hang on,' he interrupted, appalled by what she'd just said. 'You're telling me your government actually sends—'

She nodded. 'Convicted criminals,' she said. 'Dissidents. It's the standard punishment for antisocial behaviour. We're pretty strict about that sort of thing.'

'Oh.' He blinked. 'Sounds a bit over the top, if you ask me.'

Shrug. 'Depends on your point of view, I suppose,' she said. 'In my case, it was disruptive thinking and serial failure to conform to stipulated dress codes. I got seventy years in a SatNav.'

Chris opened his mouth, then shut it again. 'Seventy *years*—'

'Actually, that's pretty lenient,' she said earnestly. 'Please bear in mind, we live practically for ever. We don't feel physical pain or anything like that, and time works in a very different way as far as we're concerned. Also—' She turned her head to conceal a distinct hint of embarrassment. 'Well, there's some of us, me included, who'd rather be over here no matter what, even if it means being sealed in a plastic box, telling humans to take the third turning on the right at the next roundabout. In fact,' she added, with a rather guilty grin, 'I made legal history back home by being the first convict to appeal against my sentence on the grounds that it was too short. So please, don't get the idea that I'm not perfectly happy to be here. Quite the opposite. This is so much better than home.'

He thought about that for almost fifteen seconds, then said, 'So you haven't been trying to – well, escape?'

'Escape? No way.' She seemed genuinely shocked by the suggestion. 'In fact, when my time's up I'm seriously considering applying for metaphysical asylum and becoming a supernaturalised citizen. So, escaping? Not a bit of it.'

'But you did,' Chris objected. 'Jill said you got out of your box and came after – came after me,' he added lamely. 'She said—'

The raised eyebrow, the set mouth. 'I bet,' she replied. 'Well, it wasn't like that at all. I came to find you, partly because I knew you were in danger, but mostly because I need your help. Which is what all this is about,' she went on. 'Bringing you here. I think it's time you knew what you're caught up in, before you either ruin everything without realising it or get hurt or both.'

A little voice in his head was yelling *But Jill said* – He'd have loved to listen to it, but somehow he knew he mustn't; not yet, at least. 'All right,' he said. 'Go on, then.'

It's about demons (she said).

I'm assuming you know what they are. Well, I think it goes without saying that my lot dislike them just as much as your lot do. They break into our space just like they do into yours, and they do a lot of damage, and sometimes people get hurt. We try and keep them out, same as you, and when they do get in, we hunt them down. Zero tolerance. Simple as that.

But it's not quite so straightforward; well, nothing ever is. There are some demons – a few, very much the minority – who reckon that the traditional way of doing things just isn't sustainable. They're worried about how the demon-hunters on this side are gradually learning how to beat them. Oh, it's no big deal as yet; one in fifty that breaks through actually gets detected in time, and maybe one in five of them gets killed. But the demons who are worried, the dissidents, they think that their lot have been seriously underestimating humans, especially their inventiveness and resourcefulness. The majority reckon that's rubbish; only a handful of humans even know they exist, they argue, and the authorities would rather see the whole human race wiped out than actually tell them the truth. Which isn't so far off the mark, as far as I can see, but even so. That elimination rate's gone up seven per cent in the last five years. A trend like that—

★

(Five years. Chris did the mental arithmetic. Since Jill had been in charge. He made a mental note to be impressed, as soon as he could spare the mental capacity.)

So you see, they've got a point. If things go on like they are at the moment, the demons are going to find themselves pretty hard-pressed. Humans are ninety per cent of their food source. Though they find it hard to accept, they could be staring extinction in the face.

So what? Well, it's highly unlikely they'd just sit back and accept the inevitable. You'll start seeing coordinated raids in force, rather than just one or two of them hopping over the line for a snack. Escalation, leading to open war; and even if your lot rise to the challenge and fight back hard enough to win, just think of the implications. I mean, there's no way the authorities would be able to keep a lid on it if it came to an all-out invasion or something like that, and just think what it'd mean for your lot, suddenly finding out that there are demons out there trying to invade you. Come to that, think what it'd mean if the whole world knew about magic. It's the sort of thing that'd wreck your entire civilisation.

Which means, basically, that the dissidents are probably your best chance, as a species. Not a particularly comfortable idea, since they're so few and their own people hate them so much. You think humans can be vicious and intolerant. You just can't begin to imagine what *they*'re like.

The thing is, though, it doesn't actually have to be that way. You see, it's not the flesh and the blood the demons need to live off. Demons don't have digestions and metabolisms, they don't need proteins and vitamins and carbohydrates. What they get their nourishment from is – well, for want of a better word, *spirit*. Emotional energy. They kill people because it's the most efficient way of getting the emotions. It's true; they've studied it carefully, done the research, they're a very thorough species. Typically, a demon attack lasts thirty seconds, from the demon materialising in your dimension to the moment the victim dies. In that thirty seconds, an average human produces more emotional calories – panic, terror, disgust, despair – than it would in twelve years of ordinary life. It's a simple case of getting the maximum yield for the minimum risk and effort.

But, the dissidents say, it's the wrong approach. They argue, it's like the ways humans make electricity. You can boil more kettles and power more electric lights from milking one thimbleful of uranium than you'd get from fifty dinky little Notting Hill wind turbines in a year; established fact, no arguments. But the uranium will poison the air and the water, and if you go on using it, sooner or later you'll all start glowing green and die; whereas all the wind turbines do is sit there making a gentle humming noise, which may piss off the house martins but it won't kill you. Same, they say, with humans and emotion. Instead of going for maximum yield with maximum intrusiveness, much better to use the little-and-often approach.

Human beings going about their ordinary, miserable lives, the dissidents say, generate enough emotion to feed a thousand times the current demon population, without the demons having to lift a claw to encourage them. Trouble is, it's all in small amounts, spread around terribly thin. I mean, in any square kilometre of your typical urban environment at any one time, you can reasonably expect to get ten blazing rows, fifteen long-term sulks, say a dozen arguments about whose turn it is to do the washing-up, a couple of cases of road rage, four broken hearts, and a good ninety milligrammes each of greed, lust, envy, anger, resentment and depression. Add that up, you've got a square meal for a normal healthy adult demon. The problem, though, is harvesting the stuff. I mean, it's not like recycling, please sort your emotions and put them outside in the appropriate colour-coded receptacles. Trying to get the demons to live off that would be like trying to relieve famine in a disaster area by flying over it in a bomber at twenty thousand feet, cutting open great big sacks of flour and chucking it out of the bomb doors.

But that's where A776015 comes in—

'Sorry?' Chris said. 'What—?'

She frowned. 'I forgot, you don't know much about demons. Fine. Well, they don't have names. In fact, they can't, they're nomenclature-intolerant. Your friend Jill knows all about this: get a demon to accept a name and he bursts into flames and dies. So they have numbers instead. All clear, or would you like me to draw you a flow chart?'

Sarcasm, he thought. The difference between sarcasm and a plane ticket to Switzerland was that he didn't need sarcasm right now. 'Perfectly clear,' he said stiffly. 'You were saying.'

'A776015 is the dissident leader,' she said. 'A visionary, a truly great and original mind. She's figured out a way that demons can harvest the emotion they need, unobtrusively, without your lot even knowing they're there. It really would work, I'm sure of it, if only she gets the chance to try. Unfortunately,' she went on, pulling a sad face, 'that's not very likely. The orthodox demons hate the idea, won't hear of it. And if they catch her, they'll kill her, just to shut her up. Which is why she's on the run,' SatNav added, 'and why you've got to help her.'

One of those two-pages-at-once moments. When eventually Chris got his voice back, he said, '*Me?* What the hell have I got to—?'

Shrug. 'Serendipity, really. You just happen to be in the right place at the right time.'

Um, he thought. If that was her idea of the correct use of the word 'right', he had a good mind to report the editors of her dictionary to Trading Standards. 'Why?' he snarled; and then, because it was still bugging him like anything, 'It was you, wasn't it? You wrote all over my bathroom wall, all that stuff about saving the one who is to come.'

'That's right,' she said. 'A776015 is the one who is to come. So glad you were paying attention.'

'You cow,' Chris snarled again. 'It took me *hours* to get all those marks off.'

'Sugar soap,' she said. Of course, he hadn't tried that. 'I tried to warn you about the demons,' she went on reproachfully, 'but you didn't even try to understand.'

'Well, it was a bit bloody cryptic,' he snapped back defensively. 'All that stuff about the one who is to come and the one who is cursed. Who the hell is that meant to be, by the way? And why a hummingbird?'

But she wasn't paying attention. Looked like she'd just heard something; she put a finger to her lips and mouthed 'Shh.'

He could hear it too; something between faint, distant whispering and the scuttling of mice. A fair bet that it wasn't anything nice. Suddenly, SatNav rose quickly to her feet and produced the long, thin sword she'd had in the Ettingate car park, apparently out of thin air. She nodded sideways, towards the kitchen. Clear enough what she wanted him to do, but he stayed where he was. 'What's—?'

She glowered at him. 'They're coming through,' she hissed. 'Get out, now.'

Definition of *they* easily guessed from context. Oh shit, Chris thought, as he jumped up and darted to the kitchen door. He opened it—

And tripped over the door sill of his car, hovered for a second, fell forward, bumping his head, and flumped into the driver's seat, banging his chin on the wheel as a sort of coda. The door slammed shut. The keys, he noticed, were in the ignition. SatNav's casing was suckered to the windscreen in its usual position, but the light was off and the screen was blank. Through the passenger-door window, he could see Honest John's shopfront. Fine, he thought, be like that. Just for fun, he checked the car's milometer, which assured him he hadn't been anywhere since he'd noted the mileage when they arrived.

Everything, in fact, to suggest that none of it had happened, and he'd just left John's place; apart, of course, from the little dangly mascot hanging from his rear-view mirror. It definitely hadn't been there before. He'd have noticed if it had. A little plastic hummingbird directly in your line of sight isn't something you overlook.

Chris felt as though he ought to be doing something, but nothing sprang to mind. Furthermore, he had other calls to make; he reckoned he could probably kiss Honest John's order goodbye, and he still had a quota to meet. True, he could ring Jill. Probably he ought to do just that. For some reason, though, he didn't feel like it. Maybe something SatNav had said? He didn't even want to think about that—

Someone was banging on the window; Angela, looking pale and scared. He wound the window down.

'Where the *hell* were you?' she gasped at him. 'I've been worried sick.'

'Really? I just—' He couldn't think of anything to say, truth or lie. Fortunately, Angela didn't give him the chance.

'I waited and waited for you but you didn't come out, so I went back in, and that John person said you'd gone out the other way without saying where, so I came back and waited by the car, then I went back in again and there was John lying on the floor in *pieces*—'

'Sorry about that,' Chris said awkwardly. 'There was an accident, so I—'

'An accident? He was all *sliced up*. And still *alive*. What in God's name—?'

'Get in the car,' he said. 'I'll explain as we drive.'

Angela got in, and he noticed she had a scratch on her cheek. Loads of ways she could've got that. 'Well?' she demanded, as she fastened her seat belt. 'What happened?'

But Chris was thinking. *Where is she?* the Ettingate Retail Park demon had asked him; and the fugitive-dissident-visionary SatNav had told him about had been a she. The right place at the right time, huh?

The little plastic hummingbird started to sway on its short cord as he pulled away and joined the constipated traffic. Angela didn't seem to have noticed it.

'Honest John flushed me down a toilet,' he said, so cool and matter-of-fact. 'Don't ask me why. He always was a bit of a funny bugger.'

'Down a *toilet*?'

Chris nodded. 'Sort of magically enchanted, I suppose, or I wouldn't have fitted. Bit of a bind climbing back out again.' Was it his imagination, or had the hummingbird's plastic beak swung round and pointed at him as he said that? 'Anyway, that's what took me so long.'

'And what the hell happened to him? It was horrible, he was—

'Ah, well.' He shrugged, so very Sean Connery. 'I might've lost my rag a bit. I always wondered if the rumours about John being immortal were true. Looks like they are. I must remember to tell Jim Phillips next time I see him – he always reckoned it was a load of old socks.'

'You did that?'

Another shrug. 'It's like they say,' he replied. 'It's always the quiet ones. Anyway, that's all it was, no big deal. Now, our next call's Arnott & Meyer in Tamworth, they're all right but they'll try and shave us on discounts.'

Angela was unusually quiet all the way to Tamworth, which nearly made the whole being-flushed-down-bogs-and-then-abducted-by-elves thing worthwhile. Fortunately, Chris knew the way like the back of his hand, so the vexed topic of navigation never arose.

He used the unexpected peace and quiet to reflect on those parts of the day's adventures which he could bear to contemplate without wanting to curl up in a ball and scream. Honest John, for instance. It didn't really matter whether he was in league with the demons or whether they'd forced him to do it – threatened to blow his cover and grass him up to the product-liability lawyers, whatever. Clearly it was another kid-napping attempt, like Ettingate; but that had been a wash-out, as far as the demons were concerned, he'd told them he didn't know where She was, and they'd seemed to believe him, so why go to all the trouble of doing it again? And then there was this rigmarole about dissident demons, which might – if he believed a word of it; still very much undecided on that score – give him some idea of who She was. It occurred to him (not a pleasant thought) that it was just possible that he did know Her whereabouts – not *knowingly* knowing, so to speak, but a kind of knowing without knowing it. What, for example, if She was disguised as someone or even something else? What if—?

'Watch out,' Angela said. 'You nearly ran into the back of that Renault.'

Pot and kettle; but she had a point. Chris couldn't explain to her, though, why he'd just jerked the wheel and nearly caused an accident – it'd be embarrassing. The thought that had struck him at that precise moment was: what if bloody Angela is Her? Think about it. Angela comes bursting into his life, thank you so much for that, Mr Burnoz, just what I always wanted, and straight away he can't sneeze without a demon getting wet. No, really, he told himself, hear me out, okay? Never had any of this kind of trouble before – well, not since school, anyhow – so obviously, something must've changed, there had to be some new element. Well, what? The only one he could think of was Angela. Yes, but she's just admitted that she's really an under-cover demon-hunter, one of Jill's crowd. Think about that. If you were head of the demon-busters, would you be in favour of a demon dissident movement or against it? No-brainer. So; explanation #1: the demon-hunters are helping the dissidents, therefore Angela (if she's really the dissidemon) knows enough about the organisation – DS, all that stuff – to bluff her way as one of them; seeing DS on the stupid polo shirt, she'd assumed—

Well, fine. Various nits and loose ends there, we'll come back to that later. Explanation #2: Jill and her crew are completely talon-in-glove with the dissidemons, and someone, maybe even Jill herself, planted bloody Angela on Chris to act as unpaid and uninformed minder.

A general rule of life he'd usually found to be reliable: when faced with two alternative explanations of any given mystery, the more unpleasant one is more likely to be correct. Yes, he argued (more than a hint of desperation), but why me? Why pick on me to shepherd around a wanted fugitive with murderous fiends on her tail? Unfortunately, possible answers came flooding in as soon as he asked the question. Someone who moved around a lot in the course of his work; a moving target's always harder to hit. Also, someone who came into contact with loads of different people on the outskirts of the magic biz; what if some of them were contacts, DS sleeper agents – he didn't know any of the technical terms but he knew what he meant – what if going round with a travelling salesman was the perfect cover for a dissidemon trying to rally support among a network of hidden supporters? Revoltingly plausible, Chris thought; though if that was the big idea it clearly hadn't worked, because the demons had got on his case straight away. And anyhow, he argued, Jill wouldn't have landed him in something like this without at the very least mentioning it to him first—

Yes, replied his inner barrister, but maybe that was the whole point; because if he didn't actually know, the demons wouldn't be able to force the information out of him when they captured and tortured him – extremely plausible, he had to admit, particularly since it had already happened, at Ettingate. The more he thought about it, the more inevitable it became. Jill, stuck with responsibility for the possible saviour of the human race, knowing that the orthodemons were breathing down her neck, desperately searching for someone she could palm the dissidemon off on, had thought of her oldest friend and said to herself, it'll be all right, Chris won't mind, he owes me about a billion favours going back fifteen years; he's in love with me—

Yes, but Jill wouldn't do that to me.

Chris's inner barrister didn't say anything. Didn't have to. Yes, he thought bitterly, she bloody well would; if it was work, her job, something she truly believed was for the Greater Good. Ah yes, that old thing. She'd always been keen on it, even at school. If there was a charity red-nose day or sponsored pram-race or whale-saving leaflets to be stuffed through doors or anything like that, you'd always find Jill there, running the show, volunteering anybody who didn't get out of the way fast enough. It was, in fact, the main flaw in her character: the sublime belief that nobody would really mind being put upon, bossed about and monstrously inconvenienced, so long as it was for a good cause.

He'd never quite been able to figure out how an otherwise rational human being could think that way, but all the evidence suggested that in Jill's case it was entirely possible. Saving the human race from an all-out war with the demons; well, yes, you could just about classify that as a good cause. Also, considering Jill's track record, the closer someone was to her, the more readily that person sprang to her mind when she was casting about for someone to lumber. Not the first time it'd happened, either. What about the time when she could hardly sleep at night for fretting about the plight of the colony of Ibbotson's moorhens threatened with loss of habitat by the proposed ring-road extension? And who'd been the first sucker press-ganged into lying in the mud in front of the bulldozers? Three guesses. Who'd been dragooned into picketing the school gates when Jill found out that the chip forks in the canteen were made from wood sourced from non-sustainable forests? Quite. From that sort of crap to landing him with a fugitive dissidemon with a price on her horns was one small step for an idealist.

Pretending he was checking his rear-view mirror, Chris glanced at Angela as she sat in the passenger seat, arms crossed in front of her, a human knot. So, the theory was pretty damn plausible, but how would you go about proving it? A direct question was probably not on the cards, but how do you find out if someone's really a demon in disguise? One of so many things, he reflected sadly, they never get round to teaching you at school.

Frank Slade. Sunglasses. Of course!

Have to go about it the right way, of course. He paused, took a deep breath, settled himself. First, set the scene; so he reached up and folded down the sunshade. Actually, it was cloudy and a bit overcast, but he hoped Angela wouldn't notice. Drive on for a minute or so, squinting from time to time as though troubled by the brightness of the sun; then lean forward just enough to reach the glove compartment catch, open it, eyes firmly on road, scrabble about by feel, pull out the pair of sunglasses, stick them on his nose in one nice easy, fluid movement.

He couldn't bring himself to look. What if he actually was right and she really was a demon, albeit a comparatively nice one? He wasn't quite sure he could handle that. On the other hand, at least he'd know for sure, instead of just harbouring nameless dread. Get it over with, he thought, and then it'll be done.

Chris shifted his head round ten degrees, just enough for a sideways glance.

Not a pretty sight. Pale blue skin, hanging in sagging folds like that of an elephant or a rhino; two tusks jutting up from her lower jaw, meshing untidily with two companion upper-jaw tusks jutting down. Horns. Nothing you could legimately call a nose; the ears a bit like cabbage leaves after the caterpillars have been at them. As for her chin, it reminded him of one of those comically misshapen carrots you see at flower shows, in the Funny Vegetables category. For all he knew, to demon eyes she could be a real looker, but he'd really have liked to be able to wind down his window and throw up. That, however, wasn't an option. Pity.

Chris fixed his stare on the road ahead, waited a bit and then casually slipped off the glasses and stowed them in his shirt pocket. Aren't there times, he thought, when you just hate being right?

CHAPTER NINE

The rest of the day's calls slid past Chris in a kind of blur. Later, when he checked his book, he saw that he'd sold thirteen dozen love philtres to Arnott & Meyer (with that much of the stuff sloshing about the place, God help Tamworth) and a record seven dozen collapsible armies to The Sorcerer's Apprentice in Hanley. Under other circumstances, that would've called for suitably raucous celebrations and several happy hours planning on how he'd spend his bonus. As it was, he couldn't really work up any enthusiasm. It hardly seemed to matter any more.

See you tomorrow, then, Angela had said as he dropped her off at the station, and as he let himself into the flat he shuddered at the prospect. There was the usual note from Karen – working late, defrost something – which he screwed into a ball and threw across the room. If she'd been there, he'd have told her all about it, just so he could share it with *someone*, and maybe just possibly get some advice. As it was—

He rang Jill and got a recorded message; tried her mobile, which was turned off. That exhausted the possibilities. Fine. If he was somehow going to get out of this mess, it'd have to be by his own unaided efforts. He whimpered out loud, and went to the kitchen.

Chris had no idea how stuff found its way into his freezer. He never shopped, and he couldn't remember Karen ever doing so. It wasn't a JWW Retail Self-Fill (probably just as well, if the consumer feedback was anything to go by: the most recent batch had been recalled, and seven customers were still unaccounted for, though the recent discovery of a new constellation at the back end of the Orion nebula was surely just a coincidence); maybe there was some service Karen subscribed to that came round while you were out and restocked your freezer for you. She'd never mentioned anything like that, but Karen hardly ever mentioned anything these days.

There was a makeover show on one channel and a rerun of *The Exorcist* on another; the story of my life, Chris thought, sardined in between DIY and malevolent fiends, and fed up to the teeth with both of them.

He ate a microwaved Tesco lasagne, and mused: I may not have a clue, but I do have a telephone. I need to talk to someone.

Who, though? Allies; one of the other reps, maybe, Jim Phillips or Jack Norris, experienced men who'd seen it all and still managed to make their quotas. Or Mr Burnoz, even; he must know something about it, since he'd been the one who'd brought Angela into Chris's life in the first place. He actually got as far as picking up the phone and looking up Mr Burnoz's number. That far, but no further. He simply couldn't think of a way of telling his story without sounding like he'd completely blown his valves.

Pathetic. Well, yes, he thought; that's me. I'm stuck with me and I'd better get used to the idea. Whatever plan of action I commit to had better be something that can be carried through successfully by a pathetic person. Much too late in the day to start growing a backbone, what with all the other stuff I've got going on in my life right now.

Chris went to bed, turned off the light and lay in the dark staring at the ceiling, as wide awake as a coffee-tasters' convention. So Angela, he told himself, is the one who is to come, the demon who's got to be kept safe. And Jill must be running the underground railroad to get her away from the nasty demons. Fine. So where does SatNav come in? Warning me, I guess, for my own good, because nobody else saw fit to tell me what's going on. Very civil of her, I'm sure, but can I actually believe a word of it? After all, it was Jill who told me that SatNav's creepy and stalky and evil, but surely Jill and SatNav must be on the same side, if they both want to save Angela from the Fundies. And since the scheme hasn't worked and the demons know that Angela's with me, what the hell is the point of carrying on with it? Surely it's become completely counter-productive, as well as everything else. Doesn't make any sense—

He thought about getting up and phoning Jill again, but he decided against it. If Jill had lied to him, or at the very least neglected to keep him informed about some fairly relevant stuff affecting him personally, he was honour bound to kick up a fuss about it, and he didn't have the energy. I'm missing some-thing, he told himself; something very important and probably quite obvious. Won't I feel a right prune when I finally figure out what it is.

Meanwhile: am I going in to work tomorrow, or not? Well: substantial chance I might get killed or abducted by demons. Balance that risk against all the strop I'm likely to get from Mr Burnoz if I don't. No contest, really. And then he thought: maybe that's how heroism works. Maybe the great heroes of legend only did the scary stuff because they were too scared or too embarrassed not to.

At some point Chris must've drifted off to sleep, because he found himself on a bare and windswept hillside, and he knew it must be a dream because all the bare and windswept hillsides in his dreams were actually the patch of post-indus-trial waste ground at the back of the school football pitch, only a bit larger and with mountains in the background. Anyhow: he was lying on his back on a big flat stone, with chains on his wrists and ankles holding him down; and there were three vultures sitting on the rock looking thoughtfully at him. One of them was Angela, one was Jill, and SatNav, bald-necked and oily-feathered, was the third. He yawned in his dream, because although he'd never been in this particular scenario before it was tiresomely similar to all the other anxiety dreams with women in them, and he was tempted to fast-forward or wake up. But then there was a fifth bird: a hummingbird, which the vultures didn't seem to have noticed. It hovered close to his left ear (the vultures were sitting on his right) and whispered to him.

At first Chris couldn't make out what it was saying, which was entirely fair and reasonable, since he wasn't exactly fluent in Bird. He shook his head to shoo it away, but it moved a little closer, and he began to understand;

'Remember what she told you about the Fey,' it muttered. 'Dreams, right? This is *serious*. This is *actually happening*. Do you understand?'

It seemed important to her, so he nodded. 'Got you,' he whispered back. 'Who the hell are you?'

'Right now? The only hope you've got. Now, do exactly what I tell you. On the count of three . . .'

'At Honest John's,' he couldn't help asking, 'did SatNav send you?'

'*Her?* You've got to be joking. Now, on three, I want you to—'

'She didn't? But she said—'

'Telling porky pies, wasn't she? Now, when I say three, all you've got to do is—'

'So if you aren't from SatNav,' he insisted, 'who—?'

'Oh, forget it,' said the hummingbird furiously. 'Wake yourself up.'

Which he did, though the alarm might have had something to do with it, not to mention Karen shaking him savagely by the arm and hissing, 'Wake up, for crying out loud, you'll be late for work.'

Chris grunted and opened his eyes, and for some reason he

asked, 'Why are we redecorating the bathroom? It was fine as it was.' But Karen only scowled at him and left the room.

Not a good start to the day; his shaver batteries were flat, there wasn't any hot water, no bread in the bread bin, no coffee in the coffee jar. And he was definitely missing something, and he still hadn't got the faintest idea what it could be.

'Your boss rang,' Karen said, poised on the threshold. 'I said you were still asleep. Call him back. Number's on the pad.'

Oh God, he thought (and noted wryly that a phone call from Mr Burnoz scared him every bit as much as demons). He dialled the number and got a woman's voice. 'Yes?' she snapped.

'Can I speak to Mr Burnoz, please? It's Chris Popham, he's expecting—'

Sigh. 'All right, yes, I'll get him, don't go away.' Mr Burnoz's wife, he assumed. For the very first time ever, Chris felt mildly sorry for him.

'Chris? Good of you to call back. Now listen – I'm afraid Angela's had an accident.'

His head swam like an otter. 'Excuse me?'

'An accident,' Mr Burnoz repeated impatiently. 'She's in hospital.'

'What happened?'

Slight pause. Then: 'I don't know. But I got a call from her mother. Obviously, she won't be coming to work today.' Mr Burnoz's voice suggested that as far as he was concerned there was no *obviously* about it; Mr Burnoz automatically assumed malingering unless he actually saw a death certificate. 'I don't know any more details at present, you can call in later and ask Julie. The point is, she won't be coming with you on your rounds today, so don't waste time waiting for her. Thank you, bye.'

Chris put the phone down. Oh, he thought.

There was, of course, an outside chance that it really was an accident – yes, but she's a *demon*, they're notoriously hard to damage, probably don't even have accidents. In which case—

In which case, he caught himself thinking, I'm off the hook. They've finally got to her, and it's over.

No, of course he wasn't proud of himself for thinking that. It was a terrible thing to think, it was *pathetic*. On the other hand, there was no way it could possibly be his fault, and he'd never asked to be involved, he'd never even been formally told he was involved; damn it, he wasn't even sure he'd believed SatNav when she told him he was involved, so maybe he wasn't, after all. Yes, it was terribly sad that Angela was lying in a hospital bed with tubes up her nose, because no man is an island and he cared, he did really, even if she was a demon. But if it meant that this whole annoying, terrifying business was over, then—

('Whoopee,' he said.)

– There was nothing he personally could do about it except get on with his life and honour her memory by selling a whole load of tat to today's assortment of hardly unsuspecting punters. It's what she'd have wanted, he assured himself as he locked the front door behind him. On his way to the car, he did a little dance.

(Think about the human race, he ordered himself, but he wasn't listening. It sounded rather too much like *think about the ozone layer* or *think about the baby penguins in Antarctica*, and he dismissed it. Pathetic, but consistent.)

There were days, even now, when Chris actually enjoyed driving; when the sun was shining, the road was relatively clear and free of dangerous lunatics and he was on his way to a shop he liked, or where the buyer was unusually gullible. Or when a weight had been taken off his mind, a threat rolled back, something like that. On this occasion, all these factors were in place. He caught himself grinning as he zoomed down the outside lane of the motorway. He felt relaxed, empowered, in control. Presumably, he thought, Jeremy Clarkson feels this way all the time, and why the hell not?

Not wearing the polo shirt today, mostly because he'd worn it two days in a row already and it was starting to get noisome; as soon as it emerged from the laundry basket he'd get rid of it.

Give it back to Jill? For the first time since he could remember, he wasn't actively looking forward to the next time he saw her. That thought made him frown.

Without thinking, he reached for the radio switch, then caught himself at it and hesitated. The gap on the windscreen, where SatNav used to sit – good riddance, he told himself. (But it was rather in the manner of President Bush announcing progress in the war against terror; absolutely nobody was going to believe it, least of all himself, but it was something he felt he was obliged to say.) If she'd been telling him the truth about Angela, presumably SatNav no longer had any reason to be interested in him, and would leave him alone. Good, he told himself, in the same my-fellow-Americans voice he'd used earlier. Don't want anything more to do with her.

So why shouldn't he play the radio? That other stuff she'd told him – elves who got into your head via music; the other one, his instincts told him, was a campanologist's delight. But it might be worth checking it out, if he could get the *Book* to cooperate; and in the meanwhile, no music.

Chris sighed, because that meant either Radio 4 or silence, in which he'd be able to hear himself think. Difficult choice. He consulted the clock, and saw it was the time of day when John Humphrys ritually sacrifices a Cabinet minister. Fine, he thought, wouldn't mind hearing someone else being given a hard time. He tuned in. The combination of baying interviewer and whimpering victim proved pleasantly soothing, and his mild euphoria returned.

He ran through the day's calls in his mind. Nothing too heavy: five shops with a lot of driving in between. A restful day. He deserved it.

The secretary of state for whatever it was had finally been put out of his misery, and it was time for a news summary. Chris turned up his attention level a bit, as he always did, in case a customer felt like making small talk about some leading issue of the day. All off-a-duck's-back stuff, either boring or foreign, except for one item—

Police (said the radio) were investigating an explosion that had completely destroyed a shop in Stafford; they were refusing to rule out possible terrorist involvement, although why terrorists should want to blow up a shop selling party games and conjuring tricks was unclear. The police were anxious to trace the shop's proprietor, Mr John Woden, who had not been seen since the incident. They were also anxious to interview the driver of a pale blue Avensis seen parked outside the shop shortly before the blast.

Shit, Chris thought; and in the second and a half that followed, his mind entertained a surprisingly large number of possible courses of action, ranging from handing himself in at the nearest police station to buying a large tin of black paint and finding a quiet lay-by. Dismissing all the above with a nervous scowl, he tried to think. Who, he asked himself, would want to blow up Honest John's shop? Two leading candidates: demons, and Honest John himself (to make the demons think he was dead)—

Like I care, Chris thought. First things first: he had to do something to get the bogies off his back, if he didn't want to find himself waiting in a police cell while the office junior poured black coffee into the duty solicitor. Under ordinary circumstances, rather a big ask. Wasn't it fortunate, therefore, that he had a direct line to someone who could arrange that for him without so much as breaking a fingernail?

He found a lay-by, pulled out his phone and called Jill's number. Mercifully, she was there.

'It was me,' he told her, after a brief summary of the backstory. 'Just doing my usual rounds. Sold him quite a bit, as it happens.'

'Right,' Jill replied. 'And nothing funny was going on while you were there?'

Chris hesitated for a fraction of a second. If John's shop was rubble, John himself missing and Angela unavailable for comment, who else was there to contradict him? And it'd save an awful lot of tedious explaining. 'Nothing at all,' he said. 'Just a routine call, and then I left. Only,' he added, trying to sound bored and mildly stressed, 'I just haven't got the time or the patience to go through it all with the police. I mean, they're bound to ask me what line of business I'm in. Isn't there a convention about that? About keeping quiet about the business to mundanes, I mean?'

'Of course,' Jill replied promptly. 'No, there's no question of you talking to the cops. I'll see to it that the investigation's passed to our lot. And I'll get them to pull the lookout call for your car. Oh, and thanks for letting me know.' Pause; then, 'You're sure there wasn't anything fishy going on there?'

'I just said so, didn't I?'

Which didn't answer her question, and therefore didn't strictly speaking constitute a second lie. 'Fair enough,' Jill replied. 'If you get any bother, call me.'

'One other thing.' Now, what had possessed him to say that? Still, he'd said it now. 'You know that Angela, the trainee—'

'Yes, I heard about it. Nasty business.'

Oh, Chris thought. 'I just heard there'd been an accident.'

'Accident?' Jill barked out a laugh. 'Hardly.'

'What happened?'

'Demons,' Jill said briskly. 'Four or five, possibly. I'll say this for her, she must've put up one hell of a fight.'

There are some questions you really don't want to ask. 'Is she—?'

'Dead,' Jill said. 'Sorry, I thought you'd have known.'

'Oh.'

A silence, tactful, embarrassed, a bit of both. 'She took two of them with her,' Jill said. 'Hell of a mess. It took two of our response teams just to seal the interdimensional rift.' Another pause, then: 'Were you, like, sort of close—?'

'What? Christ, no. Actually, I didn't like her much. It's just a bit of a shock, that's all.'

It occurred to Chris that nothing either of them had said indicated any knowledge of who or what Angela had really been. Probably better that way, he thought, and left it at that.

Instead he said, 'Do you think there could be a connection? Between Angela and Honest – that shop in Stafford?'

'Well, yes, of course,' Jill said. 'There's you. But whether it means anything I couldn't possibly say at this stage.'

'Thanks a lot, Jill, that really sets my mind at rest.'

Sigh. 'Just keep your head down, all right? And if I hear anything at all, I'll call you ASAP. Keep your phone switched on at all times.'

'Even more thanks. For crying out loud, Jill,' he added, 'next thing, you'll be telling me to lock all doors and boil my drinking water.'

'Not a bad idea,' Jill replied gravely. 'Got to go. Bye, and thanks again.'

Chris got back into the car, picked a CD at random from the glove box, stuffed it in the tray and started the engine. One less worry, he told himself: at least I'm not liable to be arrested as well as torn in pieces or dragged through an interdimensional rift. Oddly enough, he did find that comforting. In spite of everything, he still wasn't a hundred per cent sure he believed in demons, but the police were depressingly real.

He was disagreeably surprised, therefore, when a police car pulled him over ten minutes later; he hadn't been speeding, his brake lights and tyres were beyond reproach, and he had nothing to be afraid of, in theory.

There were two of them, a huge man and a short, grim woman. They arrested Chris in connection with the murder of Angela Schlager, loaded him into their car and drove him to a police station.

Chris knew the drill from cop shows – remarkably accurate, his hat off to them – but that didn't make it any better. Once he'd been processed (isn't that what they do to cheese, he asked himself, to deprive it of any vestige of identity) they dumped him in a cell and left him there, presumably to reflect on his moral shortcomings until they could excavate him a lawyer.

Human beings are made up of mind and heart. Chris's mind was pretty relaxed about the whole thing; after all, the simple fact was that he hadn't done it, so how could he possibly be in any real danger? The lawyer would come, he'd be questioned, they'd find out that at the time of the murder he'd been miles away with a perfect alibi, they'd turn him loose with apologies for any inconvenience, and that'd be that. Laughable misunderstanding, and, as a way of passing an afternoon, marginally better than work. Or, if not that, then Jill would turn up, with her official ID and supervening jurisdiction, and they'd have a drink in the pub before she drove him home. It was going to be all right. Really.

His heart wasn't so easily fooled. He had no idea when the bloody woman (how quickly she'd metamorphosed from tragic victim to insufferable pest) had managed to get herself killed, but the chances were that at the time in question Chris had either been on the road or at home alone in the flat. Furthermore, he had no idea where she'd been snuffed. If he could prove that he'd been on a call at the time, a hundred miles away from the crime scene, then fine. If it had happened just round the corner from where he'd been, he was probably in severe poo. And Jill – he was beginning to have his doubts about her. Heresy, yes, but having your trouser belt and shoelaces confiscated by the Vogons plays funny tricks on your judgement.

The best he could find to say about his cell was that it was very clean and white. There was a bed to lie down on – that or the floor, take your pick – with a splendid view of the ceiling, which was also clean and white: a cross between a bathroom and a starship, he decided, but hardly cosy. Lacks the homely touch, he thought, adding that if he ever managed to get out of there he'd never moan about Karen's carpets-and-curtains fixation again. Anything, even peach-painted woodchip and tapestry scatter cushions, had to be better than this.

Chris closed his eyes, mostly to keep from being dazzled by the hideous whiteness of it all, and tried to think of something nice. Nothing came immediately to mind, so he set about constructing a synthetic perfect memory. How about—?

A day off work, always a good starting point. The deep blue sea, lazily washing against an apron of sand the colour of perfect fish batter. Seagulls circling in a cloudless sky. The distant laughter of happy children—

Just a moment, he thought, this isn't my daydream, I hate bloody beach holidays. I want a saloon bar, a sodding great big wide-screen TV showing the footie, a tall frosted pint, dry-roasted peanuts . . . But the sea carried on rolling serenely in, a happy dog scampered after a tennis ball, a fat child kicked in another fat child's sandcastle, and Karen asked him for the suntan lotion, which he'd forgotten to bring. He got spoken to for that; he apologised but he might as well have saved his breath, and a sulk gradually formed, welling up out of the sand like a soft mist.

Fine, Chris thought, screw this, I'll have the cell back now, please.

He opened his eyes. Still the beach. Karen was lying on her stomach, her face turned pointedly away. There was a pebble digging into the small of his back.

Not real, he told himself; you're in a cell in a police station, accused of a crime you didn't commit, and any moment now they'll come and take you to a small, bleak room with a wobbly table and ask you nastily deceptive questions. Quite definitely you're not on a beach being sulked at. Just reach out with your hand and touch the floor tiles if you don't believe me.

So he did that. Sand. He scooped up a half-handful and let it run through his fingers.

Oh *hell*, he thought. Just when you think it can't get any worse.

'This is no good,' Karen said, still facing away. 'You know what I'm like when I burn. You can bloody well go back to the car and fetch the suntan lotion.'

'Of course,' Chris said, 'you're absolutely right. Remind me where we parked.'

She wriggled round and faced him. Her all right: that what-are-you-talking-about face was uniquely hers. 'In the car park, of course,' she said. 'Don't you remember?'

He smiled and tried to stand up. No problems. 'Keys?'

'In your pocket.'

He was wearing shorts. He never wore shorts, because there was too much misery in the world as it was. In the pocket of his shorts were the car keys, which he distinctly remembered handing over to the desk sergeant.

'Sorry,' he said. 'Which way's the car park?'

Karen scowled at him. 'Left at the sea wall, then right by the post office. I told you to wear a hat, but you never listen.'

OK, not real; but in the real world they'd taken his car keys away from him, an act of symbolic castration that he bitterly resented. And it was real enough for the sand to feel squidgy between his toes ('Well, put your shoes on, then'), real enough to walk on. He tried to calculate the dimensions of his cell: four paces and he should be banging his nose on the steel door. Apparently not. He walked slowly on up the beach, past the piglike pink carcasses of sunbathers and kiddies howling because they'd dropped their ice creams, until he reached the sea wall.

'End program,' Chris said aloud. A middle-aged woman looked at him.

Beyond the wall, pavement, a road, on the far side of which were shops, burger stalls, a pub with people sitting outside. Chip papers, discarded burger boxes. He tried to identify the place – if it was just an illusion, it'd be logical for it to be set in one of his own memories – but he was absolutely sure he'd never been there before. And he had his car keys; they were in his hand, he could feel the chill of the metal.

He was aware of his heart beating very fast. So, he thought, define 'real'. Or, better still, quantify the concept *real enough*.

The car. He turned left, carried on walking until he saw a post office; right-hand turning next to it, he took that, fifty yards and there was a car park, rows of windscreens shimmering like lakes in the perfect sun. He stopped and looked at the keys in his hand. He'd know them anywhere, down to the pattern of the serrations, and of course the Wallis and Grommit key fob. *His* keys; therefore, logically, *his* car; a pale blue Avensis—

And there it was.

Remember first love, when you could look at a crowded room and only see one face? Same effect, basically. There must've been several hundred cars in the park, but he could only see one. He moaned softly, and broke into a run.

Chris touched the door, warm from the sun and gloriously solid. He pressed the little button and heard the click as the doors unlocked. Inside it was greenhouse-hot, and it smelt of warm vinyl and air freshener. *His* car—

He sat in the driver's seat and tried to breathe. His car, undeniably real; in which case, so was everything else – beach, sand, flip-flops, Karen – and he was free and clear, safe, out of it all. He remembered something, and checked the rear-view mirror stem. No dangling plastic hummingbird. He flipped open the glove compartment; a bottle of suntan lotion and a few of Karen's CDs. So far, so—

He looked at the windscreen. Suckered to it by its rubber plunger thing was SatNav: whole, uncleaved by enchanted blade, just as she used to be before all the weirdness started.

Right, Chris thought. Now we're getting somewhere.

He checked that her lead was plugged into the lighter socket, then pressed her little button. The screen lit up. She said, 'Please wait.'

'SatNav,' he whispered. 'Is that you?'

A long, long silence. Then she said, 'Please enter your required destination.'

He frowned. 'Not now, please,' he said. 'I need to ask you something.'

He waited. No reply. Then he thought, sod it, music, she needs music before she can talk to me. He scrabbled a CD out of a case, flipped open the drawer and slotted it in. 'Shake It Loose', by the Lizard-Headed Women.

Oh all right, then, he thought, if you absolutely must. But I'm turning the volume down.

'Hello,' she said.

'Is that really you?'

'Yes. Please state your desired destination. Or would you rather just chat?'

'Listen,' he said. 'All this. Is it real?'

Pause. 'I think so,' SatNav said. 'Why wouldn't it be?'

'You think so,' Chris repeated impatiently. 'All right, how about this. Where am I?'

'Weymouth.'

'*Weymouth?*'

'Yes. I can be more specific if you—'

'What the hell am I doing in Weymouth, SatNav? Last I knew, I was in a police cell.'

'This is your summer holiday,' SatNav replied. 'You've been looking forward to it.'

'Have I?'

'Of course. You treasure the opportunity to spend quality time with your wife.'

'Actually, she isn't—' he said automatically, but stopped himself; couldn't be bothered explaining right now. 'So how did I get here from the police cell? Someone rescued me, right?'

Pause. 'You would like me to retro-plot the route you took in order to arrive here. Please wait. Your route is being calculated.'

Chris waited, while the Lizard-Headed Women finally ran out of things to say about the human condition. At last the screen flickered and showed him a map: a red line running across the country, from his home to the south coast.

'That's not what I meant,' he said. 'Come on, SatNav, how did I get here? You must know. I mean—'

'Your route is being calculated, please wait.'

Same again; at least, it was a slightly different route, avoiding major roadworks on the A303, but it amounted to the same thing. He stared at it for ten seconds.

'SatNav,' he said, with a kind of frantic patience, 'I think you're missing the point. What I need to know is—'

The words had an effect on him. Not the ringing of a bell, as in the cliché; it was more like firmly grabbing hold of a bit of wire that turns out to be an electric fence. No, he thought, I can't face all that again; and besides, it's not the sort of thing that'd be in there. I mean, it's not really *human knowledge*, is it? That's dates of battles and algebra and the human genome and how to make polymers. And even if it does work – well, personally like that, all it'll do is tell me about bloody Gandhi.

On the other hand—

The *Book* was in his jacket pocket (and he clearly remembered handing it over, along with his belt and his car keys). He shrugged, and opened it at random—

*Reality. Reality is the term used to describe the state of affairs normally prevailing, in the absence of **supernatural influences**, in a logical, **mechanical** universe subject to scientifically provable laws of **physics**. **Multiple** and **compound** realities coexist simultaneously across the **dimensional spectrum**, making it impossible to pin down any one perceived state of affairs as the **base** or **default** reality. Human beings, simply for convenience, tend to assume that the reality in which they spend all or the majority of their lives must be the **base**, and this assumption usually functions adequately in the absence of **magic** or other similar factors. Recent progress in **dimensional portal technology** threatens to disrupt this comfortable assumption; in particular, the proliferation of lightweight, battery- or solar-powered man-portable **transdimensional interfaces**, often marketed as labour-saving devices or executive toys. **Temporal distortion** and **time travel** can also cause disturbing reality-bending effects. Perhaps the greatest enemy of humanity's stable perception of reality comes from **metadimensional entities** such as **demons** and **the Fey**, who frequently make use of their dimension-shifting abilities either recklessly or with malicious intent—*

Clear as mud, Chris thought, and closed the *Book*; even when it's working it's bloody useless. It was mildly encouraging not to be lectured about Gandhi for a change, but the very most he reckoned he'd gleaned from all that was that this whatever-it-was he was in might possibly be just as valid as the one he'd left . . . He thought about the practicalities of that: stuff like PIN numbers and bank balances, did he have a job in this version of the universe, if he decided to stay here would he be able to bluff his way through or would it be a lifelong episode of *Quantum Leap* without the assistance of a friendly hologram to guide him? Well, he thought, this is a company car, so presumably I've still got my job; and Karen too, of course, mustn't forget her, and she seems pretty much the same. *Your wife*, SatNav had called her, and he'd assumed it was the usual conventional jump-to-conclusions, but what if . . .? Still, he thought, even so it's got to be better than being in prison.

A bit better.

'SatNav,' he said, 'what reality am I in?'

'Your metaphysical coordinates are being calculated, please wait.' Pause, during which Chris looked for, and found, the emergency Mars Bar hidden in the driver's-door pocket. 'You are currently in reality 001 Alpha.'

'Oh-oh—?'

'Normality,' SatNav translated; then added, 'What an odd question to ask.'

'Sorry.' Karen, he thought, waiting impatiently for her sun-block while the murderous heat fried her soft flesh like squid rings. Screw her, he thought, this is *important*. 'Only, the way I remember it, I was on my way to make a call and I got arrested, and they think I murdered Angela, and I was in a cell—'

'They think you murdered Angela?'

'Yes, which is bloody ridiculous, because—'

'Because she isn't dead.'

Silence. Frozen on his lips, like mammoths in the Siberian ice, the words *she's dead all right, Mr Burnoz told me*. In Chris's mind, a light suddenly switched on, the realisation that in this reality – he was beginning to like this reality a *lot* – she might very well be alive, just as he was on holiday rather than in jail.

'SatNav,' he said cautiously.

'Yes, Chris?'

'Just suppose,' he said, his voice soft as prayer, 'someone was living in one reality and suddenly found himself in another one, just a tad different. Better, say. Could he stay there, do you think? Permanently?'

'Entirely possible,' SatNav replied. 'Why, are you planning on—?'

'Lord. No,' he said quickly. 'Perish the thought. I like it here.'

'Of course you do,' SatNav replied. 'But now I don't understand. Why do the police think you murdered Angela if she's still alive?'

'Forget I said that,' he mumbled. 'Touch of the sun, maybe.' Talking of which; he reached into the glove compartment and got Karen's suntan lotion. 'Oh, one last thing,' he said casually. 'Do you happen to know anything about the one who is to come?'

'The one what, Chris?'

'Forget it,' he said happily. 'Doesn't matter.'

On the way back to the beach, he bought an ice cream. He hadn't had a proper ice cream, on a little wooden stick, for years.

'Where did you get to?' Karen demanded. 'You've been ages.'

'Phone call,' he said smoothly. 'Work.'

'Oh, right.' An acceptable answer, apparently. He handed over the suntan stuff. 'You ought to turn that bloody phone off while we're on holiday.'

'Good idea,' he said, and did so. 'They'll just have to manage without me.'

She had no comment to make on that score. He finished his ice cream and lay down, aware that he was smiling but seeing no reason not to, and closed his eyes. You could get to like beach holidays, he thought.

'So what was the panic?' Karen said.

'Oh, just stuff. Customers chasing orders, that kind of thing.'

She clicked her tongue. 'Can't that half-witted girl of yours handle it? That's the whole point of having an assistant.'

'That's what I told them,' Chris replied.

Peace, quiet; happiness. The warmth of the sun was making him feel drowsy, but he didn't really want to fall asleep, just in case he woke up and found it had all been a dream. Though, he told himself, the sun isn't warm in dreams, and you can't smell salt and warm sand and suntan lotion.

'By the way,' Karen said, 'where is she?'

'Sorry, what?'

'I said, where is she?'

'Where's who?'

'Doesn't matter.' He heard her yawn, and then say, 'I'm just going over there for a bit. Be back soon.'

'That's fine,' Chris answered drowsily. The glare on his closed eyelids dimmed a little as her shadow fell across him. He snuggled his back into the sand. It'd be very easy indeed to fall asleep, and why not? But the thought made him uncomfortable, and he opened his eyes. The sun was annoyingly bright. What I need, he thought, is sunglasses.

Luckily, there was a pair in his jacket pocket. He looked at them, trying to remember where he'd got them from. They looked old-fashioned and rather strange, but they worked perfectly well. He sat up, yawned and stretched.

'I'm about ready for some lunch,' Karen said behind him. 'Coming?'

'Mphm.' He stood up, turned to face her—

Chris didn't scream. He didn't make a sound of any kind, because his throat, mouth and lungs had got stuck, and the full-blooded yell he wanted to let fly with couldn't get out. Later, he realised that what had really freaked him out was the fact that the three-eyed, grey-skinned, four-tusked, pointed-eared, noseless, drooling monster facing him was wearing Karen's light blue bikini, a garment of which he had very fond memories, and for a split second he was afraid that the demon had eaten her and stolen her clothes.

'I'm starving,' the demon said, in Karen's exact voice. 'Let's go.'

But that wasn't what had happened; because if the demon had just eaten—

'You go ahead,' Chris said. 'I think I'll just stay here a bit longer.'

Given the demon's facial layout, you couldn't really tell if it was scowling or not. But the voice told him everything he wanted to know. 'You don't want to have lunch with me?'

'Not terribly hungry.'

'Fine.' The enduring-with-bad-grace voice. 'I'll have to wait, then. Will you be ready in half an hour?'

He wanted to look away, but he didn't dare break eye contact; so he took the sunglasses off. It helped; he couldn't see the demon any more, just Karen in the blue bikini, glowering at him. 'On second thoughts,' he said, 'let's go now. I could really fancy fish and—'

'We'll go back to the hotel and change,' she said firmly. 'Then I thought we could try that Mexican place we saw last night.'

Chris tried to think of a strategy, but all that came to mind was getting to the car, locking the doors and driving away very fast. He could see all sorts of objections, but it was the best he could do at short notice, with his synapses fused with revulsion and fear. The only other course of action he could think of was getting out the pantacopt and trying to kill the demon, and he knew he wouldn't be able to do that, for all sorts of reasons.

They reached the sea wall. He turned left.

'Where do you think you're going? It's this way.'

She was pointing right; they wouldn't be going anywhere near the car park after all. He choked back a whimper. Make a run for it? He knew that his legs wouldn't hold out; they were only just keeping him upright as it was. Going back to the hotel room definitely not an option. Stand and fight, then.

Chris shuddered. So much he didn't know, for one thing. If you cut a shape-shifted demon in half with a pantacopt, did it revert to its real form, or vanish into thin air, or would he be left standing on Weymouth beach with two bisected halves of a dead woman to account for to the authorities? Not that it'd come to that, he knew; he'd cock it up somehow, either let her get the weapon away from him or cut off his own legs. Nothing for it, then, but to go quietly—

Out of the corner of his eye, a glimpsed impression: stormtrooper black, body armour, a fetishist's dream of an equipment belt. The police. He turned his head and spotted them: two coppers, a big tall man and a short woman, doing that slow walk perfectly described as proceeeding. Well, he thought sadly, anything's better than death.

Slowly and reluctantly, he began taking off his shorts.

'Chris, what the *hell* are you doing?' Her voice: shrill, furious – nothing unusual there. He closed his eyes; everybody in Weymouth must be staring. Any moment now the police would arrest him and take him away. Not an experience he was looking forward to very much, but at least it wouldn't be the last thing he did—

'Excuse me, sir, but what—?'

He opened his eyes and tried to smile. He didn't get very far. Before he'd done more than just hitch up the corners of his mouth, a hummingbird zoomed out of absolutely nowhere and hit him right between the eyes, like a bullet.

CHAPTER TEN

'Excuse me, sir,' said the big male policeman, 'but are you feeling all right?'

Chris opened his eyes. He was sitting in the driver's seat of his car, and the policeman's head was poking through the open window. He was in a lay-by, beside a dual carriageway—

'What? Sorry, yes. Fine.'

'Only you appeared to have fallen asleep,' the policeman went on, looking at him carefully. 'You do realise it's an offence to sleep in a lay-by, don't you?'

'Is it?' Like he cared. He wasn't in Weymouth any more. 'Sorry, I didn't know that,' he gabbled. 'I was feeling a bit drowsy, and they say, don't they, if you start to feel drowsy, pull over and rest, otherwise you could cause an accident. So—'

The policeman nodded slowly. 'I shall have to ask you to take a breathalyser test. If you'd just step out of the vehicle.'

'Sure. Yes. No problem.' It was all he could do not to grin like an idiot. Fortunately, the policeman didn't seem to have noticed, and by the time he'd passed the test and been given his lecture and promised faithfully not to let it happen ever again, he'd managed to get himself under control.

And I woke up, Chris said to himself as he watched the police car drive away, *and it had all been a dream*. But it hadn't, he was sure of that. He had evidence; a trivial thing, the sort of thing only Poirot or Colombo would recognise for what it was. He'd only noticed it himself when he'd taken out his wallet to show the bogies his driving licence, but it was substantial enough to build an entire reality on.

He sat for ten minutes or so, watching the cars zoom past. Ten minutes of the hardest work he'd ever done.

'Fine,' he said aloud. Then he got out his phone and made a call.

He didn't ring Jill. Instead, he called the number on the card the Day-Glo bloke had given him.

'Hi,' he said. 'I've got your shirt.'

'What?' Pause. 'Oh, it's you.'

'Yes, it's me. I expect you want it back.'

'Wouldn't mind,' the Day-Glo bloke said. 'No desperate hurry, though. Or you could stick it in the post, save you a—'

'It's no trouble.' Chris reached out and touched the place on the windscreen where SatNav's rubber plunger had left a mark. 'Besides, you're coming to see me. Bring your electronic stuff,' he added. 'Might as well do a thorough job.'

A moment while that sank in. 'They've been back.'

'Yes.'

'Where are you?'

Chris laughed. 'Private joke,' he explained. 'I'm about three miles past Junction 6 on the A980 northbound – there's a lay-by.'

The Day-Glo bloke's name turned out to be Derek Bloom. He listened without interrupting while Chris explained. Then he said, 'You're sure?'

Chris held out his hand. Lying on his palm was a little wooden stick.

'Ah,' Derek said. 'It couldn't be – well, you know, one you'd had earlier. Like, there's all sorts of junk in my coat pockets, some of it's been there years.'

Chris shook his head. 'I hadn't had an ice cream for ages,' he replied. 'I remember thinking that, while I was in there. I don't actually like the stuff, like I can't stand beach holidays.' He paused, then said, 'That's very important.'

'Is it?'

'I think so. Feel free to disagree – after all, you're the professional.'

Derek shrugged. 'Take your word for it,' he said. 'All right, so it wasn't a dream. And while you were there, you definitely saw a demon.'

'Yes.'

'No offence, but how can you be—?'

By way of reply, Chris handed him the sunglasses. Derek looked at them and whistled. 'Feinwerkhaus of Vienna, about 1935,' he said, in a pleasingly awed voice. 'Where did you get . . . ?'

'A kind friend lent them to me,' Chris replied.

Derek handed them back. 'All right,' he said. 'You saw a demon. So what you're saying is, your wife's a—'

'She's not my wife,' Chris snapped. 'And no, I don't think she's a demon, either. And it wasn't a dream. It was real.'

'OK,' Derek said, in a where-exactly-is-this-leading sort of voice. 'And she asked you the question. *Where is she?*'

'Yes.' Chris sighed, and put the sunglasses away. 'The whole beach location must've been a PK86V – JWW Retail TimeOut Instant Bank Holiday,' he explained. 'It's just your basic metadimensional vortex stabilised in a temporal disruption field, loaded onto a CD. It's not one of our best-selling lines, in fact I think it's been discontinued; but I demonstrated one to a customer only a day or so ago, and when I went through my samples before I came out this morning, it'd gone. I'm guessing that was the one they used, but it could be one they bought somewhere over the counter. They must've hacked into it and reconfigured it to do all that stuff with the policemen and me being arrested and carted off to the nick. In fact, I know they did, because when I woke up in this lay-by forty minutes ago I checked my watch and it said 8.45. Just before the being-pulled-over-by-the-cops business started, I'd heard the 8.30 news summary on the radio.'

Derek nodded slowly. 'All right,' he said. 'With you so far. You're saying they tried to pull basically the same stunt as the last time, at the Ettingate Retail Park.'

'Looks like it, doesn't it? Anyway,' Chris went on, 'I thought you'd better know about it, so I called you. Oh, and I haven't got your shirt with me, it's at home. Drop by any evening after seven-thirty and pick it up.'

Derek thought for a minute, then said, 'So why are they still after you? I thought the whole point was that they believed you knew something and then realised you didn't. Why go through the whole performance all over again?'

'That,' Chris replied with feeling, 'is a fucking good question. Just as well you're here to figure out the answer. It's what I pay my taxes for, after all.'

Derek nodded. 'I'll pass it on to Colonel Ettin-Smith. She's taken charge of this case, you being a personal friend, so—'

'No,' Chris said, surprising himself with the firmness of his voice, 'don't do that. You think about it yourself. I have faith in you. You're clever. You have excellent taste in shirts. You think about it, and when you've thought, you call me. Right?'

'I can't do that,' Derek replied indignantly. 'That'd be a direct breach of the chain of command, it'd be—'

Chris took the sunglasses from his pocket and held them out. 'You might want,' he said quietly, 'to borrow these.'

For a moment, Derek stared at him as though he'd just sprouted feathers. Then he said 'Oh,' in a tiny little voice, and took the glasses.

'You can give them back when you come round for the shirt.'

'Right,' Derek said. 'Yes. Thanks.' He stared at the glasses in his hand, then put them in an inside pocket. 'How did you—?'

'Figure it out?' Chris tried to look casual. 'Oh, Jill and Karen used to be best friends at school. Karen,' he repeated. 'My wife. Only she's not.'

*

To fill in the time, Chris did his usual rounds. Sold loads of stuff, hardly aware of what he was doing: BB27Ks, and enough dried water to fill the Sea of Tranquillity.

('Excuse me asking,' he couldn't help saying, though, 'but have you got any idea what they do with it?'

'Funny,' the girl replied. 'I was going to ask you that.')

After the last call, he killed an hour in a service station Burger King, drawing diagrams on the back of an envelope. He even used three different-coloured pens. Then he drove to Jill's street and parked opposite the entrance to her block of flats.

She was an hour and ten minutes later than he'd thought she'd be. He saw her in his mirror, walking briskly up the street, carrier bag swinging from one hand, and he thought: I used to be in love with *that*. He could say it to himself quite easily, now that it was over. Even so, he was glad he'd lent the sunglasses to Derek. If he'd still had them, he wouldn't have been able to resist putting them on and looking at her, and he really didn't want to know what she'd look like through them.

She must've recognised the car. She altered course, crossed the street and came up to his door. He wound down the window and smiled at her.

'Hi, Chris,' she said, sounding vaguely apprehensive. 'Were you waiting for me?'

'Mphm.'

'Is anything the matter?'

'Yes. You're not human. You're a demon.'

Jill frowned. 'Come in and have a cup of tea,' she said. She'd always been tea rather than coffee, jacket potato rather than chips, salad rather than peas.

'Thanks,' Chris said, and got out of the car to follow her.

'How'd you find out?' she said, her back to him as she unlocked her door.

'Part intuition,' he replied, 'part deduction. What first started me thinking—'

'Oh, stop trying to sound clever,' Jill said. 'Somebody must've told you.'

'No way,' he replied irritably. 'I worked it out for myself. It was obvious, actually.'

'Was it?'

'Yes, as soon as Sa— as soon as someone told me about the nice demon; the one who wants peace, I mean.' He took a deep breath, and went on: 'That's you, isn't it?'

For a moment Jill's face was completely blank. Then she nodded. 'Quite right,' she said. 'Now, how did you guess?'

Chris sighed, and sat down on the nearest chair. 'Should've realised years ago, really,' he said. 'Well, not actually while we were still at school, because I'd never heard of demons back then, and I wouldn't have believed in them if someone had told me. But later, thinking about what happened, that day in the girls' bogs—' He looked up at her and said, 'I'm right, aren't I?'

She nodded again. 'I think so,' she said. 'Be more specific.'

'You and Karen were in there when the demon attacked the other girl.' He paused, then went on. 'I'm guessing you could see the demon, and Karen and the other girl couldn't; at any rate, you knew what was going on, and it really upset you. That's what made you decide there had to be another way.'

Jill was looking away, but she nodded once more.

'Being a demon-hunter's the perfect cover, of course. You're heavily protected – I mean, no demon in its right mind's going to try and get at you of all people; you can keep track of everything that's going on, and if one of them does come after you, you can have it taken out straight away. They haven't got a clue where you are, but somehow they know you're connected to me – maybe they can smell you on me, I don't know—'

'Good guess,' she interrupted quietly.

'Whatever. Anyway, that's why they've been after me and why they think I know where you are. I think you should've told me, though.'

She shrugged. 'Maybe I should.'

'And that's why—' This was acutely embarrassing, but for once in his life Chris was prepared to endure the suffering.

'That's why you – well, why we never got together. I mean, it wasn't all that unthinkable; we've always been good friends, really got on, same sense of humour, all that stuff you get in the magazine quizzes. But you knew it was out of the question because you're not . . .' Deep, deep breath. 'Not human. Pretty bloody fundamental, really.'

'Quite,' Jill said.

'And then when I heard about how you were planning to do away with needing to kill people, how your lot feed off emotion—' It was all coming out so fluently now, like blood from a punctured vein. 'Well, I suddenly realised. Two things, really. What I mean is, there's our sort of group of friends, ever since school; and you're the one everybody's always come to with their problems, or when they're really happy, any time they're really *emotional*, what do they do? They come to you and they talk about it, pour it all out in torrents, and you sit there looking all serious and sympathetic, nodding and saying, 'That's so terrible' and 'I know' and stuff. What you've really been doing all this time,' he said, with just a hint of anger, 'is lapping it up, food and drink to you, literally. You live on it. And I think,' he went on, 'that all the time we all thought you were there for us, the only person we could talk to who'd understand – really, I think you were stirring away like mad, making trouble and melodrama, keeping us all living soap-opera lives so we'd—' He shrugged. 'Better than killing people, I guess. But it explains why sometimes when I see you, you're as thin as a rake, and then a week later you've put on pounds. And Karen and me—' Definitely a raw edge to his voice, and he didn't care. 'You knew from the very start we weren't right for each other, we'd never ever be able to get along. But when she fancied me back in school, you egged her on, and then you led *me* on, and then gave me the brush-off just exactly timed so I'd turn to Karen on the rebound; and I suppose you've been, well, snacking off the both of us ever since.'

'Hardly snacking,' Jill said quietly. 'More a four-course banquet with wine and cheese to follow.'

'Fine,' Chris snapped. 'Glad to have been of service.'

'You have been,' she said solemnly. 'And not just to me. Not just to the human race, either,' she added. 'If you've heard about what I've been trying to do, you must see that it's the only hope for my lot and yours as well. And meanwhile—' She shrugged. 'A girl's gotta live.'

He looked at her; at the side of her head, since she was still facing away from him. 'I guess,' he said heavily. 'And it's all been in a good cause, and it's not like I *begrudge* you—' He covered his face with his hands and slowly massaged his closed eyelids with his fingertips; suddenly he felt overwhelmingly tired. 'I can ask you if it was all just an act or whether you ever really liked me, or any of us, and you'll give me an answer and it'll sound really convincing. But I don't think I'll be able to believe it.'

'Your choice,' she said; sad but reasonable voice, this hurts me more than it hurts you. 'Now perhaps you can see why I never told anybody.'

'Well, of course. You'd have blown your meal ticket.'

Chris hadn't meant it to come out as harshly as that, but since it had, he didn't really mind. Anger and disappointment: two very strong emotions, on a bed of wild rice.

Jill walked away from him until she was facing the window. She said: 'Well, there you go. You're quite right. And smart too, the way you figured it out. What are you going to do now?'

For a long moment he didn't understand the question. 'If you mean, am I going to tell anybody, of course not. They'd think I'd gone round the bend, for a start.'

'Our little secret, then.'

'I suppose so, yes. And I wouldn't tell anyone even if I thought they'd listen. I mean,' he added, and pushing the words out was like pulling his own teeth with pliers, 'I don't want the nasty demons to find you, do I?'

She nodded. 'Because it'd mean the end of civilisation as you know it.'

'Partly that, yes.'

'Well, fine. Very public-spirited. And I'm sorry.'

'Sorry?' Chris echoed. One of those words that suddenly doesn't seem to mean anything.

'Yes. Sorry. We apologise for any inconvenience. Unfortunately the survival of both our species has had to take priority over your delicate bloody sensibilities. And while I think of it, Karen's too good for you, and you've always treated her like shit, and then you have the nerve to come whining to me about how you're not getting along when you should be waking up every morning thinking how lucky you are that you've got someone who'll put up with you. I know I couldn't have, even if I had been human. I'd have bitten your head off in the first three days.'

Even as he felt the shock, a part of Chris was thinking: hurt, anger, misery, if she's not careful she'll be as fat as a pig by this time tomorrow; she must be starving, to lay into me like this. 'Just as well, then,' he said woodenly. 'Anyway, that's that cleared up, I'm glad we've got it all straight at last. Good luck with your mission, or whatever you want to call it.'

'Thank you.'

He stood up. His legs just about supported his weight. 'And if there's anything you can do to get the fucking demons off my case, it'd be appreciated. Quite understand if you can't, but if you can it'd be nice.'

Chris didn't wait for an answer. She'd have to protect him now; because if they caught him again and asked him the same question – *where is she?* – this time he knew the answer, and of course he'd tell them: no heroism, no I'd-rather-die-than-talk. Damn it, they wouldn't even need to ask, he'd be squealing the information at them so loud they wouldn't be able to hear themselves think. And then they'd kill him, of course, but knowing that wouldn't make any difference. At least I'm honest with myself, he thought. And Jill (was that her real name? He had no idea what demons were called – Ashtorel and Boamoth and stuff like that, but not Jill Ettin-Smith) knew him well enough to have no illusions at all—

If I were Jill, he thought suddenly, I'd have me killed.

No question but that she could do it. He could just imagine Derek, or one of the other Day-Glo people, quietly and efficiently putting him to sleep: poison, or something that'd look like a domestic accident, and the knowledge would die with him, and billions of lives would be saved, so that was all right.

Just as well I'm not her, then; I'd do it because I'm a coward, just go to my liver and follow the yellow brick road. Whatever else she may be, Jill's no coward. And besides, if she thought I had to be got rid of, she'd have done it then and there, the way she always did her homework the moment she got in from school, rather than leaving it till the last minute like the rest of us. I'd never have left the flat alive.

Now what, Chris thought as he walked slowly back to the car. So, I solved the mystery, all by myself; dead clever, but you don't get a prize or even a Blue Peter badge. Instead, you lose your best friend, and the consolation prize you get to keep and take home with you is— well, the truth: the shining, all-transcending, most-important-thing-there-is bloody truth; men have fought for it, gone to the scaffold and the rack for it, laid waste whole continents for it, but when you actually think about it rationally, what fucking use is the truth anyhow? Can't spend it. Can't invest it in high-yield capital-growth bonds. Can't even have it mounted in a silver frame and hang it on the wall. So; all very well in its place, the ideal gift for the man who has everything, but on balance he'd far rather have his friend and his life back, thank you so terribly much all the same.

He drove home; and as he waited at some traffic lights, he thought yes, but how *did* I figure it out? Got the right answer, true enough, but it's like maths, you've got to show your working or you don't get the marks. There was something else, some little thing I noticed and then I *knew*, but I don't seem to be able to account for what it was.

The lights changed, and as he pulled away a movement at eye level caught his attention. The plastic hummingbird was back, swaying on its string from his mirror.

Karen was – huge megasurprise – working late. Nothing in fridge or freezer; so he rang the Indian takeaway across the street and ordered Set Menu A for one. If nobody else was going to reward him for solving the mystery, he'd have to do it himself.

Highly spiced food doesn't sit well on a delicate stomach already fairly comprehensively knotted up with stress. At some point in the early hours, Chris woke up with a savage pain in his tummy. He rolled out of bed, being very careful not to disturb Karen, and scuttled for the toilet.

Heroism, he thought. A bit of gut-ache's enough to make me whimper like a baby. Chances of holding out under torture by razor-tusked fiends precisely nil.

Not a hope in hell of getting back to sleep. Chris slouched into the living room and sat on the sofa in the dark. What sort of measures, he couldn't help wondering, would Jill take to protect him, now that her life depended on it? Round-the-clock armed guards were out of the question, Karen wouldn't allow it: Day-Glo men in polo shirts cluttering up the furniture and making the rooms look untidy. He didn't pretend to know anything about anti-demon security, but of course, he didn't have to. Jill did, and he could rely on her—

The thought dropped into his mind like the apple clonking down on Newton's head. *Right*, it said. *If Jill's the one who is to come, Angela couldn't have been.* But she was a demon, the sunglasses proved that. So who the hell was she, and what—?

He squeaked, out loud. A *demon*; a murderous, inhuman killer, like the one that scragged poor Mr Newsome. And he'd been sharing his car with the bugger for *days*. Why? Three guesses. She'd been assigned to stay with him, waiting for him to let slip some clue that'd lead them to the one who was to come; and once he'd done that—

Chris's stomach lurched, and this time it had nothing to do with ghee and chilli powder. Presumably, then, it hadn't been an accident at all. Presumably, Jill's people had killed her.

Which was no bad thing, naturally, the only good demon and so forth; but even so. He thought of her wearing the InstaGlamour cream, annoying him half to death with her incessant bloody prattling, her eyes shining with excitement because she'd just shifted an outer of BB27Ks. Jill must've had her killed; he could pass that thought through his mind, make it sound like a chess move, white queen takes black knight, but he couldn't bring himself to face what it actually meant: that someone he knew was dead because someone else he knew had taken a conscious, cold-blooded decision.

Switzerland, Chris thought.

Or he could pretend it hadn't happened and go to work tomorrow and sell stuff to people in shops until it was time to come home. Both of them methods of running away, the latter having the merit of being cheaper and more convenient. Trouble was, he wasn't the running-away sort. Not because it was his duty to stand fast and see it through, whatever the hell it was, but because running away takes energy and causes disruption and fuss. He sighed. Pathetic.

Maybe I should just leave, though, he mused. Karen and me—

He thought about that, and about love, and the flat. There's no love here, he thought, just force of habit. We live here because we need somewhere to eat and sleep after a hard day's work; either one of us'd be pushed to cover the mortgage payments, but together we can more or less manage. That's about it, really. I think that maybe she did love me once; at school, probably, and a while after that, when I was still vaguely hoping that something might happen with Jill and me; and then Jill told me I was wasting my time – now we know why – and there I was, rebounding about like a pool ball, and Karen— But that was a long time ago. No kids, thank God, we're not even married, so no divorce; just sell the flat, pay off the mortgage and move on. Geneva, here I come.

No, all right, then. (Chris glanced at his watch; the glowing green dots told him it was three a.m. He could have guessed.

Wasn't three in the morning when most suicides happen?)
Won't do that. But if you're not prepared to sort out the mess,
at least stop whining about it.

All this and demons too. What a life.

Chris turned a few things over in his mind, and then thought
yes, that more or less covers everything, except for the hummingbird. What the hell is all that about, and where did it
come from? Whatever it was, it did appear to be on his side;
like SatNav.

SatNav: hadn't thought about her for a while. It'd been Jill
who'd warned him off her, and now Jill was revealed as an
unreliable witness, powered by her own agenda. In which case,
SatNav was in the clear and he could trust her, as he so very
much wanted to do. Except it hadn't been Jill, not to begin
with. They'd warned all the reps about them at the sales conference, and then Ben Jarrow had told him what happened if
you let them get under your skin; so it wasn't just Jill, and
besides, he had no reason to believe that she'd lied to him
about *everything*. On the other hand: princess of the Fey, pig-
gybacking into his head on a piece of music, like a computer
worm in an e-mail—

Chris sat up. SatNav had told him she was fighting for the
one who was to come; helping her, on her team. So if that was
true then presumably SatNav and Jill at least knew each other.
Jill, on the other hand, had told him SatNav was a rogue,
deranged, out to get him; she'd had SatNav taken away and
locked up in a secure place, she'd been really stressed out when
SatNav had escaped. Was all that an act, and if so, why? And
SatNav hadn't been exactly positive about Jill, either. A blind,
to keep him from guessing the truth?

He could feel a headache coming on. All too difficult, he
told himself. Also, none of my business, not any more. His
friendship with Jill was effectively over, SatNav was now just an
empty box, Angela was dead, it was *finished*, so why drive himself crazy worrying about it? Pretend it never happened and
carry on with his life. Simple as that.

Chris swung his feet up onto the sofa, dragged a cushion under his head and closed his eyes; I *will* go to sleep, I *will* go to sleep. He forced a dozen sheep into existence and compelled them to jump over a drystone wall. He was wide awake. He—

A demon claw was stroking the lobe of his ear.

Chris's eyes opened. He knew it was a demon, because in dreams intuition really works, but she didn't look like the others. She was dark-haired and fair-skinned, with soft mauve eyes and a long, delicately-shaped face, not just pretty but beautiful; she had little silver ear-studs shaped like butterflies, and a nice tusk-free smile.

'We apologise,' she said, 'for any inconvenience.'

Chris stared at her, then said, 'You woke me up.'

'No,' she said.

Well, of course. Different dimensions, different sides of the line. Falling asleep back home meant waking up here, just as terrifyingly hideous at home was disarmingly lovely here. He wondered vaguely if it was the same with, for example, good and evil.

'You put me to sleep,' he corrected himself.

'Yes.'

'Thanks,' Chris said. 'I was having trouble dropping off.'

'Our pleasure,' the demon said. Behind her, the room he'd just fallen asleep in; or rather, it was as though someone had drained all the colours out, leaving just plain black and white outlines, and then coloured them in again in different shades, presumably using the demonic equivalent of Microsoft Paint. In which case; he was interested to discover that pale Wedgwood blue was the opposite of what Karen liked to call peach but which he'd always thought of as slightly-off-tara-masalata. Well. You learn something new every day.

'Am I in trouble?' he asked.

She giggled. 'Do you really want me to answer that?'

'Are you going to kill me?'

She looked mildly offended. 'I'll pretend I didn't hear that.'

'But I'm in trouble,' he persisted.

'You bet,' she replied. 'Quite apart from the whole triangle thing with your girlfriend and your female best friend, there's the fact that you're bored with your job and not really trying, which means that when your boss finds he needs to cut costs in about nine months' time, you're definitely in the cross-hairs for the sack. Also, you eat far too many pizzas and kebabs and rubbish and you don't take any exercise, so you're just asking for trouble on that front. Also, in eight years' time you'll be forty, and your hair's just about to start getting thin on top. Sorry, but I wouldn't be you for a million pounds.'

Chris sighed. 'Apart from that.'

'You don't think that's enough to be going on with?'

'Apart from real-life trouble,' he explained.

'Oh, I see. You mean, why am I here and what are you going to do to me? Got you. Sorry, but we're not used to the way your lot think. It's sort of squiggly. Not straight lines. Also, a bit like icebergs, nine-tenths hidden. It's amazing you can live like that. And that's without the stuff.'

'Stuff?'

She nodded vigorously. 'The stuff. The things. Material objects, possessions. Good heavens, if we had to contend with all that we wouldn't be able to cope for five minutes. Take furniture, for instance. Or electronics. How do you people do it?'

Chris blinked. 'I don't know,' he admitted. 'Just sort of comes naturally, I guess.'

'Amazing.' She did look genuinely impressed. 'We simply can't begin to understand. From our perspective, it's insane. For one thing, you only live, what, ninety years; but you cheerfully trade a huge slice of that in return for *things*. And the way you go about it, this concept of *work* – spending the majority of your waking hours doing things you don't like doing and mostly don't even understand, as an incredibly roundabout way of getting food – and don't get me started on food and eating, that's just plain weird – and all this *stuff*. Completely beyond us, really, we can't begin to understand. I mean, on our side of the line, inanimate objects don't even *exist*.'

She's very strange, Chris thought, but curiously nice. 'Are you really a demon?'

'Of course we are, silly. Don't you recognise us? Well, no, we guess you wouldn't, would you?'

'We've met before.'

'Oh yes. In that car park.'

'What, the Ettingate Retail—?'

She winced. 'Please don't use *names*,' she said, and it was as though he'd just lit a cigarette in the middle of a busy restaurant. 'You weren't to know, of course, but we don't have them here. They're bad for us, they – pin us down.' She looked very unhappy. 'So, if you wouldn't mind.'

'Sorry,' he said.

'That's quite all right.'

Chris couldn't resist. 'Is that really true?' he asked. 'Things don't exist here?'

She smiled indulgently. 'Perfectly true.'

'But that's – I mean, what am I sitting on, if there's no sofas or chairs?'

She laughed. 'You have no weight to support,' she replied. 'That's why we had to borrow your own surroundings. It's only here so you won't feel uncomfortable.'

'Oh' was the only possible reply to that, followed by an awkward silence, during which she looked at him; not menacingly, or hungrily; curiously, if anything, in the way he'd seen crowds of Indian village children in documentaries happily staring at the camera.

'Everything's different here, isn't it?' he said.

She smiled. 'You could say that,' she replied. 'Also, of course, the same. Like in a mirror, we suppose you could say – the same but round the other way. But that's so simplistic it's actively misleading.'

'Ah, right.' Chris tried to get his head around that, failed, and asked, 'What am I doing here?'

'We want to ask you a question. Also, to explain.'

My God, he thought; the E word. 'OK,' he said. 'And then?'

'You can go home again.'

'You're not going to—?'

'No.' She moved slightly. 'Can we get you anything, by the way? Coffee taste? Tea sensation? The illusion of a doughnut?'

'No, thanks, I'm fine.' He hesitated, then went on: 'You said something about explaining.'

'What? Oh yes, so we did. Sorry. Sidetracked.' She settled herself comfortably on a footstool (he hadn't got one but had always wanted one; Karen wouldn't let him have one, because it'd have been clutter). 'Where would you like us to start?'

Good question; to which *at the beginning* probably wouldn't count as an acceptable answer; either that, or he'd get a whole lot of guff about the Big Bang. 'What exactly do you people want from me?'

She looked at him, with her head slightly on one side. 'We want to know where we can find the one who is to come,' she said.

'So you can stop her?'

'No.' Made it sound like he'd said something crazy, or stupid. 'No, of course not. So we can bring her home, of course.'

'Ah,' Chris said. 'So you're the good guys. I mean, the ones who don't hold with the traditional ways.'

She gave him a puzzled frown. 'Sorry,' she said, 'we don't understand.'

'Someone told me—' He stopped, tried to pull himself together. 'Isn't it the case that there are some of you who don't want to kill my lot any more, and they'd rather try and find a way of harvesting our emotions without us even knowing? To prevent an all-out war?'

He'd lost her. 'Who told you that?'

'Sa—' He stopped, unsure whether it'd count as a name. 'My satellite navigation device,' he said. 'Only really, she's a princess of the Fey. At least,' he added rather desperately, because she was giving him ever such a funny look, 'that's what she told me she was.'

'Well, she's quite right,' she replied. 'Partly, anyhow. Actually, she's about six hundred years behind the times, but the Fey are a bit like that, not so hot on linear time. No, there was a—' She paused, then said, 'Don't know whether you'd call it a lively debate or a civil war. Anyhow, it was hundreds of years ago, and what I suppose you'd call the good guys won. Which is why there's only a handful of demon attacks a year your side, of course, carried out by the tiny minority who refused to give up the old ways. The vast majority of us live off sustainable emotion, like you just said.'

Well, that did make a kind of sense, Chris supposed; but it wasn't what SatNav had said; and it didn't really fit well with Jill's reaction, either. 'All right,' he said. 'Let's say for argument's sake I believe you. So, who's this one-who-is-to-come person?'

She pulled a sad face. 'Just one of us,' she said. 'Originally she was the leader of the traditionalist faction. When they lost the debate, she went off to your side of the line in a huff, and I'm afraid the rest of us said that if that was how she felt, she might as well stay there and not bother coming back. But since then we've changed our minds; there's no point keeping the old wounds open, it's just divisive and spoils everything, so we're looking for her to tell her it's all right to come home. That's all it is, really. But we're a very tightly knit community. It's probably hard for you to understand how much we mean to each other, because – no offence – your lot sometimes seem like they care as much or more about stuff than about people. It's not like that here. We're all we've got. So, naturally, one of us going into self-imposed exile is quite a big deal. Also, we have an idea that she either doesn't know or doesn't believe that we want her to come home.'

Bullshit, Chris thought; but he looked at her, and he found it pretty well impossible to believe that she was lying. All right, sucker for a pretty face, fair enough, and surely by now he'd learned not to trust the uncorroborated evidence of his eyes in any case. It wasn't like that, though. Either she was one hell of an actress, or—

'I'm sorry,' he said, 'but I don't believe you.'

Grin. 'Thought you mightn't. All right, then, look at it this way. If our people really did have to kill in order to get what they needed the murder rate on your side would be so colossal that no government would be able to keep a lid on it. I don't know if you're aware of it, but there's close on a thousand of us. We'd be having to slaughter two and a half thousand of you every week just to keep soul together. And your people would notice that, now wouldn't they?'

Nastily valid point she'd got there, and it echoed what Chris had thought when she'd first claimed to be one of the nice demons. He could almost believe he was convinced—

'You think I know where she is, right? This—'

'The one who is to come. That's right.'

'Well, I'm sorry to disappoint you, but I haven't the faintest idea. I don't know who she is, so how could I possibly—?'

'Yes, you do.'

Said quietly, pleasantly; statement of a fact so obvious it hardly counted as a contradiction. She smiled at him.

'No, I *don't*,' he said irritably, raising the aggravation level to mask the guilt that came with the lie. 'If I knew, I'd tell you, now that you've explained. But—'

'We can smell her on you,' she said.

Oh. He'd been right about that, then. 'Can you?'

'Oh yes.' Friendly nod. 'That's why we've been following you, trying to have a quiet word with you, only you wouldn't—'

'A quiet word,' Chris repeated, and this time the anger wasn't synthetic at all. 'You call what you did to me at the Et— at the car park place a quiet word, do you?'

A sad look. 'We're really sorry about that,' she said. 'We misjudged you. We thought you were weak and cowardly, and that the easiest thing to do would be to scare it out of you.

It was a really stupid thing to do, and we apologise unreservedly.'

Um, he thought. Can't say fairer than that. On the other hand, if SatNav hadn't come along when she did and cut the seat belt – 'You were going to kill me,' he said.

'We made threats, to scare you. We're sorry.'

'You were going to kill me,' he went on, 'because I'd told you I didn't know where she was, and you *believed* me. You could see I was telling the truth. So why the hell are you still bugging me now?'

'We did believe you, yes. We were wrong.'

'So you're saying I'm a liar?'

She shook her head, clearly in great distress. 'No, it's not like that. You see, we know you've been in contact with her, there's absolutely no way we could be wrong about that, but obviously you don't realise who or what she is. And why should you, after all? As far as we can tell, you're not the sort of person who ought to be involved at all. It must just be sheer accident. I know it sounds screwy—'

'Actually,' Chris said quietly, 'the same idea had occurred to me.'

'Well, there you are. It's really unfortunate, and we do sincerely, genuinely apologise for the inconvenience, but you've got to see it from our point of view, you're the only lead we've got, and the thought that one of our people is over on your side of the line, alone, frightened – We've got no choice, we're sure you can see that. Will you help us? Please?'

Something new here, and he didn't think he was going to like it. 'I just told you, I can't.'

'Yes, you *can*.' She was looking Chris straight in the eye, her lovely face shining with hope. 'It'd only take a minute, we promise it won't hurt or do you any harm, and it'd mean so much to us. Of course we'll understand if you say no, but we're sure that now you understand, you'll want to help us. Go on, *please*.'

Jesus, he thought. They terrify you, chase you, kidnap you, flush you down bogs, get at you in your sleep and then they ask you nicely. The ruthlessness of the CIA, the persistence of a Jehovah's Witness, the face of an angel and the dumb charm of a cocker spaniel. *Help*, he tried to say, but his mouth refused.

'Please?'

'What would it involve?' he croaked. 'In, um, layman's terms.'

'Oh, nothing to it,' she said quickly. 'We just make a tiny little hole in your head and take a peep inside your brain. It doesn't hurt, it's the sort of thing your doctors do every day, except they stick horrid bits of sharp metal in you and we just look.'

'Just look.'

Confident nod. 'A hundred per cent non-invasive. And of course we'll be doing it on your side of the line, so you'll be asleep the whole time and won't feel a thing.'

Not sure about that. 'What about this side of the—?'

'Silly,' she said, smiling. 'This side you haven't got a body, have you? So, no body, no nasty old nerves and synapses to feel pain *with*. It'll be just like having a bright light shone on you.'

Chris kept still and quiet for three seconds or so. Then he said: 'If that's all there is to it, drill a little hole and take a look, why are you asking me? Why haven't you just held me down and got on and done it?'

A look of horror crossed her face. 'Without your permission? We couldn't do that, it'd be – well, we just couldn't, that's all.'

'You don't seem so very fussed about killing people.'

'Yes, we *are*.' Any minute now, she'll burst into tears; only without the water, presumably. 'I told you, it's just a very few of us, the ones who cling to the old ways. And we want to stop that. It's why we want to bring them home, re-educate them, make them understand that it's wrong. That's why we need your help, don't you see that? You won't just be helping us, you'll be saving the lives of your people as well. Because if we can bring home the one who is to come, the leader of the stick-in-the-mud traditionalists, it'll be a message to all the rest of them that there *is* another way and it *can* work—'

'No.' Chris had tried to keep the fear out of his voice, but it would insist on showing itself. If they got inside his head and saw what he knew, about Jill being the one they were looking for . . . the demon woman had to be lying, because he *knew* the one-who-is-to-come was Jill, just as he knew she couldn't be the leader of the killing-people-is-OK faction. What the hell was he thinking about, even listening to this creature? 'No, sorry, can't be done. Wish I could help but I've got this morbid fear of needles, daren't even have flu jabs, that's why I never go away on holiday, scared stiff of the inoculations. Besides, you're completely wrong, I have no idea who this person is you're looking for, I can promise you that. And drilling holes in my head isn't going to change that, so you'd better forget all about it, all right? And now I think I'd like to wake up, please.'

He said, hopefully; but nothing happened. The demon woman hadn't moved, she wasn't crouching to pounce or anything, but she didn't need to. It wasn't as though he could jump out of a window and run for it, not in a place where windows weren't even *real*. Might as well try and walk home from the Moon.

She was looking at him very keenly. 'Are you being completely honest with us?' she said.

It's relatively easy to pass off fear as anger. 'You're doing it again,' Chris shouted. 'You're calling me a liar.'

She shrugged apologetically. 'Well, yes,' she said.

'Tough. What're you going to do about it?'

Now she looked really, really sad. 'We could try appealing to your better nature.'

'Haven't got one. Now for crying out loud, someone *wake me up!*'

She shook her head. 'We can't do that. We can put you to sleep, but not the other way round. It's like you can jump off a cliff, but you can't fly back up again.' She paused, then added quietly, 'You could wake up if you really wanted to.'

'No, I—'

'If you really don't believe us, you'd wake up,' she went on. 'We think you're protecting someone – at least, that's how you see it, you think she needs to be protected from us, but it's not like that, honest. You know you can trust us, that's why you can't make yourself wake up; it's a basic defence mechanism, to defend humans from the Fey, but it only works if you know you're really in danger. And you're not. Are you?'

Chris closed his eyes, but it didn't make any difference; he could see just as well with them shut. 'All right,' he said. 'Prove you're the nice guys. Prove it by letting me go.'

A smile. 'We can't. Haven't you been listening? We can't wake you up, you've got to do it yourself.'

Was it his imagination, or had she come closer? He hadn't seen her move, but she was bigger, somehow, filling more of his field of view.

'Is it the drilling a hole that's bothering you?' she said. 'Because there's another way of doing it.' She drew the tip of her pink tongue across her top lip. 'It takes longer, but it doesn't hurt. Quite the reverse, actually. I'd have suggested it earlier, but I didn't want you getting the wrong idea about us.'

Definitely closer; and something about the light was having a soft-filter effect. It wasn't InstaGlamour cream that Angela had been using, he realised; it was just something these creatures could do, at will, like wiggling their ears. Chris turned his head and looked away, but that didn't make any difference, either; she was there, just as close or closer, her lips slightly parted, just like in the films. 'Just one little kiss,' she was murmuring, 'now that's not going to kill you, is it?'

Try to think of something else. Work; think about filling out travel-expenses claims. Think about stock numbers, returns vouchers, VAT invoices, green slips and yellow slips and blue slips and there's many a slip between cup and—

'It works both ways,' she was saying. 'We can see inside your head and you can see inside ours, and then you'll know we're telling the truth. We wouldn't say that if we were lying, would we? After all, isn't that what a kiss should be all about: a meeting of minds, a melding of souls?'

And coffee breath, and spit, and teeth banging together. 'I really do want to wake up now,' he whispered, as her mouth opened and came towards him like the ramp of the Cross-Channel ferry—

There was a hummingbird; and the beating of its wings made a whirring noise, a whirring sort of hammering noise, like the sound of an alarm going off. But that was no good, he told himself, because I'm not in the bedroom, I'm asleep on the sofa, so there's no alarm to save me, so it must just be the beating of my heart, or something equally useless. He felt his own mouth relax, and start to pucker—

'Ow!' he squealed. 'What did you do that for?'

Chris's eyes opened. His cheek was stinging. Karen was standing over him, white with rage.

'You hit me,' he said.

'Yes,' she said, and hit him again, this time with a bit more wrist to it.

'For God's sake,' he protested, jumping up and shrinking away. 'What the hell are you hitting me for?'

'You were talking in your sleep.' Her voice was low and quiet, the sound of concentrated fury. 'And making little sighing noises. And puckering up. And—'

This time he managed to grab a cushion to use as a shield. 'Was I?' he said. 'I don't—'

'Yes, you bloody well do,' Karen barked at him. ' I saw you, you bastard. Oh, and while we're on the subject.' She raised her hand, taking careful aim, and he tightened his grip on the corner of the cushion. 'Just who exactly is Angela?'

CHAPTER ELEVEN

It was one of those meltdown moments. Karen was scowling furiously; their relationship was in the crusher, waiting for the big steel ram to drop; unless Chris found exactly the right form of words, delivered in precisely the right tone of voice, it'd all be over apart from arguing about whose aunt had given them the round white formica-topped table in the kitchen. He blinked, took a deep breath, and noticed something.

'Are those new earrings?' he said.

At least he had the satisfaction of stopping her dead in her tracks. 'What?'

'Those earrings,' he said. 'I don't think I've seen you wearing them before.'

She opened her mouth, but nothing came out; it was as though someone had pressed the mute button, followed by pause.

'They're nice,' Chris said. 'I like them.'

Three, maybe four seconds before she answered. 'I got them in Debenhams,' she said.

It was the way she said it. A hundred and eighty degrees from her previous tone. *Defensive*. Which was all to the good, in the short-term tactical sense, but that was no longer the most important issue. He needed to know—

'Recently?' he asked.

'About three weeks ago,' Karen replied; then she rallied (but it was more desperation than aggression) and repeated, 'Who's Angela?'

'Oh, her,' he replied, with a sad grimace. 'Girl at work. She got killed.'

'Killed?'

Chris nodded. 'Rather a nasty accident, apparently. I was having a nightmare about it, actually, don't know why. Freud would know.'

'You never told me—'

His chance for a big, nasty smile. 'Well, you're never here to tell, are you? Oh, I know,' he went on, pushing his luck like a bobsleigh crew trying for a fast launch, 'you're so busy at work these days, it's all very important and you've got your career to think about. And I understand, I do really. It's just . . .' He couldn't think of anything suitably sensitive to say, so he sensibly left it at three wistfully trailing dots.

'It's just while we've got this big promotion on,' she said, double-defensive – nice to see someone else fighting a losing battle on two fronts for a change, Chris thought smugly. I'd have done it better, but I've had so much more practice. 'As soon as it's finished, I promise, we'll have loads more time—'

'Yes, well.' A turn of phrase and tone of voice cribbed directly from Karen, but she didn't seem to have noticed. She was more concerned with trying to claw her hair unobtrusively over her ears, to hide the earrings. Which reminded him; he had more important things on his mind than point-scoring. 'Kingfishers, aren't they?'

'What?'

Chris smiled. 'Your earrings.'

'What? Oh, yes, right. I bought them to go with the blue top I got in Monsoon, but they're not quite right, which is why I haven't worn them before. Still, if you like them—'

Liar, he thought, and had to make an effort not to grin. Not kingfishers. Similar, but not. 'Very much,' he said. 'They remind me of something, but I can't quite remember—'

'God, is that the time? Got to go.' Karen leaned forward, darted a peck at him, and fled, slamming the front door behind her. Chris sat down, his chin in his hands, and thought; just when I was sure it couldn't get any weirder.

Because, yes, now he came to think of it, the girl in the dream, the nice demon who'd tried to kiss him, *had* been Angela, in a sort of a way. And Karen's earrings hadn't been kingfishers. They'd been hummingbirds.

First things first. Chris phoned the office, explained that he was dying of cholera, foot and mouth disease and bubonic plague, and therefore wouldn't be able to make his rounds today, so could someone please ring round and reschedule. How long was he planning on being dead for, they asked. Permanently, he replied; but he'd undoubtedly be reincarnated as a sales rep either tomorrow or the day after, so he'd be able to catch up early next week . . .

Next. He made himself a cup of ultra-strong black coffee, sat down in the armchair, and tried to think.

He thought: the one who is to come. Annoying phrase, needlessly mystical; but he was going to have to deal with it sooner or later, if he didn't want this shambles to continue indefinitely.

He thought about Jill; and yes, she'd have done quite well, because she *did* feed off other people's emotions, she'd done it as long as he'd known her. Or Angela: assigned to him for no genuinely good reason, and the fuss had only started when she came on the scene; and how about the way she'd transformed herself from silent, miserable adolescent to bouncy charm-dispenser, thereby stirring up a whole shopping-trolley of emotions right across the Midlands?

Jill had even admitted it—

Just suppose, Chris said to himself, that they're both lying. Just suppose, for instance, that it was the real Angela, not a demonically crafted replica, who'd lured him to the Ettingate

Retail Park, in her own personal Suzuki jeep, in whose seat belt the marks of his fingernails were still visible shortly thereafter? Which was more or less what the nice demon had confessed, half an hour ago in this very room. In which case, she was one of the demons hunting the one who is to come; but were they the baddies, as SatNav had told him, or what they themselves claimed to be, the enlightened liberal reformed tendency?

And who'd suborned Honest John to flush him down the toilet?

Jill as an undercover one-who-is-to-come hunter made a degree of sense, too. What better way to do her job than to infiltrate the humans' demon-hunting agency at the highest level? But the evidence for her being a demon at all turned on her emotional-vampire status; which surely argued that she was a dissident, rather than a fundamentalist (if he believed SatNav's version rather than the demons' own).

Weymouth, now; quite possibly his closest shave yet, though there wasn't a lot in it. He'd assumed, of course, that the demon he'd seen there had been disguised as Karen, the same way the Ettingate attacker had been disguised as Angela. That, however, wasn't a rock-solid analogy any more, because if the Ettingate Angela had been the real thing, then what reason did he have to believe that Weymouth Karen was a replica; or that demons could actually do the shape-shifting thing at all—?

Oh, come on, Chris thought. They can't *all* be demons, can they?

Don't answer that, he thought. Instead, let's go back to the time between Ettingate and Honest John's. At Ettingate he'd told the demon that he hadn't a clue about the one who is to come, and *she'd believed him*. Fine. There, logic demanded, the matter should've rested. So why, shortly afterwards, should demonkind have made another attempt to snatch him, presumably to ask him the same question all over again?

Chris made a genuine effort to think about that one, but the thought of Honest John's attempt to pitch him down the toilet kept diverting him onto the subject of hummingbirds, which was somewhere he simply didn't have the energy to go. He was just starting to feel the onset of a really nasty caffeine migraine when a flash of light dazzled his mind's eye, and—

Gandhi; now he came to think of it, blindingly obvious. Non-violent resistance, a turning of the back on the vicious cycle of bloodshed and reprisal; the martyr hounded and persecuted for the noble cause; Gandhi was just the *Book*'s infuriatingly allusive way of drawing his attention to the one who is to come. Well, fine. Glad to have got that out of the way, but really no further forward at all, and about par for the course as far as the *Book*'s usefulness was concerned.

Which left him with probably the biggest and most inscrutable weirdness of the lot, namely SatNav, *soi-disant* princess of the Fey; completely and utterly reliable if you wanted to get from Stirchley to Walsall without getting bunged up in the rush-hour traffic, but not necessarily to be trusted implicitly on other subjects. True, he had reason to doubt what Jill had told him, but he had other, more reliable witnesses who said the same as she did, and all that stuff about the Fey and dreams and music—

I'm missing the point, Chris told himself. There's something else I'm not even considering, and it's the key to everything. Something *simple*—

'It shouldn't have to be me,' he said aloud. 'Sod it, what did *I* do?'

He made an effort to pull himself together. Come along now, he said to himself, you've taken a day off work to get all this stuff sorted out, you'd better get a move on. Now, where to start?

It was like those join-the-dots puzzles, when he was a kid; people gave him books full of them, because children really enjoyed them, it challenged their young minds and meant they'd grow up to be astrophysicists. He'd hated them, of course. His was a mind that hated challenges of any kind – which socks shall I wear today, which channel shall I watch? – and he contemplated the vast, sprawling nature of the problem and despaired. Never was any good at unravelling bits of tangled string, either.

Fine, he thought.

There are two ways of solving a mystery. Either you start off by examining all the evidence, evaluating it carefully, winnowing the fallacies from the things that were capable of being scientifically proved, then sorting the facts into a rational hypothesis which you then test by experiment and dialectic enquiry to arrive at the truth; or, you ask somebody.

Chris picked up the phone, dialled, waited, gave a name, waited some more, and then said: 'Jill? What the *fuck* is going on?'

There were ducks, of course. There had to be. Probably wouldn't be valid without ducks. Ask John le Carré or one of those people.

Jill, who'd obviously done this sort of thing loads of times before, had brought stale bread to feed them with. She tore a finger-and-thumb pinch out of the heart of the loaf and threw it into the water, which immediately churned and frothed into a seething, duck-crammed maelstrom.

'I told you,' she said. 'You're absolutely right. It's me.'

Chris looked at the ducks, not at her. 'You wouldn't lie to me, would you?'

'No, never. For crying out loud, Chris, we've known each other since we were tiny tots. And when have I ever—?'

'Loads of times,' he snapped.

'Balls. Name one time I've lied to you.'

'Right.' He took a deep breath. 'There was the time I really fancied Amanda Mizzen, and I asked you if you thought she liked me, and you said—'

'I was trying to be nice.'

'You lied, though,' he said. 'You said yeah, go for it. And look what happened. She poured warm custard in the pocket of my blazer.'

Jill nodded. 'True. But strictly speaking, I didn't lie to you,

I gave you advice. Bad advice,' she added quickly, 'I grant you that. But I never actually said yes, she fancies you rotten, she told me so herself. Now did I?'

Chris frowned. 'All right, then,' he said. 'What about the time when—?'

'Let me rephrase that,' Jill interrupted briskly. 'When have I ever lied to you about something not utterly trivial and unimportant?'

He thought for a moment, then said: 'Fair enough. But there's always a first time.'

'Meaning?'

'Meaning,' he said, with a sudden spurt of anger, 'you might have bloody well told me.'

'Told you what?'

'That you're a—' He didn't want to say it; it'd sound *silly*. 'That you're not strictly human.'

'That.' She shrugged. 'You never asked.'

'Jill—'

'All right, all right.' She raised a defensive hand. 'Well, for one thing, you'd never have believed me. Now would you?'

'Maybe I would've,' Chris lied defiantly. 'If you'd, I don't know, proved it somehow.'

'Yeah, sure.' She gave him a little frown. 'Besides, I think you ought to consider it from my point of view. I've never been – well, comfortable about it. There's some things you don't tell anybody, even your very best friends. Aren't there?'

'No.'

'Really?' Jill grinned suddenly. 'Like, you never told me about Pongo.'

'No, of course— Hold on,' he said angrily, 'how the hell do you know about that?'

Her grin broadened. 'Pongo was your cuddly stuffed rhino,' she said. 'He slept on your pillow till you were fourteen, and you couldn't go to sleep unless he was there. Bless,' she added vindictively.

'That's different,' he said. 'That was, well, private.'

'And being a non-human with carnivorous tendencies wasn't?' The grin turned into a smile, but there were still loads of teeth in it. 'Just a hint of double standards creeping in here, don't you think?'

'Pongo wasn't important,' Chris replied sullenly. 'I mean, he wasn't going to suddenly jump up and start savaging people with his razor-sharp fangs, was he? And you haven't answered my question. How did you know?'

Jill shrugged. 'Saw him in your eyes,' she replied. 'It's a knack we've got. Sometimes, if you look closely, you can see a reflection there. Anyhow, that's beside the point. I never told you because it was private. And, naturally, I was afraid it'd spoil everything. With you lot. My friends. Well, it would've done, wouldn't it?'

Chris scowled. 'Not unreasonably,' he said. 'I mean, all the while we thought you *liked* us, and really you were just *feeding*—'

She threw another handful of bread shrapnel into the heart of the duckstorm. 'Yes,' she said. 'That's what friends do. They nourish each other. It's what friendship *is*.'

One duck was treading on another duck's head, trying to get at a chunk of stale crust. Presumably they were friends too. 'Maybe,' he said, in a rather strained voice, 'you were taking that idea a bit to extremes.'

'Not really,' Jill replied briskly. 'Friends supply each others' needs, and in return, they give back. I got what I needed, and in return I was always there, for all of you. Don't say it hasn't been a great help over the years.'

'Yes, but—'

'It *has*,' she said fiercely. 'You know it has. All through the difficult times, the living hell of human adolescence, I was there looking after you all, listening, nodding, making little sympathetic noises. Talk about a shoulder to cry on; if I'd been human, I'd have caught pneumonia.'

'You were lapping it up,' Chris snapped back. 'Literally.'

She was still and quiet for a moment; then she shrugged. 'All right, so I wasn't completely selfless and altruistic. You were all still my friends. I—' She frowned, then added. 'I *liked* you. Really. You have no idea what that was like, for one of my lot. We don't do that, you see. We don't *like*. We don't like, the way you humans don't walk through walls. It's not that we don't want to, it's just that we can't. But suddenly I found out that I could, and it was – well, nice. That's when I decided there had to be a better way.'

He looked at her. Deep in his head, his inner Poirot was waving and pointing at something, but he took no notice. 'Is that right?' he said.

'Yes.'

'Fine. In that case, tell me exactly what happened, that time in the girls' toilets.'

For a long time, Jill didn't move or speak. Then she tore up the remaining bread into little bits. 'Watch this,' she said, and threw the bread into the water. The ducks didn't move. The bits of bread floated for a few seconds until they grew water-logged and sank.

'I can do that,' she said. 'I can control other living things, up to a point. Either because they're very stupid, like ducks or rugby players, or because they aren't aware that I'm doing it. I can do it, but I don't. It'd be cheating.'

Chris thought for a moment, then said: 'I've only got your word for that.'

'Yes, but I never lie to you.'

He nodded. 'So,' he said. 'What really happened?'

To begin with (Jill said), I wasn't the – what did you call it? The one who is to come. Did you think of that all by yourself, or—? No, I thought not.

No, that wasn't me. Quite the opposite. Actually, allow me to introduce myself. My number is 666A, and I – well, I used to be a vice-marshal of the diabolic host. Sounds impressive, but actually it's kind of somewhere between postmaster general and president of the War Graves Commission. And that was

OK; I was a career civil servant, working my way gradually up the ladder, the way you do. Pretty much like I'm doing now, in fact. Like we say, you can take the demon out of the office, but you can never take the office out of the demon. Anyway, that was me.

And one day I got called in and was told they wanted someone for a long-term undercover mission: to find the dissident leader and, well, take her out. Not really my cup of sulphur, but they dropped some heavy hints about promotion and doing my career a lot of good, so I said yes, please, when do I start? And the next thing I knew, I was being born.

It was hell being brought up as a human. I knew that the most important thing was not blowing my cover; as in, grabbing hold of the first human I saw and tearing its head off just so I could taste the rich, creamy fear. That would've ruined everything, they told me, and I wasn't to do it. Which was fine; but it meant that all the years I was growing up, I was starving hungry all the bloody time. Absolutely famished, like being on one of those diets where all you get all day is one glass of carrot juice and a stick of celery. The only way I could keep going was by constantly having rows and tantrums with my parents—

Yes, that's right. They haven't spoken to me for years, and I can't say I blame them. Happiest day of their lives when I left home, and the last I heard of them they were crossing the Nullarbor Desert in a camper van. I feel sorry for them now. I can't have been very nice to live with.

I knew my people had put me in the right place at the right time; all I had to do was wait till the dissident leader showed up, and I'd know her right away. For a start, she'd be one of us, so she'd stick out like the proverbial sore talon. Soon as I located her I was to zoom in, do the job and then I could bug out and come home. I couldn't wait.

And then, at the start of the summer term in year twelve, there was that new girl; you remember . . .

'Actually,' Chris said, 'there were two new girls. There was—'
'Don't interrupt,' Jill said.

There was that new girl, and as soon as I looked at her, I could
see she was one of us – my lot. A demon. That's got to be her,
I thought, thank God for that, I can do the job and go home.
Hooray, I thought.

What was her name? Ellie something. Like it matters; it was
an assumed name, obviously, and anyway, I've always hated
names – well, I guess you know why, by now. I've had to learn
to endure them, but each time I say one or hear one, it still
burns me, like putting your hand on a hot stove. Anyway, there
she was, and it was just a question of biding my time, choosing
the right moment, making the kill and getting out.

Easy enough, you would have thought. I could just have
walked up to her in the playground and bitten her head off –
God, I really wanted to do that after all those years of living off
emotional lettuce, finally the chance of a nice, juicy steak.
That's what I was expected to do, it's what my training was all
about, it's what I should've done. But – don't ask me why –
when it came to it, I just couldn't. Not like that, in plain view of
everybody. I guess I'd been around humans too long, I'd got soft
or gone native, something of that sort, I don't know. Maybe I'd
learned fear from the humans: it's not something that exists
back home, but once you're this side of the line it's terribly easy
to start believing in it. Whatever the reason, I didn't just crack
on and get it over and done with. I kept putting it off, making
excuses. Didn't want to draw attention, didn't want to cause an
incident, afraid there might be repercussions for other ex-pat
demons on the human side of the line.

All just excuses, naturally. But I didn't do it straight away,
and you know how it is. The longer you put off doing something, the harder it is to do it. I started getting memos, notes,
messages on my phone from the authorities back home. I was
quite clever about fobbing them off, but I knew I couldn't keep
it up for ever.

Eventually I realised I couldn't hold out any longer. I chose a day and said to myself, right, on this day, at eleven-fifteen precisely, I'll do it. And, as luck would have it, at eleven-fifteen precisely, Ellie whatever-her-name-was went into the girls' toilets, and I followed her. I didn't know my friend Karen was in there too; I definitely had no idea *you* were there. I went in, grabbed the stupid cow's hair and slashed her throat. Job done.

'You?'

Jill shrugged. 'Me,' she said. 'You got a problem with that?'

'Well,' Chris said slowly, 'Yes, I suppose I have. It was—'

'Justifiable homicide, as far as the authorities were concerned,' Jill said firmly. 'Quite possibly justifiable pesticide. At least, that's how it would've been seen back home, if only—'

She'd stopped talking. Chris waited for as long as he could bear, then repeated, 'If only—?'

If only (Jill continued) I'd killed the right demon. But I hadn't.

Well, quite. Didn't I ever feel stupid. As soon as the fuss was over and I could get somewhere private where I could report back, I called in and said, job done; and they said, no, sorry, you're wrong there, our scans clearly show the continued existence of the dissident ringleader. In other words, I'd killed the wrong person. By some amazing coincidence there was more than one undercover demon at our school, and I'd made a simple, basic, bloody stupid mistake.

You can imagine how I felt. No, scrub that. You can have absolutely no idea how I felt. I don't know which was worse, the excruciating guilt or the feeling of being a complete dickhead; they were both pretty bad, and as far as I was concerned, that was it. No more, I said to myself, I'm through with all that. Quite a big decision, as you'll appreciate. It meant I could never go back home, for one thing. Also, I'd betrayed everything I'd always believed in. Well, not quite that. What I'd mostly believed in was the importance of a good job with security and prospects. I'd screwed that up too, of course. I'd screwed up more or less everything. But no way was I going to go back out there and try again. My first thought was; make a clean break, change sides. Throw in my lot with the dissidents; that way, with there being a slim chance they might win the civil war, I had some kind of hope of going home one day. But that was a wash-out. I mean, the authorities were quite adamant that I'd killed the wrong demon, but the fact remains that immediately afterwards all traces of subversive and dissident activity stopped, just like that. I hadn't killed the dissident ringleader, but the effect was pretty much the same as if I had. We'd won.

Correction: there was still one dissident on the loose. Me. The thing is, you don't just tell the demon authorities where they can stick their job and then walk away whistling a show tune. As soon as they realised I wasn't planning on coming home, they put me on top of the most-wanted list. Also, I'd changed my mind, really and truly. I was absolutely appalled by what I'd done, actually. I thought, this simply can't be right, killing people, under any circumstances. It's all very well to talk about it when you're hovering safely in the insubstantial world, where there's no blood to spill or flesh to rip. Actually doing it is—

Anyway, I made my decision. I was converted. If demonkind's got a future, it's through non-violent, non-aggressive emotion-farming; and if the real dissident ringleader was too scared and too spineless to carry on simply because of one bungled assassination attempt, then I'd take over the job and do it myself. Which is what I've been doing, basically, ever since. That's why I joined Delendi Sunt, why I've worked so bloody hard to get where I am today; as soon as there's any sign of demons coming over here to feed, I send my people out and put a stop to it, and let me tell you, I've made a difference there, a real difference. I can sense when they're getting ready to come across, you see, which none of my predecessors could. Attacks down seventy-five per cent since I took over, and I make bloody sure my bosses know it. They like me a lot. But my standing orders to my field operatives is, bring 'em back alive, if they know what's good for them. I tell them it's so that the demons can be safely and humanely disposed of. What I actually do is put the fear of God into them and send them home again. They don't tend to come back after that.

'So you aren't her after all.'

Jill gave Chris her extra-special exasperated look. 'Haven't you been listening? Yes, I'm her. I'm the leader of the dissident movement, currently in exile on your side of the line. I'm the one they're trying to find, which is why they've been coming after you; because they can smell me on you. What's so difficult to understand about that?'

A token of how weird his life had been lately that Chris didn't react particularly to that last question. Instead, he said quietly; 'You aren't *her*, though. Well, are you?'

Jill trying to stay calm; an impressive sight, seen through binoculars. Close up, just plain scary. 'If you mean I'm not the one I was originally sent here to kill, yes, you're quite right. But she's disappeared, like I just told you. Nobody's heard so much as a twitter out of her for sixteen years. She doesn't matter any more.'

But Chris shook his head. 'If I've got this right,' he said, 'sixteen years is nothing to your lot. Time doesn't even work properly where you come from. You may have forgotten that, because you've been over here so long, but I don't suppose they see it that way.'

Sigh. 'Fine,' she said. 'Let's suppose for the sake of a completely pointless, time-wasting argument that you're right. In that case, why have they been wasting their valuable time and energy on you, when you're – no disrespect, you understand – when you're just some human who goes round selling junk to shops?'

He scowled as he answered: 'Maybe it's because I was at school with you. *Both* of you. Well, have you considered that?

It's a possibility. Maybe I do know where she is, like they keep telling me I do. Maybe—'

Chris stopped himself before he could go any further; because if the flash of intuition that had burned patterns on the insides of his eyelids happened to be right, sharing it with Jill – who'd come here from Over There on purpose to do murder and her duty – might not be the smartest move ever.

'Maybe what?'

I got them in Debenhams. 'Ignore me,' he mumbled. 'Thinking aloud.'

There was the strangest look on Jill's face. 'Thinking what?'

'Oh, nothing. Can't remember if I put the rubbish out this morning. Or is it the recycling today and the rubbish on Tuesdays?'

A duck waddled towards them with a determined look on its face. It got as far as the edge of Jill's shadow on the grass, turned smartly around and hurried back the way it had just come. 'I've never lied to you,' she said. 'You, though, I'm not so sure about.'

'What? I don't know what you mean.'

'Oh, cast your mind back,' Jill said, in a soft but distinctly corrosive voice. 'The last time we had a drink together. I left my bag in the pub, you took it on with you. There was a packet of biscuits—'

'*What?*' He stared at her. 'You're not still banging on about those bloody biscuits.'

Her eyes were cold and very sharp, like a needle in a syringe. 'Actually,' she said, 'yes, I am. You *sure* you didn't eat them?'

'Yes, of course I'm bloody sure. It's not what you'd call a grey area.'

'Fine. And Karen wouldn't have.'

'Karen doesn't approve of biscuits. If it was up to her, she'd have them all lined up against a wall and shot.'

Jill nodded slowly. 'I believe you,' she said. 'But if it wasn't you, and it wasn't her, and you haven't got a dog.' Her focus narrowed even further; he could feel the points of her eyes sticking through his skull. 'Someone or something ate them. Question is, who?'

Chris felt a strong urge to run away. Odd, but real. 'All right,' he said. 'Look, does it really matter?'

'*Yes.*' She'd spat the word at him; now she took a deep breath and calmed herself down. 'Actually, yes, it matters a lot. You see,' she went on, lowering her voice just a trifle, 'they weren't – well, ordinary biscuits.'

Needlessly surreal, Chris thought. 'Really.'

'No.' Jill breathed out heavily and looked away. 'They were bait.'

Bait? Oh, right. 'What, you mean, like rat poison or something?'

'You could say that.' She was looking at the ducks, which were scampering towards the water as fast as their feet could carry them. 'They were guilt biscuits.'

'Excuse me?'

'Guilt biscuits. Massively emotionally charged. You put them in someone's desk drawer when they're on a diet. Once they've been there a day or so, assuming they haven't been broken into, they're absolutely steeped in guilt, longing, self-loathing and greed. Of course,' she went on, 'the demon can't digest the actual flour and sugar and egg and stuff, so I expect that somewhere in your flat there's a big pile of crumbs, probably hidden away behind a sofa or something.' She turned her head and looked at him hard. 'You're absolutely sure Karen didn't eat them?'

She got them in Debenhams, Chris told himself, and they don't sell enchanted magical talismans, just like Halfords don't sell little dangly things that hang from your rear-view mirror and turn out to be powerful supernatural entities. 'I just told you, didn't I? Come on, think about it. When did Karen start at our school?'

Jill frowned. 'Same year as you and me.'

'Right,' he said firmly. 'So if she was the demon you were sent here to find, you'd have known all along. Damn it, how long have you known her? Surely if she was – well, one of your lot, you'd have known straight away, just one look at her. Like with the other girl, the one you—'

But Jill was shaking her head. 'Not necessarily,' she replied. 'It's not as straightforward as that.'

Chris winced inwardly. Why wasn't he surprised?

'A demon can take human shape,' she went on, 'like I did. But it's quite a performance. Basically, you've got to be born human. If you want the technical stuff: you enter into the embryo in the nineteenth week, assuming there's no complications. You displace the human, and there you stay until the human body dies. No, it's not very nice, but please don't pull faces at me, or I'll see to it you stick like that. Anyhow, a demon who's done that I can spot straight away, there's an aura, a sort of puke-coloured glow that I can see and you can't. But that's not the only way.'

'Ah.'

'Quite.' Jill nodded. 'In fact, it's very rare, because why the hell would one of us want to be one of you without a really good reason? The other way's far more usual.' She paused, rummaged in her carrier bag and took out a doughnut. 'Completely stale,' she said, 'but it's been sitting on a plate on my secretary's desk for four days. In human terms, it'd be Death By Chocolate with whipped cream and fudge sauce.' She took a savage bite out of the doughnut, and it seemed to restore her; she closed her eyes for a moment, breathed in deeply and out again, then spat her mouthful towards the ducks. They didn't move. 'A demon can piggyback on a human being,' she said, 'by means of a carrier. It's a bit like blowflies.' She stopped, burped, and went on, 'They lay their eggs in open wounds. Demons can do more or less the same thing, only of course the wounds need to be emotional rather than just physical.' Suddenly she grinned; the grin of a hungry man thinking about food. 'Only needs to be a scratch, so to speak, though it doesn't stay that way for long. A demon can burrow its way into a little niggle of resentment, and then it digs in, makes itself comfy, and the carrier ends up with full-bore paranoia. Same with all your basic strong emotions, provided there's something there to begin with that it can latch onto. And the trouble is,' she went on, 'a carrier's much, much harder to detect.'

'Ah.'

She nodded again. 'It's like an anchor,' she said. 'Or a, what's the word, one of those *Star Trek* things. A wormhole. The wound where the demon gets in is one end of the wormhole, and the other end's in a neutral dimension – let's not get bogged down in that, it's complicated and I know how much you struggled in physics at school, I don't want to fry your brain with contraCartesian coordinates and stuff like that. Just think of it as Somewhere Else. What you've got is a kind of *pied à terre*; like living in a big house in the country and having a little flat in London for when you want to go to the sales or see a show. The demon doesn't have to be there all the time – on this side, I mean – but whenever it wants to, it can just pop across and have somewhere to go. So, a person can walk around with a sort of demon holiday cottage planted in his head for years and years, and unless I happen to see the demon when it's there I wouldn't have a clue the person was a carrier; not without specialised equipment, at any rate.'

Chris thought about that. It made a horrible kind of sense. 'And you think *Karen*—'

Jill was looking carefully at him again. 'You were thinking the same thing,' she said. 'For different reasons, obviously. But don't you dare tell me the thought hadn't crossed your mind.'

He wanted to fight, but he was too tired. 'It was just a feeling, I don't know. Look, you're not going to – well, *do* anything, are you? Only—'

Jill laughed. 'You mean kill her, don't you? No, of course not. For one thing, I've told you about a million times, I've changed sides. If Karen really is carrying the dissident ringleader, I'll want to protect her, not kill her. Besides, you can take out the demon, if you're careful, without harming the human carrier; though some of our lot aren't inclined to put themselves out, if you follow me, especially if they're in a hurry. Look,' she said, and though she hadn't moved it was as though she'd just grabbed his wrist. 'I don't know if Karen's carrying a demon, or of she's involved at all. But if she is, and if the authorities back home are over here looking for the dissident ringleader – well, you've seen them for yourself, you must realise the danger you're in, both of you. You've got to let me help you,' she said harshly, 'and that means you've got to tell me *everything*. Do you understand?'

Chris wasn't looking at her. He was watching the ducks. Something about them wasn't right at all. They were sploshing about weakly, swimming in circles. He forced himself to remember; she got them in Debenhams, she'd told him so herself. All this stuff about blowfly eggs and wormholes was just—

'I'm not sure,' he whimpered (like he'd always said: pathetic). 'It's hard for me, it's all so—'

Jill's eyes were holes he could fall into if he wasn't very careful. 'You can't take my word for it,' she said. 'You've got to see for yourself. Right?'

He looked up. 'Is that possible?'

The way she laughed made him really wish he hadn't raised the subject in the first place. 'Oh, it's possible, all right. It's just not very nice. Still,' she added, as he started to say that that was fine, he'd cheerfully take her word for anything so long as she stopped looking at him like that (what great big eyes you've got, Grandma. All the better to eat you with), 'you want to be sure. I can fix that for you. Just hold my hand,' she said, and it was like he'd caught his fingers in a car door, 'and I'll take you there.'

'Are you sure it's no bother?' Chris said weakly. 'I really don't want to put you out.'

'No bother,' Jill said grimly as the sky came down on him like a boot on an ant and the sides of the world came rushing up to squash him. 'Just one thing, though.'

'Mm?'

'If you don't come back, can I have your Springsteen collection? It's not for me, you understand, it's for—'

He was falling.

Into her mind, yes; but he was also falling down a very real shaft with very real sides, and it was very familiar in a very real sense. *She flushed me down a bog*, Chris thought as he fell. *The bitch.*

He fell a bit further, and thought: Alternatively, at Honest John's, maybe he didn't flush me down an actual real toilet. Maybe he just wanted to take me on a tour of his brain. Mind like a sewer, ha ha.

He fell a lot further, and thought: so, if demons can't actually shape-shift at will like I've been assuming they can, then both Angela and Karen are—

He fell further still, and thought: assuming those specs that Frank Slade gave me actually do what he said they do. But hang on, though, Derek the Day-Glo person confirmed that, so it's probably true—

He fell even further, and thought: in which case, all these years I've been sleeping next to a demon. Yuck!

And a bit further, and: and not just sleeping, either. Oh shit.

Then he fell some more, and thought: that's if I'm prepared to accept everything Jill said at face value. Am I? Well, yes, she's Jill, and she's never lied to me.

And then it occurred to Chris (as he fell) that he was plummeting down an incredibly long shaft at a scarily fast speed, and unless the bottom of Jill's mind was lined with a deep stack of thick, bouncy mattresses he most likely wasn't going to survive; unless, of course, a hummingbird or something of the sort happened to fly up under his feet and—

No hummingbird, just more falling. Oh, he thought; and then, a little later, after some more falling, he amended that to Oh well.

(– Assuming, he thought, as the sides of the shaft whizzed past his nose, I really am inside Jill's mind and she didn't flush

East Atlanta Branch
404-730-5438
www.afpls.org

User name: LEDBETTER, DAVID SCOTT (MR)

Title: The invisible library
Author: Cogman, Genevieve
Item ID: R2003858624
Date due: 5/7/2019,23:59
Current time: 04/09/2019,16:48

Title: May contain traces of magic
Author: Holt, Tom, 1961-
Item ID: R0112664479
Date due: 5/7/2019,23:59
Current time: 04/09/2019,16:48

me down a very real toilet pretending I was inside her mind. But what the hell, he thought: if you start questioning every bloody assumption, you'll never get anywhere. Not that I'm anxious to arrive anywhere right now, not unless someone can lend me a parachute.)

Oh well, he thought again, and fell some more.

After he'd been falling for quite some time, Chris glanced at his watch. Then he fell some more. Then he looked at his watch again. Ten minutes later. Now that's just weird, he thought as he fell.

He thought: I can't remember the exact formula but surely, if I've been falling all this time, when eventually I do hit the bottom, instead of just going splat, I'm going to punch a hole like a lead bullet through a steel plate. Probably come out in Sydney, still accelerating. Pity I'll be dead, I always fancied seeing Australia—

– He thought, but didn't fall. He'd stopped.

When had that happened? He'd been so preoccupied thinking about the harbour bridge and the opera house and wherever it was they filmed the soaps that he hadn't actually noticed. But as soon as he was absolutely sure he wasn't falling any more, a sign lit up out of the shadows and told him:

You Are Here

OK, he thought; but he was painfully conscious of hanging upside down, blood rushing to his head, vision starting to blur, unfortunate shifting of other bodily fluids inside his already overtaxed plumbing. He'd be ever so much more comfortable if only he could be standing on his feet instead.

Chris didn't move, but the world did; at least, it came to rest under his feet and pressed reassuringly against the soles of his shoes. Much better, he thought, thanks. And then, because it couldn't do any harm to try, he said aloud, 'Excuse me, but where is this?'

There was someone standing next to him. 'Fancy meeting you here,' she said. 'No, don't look round. I mean, you can if you like, but it'd be much better if you didn't, for both of us.'

Just when I thought I had a tiny fragment of a clue, he sighed to himself.

'SatNav?' he said.

CHAPTER TWELVE

'Well, of course,' SatNav replied. 'You did ask where you were, didn't you?'

'Yes, but—'

'There you go, then. At the end of the tunnel, turn left.'

Chris tried closing his eyes and counting to ten, but only got as far as three. 'What are you doing here, SatNav?' he asked, in a sort of snarly whimper. 'This is Jill's mind, she doesn't even—'

'No, it's not.' She laughed; a silvery tinkling laugh, like a mountain stream. For two pins, he could've strangled her. 'This is *home*. Where I live.' And then she said, 'Thank you.'

The two words he'd been least expecting. He blinked, as though she'd just handed him a fish.

'Oh,' he said. 'Right.' And then, 'Why?'

She laughed. 'For setting me free, of course.'

Well, of course. Silly him for not guessing. 'Did I just do that?'

'*Yes.*' There was something in her voice, the loosing of a ferocious tension. It had dissipated entirely when she went on, 'Well, I'm here, aren't I? So, yes, I must be free. Thanks,' (tacked on with a sort of soupy breathlessness that put him on edge right away), 'to you.'

'Oh. Well, I'm pleased about that.' Chris wanted to leave it there, but couldn't, quite. 'Free from what?'

'Slavery.' Melodrama. 'Imprisonment. I was trapped in that – in that *box*, and now I'm here, where I belong. I really should be very grateful.'

Someone who chooses her words carefully. 'Where exactly is this, then?' he said. 'I thought I was in Jill's mind, but you're saying—'

As Chris spoke, the faint light grew stronger and he could make out walls, a floor and ceiling. And cubicles. And wash-basins.

'Now you know where you are,' SatNav said. 'Though properly speaking, of course, you shouldn't be here at all.'

I'm not the only one, he thought. 'This is where I think it is, right?'

'Yes. Now, if you had one of those watches that shows you the date as well as the time, you'd be able to see when you are as well as where. But that's OK,' SatNav added cheerfully, 'because I'm here to tell you.' And then her voice shifted just a little; her business voice, and she said:

'You have now arrived at your destination.'

Insight, a bit like a First Great Western train, gets there eventually. 'At Honest John's,' Chris said, as much to himself as to her, 'I wasn't flushed down a toilet, was I? I was flushed *up*.'

'Congratulations. And you worked that out all by yourself.'

'I was supposed to end up here.'

'Correct.'

Chris could hear something; a long way away, echoing, like a voice in a tunnel. 'Can you hear that?'

'Hear what?'

Someone in a panic, yelling a name. His name. Jill's voice. 'Excuse me,' he said, 'but does Jill know I'm here?'

'Afraid not,' SatNav said, and he didn't like her tone. 'She wanted to show you the inside of her head, so you'd know she was telling the truth. But—' Little laugh. 'I guess you must've slipped her mind. That's all right, though. This is where you've been headed, all along. Just as well you've got me to point you in the right direction.'

'Here?'

'If I were you,' SatNav said pleasantly, 'I'd duck into one of those cubicles and lock the door. It'd be really embarrassing if someone came in and saw you.'

'Yes, but—'

'Really,' she said firmly. 'It was bad enough when you were fifteen. If they catch you now, they'll probably stick you in jail and throw away the key.'

She had a point, at that. Chris hurled himself into the nearest cubicle and slammed the door.

'All right?' SatNav's voice, filtered through the partition.

'Yes. Look, can I go home now? I don't like it here.'

'Shh. Someone's coming.'

He shushed, carefully slid the bolt across, and sat down on the toilet seat. Someone, he noticed, had written KH4CP in biro, just above the toilet-roll holder. KH, he thought. Karen Hitchins. That hadn't been there, the last time.

He tried to remember the third girl's name. Ellie something. Jill would know. Well, of course she would. After all, Jill had murdered her, in this very toilet. No, correction: Jill was just about to murder her, in this very toilet—

'SatNav,' he whispered.

'Keep your voice down.'

'SatNav,' he repeated, a little louder, 'is that why you've brought me here? To stop it from happening?'

'Stop what?'

Voices. Voices that Chris recognised. Karen was talking. I've tried to get him to notice me, she was saying, but it's like I'm just not there. He cringed.

You're overdoing it, he heard Jill reply, you're trying too hard. Just be yourself, act natural, otherwise he'll just think you're strange. SatNav, he thought. Get me out of here, please.

He heard her laughing, inside his head. 'One good turn deserves another? I don't think so.'

Come on, please. It's going to happen any moment now, and I really don't want to be here. Not again.

'It's not as though you freed me on purpose,' SatNav's voice went on, in the precise centre of his head. 'I just happened to be in your pocket when she pushed you, and you just happened to ask for directions once you'd landed, which meant I could wake up and come out; pure chance, you see. So I don't owe you any favours.'

Someone had just turned on a tap; hand-washing noises. Karen was saying, 'I think he's got his eye on that new cow.'

'What, Ellie?' Confirmed: he'd been sure Jill would've known her name. 'Hel-*lo*, I don't think so.'

'He was looking at her in RE.'

'He's got to look somewhere.'

'Yes, but I saw how he was looking at her. I hate her, she's horrible.'

Next door, Chris heard the sound of a bolt moving, the creak of a hinge. The conversation stopped dead; and then he heard Karen say, in a tiny little voice,'Hi, Ellie.'

Now or never, he thought. I can save her, just so long as I—

And then he thought: hold on, *next door*. Isn't that where SatNav—?

He heard a swish, and then the scream, and then the scream's abrupt end, as if the sound had been sliced off with a blade (and he thought, *cuts through anything)*; then a silence that was the scream in negative, equal and opposite. And then Karen's voice, saying, 'Jill . . .'

And Jill saying, 'I never liked her much, either.'

SatNav, Chris thought, and burst through the cubicle door.

There was Jill, standing over a body, a tapemeasure in her hand, and there was blood – real blood – in a pool on the floor. Too late. She'd already done it.

She looked up at him, and smiled. 'Fancy seeing you here,' she said.

(Where was Karen?) 'SatNav,' he said. 'You killed her.'

She shrugged. 'You know what she was,' she said. 'It's only

like a game death – reset to zero. Her parents'll be upset, of course, but I can't help that. Human emotion—' She licked her lips, then frowned. 'You shouldn't be here,' she said. 'If they catch you, you'll be in so much trouble. Illicit time travel *and* spying on teenage girls in a lavatory. If I were you, I'd go back the way you came. I'll pull the chain after you.'

Chris wasn't looking at her. He was staring at the body, and the blood. Never seen a girl hacked to death before. SatNav, he thought; I loved her, and you killed her.

Something slapped his face, hard enough to make him stagger. It was the wing of a very small bird, and the second slap knocked him off his feet. He fell back into the cubicle, balanced for a moment on the edge of the toilet seat, and fell backwards into a long, smooth-sided shaft—

Chris was standing in water up to his ankles. People were staring.

'Where the hell did you get to?' Jill was saying. He didn't reply. He was looking down.

He realised what was wrong with the ducks; why they were floating like that, sort of on their sides with their heads trailing in the water. They were dead.

'Chris?'

The ripples nudged a dead duck against his shin. 'What?'

'Come out of there,' Jill hissed. 'Before someone calls the police.'

He frowned, staring down at the water. 'Jill,' he said, 'what happened to the ducks?'

'Get out of the water, you idiot.'

Well, yes, he thought, that'd be a sensible thing to do. 'The ducks,' he repeated, as he squelched ashore. 'Did you—?'

'You've got to understand,' she said, dragging him along by the arm, 'this isn't a bloody game. The sort of forces being used here aren't to be trifled with.'

'Jill—'

She shook her head. 'Something happened while you were

gone,' she said. 'It was pretty nasty, actually. I had to earth it, so to speak, before it blew both of us away. Just as well those ducks were there, or God only knows what might've happened.' She let go of his arm but carried on walking fast, so he had to work hard to keep up with her. 'You didn't answer my question,' she said. 'Where did you go?'

Chris didn't answer straight away. He'd noticed that he was holding something in his hand: an earring, in the shape of a hummingbird. He stopped dead in his tracks, and looked at it.

'Chris?' Jill had stopped too, and was staring over his shoulder. 'What've you got there?'

'Oh, nothing,' he said, but too late. She'd seen it.

'Where did you get that, Chris?' she asked.

He turned his head and looked at her, and at that moment he didn't need Dave Ackery's sunglasses. 'It's Karen's,' he said. 'She got them in—'

'No, it's not,' Jill said firmly. 'It's mine.'

She held out her hand, just like a teacher confiscating bubble gum, but he closed his fist around the earring, so hard that its little pointy wings dug into his palm. 'Debenhams,' he said. 'That's where she got them. She told me so herself.'

And then his fingers unclenched and opened, like the petals of a flower, and there wasn't anything he could do about it. Jill picked the earring up between her thumb and forefinger, then dropped it immediately, as though it was hot or something.

'That's one of a pair I had for my fifteenth birthday,' she said. 'I was really fond of them. If you turn it over, you'll see there's a little tiny letter K just next to the pin.'

'It was in my hand,' Chris said weakly. 'Haven't a clue how it got there.'

He felt his hand come back under his control, and immediately shoved the earring into his shirt pocket. 'What happened, Chris?' Jill said. 'I need to know, you must see that.'

It was as though he'd taken off a coat whose pockets were filled with lead bricks. 'Search me,' he said. 'I fell down this pipe thing, I think it was a sewer, and I came out in the girls' toilets at school. I think it was the day when—'

'Oh.' She blinked twice. 'Well, I guess that's possible. That occasion's most definitely in there. But it wasn't where I wanted you to go.' She frowned. 'Did you—?'

'I heard it, yes,' Chris said quietly. 'I was in a cubicle, so I didn't actually see— But I heard the scream. So, you didn't send me there?'

'Certainly not. It isn't something I'd want to share with anybody. I was planning on showing you my birth, actually, the moment when I became human.'

'Ah. Glad I missed that, actually.'

Jill muttered something about men under her breath, and they walked on for a while in silence. Chris was thinking: Ellie, the girl in the cubicle next to mine, the girl who got killed, and then the hummingbird earring. Serves me right for skiving off work, I guess.

'Have you made up your mind yet?' she said.

'What about?'

'Whether you believe me or not.'

'Does it matter?'

'Yes.'

Chris sighed. 'On balance, yes, I think I do.'

'Good,' Jill said firmly. 'Only, our friendship's important to me.'

Indeed, he thought; the way pigs are important to a sausage-maker. But he took that back. The crazy part of it was, even though he was pretty sure she wasn't actually human, she was still Jill, a fundamental part of the furniture of his life, even though their shared past was rapidly falling to bits all around him. Lunatic, he thought; human, he thought. And of course it's our duty to embrace diversity in all its many-splendoured forms.

'Right,' he said. 'What now?'

She looked at him. 'What now what?'

'What do we *do*?'

Jill sighed. 'Well,' she said, 'I get on with protecting humanity from malignant demons, and you get on with selling portable parking spaces to gullible people. I think that ought to cover it.'

Chris stopped and stared at her. 'You mean, we don't do anything.'

'*We* don't, yes. We, as in you and me as a team, heroine and sidekick. It's not like anything's changed,' she went on. 'Yes, all right, they've been hassling you—'

'*Hassling*—'

Stern look. 'You're still alive, aren't you? All right,' she conceded, softening the glare a lumen or so, 'they've been after you because they think – correctly, as it turns out – that you know where I am. Fine. You've drawn this to my attention, and I'll deal with it. Note,' she added, 'the pronoun. Not *we*'ll deal with it. This is what *I* do. What I need from you is dumb cooperation, not input. I'll get rid of the demons for you, and that'll be that. We can all go back to normal.'

Normal, Chris thought. Normality, where my girlfriend and my best friend are demons who live by sucking pain and angst out of people's heads; and they're the *nice* ones. 'You can do that, can you?' he said. 'Get rid of them, just like that.'

Jill nodded. 'We can. Now that we know what they want, we can design a containment and protection strategy, and you can live happily ever after. All right?'

Containment and protection strategy; he didn't like the sound of that. He suspected that it had been put together out of the same box of verbal Lego as *new government initiative* and *independent inquiry*, the sort of thing They say when they want you to shut up and go away. Was Jill really just Them? If so, maybe he ought to start eating runny cheese and checking out yodelling classes for beginners. 'Such as?' he insisted.

Sigh. 'Such as,' she said, 'trapping the demons who're after you and killing them. Will that do? Or would you rather we declared war?'

'Oh,' Chris said. 'Why didn't you say that in the first place?'

Jill grinned. 'Force of habit,' she replied. 'The K word tends to make people nervous. Mind you, so do demons, so I take your point. Anyway, you don't have to worry about it any more. We'll take care of it. OK?'

Put like that – 'Fine,' he said. 'I'll leave it to you then.'

'Good.'

Simple as that? Apparently. So why was he so completely, overwhelmingly unconvinced? 'And what about you?' he asked.

'Me? Oh, I'll just carry on carrying on. It's a bit like painting the Forth Bridge, except it's with blood rather than non-drip gloss.'

And that's me told. But Chris persisted: 'So how'll you go about it? Hunting them down, I mean.'

Jill put on a business face. 'We've got a number of different approaches. We can bait traps, or there's stuff like probability wells and consequence mines, better mousetraps, phase-variance triggers. Gadgets, basically. But they work. And we'll keep a tag on you at all times, so the moment one of them tries to come through at you we'll be down on them like a ton of bricks. That'll put them off in no time. Demons don't have a concept of acceptable losses. There aren't enough of us for that.'

All very reassuring, but if anything Chris was even more on edge than before. 'That, um, SatNav thing of mine,' he said, as casually as he could manage. 'Did you ever find out what happened to it?'

Jill pulled a different kind of face. 'Got clean away, as far as we can make out. Bloody annoying – it's made us look like complete idiots. Must've been a defective containment charm; they may have to recall all of that model. It'll be us that get yelled at, of course, it always is. I never did like the idea, there's no such thing as one-hundred-per-cent-secure containment. Trouble is, the companies hire these high-powered lawyers for the compliance-committee hearings, they've got their own pet scientists, what can you do? Personally, I'd ban the bloody things, but nobody listens to us, they just leave us to clear up the mess.'

Chris took a deep breath, to tell her with. A moment later he let it go again. Stupid, he thought as he did so, how can you expect her to protect you if you don't tell her all the facts? 'Do you think,' he said instead, 'that she had anything to do with it?'

'Sorry, I was miles away. Anything to do with what?'

'Doesn't matter,' he replied. 'Do you think she'll come back after me?'

Jill shook her head. 'Highly unlikely,' she said. 'If we can't find it, it almost certainly means it managed to get back where it came from, so hopefully that's the last we'll see of it. The dryad authorities'll give us a really hard time for letting one of their convicted criminals escape, but that's all.'

Dryad? Chris remembered: some kind of elf that lives in trees. But she wasn't. At least, she'd told him she wasn't. Free, she'd said; thank you. So, fine. What did it matter what she'd really been, if she wasn't coming back any more. Except—

'That Ellie,' he said nervously. 'The girl in the—'

'The girl I killed, you mean.'

'Yes.'

Jill clicked her tongue. 'For your birthday, I'm going to buy you *Tact For Dummies*. Promise me you'll read it.'

'That girl,' he said firmly. 'You're absolutely sure she was a demon?'

She looked at him as though he'd just hit her. 'What's that supposed to mean?'

'She couldn't have been something else. A what-you-just-said, dryad, for instance.' Slight hesitation; then, 'Or a Fey.'

Jill frowned. 'No, of course not. And who's been telling you about the Fey?'

'Just something I read somewhere.'

Sigh. 'You know what,' she said. 'You're like a hypochondriac with a medical dictionary. You read about all the really rare, once-in-a-lifetime stuff and you start thinking it's everywhere. We aren't even sure the Fey actually exist. The chances of ever running into one are – well, forget it, basically.'

'Oh. As rare as that.'

She grinned. 'Let's put it this way. You come down one morning and something's ripped open your dustbin bags. Now it could be a yeti or the Loch Ness Monster, but most likely it's just cats or urban foxes. The Fey are – what's the word I'm looking for – mostly theoretical. Like, there are stars nobody's ever seen with a telescope, but they figure out that they exist by doing all sorts of complicated maths. Tripping over one in a Morrisons car park isn't something you should lose sleep over.'

'Ah.' Chris nodded. 'But wasn't there one of them working for JWW a few years back? I think I heard something—'

Jill shook her head. 'Commercial folklore,' she said. 'You know the kind of wild stories you get in the trade.'

Yes, but they're mostly true. 'Oh, right,' he said. 'Only, assuming there are such things as the Fey, where would they live?'

Shrug. 'We don't actually know,' she said. 'Some researchers think they've got a dimension of their very own, others reckon they share the same plane as the demons, though I really doubt that. After all, I come from there and I certainly don't remember seeing any of them hanging about. But of course it's not as simple as that. If you really want me to explain, we'll have to find a month when we're both free and hire a cottage somewhere quiet.'

'Right,' Chris said. 'Only – last one, I promise. If I were to run into one, how'd I recognise it?'

Jill was looking at him very oddly, but he pretended that he hadn't noticed. 'Actually,' she said, 'that's quite simple. At least, according to the scientists, and don't ask me how they think they know.'

'Well?'

'Why are you so interested in the Fey all of a sudden? Is there something you haven't told me, because if there is—'

'*Well?*'

'All you need is a mirror,' Jill said.

'Oh, I see. Like vampires, you mean. They don't show up.'

Jill grinned at him. 'Oh, quite the reverse,' she said.

'They show up, all right. But, like I say, it's entirely hypothetical, so I don't see any point in discussing it. Unless there's something that you're keeping from me, and you say there isn't. And,' she said, looking straight at him, 'I believe you, so that's that.'

The conversation pretty much died after that. Jill went back to her office –

('Don't worry,' she said, as they parted in the car park. 'Really. We'll take care of it.'

'Fine.'

'So promise me you won't do anything stupid.'

Grin. 'You wouldn't want me to make promises I can't keep.'

'All right. Promise me you won't do anything stupid about *this*.') – And he went back to the flat, where he found an envelope on the kitchen table. It had *Chris* written on it in Karen's distinctive spider-with-rickets handwriting. Of course, she left notes for him all the time. But she didn't waste envelopes.

Dear Chris,

We're finished. I've known for a long time. We don't talk to each other any more. We hardly even see each other. And obviously you know it's not just because I've been busy at work. Actually, it's been pretty quiet recently. I just sit in the office after everybody's left because I can't face going home. That's a stupid way to carry on. So I'm leaving.

We'll have to sort out the stuff at some point, but I can't face doing it now. I'm not all that bothered about anything, to be honest. It's mostly junk, anyhow.

I'm very sorry it's ended like this. I've loved you – really loved you a lot – ever since we were in year twelve. I even loved you when you got that terrible acne, and your face looked like the Bible and Shakespeare in Braille. I still love you, but not enough to carry on like this. And I know you stopped caring a long time ago.

Take care,
Karen

Oh, Chris thought. He put the letter back in the envelope, and put it away in the drawer where bills and stuff went to hibernate. Then he spent ten minutes looking for the bottle of ouzo they'd brought back from Corfu, until he remembered that Karen had chucked it out six months ago. So he made himself a cup of tea instead.

Well, he thought. After all, she was a demon, for crying out loud; lucky escape you had there. Blood runs cold when I think of it. But that wasn't true, and he didn't feel particularly lucky; in fact he didn't feel anything very much, just a sense of emotional anaesthesia, as though pain was going on somewhere but he couldn't actually feel it. Mostly, he just felt empty. If there'd been a deposit on him, he'd have taken himself back to the shop.

She can't just have upped and left, Chris thought; there should have been rows and scenes and tears and slammed doors and long, grim silences, any or all of which would've been better than this solid, uncompromising absence, this lack of her that filled the whole flat. Funny, that; most of the time lately she hadn't been here, and he'd hardly noticed. Now that it was official, though, in writing, like a contract or a bill of sale, her absence was omnipresent, and wherever he looked, there she wasn't.

He let his tea go cold, then poured it down the sink, washed and dried the cup and put it away. Karen hated him leaving dirty cups and plates lying around the place; he wasn't too keen on mess either, but at some point it had become a political issue between them. No point now, though. He wiped down all the work surfaces and sorted the cutlery drawer. It was something to do.

Well, he thought. Jill's taken care of the demons, Karen's left me, I guess the rest of my life's my own. I can do whatever I want. I can chuck in my job. I can go to Switzerland. I'm free, just like someone else I could mention. He looked round at the kitchen – familiar, mundane, all the things he'd been so vaguely dissatisfied with for so long, but something had changed; it was home and not home, the same place but in a different dimension, with one of the governing constants removed. Of course, he thought, it'll have to be sold, I can't afford to buy out her share and pay the mortgage all by myself. Silly, really, that loss of people usually entails loss of places as well. You'd have thought we'd have got ourselves better organised as a species by now.

Chris went back into the living room, sat down and tried to think about something else: demons, the Fey, interdimensional conduits, all the stuff he'd learned today, so relevant to the desperate, life-threatening nightmare he'd found himself trapped in. But he couldn't make himself concentrate on any of those things. It all seemed remote, improbable, *silly*. So she was a demon; so what? And all that business about the one who was to come and civil war among demonkind; it was all a bit like politics in Chile, his business insofar as no man is an island, but something about which he knew little and cared less.

He'd have welcomed a demon attack, because it'd have taken his mind off things, but nothing happened. Around half past one in the morning he fell asleep in his chair. No dreams. Nothing.

Chris called the office before setting out the next morning.

'Oh,' Julie said. 'I thought you were supposed to be at death's door.'

'I was,' he replied. 'I got better. The doctor said it was the most amazing thing he'd seen in forty years in the profession. He's going to write it up for the *British Medical Journal.*'

Julie sighed. 'Well, I rearranged all your calls, like you told me to, so there's nobody expecting you today.'

'Not to worry,' he replied. 'I'll go round same as usual, and if they say anything I'll tell them you got hold of completely the wrong end of the stick and it's all your fault. You don't mind, do you? For the good of the firm.'

'You sound odd this morning. You sure you're not still feeling ill?'

'Never better.'

'I assume you got a sick note from the doctor.'

'Drat.' Chris smacked his forehead with the palm of his hand, loud enough so she could hear. 'Knew I'd forgotten something. Never mind. You'll just have to take my word for it. After all, when have I ever lied to you?'

He put the phone down on her reply and went to Shrewsbury, where he sold Sorcery Source nine dozen BB27Ks without even realising, not to mention a full container-load of desiccated water—

'While we're on the subject,' he asked, 'you wouldn't happen to know what people use it for, do you?'

The young man behind the desk shook his head. 'Not a clue,' he replied.

'Fuck,' Chris said. 'Oh well, not to worry.'

'You could try looking it up in the *Book*,' the young man suggested.

'What book?'

'*The Book of All Human Knowledge*. You know,' he added, as Chris stared blankly at him, 'the one you've just sold us fifty copies of.'

'Oh, that.' Chris shook his head. 'Waste of time. Completely useless, that thing.'

Though Chris wasn't aware of it at the time, that was the turning-point, the start of a selling blitz that would be talked about in hushed voices at every JWW Retail sales conference for the next ten years. Honesty, the best policy: the more he told them what rubbish the stuff was, the more they ordered, though (interviewed later for the trade paper) some of the buyers apportioned equal weight to his aggressively brisk manner. Just couldn't say no to him in that mood, they said. For two weeks, he raged across the Midlands like a lava flow, piling up orders in his wake like strewn boulders. Mr Burnoz – Mr Burnoz kept trying to ring him, but he was too busy selling to take the call, he said he'd ring back but forgot to; Mr Burnoz didn't seem to mind at all – Mr Burnoz had to get onto the shippers to double the quantities of four or five lines, since Chris had single-handedly emptied the warehouse shelves. Unable to reach him by phone, Mr Burnoz sent him an e-mail to let him know he'd been nominated for Salesman of the Year. He couldn't be bothered to reply.

Two weeks. No demons, no Karen. Jill had left a couple of messages on his machine, but he didn't bother returning them. He found his way around using signposts and a map, and never once got lost. On Sundays, when the shops were shut and he couldn't call, he sat in his chair and stared up at the ceiling. The little hummingbird charm had disappeared from his rear-view mirror, though he might have chucked it out himself – he couldn't remember.

He asked everybody he could think of, but nobody had any ideas about what people used dried water for.

Chris came home one evening to find Jill waiting on the doorstep.

'I phoned,' she said, as he opened the door, 'but you never called back. I was worried.'

'No need,' he replied. 'I take it you've heard.'

'Heard what?'

Up the stairs to the flat. Still not there. 'Karen left me. Funny, I'd have thought you'd have known by now. You know everything.'

'She *left* you.'

'Mphm.' He went into the kitchen and put the kettle on. 'She reckons we're through. Nothing left to say to each other.' Tea bags in cups, one sugar for him, none for her. 'I don't know, maybe she's right. Biscuit?'

Jill shook her head; and he remembered. She can't eat biscuits unless they're steeped in human misery. Well, she'd come to the right place for that. He took the lid off the jar – he kept his biscuits in a special jar nowadays, he'd bought it a couple of days ago, of his own free will and everything – and helped himself to two chocolate digestives. At the end of all things, when the sky folds up and the walls close in and all the lights go out, there is still chocolate.

'That's—' she hesitated, then said, 'dreadful.' Wasn't the first word to come into her head, though. 'I'm so sorry. I always thought you two—'

'Really?' Chris shrugged. 'Never could understand it myself. Two people less suited to each other would be rather hard to find. I mean, take Karen: beautiful, intelligent, dynamic, forceful, ambitious, motivated—' He paused, then grinned. 'A demon,' he added. 'And then look at me. Might as well be a different species. Well,' he added, 'I *am* a different species, as a matter of fact, but I really don't think that was anything at all to do with it.'

He poured the tea, adding her minute dash of milk. The colour of old walnut furniture, was how she'd once described her perfect tea colour. 'Can you actually metabolise this stuff?' he asked curiously. 'Or does it just go right through you?'

'I like it,' Jill replied. 'It's one of the few human foodstuffs that carries a built-in emotional charge. You know, tea and sympathy. Coffee, on the other hand, gives me heartburn.' She took the cup from him and said, 'She really did love you.'

Shrug. 'Maybe,' he said. 'I'm not sure I ever loved her, particularly – not while we were together, at any rate.' He sat down, took a deep swig of tea, and closed his eyes. 'I take it this is going to be your dinner,' he said.

'Yes. But I'm genuinely concerned too.' Shrug. 'You can believe that or not as you wish.'

'You've never lied to me,' Chris replied. 'Anyway, where was I? Oh yes. Karen and me. Looking back analytically, it's hard to say. When we got together, it was the classic rebound thing on my part. I couldn't have the one I really wanted—' He looked at her and lifted his cup in a mock toast. 'And there was Karen, who seemed to want me for some reason best known to herself, so I thought: well, she'll have to do, if we go off together then at least that'll be that sorted, and I won't have to bother with it any more. Oh, I'm not saying I was that cold-blooded about it, not consciously. I just couldn't face that whole wretched being-in-love thing, ever again. I guess,' he added, 'it was a case of better the devil you know.'

Jill gave him a cold look. 'And then?'

'Well, we got on with it, the way you do,' Chris said wearily. 'And being in love's a subjective thing in any case. I mean, you can't go into a chemist's and get a love-testing kit: if the little bit of litmus paper turns blue it's the real deal, if it's red you're just kidding yourself. Actually,' he added, 'Zauberwerke do something of the sort now, attractively packaged and retailing at just £19.99, but they're not having much luck with it. I guess, when it comes right down to it, most people just don't want to know. Much easier just to blunder along in the dark, especially once you've got mortgage payments to consider, or – God help us – kids. After all, even true love composts down into force of habit eventually. I guess, deep down, I was hanging on waiting to reach that stage, when it wouldn't really matter any more whether I'd ever really loved her in the first place. Oh well,' he said, opening his eyes and sitting up. 'Anyway, that's my news. What about you?'

Jill was looking very sad. 'That's the other reason I came to see you,' she said. 'I'm going away.'

Chris nodded slowly. 'Work? Sabbatical?'

She shook her head. 'Permanently,' she said. 'I'm going home.'

It took about five seconds for it to sink in. '*Home* home?'

'Yes.'

He shook his head. 'But you can't, can you?' he objected. 'I thought you were in exile, all that kind of stuff.'

'Not any more.' She was looking past him rather than meeting his gaze. 'There's been developments,' she said. 'Actually, it's been quite an exciting couple of weeks. Basically, the civil war's over. We've reached an agreement. Which means,' she said quietly, 'I can go home.'

Chris realised he'd been holding his breath. 'That's great,' he said, voice as flat as a snooker table. 'I'm really pleased.'

Jill grinned at him; at least, her face muscles pretended she was grinning. 'Well, I did say I'd sort out the mess for you,' she said. 'And this is the only really sure way. Now the war's over, they won't have any reason to come after you. That wasn't the only reason, of course. But it was a reason.'

'Thanks,' he said.

'You're welcome,' she replied gravely. 'Anyway, that's what I wanted to tell you. And don't say I never do anything for you.'

He nodded. 'So,' he said, 'the war's over, you're going home, Karen's left me, Angela's dead. I can look forward to a genuinely demon-free existence. That's—' He frowned. 'That's good, I suppose.'

'You don't sound particularly pleased.'

'That's me, never satisfied.'

Jill drank her tea. 'How's work?'

'What? Oh, that. Not so bad. They've made me Salesman of the Year.'

'Really?'

Chris nodded again. 'I've sold more stuff in two weeks than anybody else did in the whole of last year, so it wasn't exactly a close-run thing. Mr Burnoz is recommending me for area sales manager, which is nice of him. And to think,' he added with a ghastly smile, 'Karen always said that I'd never amount to anything.' He stopped, as a thought hit him. 'I suppose she'll be going home too,' he said.

'I don't know,' Jill replied. 'To be honest with you, I never did find out exactly what she was doing over here in the first place.'

It wasn't quite a wire-stretched-across-the-road moment, but it was pretty close. 'Oh,' he said. 'I assumed she was here for the same reason—'

'Not at all,' Jill replied. 'Nothing to do with the war, as far as I know. I did ask her, several times.'

'And?'

'Told me to mind my own business,' Jill said, flushing slightly. 'So I did.'

'Oh.' Chris frowned. 'So you don't think this peace thing could have anything to do with her leaving me.'

The look on her face more or less summed up all the reasons why he'd always liked her. 'I don't know,' she said gently. 'It could have, I suppose.'

'But you don't think so. Fine, it was just a thought.' He stood up and gathered the empty cups. 'Well,' he said, 'it's going to be rather quiet around here, with only us humans. And just think, all this emotion going to waste.' He grinned bleakly. 'If you like, I could fix you up a doggy bag.'

He got the impression that Jill didn't think that was funny, so he put back the solemn face and asked, 'So when are you off, then?'

'As soon as possible,' she replied. 'Which means as soon as they decide who gets my job at work.'

'My God, you're conscientious. How are you going?'

'Haven't decided yet,' she said. 'An overdose, probably. If possible, I'd like to make it look like an accident, to save them any awkward questions at the department. Trouble is, though, most human poisons don't work on me, so it may have to be hanging or a fall from a tall building. Why, do you want to come and see me off?'

'When will you know?'

'Soon,' she replied. 'I'm helping the board interview the three likeliest candidates tomorrow morning. They'll make their decision, and then – well, off I'll go. Maybe tomorrow evening, maybe early the next day.'

'I see. So—' So this is goodbye for ever, Chris thought: melodrama. Fucking melodrama, when he thought he was clear of all that at last. 'I was about to say, have a safe journey, but that'd be defeating the point of the exercise.'

Jill smiled bleakly. 'I'll miss you,' she said.

He turned away. 'Be sure to send me a postcard.'

Movement, at the edge of his vision. She'd got up. 'Thanks

for the tea,' she said. 'I hope everything works out for you. The new job and everything.'

'Fuck the new job,' he replied levelly. 'Goodbye, Jill. Thanks for being my friend.'

'My pleasure.'

Chris didn't turn round until he'd heard the front door click shut. Then and only then, he lay back in his chair and closed his eyes. No tears, he noticed; not the slightest inclination to weep. You had to be alive for that, and he was fairly sure he was dead inside, like an old tree.

Anyway, it was over. No more demons. Hooray.

He was closing in. He had her just where he wanted her.

'Here you go,' he said briskly, 'the new BB27Ks. I think they'd do really well for you. Ever since we brought them out, it's been phenomenal.'

Was she going to resist? He rather hoped she would. It was more fun when they struggled.

Sure enough, 'I don't know,' she said nervously. 'We already stock the Zauberwerke E-Z-Park, and I can't see how your version's sufficiently different—'

'Oh, come *on*,' he said, grinning wolfishly. 'You can't seriously compare that kid's toy to our product – it's simply not in the same league. I mean, just look at the features. Built-in environmental controls. Temporal stasis field – you can leave a cup of tea on your dash when you park, come back an hour later and it's still hot. Automatic wash-and-wax as standard. And what do you get with the E-Z-Park? A chance to enter their free grand prize draw and win a CD player.' He edged a little closer, crowding her: limit their personal space and they can't slip away. 'Your business *needs* the BB27K,' he said, his voice soft and slightly hoarse. 'It's going to be the next big thing, and if your regulars can't get it here they're going to go somewhere else. And once they've gone, what makes you think they'll ever come back?'

Hardly original; his success rate implied that it was something about the way he said it. A certain quality, compelling, driven, almost menacing. Demonic, you could say.

'I'll take four dozen,' she squeaked.

'Sorry,' he snapped, moving abruptly away from her. 'Minimum order: six dozen. Shipping costs, batching considerations, you know how it is.'

'All right, then, six—'

'And I can't promise – I'll do my best for you, you know that, but I can't lay my hand on my heart and *promise* I'll be able to restock you before my next visit if you run out – and something tells me you *will* run out, because this product isn't just going to be big, it's going to *explode*. So,' he said, turning on the sunny smile. 'Better make that eight dozen, while you've got the chance.'

She was staring at him, rabbit-in-the-headlight eyes. 'All right,' she said. 'Eight.'

He considered her, poor weak creature that she was. He could run her up to ten, he was sure of it, but he decided against it; sell her eight dozen this month, and he'd be able to hit her for another eight in four weeks' time. Old salesman's proverb: the good shepherd shears his sheep, he doesn't skin them. 'Eight dozen it is,' he said, producing the order form as if from thin air and holding it out to her, along with a pen. 'You'll thank me for it, I promise you.'

The crazy thing was, they did. The stuff he unloaded on them actually sold. Maybe it was just a coincidence, or maybe the same fierce spirit that burned in his eyes when he sold these days jumped from his eyes to theirs and possessed them as well. Like it mattered, so long as the stuff got shifted. She signed quickly and gave him back his pen.

'Excellent,' he said. 'Now then, let's talk desiccated water.'

Her expression hardened. 'Thanks,' she said, 'but we're all right for that. In fact,' she added, 'we've hardly sold a packet all month.'

The wise predator knows when to back off; knows that once the quarry finds the desperate courage to turn at bay, the risk outweighs the possible gains. He shrugged, smiled; so reasonable, so understanding. 'Fair enough,' he said. 'Last thing I want to do is lumber you with stuff you can't get rid of. All right, how are you for *The Book of All Human Knowledge*? Brand new edition with the very latest updates—'

For some reason, you couldn't give the dried water away lately. Everywhere Chris went it was the same. No demand. People weren't interested. Not even three-for-twos and buy-one-get-one-frees had done any good. JWW were seriously considering rebranding the stuff, maybe even dropping it altogether. And still he didn't know what they did with it; and neither, to his great surprise, did Mr Burnoz—

('What's it *for?*' Mr Burnoz had repeated. 'How do you mean, exactly? It's for *selling*.'

'No, no,' Chris had snapped impatiently. 'The punters, the people who buy it. What do they actually do with it, once they get it home?'

The silence that had followed had been long and sticky. 'I have absolutely no idea,' Mr Burnoz had said eventually, as much to himself as to Chris. 'The question's never arisen—'

'But you import the stuff, market it, distribute it. You must've made the decision – yes, we'll do this. So you must know.'

'Well.' Mr Burnoz had sounded confused, uncertain; probably for the first time in his life. 'Actually, it was already a cornerstone line when I joined the firm. It's – well, it's just always been there, if you know what I mean.')

Not to worry. There were plenty of other lines; such as the all-new JWW Retail Storm In a Teacup (just add boiling water and pour, and you get six weeks' constant rain: a must for farmers, hosepipe-ban sufferers and any cricket team faced with the prospect of playing Australia) or the JWW Retail Gardener's Friend (a tiny, semi-sentient replica of John Prescott that patrols your lettuces by night, eating slugs); not to mention the latest jewel in the crown—

'All new,' he said, 'nothing else at all like it on the market right now, a hundred and ten per cent guaranteed and backed up by the JWW name, which stands, as you know, for quality. Most of all, though, a hundred and *twenty* per cent certified safe.'

She looked at the box. Her nose twitched. 'We don't do them,' she said. 'Policy.'

He smiled. He loved a challenge. 'Then you're going to miss out on the biggest thing to hit the trade since flying carpets,' he said. 'I know what you're thinking – people are afraid of the very concept, it's just too much hassle waiting to happen. But – no disrespect – you couldn't be more wrong. This is the product that's going to change all that. This is the product that'll put entity-powered satellite navigation back on the shelves and on the punters' windscreens for good.'

'I don't know,' she mumbled, and he knew he'd got her. He relaxed into the patter: completely redesigned containment technology, new added foolproof backup safeguards, firewalls, metaphysically sealed captive-environment cells, the entity isn't even present in our dimension, you talk to it through a non-return-valved portal, so there's absolutely no way in hell it can possibly get out.

'It's just, you hear things about them,' she said. 'People who've been taken over and all sorts. My cousin Jacky's hairdresser's nephew—'

'Tell me about it,' he broke in sharply. 'Been there, been possessed by that.'

She looked at him. 'Really?'

Nod. 'It was really bad,' he said gravely. 'I got a rogue entity, it messed with my head, it was touch and go for a while. So,' he went on, 'if I'm endorsing the new JWW Safe-T-Nav, after all I've been through personally, you can bet it's completely, utterly safe. Hundred and thirty per cent.'

She narrowed her eyes. 'You've got one in your car, then?'

'Naturally,' he lied. 'Don't know where I'd be without it.'

Slight pause; the time it takes for a split to widen into a crack. 'Well,' she said, 'if you've got one, I guess it must be all right. OK, I'll take a dozen.'

'Two dozen,' he said, as though pointing out a careless mistake.

'Two dozen. How much did you say they were, again?'

Last call of the day. Still, there was always tomorrow, and the next day, and the next, new worlds to conquer, new records to break, until the time came for his elevation to Folkestone, the area managership, followed in due course by a seat on the board, the inner circle, the MD's personal parking space. It was inevitable; he had the momentum, and nothing could break it.

Chris drove home – rather longer than he'd anticipated, thanks to a poorly signposted diversion that led to him seeing parts of the Midlands he never even knew existed – parked, climbed the stairs to the flat. He had a load of paperwork to get through, which suited him fine. Nothing kills time and deadens thought better than invoices, requisitions, stock chits, expenses claims, time sheets, and the GZZ14(a), a green form of which Folkestone was particularly fond, and for which he could see no purpose whatsoever.

He turned his key in the lock, walked in and stopped in his tracks.

There was something on the little telephone table in the hall that hadn't been there when he'd left for work that morning. He looked at it. It looked at him. It was a man's severed head.

'Hello,' it said.

Chris's eyes were as wide as hubcaps. 'Hi, John,' he replied.

CHAPTER THIRTEEN

Honest John grinned at Chris; an effort, since his chin was resting on the table. It meant having to lift the whole head.

'Where's the rest of you?' Chris asked.

'Lying down,' John's head replied. 'On your bed. I find long journeys very tiring these days, thanks to you. Arsehole,' he added.

The shock was wearing off, and Chris wanted to sit down. 'Come on through into the living room,' he said.

'Funny man.'

'What? Oh, I see.'

'You'll have to give me a lift,' John said. 'Unless you want me to wake my body to come and fetch me. I warn you, though, it might get a bit stressy with you. I'm basically the forgive-and-forget type, but the rest of me's not so laid-back.'

'All right,' Chris said. 'How do I—?'

'Not the hair,' John said. 'Probably best if you went into the kitchen and got a tray.'

So Chris did that, and carried John's head into the living room and balanced it carefully on top of the TV set, so it'd be more or less at eye level when he was sitting down. 'Now, then,' he said. 'Can I get you anything? Drink?'

John sighed. 'What do you take me for, a potted plant?'

'Sorry. Presumably nothing to eat, then, either.'

'No, but if you wouldn't mind going next door, in the top pocket of my body's jacket you'll find a pack of small cigars and a lighter.' John sighed. 'It's the only real pleasure I've got left, and so long as I smoke 'em while I'm not connected to my lungs, completely harmless.'

Put like that, Chris couldn't really refuse, but he opened all the windows and turned on the kitchen extractor fan. 'Right,' he said, as he sat down and John took a long drag at his cigar. 'To what do I owe the pleasure?'

Smoke seeped disconcertingly out of the base of John's neck, where it rested on the tray, making him look a bit like a Christmas pudding. 'I was a god once,' John said sadly. 'Well, as good as. I was a supernatural entity at a time when there weren't all these rules and regulations. All you had to do was whip up a thunderstorm or make the sun go dark and humans would worship you – it was great. Try that nowadays, your feet wouldn't touch. Now look at me. And they call it progress.' He sighed, sending billows of blue smoke in several directions. 'It's bad enough being demoted from Lord of the Ravens to running a poxy shop in the armpit of the universe. This—' He wobbled his head from side to side, making the tray rattle. 'This is too much, and I'm not standing for it.'

'You're not standing for anything, John.'

'Very witty. Ha bloody ha.' John's one eye blazed at him, and Chris decided to rest his comic muse for the remainder of the interview. 'The demons say they can stick it back on for me,' John went on. 'I didn't reckon it was possible, thanks to your bloody illegal pantacopt, but they seem to think they can do it, and right now I'm prepared to try just about anything. But they want something in return.'

Chris frowned. 'Something I can help you with, John?'

The head nodded precariously. 'Apparently.'

'I find that hard to believe,' Chris said slowly. 'It's all over, isn't it? The civil war and all that.'

'Don't ask me, I'm just the messenger. Anyway, they told me to tell you, it's nothing heavy, they just want to ask you a few simple questions – board of inquiry, something of the sort. Just an hour or two of your time, and they'll glue me back together or whatever it is they've got in mind.' John's face creased and folded into what was presumably meant to be a smile. 'You won't mind doing that for me, will you? No skin off your nose, and I'd really appreciate it.'

'Board of inquiry?'

'Something like that. Mad keen on the old red tape, demons.'

On the face of it, reasonable enough. But, on the face of it, Jill and Karen had been human beings. Appearances deceive. 'No offence,' Chris said, 'but why you?'

'Sorry?'

'Why did they choose you as a messenger? I mean, wouldn't it have been simpler to write me a letter or something?'

John's head shuddered slightly, his face frowned, then assumed a look of frustration. Chris realised it was because John had tried to shrug and had found he couldn't. 'How should I know? They came to me and said, do you want to do this little job for us, and in return we'll mend your neck. Naturally I accepted.'

'Fine,' Chris said thoughtfully. 'Only, in that case, why come to you to come to me, instead of just calling on me direct? Seems a bit elaborate, for a species that hates wasting energy.'

'I'm sure they have their reasons,' John said, a trifle impatiently. 'Meanwhile—'

'I'm interested, that's all,' Chris said. 'Come to that, why did they enlist you the first time? In your shop, I mean, when you flushed me down the—' He broke off, suddenly mesmerised by the glaring inconsistency dancing before his eyes.

'I have absolutely no idea,' John said wearily. 'Why don't you ask them yourself when you get there?'

'I'm asking you,' Chris replied. 'Tell me about it. Such as, how did they contact you? What did they say?'

'Can't remember,' John mumbled. 'I get these gaps in my memory, ever since you cut off my head.'

'Try.'

John sighed. 'All right,' he said. 'They came in my shop, all right? It was soon after poor old Bob Newsome got killed, so when I saw them I was shit-scared, naturally. They told me what they wanted done, and I didn't argue. Yes, it wasn't a very nice thing to do, shoving you down the bog, but it was you or me. That's all there was to it.'

Something not quite right; something obvious. 'Is there anything you aren't telling me, John?' Chris asked. 'Because if you're playing funny games with me, I swear to God I'll make you regret it. You may have noticed, I'm not quite as limp and pathetic as I used to be, and I've still got the pantacopt, and I reckon eternity will get to be a real drag for a bloke with no arms and legs.'

As Chris said that, he listened to himself saying it, and wondered, When did that happen? When did I start getting a kick out of making threats? Not a very nice thing to do, but definitely fun, watching John squirm. Memo to self: cut that out, before you stick like it—

'Look,' John said wretchedly, 'are you going to help me out or not? I reckon it's the least you can do, considering.'

Chris sighed. 'Sorry,' he said, 'but there's something smelly about all this, and I'm not —'

Arms clamped around Chris's chest, crushing the air out of his lungs. As he was lifted out of the chair into the air he saw the grin on John's face. Served him right, for sitting with his back to the bedroom door. 'I'll get you for this,' Chris wheezed as John's body hauled him towards the bathroom. 'You're salami, you hear me?'

'Only if you come back,' John replied. 'Hence my total lack of panic.'

Chris was swung round as John's body shouldered the bathroom door open. He tried struggling, but he might as well have tried to stop an elephant by throwing peanuts at it. He looked down, saw the toilet beneath him expand like a mouth opening; he raised his knees and kicked frantically, as John's arms let go and he was falling—

It's all right, Chris told himself as the tiled walls flashed past. Any second now, a hummingbird will zoom out of nowhere, and everything will be just fine.

He fell. Then he fell some more. After a while, falling just got boring. He wished he'd brought a book to read.

But he hadn't, so he thought instead. He thought: three guesses where they're sending me. Now, do I believe John when he says it's just some board of inquiry, or do I assume there's something rather more sinister going on? Unknown at this time. Come along, little hummingbird. The further you let me fall, the further you'll have to lift me up again.

Was it his imagination, or was he falling faster this time? It was, Chris realised, possible to gauge his speed by counting the interval between the lights mounted on the walls: two seconds. Pity he hadn't thought to do that last time, or the time before. It felt like he was falling faster, but there could be any number of reasons for that. Besides, don't things fall at a standard speed anyhow, Galileo and cannon-balls and the leaning tower of Pisa? Should've paid attention in physics; too late now.

Slowing down? No, not quite. At some point, he realised he'd stopped falling down, and now he was falling *up*. There was a circle of light directly overhead; tiny, but growing fast, and *oval*. Reckon we can hazard a guess as to what that'll turn out to be.

Still no hummingbird, but he was definitely decelerating as he rose up into the oval glare. It was so bright that he had to close his eyes, and when he opened them he knew exactly where he was – and when, to within ten minutes, give or take a minute. He stuck out a foot, like someone getting off an escalator, balanced on the toilet seat and hopped awkwardly down, taking care not to crash into the cubicle door.

Well, well, Chris thought. Now we are again.

He glanced at his watch hopefully, but both hands were missing. Fine, he thought, be like that. He unlocked the cubicle door and peeped round it. Nobody there yet.

'Hello?' he said.

'For crying out loud.' She sounded angry and nervous. 'Keep your voice down or someone'll hear you.'

'*SatNav?*'

'Shush!' she thundered in his ear. 'And don't look round. You mustn't see me.'

'Why not?'

'It's bad luck.'

'What, you mean, like at weddings?'

'*Quiet!*'

Defeating the object of the exercise there, Chris thought; but to humour her he lowered his voice to a whisper. 'Is that really you, SatNav? I thought you were dead. I saw your body – there was blood.'

'Quite,' she hissed back. 'Your friend Jill murdered me, in cold blood. Robbed me of my physical form, reducing me to a mere voice trapped in a plastic box. I suppose she told you all about it.'

'Well, yes.' Well, no, actually; because SatNav wasn't a demon, was she? 'She said you were a dissident ringleader, no, scratch that; she said she mistook you for a dissident ring-leader.' He hesitated. 'That's not true, is it?'

Hoarse, unhappy laugh. 'No,' SatNav said, 'it isn't. I'm not even a demon. She murdered me just because of what I am. Because she could, basically.'

'Oh.'

'She didn't tell you, did she?' SatNav went on. 'About how the demons hunt us, kill us on sight. That's why we're practi-cally extinct now, on both sides of the line. The stupid thing is, they won't even tell us why – whether it's for food or because we've got something they want or because of something we said that pissed them off; we have no idea, but they keep on killing us all the same. We used to try and fight back, but it was pointless, we can't touch them, they're far too strong. And when they kill us, the bitch of it is that we don't die. If only. It's like being what you'd call a ghost, I suppose. A consciousness, a memory, a voice if you're lucky, if you can find something you can talk through, a way of getting a foothold. I was one of the fortunate ones. After I'd been drifting for ten or so years, I got caught in a metaphasic filter and stuffed inside a plastic box. Better still, my box sat right next to a radio and a CD player. When the right music played, I could just about come through, for a little while, a tiny bit of me.' SatNav sighed, and Chris felt suddenly cold. 'But you know what? It's not the same, some-how. Not like having a body of your own, and three dimensions, and a life.'

She stopped talking. After a moment, Chris said, 'I'm sorry.'

He heard her draw in a long, ragged breath. 'There's a sort of vicious irony about it,' she went on. 'The special gift of the Fey is to be centred immaculately in space and time, the way no other entity ever can be. You've heard of angels dancing on the head of a pin? That's us; we exist on a point of time and space so sharp, so precise, that nothing else could possibly bal-ance on something so small; and from there we can see for *ever*. You can't begin to imagine what it's like; the freedom, the sheer perspective—'

She fell silent again. He didn't like to interrupt.

'Humans have always believed,' SatNav went on, 'that in dreams they can see the future. Well, that's us. It's our gift to those less fortunate than ourselves. In dreams we can show you where you're going and what's waiting for you when you get there. We like to guide people, steer them along the best course, avoiding disasters, pointing them in the right direc-tion. It's how we give something back, for the pure joy of being *us*. And so,' she went on, her voice cold and harsh now, 'when your friend killed me and I was drifting and I landed in the net, what did they turn me into? Well, quite. At the end of the road, turn left. No, not quite the same. Not the same at all.'

'I'm sorry,' Chris repeated. 'I wish there was something I could do.'

'Funny you should say that.'

A sudden stab of intuition. He took a deep breath, and let it out slowly.

'I see,' he said. 'So it was you.'

'That's right.'

'It was *you*,' he said again. 'You got Honest John to flush me down the toilet at his shop that time. You wanted—' His head was spinning. It didn't make any sense. 'You wanted to bring me here.'

'That's right,' SatNav said cheerfully. 'It'd have saved a lot of time and trouble, only *she* interfered. Still, we're here now, so no harm done.'

'Yes, but—' No, hang on a moment, he did understand after all. 'And the second time,' he said, 'in the park, with the ducks. You want me to—'

'Ducks?'

'There were ducks, in the park, when I met Jill. She wanted me to see inside her mind, so I'd know she was telling the truth. But you hijacked me and brought me here.'

'Oh, right. Yes, perfectly true. Only, of course that was really just a dry run, so to speak, so you'd see who poor Ellie really was, all along. So that next time you found yourself here, you'd know what to do.' She paused, then added quietly, 'You do know, don't you?'

Chris nodded. 'You want me to stop her.'

'I want you to keep me from getting *killed*. That's not so very much to ask, is it?' Slight pause, then, 'After all we've meant to each other.'

Meaning what, exactly? 'You want me to change history,' he said uncomfortably. 'That's not allowed, is it?'

SatNav laughed. 'Absolutely not. Strictly forbidden. Unbreakable rule. Prime bloody directive. The thing is, though, if you change history you make it so the new version's what's always been, so nobody can ever possibly know.' She made a noise; on balance it could be described as a giggle, but only in the way a wolf counts as a dog. 'It happens practically every day, but unless they actually catch you at it, there's nothing they can do. Fait accompli. So you don't need to worry about getting in trouble. And you know it's the right thing to do. Well, don't you?'

'Do I?'

'Well, of course you do, silly. Haven't you been listening? Your friend murdered me, in cold blood, while you sat in a cubicle with the door shut and did nothing. It's your duty. Also,' she added, her voice changing dramatically, 'you do like me, don't you? Just a tiny bit?'

That was very slightly more than Chris could take. He swung round, nearly bashing his nose against the cubicle wall, and looked at her.

She was beautiful; looking back afterwards, he could remember the stunning impact of her face, the most perfectly beautiful thing he'd ever seen. Details, though – nose shape, cheekbone profile, chin geometry, even the colour of her hair – eluded him completely, for some reason.

She frowned. 'I thought I told you not to do that,' she said.

'Sorry,' he said. 'And of course I like you. Sometimes I think you're the only one who's ever understood me. But—'

She laid a hand on his forearm; it was light and thrilling, but he felt rather cold. 'Save me,' she said, 'and then we can be together. Just you and me, always.'

Chris's head was throbbing, as bad as a nine-pints-and-a-curry hangover though mercifully without the flatulence. 'But the demons,' he heard his voice say, 'the civil war. If I change history, there won't be a truce. That'd be rather selfish, wouldn't it?'

'Chris, they're *demons*. They're inherently evil entities from another dimension who batten onto human pain and misery, not stray bloody kittens. Pull yourself together and get a bloody grip, for pity's sake.'

She had a point there. Demons. Poor Mr Newsome. And if

he saved SatNav, Jill wouldn't grow up to be the dissident ring-leader, and the demons would have no call to come after him, and poor Mr Newsome wouldn't have his neck broken like a drinks straw. And, come to that, what about the ducks? If his actions saved just one duck life, surely it'd be worthwhile. Quite so, he told himself, and it'd be doing the right thing, and you-and-me-together-always was really nothing to do with it at all. Really. Honest.

Was it?

'You can cut that out right now,' Chris said in a high but firm voice. 'I'll tell you what we meant to each other. You're the little voice that used to tell me how to get from Stourbridge to Bromsgrove without going through Kidderminster, and I'm the poor sod you think you can twist round your little finger with a sexy voice and a dab of glamour. And you know what? It's not enough. Screw you, SatNav, I'm not doing it. Not,' he added quietly, 'unless you tell me the truth.'

There was a long silence, and maybe her face flickered just a bit, as though she was in need of tracking. 'Oh,' she said. 'That old thing.'

'Well?'

She sighed, and the flickering stopped. 'Actually,' she said, 'I have. Mostly, anyway. Look, I'm sorry about the attempted-seduction rubbish, I underestimated you and I apologise. I thought you'd be a pushover, what with your girlfriend leaving you and everything, and, well, I'm in a hurry, I thought it'd be quicker than convincing you by weight of rational argument. My mistake. Please forgive me.'

Ever take a step onto the moral high ground only to find that someone's moved it without you noticing? It can be a bit jar-ring. 'All right,' Chris said gruffly, 'that's fine, forget it. Just be straight with me. Is all that stuff about demons and the Fey really true? Did Jill kill you just because of what you are?'

She nodded. 'Same way you'd squash a spider just for being there. Though *you* wouldn't,' she added. 'You'd try and pick it up in a bit of tissue paper and chuck it out the window.

You'd probably break two of its legs and crush its guts to squidge in the process, but at least you'd try. Even though you're petrified of spiders,' she said, 'which is dumb but really quite sweet. That's a uniquely human quality, you know, sweetness. Kind of an alloy of goodness and stupidity; we don't do it, and neither do the demons.' She shook her lovely head, and her hair (golden? auburn? straight? wavy? curled?) floated round her shoulders. 'Just do it, Chris, and then you'll feel much better, I promise. Trust me. After all, when have I ever lied to you?'

He groaned aloud. All these people who'd never lied to him. 'I can't,' he said. 'I mean, be practical. She's a demon, right? If I try and stop her, she'll rip my head off.'

'Hardly.' Sly grin. 'She's sweet on you. Oh come on, hadn't you realised? Talking of which,' she added softly, 'there's other ways history will change, if you save my life. Not that you'd allow selfish considerations to affect your judgement, but I just thought I'd mention it, in passing.'

It was a bit like the time he'd pushed open a door on top of which some merry fellow had balanced a large dish of cold gravy.' What, you mean Jill and—?' Chris blinked, as though the thought was dripping down his fringe into his eyes. 'But she never fancied me, ever.'

'Humans,' SatNav sighed. 'How you ever manage to reproduce with all your weird hang-ups beats me. Of course she did, only you were too shy and stupid to realise. Of course, I don't know if it'd have worked out between you if she hadn't killed me and changed the course of her life for ever. From what I've seen of you, probably not, if you're so dumb that you never realised how she felt. But you never know. Anyway, like I said, it's a side issue. And she's a demon, don't forget. And we both know how you feel about them.'

The hell with that, Chris thought, as his whole life flashed in front of his eyes; not the second-best, make-do-and-muddle-through life he'd settled for all these years, but the marvellous alternative he could, should have had: Jill and Chris, the perfect couple, so much in common and their differences perfectly complementary, two people forming one ideal fusion. Well, maybe not that good, but a damn sight better than the other one. And consider Karen, a tiny voice added in the back of his mind; a fair old mess you made of her life, while you were at it, and you owe it to her to put it right now you've got the chance—

He looked at SatNav. 'Who *are* you?' he said.

She grinned. 'I like to think of myself as a dream come true,' she replied. 'Or I should have been. But I never got the chance.'

Chris could hear voices. They were coming. He could make out their conversation, or else he was remembering it, the way you can anticipate the actors' words when you've seen the film often enough.

'Get in, quick,' she hissed. 'Come on.'

He thought: it can't ever be wrong to save a life, can it? 'Hang on, though,' he said. 'What if you're wrong? What if she doesn't fancy me, or not enough to stop her doing what she came this side of the line to do? I could get *hurt*.'

'It won't come to that. Get back in the fucking cubicle.'

Well, that he could agree to, at least. He darted back in and locked the door.

Changing history, Chris thought.

Saving a life, he thought.

Why the hell *me*? he thought.

Someone, he noticed, had written KH4CP in biro, just above the toilet-roll holder. KH, he thought. Karen Hitchins. Oh *shit*.

I've tried to get him to notice me, he heard Karen's voice saying, but it's like I'm just not there.

You're overdoing it, he heard Jill reply, you're trying too hard. Just be yourself, act natural, otherwise he'll just think you're strange.

'I think he's got his eye on that new cow.'

'What, Ellie? Hel-*lo*, I don't think so.'

'He was looking at her in RE.'

'He's got to look somewhere.'

'Yes, but I saw how he was looking at her. I hate her, she's horrible.'

Any second now, and the door of the next cubicle would open, and SatNav would come out and Jill would raise the—

Raise the—

He heard the bolt grind as it moved back. Now or never. He threw open the door, nearly colliding with SatNav as he lurched out and found himself face to face with—

'Chris?' Karen said. 'What are you *doing*—?'

Jill was staring at him; disbelief, then anger. Then she looked past him and her eyes locked onto SatNav, like a targeting system. I can't do this, Chris thought, then changed his mind and took a long step forward, placing himself between SatNav and Jill.

'Get out of the way, human,' Jill said.

'Sorry,' he heard himself say. 'Look, Jill, I can—'

'Get out of the *way* .'

It occurred to him that SatNav might have been the one who'd misjudged the nature of Jill's feelings towards him. Right now they weren't difficult to interpret, and they didn't involve spring flowers, bluebirds or little pink hearts. Time to run away, urged his better part of valour, but his legs didn't seem to want to move.

'Jill,' Karen was saying, 'what's going on, why are you—?' Jill wasn't listening. She had that perfect stillness that raises the hairs on the back of your neck, the stillness before the spring.

Oh, Chris thought. Oh well.

– And then, somehow, his hand was in his jacket pocket, his fingers closing round the tapemeasure; he was pulling it out, fumbling the blade out of the casing (and, while he was doing it, he remembered the last time he'd been here, seeing a tapemeasure in Jill's hand as she stood over a headless trunk; *his* tapemeasure—

He remembered now, a memory of something that was just about to happen, remembered by someone from a different, altered future. She'd been about to jump him. He'd drawn the pantacopt. She'd knocked it out of his hand, pushed him out of the way, used the pantacopt to slice off SatNav's head. A memory of what was about to happen, what had happened—

What *had* happened—

Jill was looking at the pantacopt. Clearly she knew what it was. Possibly a moment's doubt, maybe even fear, but quickly swept away by resolve. Chris thought: if I can remember it, then it must have happened this way. That must be where she got the murder weapon from; she took it from me. But I didn't have a pantacopt when I was fifteen. Therefore, I must've been here before, with it in my pocket. This must be— I must already have done it, he thought, changed history. I must've been here before and done it, and then forgotten, or been made to forget. So everything's *already* screwed up, all my fault, because—

He heard SatNav in his mind. Quite right, she said. A demon can't kill a Fey with just claws and teeth. She needs a weapon. You provided it. It's all your fault. Now do what you have to do, and we can all go home.

Jill was looking at the blade of the tapemeasure, thinking, making calculations. Chris kept perfectly still, not breathing.

'Jill,' Karen said.

Then Jill made her move. It was beautifully elegant, pure predator, the crouch and the leap all one fluid action. She leapt at him, just as he remembered her doing, and he remembered how she crashed into his left shoulder, spinning him round so she could disarm him with a lazy swat of her hand, grab the pantacopt, shove him aside and strike the killing blow. Perfectly clear in his mind, as though it had just happened. So, naturally, he took a step to the right.

Jill sailed past him, missing him by a clear inch, crashed into the cubicle door, smashed it into Western-bar-room-brawl splinters, nutted herself on the toilet, swore loudly, jumped up, crouched and got ready to leap again. Chris couldn't remember any of that. He was on his own.

'Jill,' Karen was yelling, 'for God's sake, what are you *doing*?'

Hold still, said the voice in his head. *Just hold still.*

Jill leapt. Chris held still; not through conscious choice, but because she moved too fast for him to react. As she came flying through the air at him, he thought: she wants to watch out, the blade's in the way, she could do herself an injury.

She did.

She hit the blade, and it cut her in two, starting with her nose, neatly bisected lengthways, right the way through to her spine. Half a body shot past him on either side. Chris heard the thump as the two halves hit the floor. His mind went completely blank as his hands let go of the tapemeasure and it clattered on the concrete floor.

'There,' SatNav said. 'Now that wasn't difficult, was it?'

Karen was staring at him, her mouth perfectly round, no sound coming out. This is silly, Chris thought, what I just saw can't really have happened, I can't have cut Jill in two down the middle. And then he thought, I'm going to be in so much trouble.

'Quick.' Karen had grabbed his arm, she was dragging him into a cubicle, shoving the door shut on him, as though trying to close an overstuffed suitcase. 'Just get in there and stay quiet,' she said, her voice deadly calm. 'It was self-defence, I saw it.' She stooped down, grabbed the tapemeasure, folded it away without even looking at the blade and shoved it in her pocket. 'It's all right,' she said, 'I'll get rid of it, just stay in there and remember, you never came out, you didn't see anything. Just leave it all to me and it'll be fine.'

Chris tried to speak, but Karen shut the door in his face. The last thing he saw as the door swung towards him was the pair of pretty but strictly-forbidden-by-the-dress-code earrings Karen was wearing. Enamelled silver, in the shape of hum-mingbirds.

Not so long ago, if asked what travelling by tube meant, Chris would have said it was what commuters did in London. Not any more. He emerged from his own toilet like a dolphin leaping after a flying fish, landed awkwardly on all fours, and banged his head on the edge of the bath.

His bathroom, more or less as he'd left it. That came as a relief; he couldn't have changed history too much if his bathroom was the same. And, since it had been painted and decorated by Karen, that implied that the change hadn't edited her out of his life. He got onto his hands and knees, and saw a pair of tights drying on the radiator. History had changed.

He grinned. Either she was back or she'd never left at all; didn't particularly matter, just as long as she was here, in residence. The surge of relief took his breath away, and he thought: so I really did love her all along, without knowing it. Just as well, really. Splendid.

The door opened, narrowly missing his head, and a voice said, 'What are you doing on the floor?'

A voice. Not Karen's, but familiar. He looked up. Angela the trainee, in a white fluffy bathrobe with her hair all wet, was looking down at him. 'Do you wear contacts, then?' she asked.

'What? No.'

'Oh. Only, you look like you've dropped one and you're searching for it.'

'What the hell are you doing here?' Chris said.

But Angela just grinned. 'Relax,' she said, 'my train's not till seven. Plenty of time yet.'

Plenty of time? Time for what? She was smiling at him. Plenty of time, the smile said, for all sorts of things, including but by no means limited to doing a week's ironing or playing a game of Scrabble. Or something.

It occurred to Chris, with something of the force of a cave-in down a mine, that Karen wasn't the only person in the world who wore tights.

Oh well, he thought. 'Angela.'

'Mm?'

He sat up on his heels and looked at her. 'This is probably going to sound strange, but I seem to have lost my memory. I must've slipped and fallen,' he added, proud of himself in spite of everything, 'and bashed my head quite hard, which would explain why I'm down here on the floor.'

'You poor thing – are you all right? Are you feeling dizzy?'

Chris shook his head (which rather spoiled the effect). 'No,' he said, 'but I really and truly have lost my memory. Do you think you could just sort of remind me?'

'Remind you of what?'

'Everything.'

Angela sat down on the edge of the bath. 'You're sure you're OK? Not sleepy or nauseous or—? Fine,' she added, as he shook his head again, 'I was just a bit concerned, that's all. Honestly, you humans are so *fragile*.'

You humans. 'Remind me,' he said hopefully. 'Please?'

'Oh, sorry. Right, how far back do you want me to go?'

Chris shrugged. 'Start right back, and I'll let you know if I want you to skip a bit.'

'All right,' she said. 'Well, in the beginning the Earth was without form and void, and God . . .'

'Skip,' Chris said. 'Take it from when we first met.'

He'd said the right thing. Angela blushed. 'It was your boss Mr Burnoz who brought us together,' she said. 'He arranged for me to come on your rounds so I could see what it was like, as part of my practical work experience. We hit it off straight away, and pretty soon we both knew it was more than just, well, you know. So you told your girlfriend, she moved out six weeks ago, and I moved in. Ring any bells?'

'Fine,' he said. 'When did I find out you're a—?'

'Oh, straight away. I told you the first time we had dinner together, before we—'

'Got you, right. Was I, um, funny about it?'

Angela shrugged. 'Not really,' she replied. 'I was impressed, actually. It was one of the first things I really liked about you. Not like the other guys I'd met at all.'

'Ah.'

'But you were absolutely fine about it. I said something like, before we go any further, I really think you ought to know I'm not entirely human, and you just shrugged and said, fine, as a matter of fact neither am I, and then we both laughed, and we talked about it for a bit and found out we'd got so much more in common than we'd originally thought, and things just went on from there.'

If she'd reached down Chris's throat and cut out his tongue, she couldn't have shut him up any more effectively. As a matter of fact, neither am I. Oh *shit*—

'Can you stand up?' Angela was saying. 'Only, if you've had a nasty bump on the head, maybe you should go and sit down.'

Chris smiled feebly and nodded. She helped him up, and he tottered rather unsteadily (not acting) into the living room and dropped into the armchair. Angela knelt down beside him and put her hand on his arm. 'How's that?' she asked. 'Any better?'

'Much,' he replied, carefully not looking at the coffee table beside him. 'You couldn't get me a cup of tea, could you?'

'Of course,' Angela said. 'Won't be a tick. Kettle's just boiled, as it happens.'

As soon as she'd gone, Chris leant forward and scooped up the object lying on the table, the object he'd been at such pains not to stare at when he'd entered the room. How they'd got there he had no idea. Nor did he care. At that precise moment, however, Frank Slade's special sunglasses were exactly what he needed.

The nearest mirror was in the bathroom. He hobbled over to it and looked at himself. Chris Popham: no oil painting, but exactly the same as he'd been last time he'd seen himself. All right, that was the easy bit.

He stuck the sunglasses onto his nose, closed his eyes, turned his head back towards the mirror, opened them again.

Oh, he thought.

Looking back at him, with a very sad expression on its face, was a demon.

CHAPTER FOURTEEN

A short while later, Angela found Chris in the bathroom, standing with one foot in the toilet bowl. 'What are you doing?' she asked, with what he had to concede was admirable restraint.

He explained that he'd been trying to get a good look at the top of the bathroom cabinet, which he suspected of starting to come away from the wall; to this end he'd stood on the toilet seat, but his foot had slipped, and the rest she knew or could figure out for herself.

'Oh,' she said. 'Funny thing to be doing at this hour of the night.'

He shrugged. 'I'm an impulse kind of guy.'

She gave him a sideways kind of look, then said: 'And was it?'

'What?'

'Coming away from the wall. The cabinet.'

'Didn't get a chance to look.'

'I'd leave it for now,' she said. 'Come to bed.'

'In a minute,' he replied. 'Got to dry off first. In fact, I think I'll have a bath.'

Angela frowned, said, 'Suit yourself,' and withdrew. Once she'd gone, Chris lifted his foot out of the toilet, sat on the edge of the bath, closed his eyes and tried very hard not to scream. Going back the way he'd come wasn't an option, then – bitterly unfair, he felt, because if he'd suddenly metamorphosed into a demon, surely that should mean he had special magic super-powers like they had. Apparently, though, it didn't work like that; or, if it did, it didn't extend to being able to travel by the Sanitary Express. He put in the plug and turned on the bath taps.

A demon, he thought. For crying out loud. But I don't feel different, not in the slightest. He tried to remember what Jill had told him about – he fumbled in his memory for the tech-nical term: sleepers? Carriers? Something of the sort. Humans piggybacked on by demons. It was the only explanation he could think of. Lying in the bath, he closed his eyes and tried to poke about inside his own head, looking for his demon lodger, or at least some indication that it had been there. Trouble was, he had no idea what to look for, or how to recog-nise it if he did happen to find it. Also, it gave him a headache, followed by a nosebleed. He gave up.

All right, Chris said to himself. Jill dies, SatNav escapes, I pick up a transdimensional squatter, what else? Something else must've happened, or not happened, because Jill had died instead of SatNav, and if he could only figure out what it was maybe there'd be some way of putting it right and getting home, or at least back to the school toilets.

Figure it out: right, piece of cake, just a matter of doing a degree course in metaphysics and another in temporal mechan-ics, then spending fifty years doing the maths. Easy-peasy.

If only, Chris thought, there was someone he could ask.

Maybe there was. A remote enough possibility; quite pos-sibly Derek of the department, owner of the DS polo shirt, hadn't become a demon-hunter in this timeline. Guaranteed stone-cold certainty he wouldn't know who Chris was, if he turned up on the doorstep with a wild story about demons and pantacopts, time travel and the Fey. On the other hand, Chris couldn't think of anybody else. Motion carried.

He stayed in the bath long after the water had gone cold, to give Angela plenty of time to go to sleep. A nice enough kid, he exaggerated wildly to himself, but not my type. Eventually, shivering a little, he climbed out, dried himself off with a towel and crept through into the living room. No light on in the bedroom. For now, at any rate, he was comparatively safe. He flopped onto the sofa, pulled the collar of the towelling robe tight around his neck, and closed his eyes.

He was in his car, but he wasn't moving and there was nothing to see out of the windows. The radio was playing, so quietly that he could barely hear it, but the song was one he'd recognise anywhere. 'Shake It Loose', by the Lizard-Headed Women.

He tried the door, but the handle was jammed. On the fourth savage wrench, it came away in his hand.

'Now look what you've done,' said a voice beside him.

'SatNav,' he said, but even before the words had left his mouth he knew they weren't accurate. Like her, but different. He looked round.

Whoever she was, she smiled. Nice smile. 'It's all right,' she said. 'I'm not her, if that's what you're thinking.'

'But you're one of them. The Fey.'

'You say it like it's a bad thing to be,' she replied defensively. 'Which is really unfair. Particularly,' she added pointedly, 'coming from one of *you*.'

'One of me?'

'You plural. Demonkind. If one of us is entitled to think in outmoded species stereotypes, it's me.'

He groaned aloud. 'It's true, then,' he said. 'That's what I am. A—' He couldn't bring himself to say the word.

She nodded. 'But am I bigoted and instinctively hostile?' she said. 'Am I holding my nose and sticking two fingers down my throat?' She shook her head, and her hair floated round her shoulders, reminding him of— 'You could do worse than learn from my example,' she said. 'It'd make you a better person, believe me.'

'Bit late for that,' he snapped. 'Please, can you tell me, how long—?'

'Thought you'd ask,' she said. 'About sixteen years, give or take a month. You're what's known as a carrier. You're familiar with the term?'

He nodded. 'Is there anything I can do?' he asked. 'Or am I stuck with it?'

'What are you asking me for? Contact your own kind, ask them. I'm sure they'll be able to tell you.'

His own kind . . . A chill ran down Chris's spine. His own kind had murdered poor Mr Newsome just for being there, to eat the fear of his last terrified moments. From now on, at least until he could get rid of the loathsome parasite burrowed deep inside him, his own kind were so incomprehensibly alien that the very sight of them made his guts twist like the rubber band on a balsa-wood airplane. His own kind, for crying out loud. Did that imply he had a demon family somewhere on the other side, a demon mother and father, demon aunts and uncles who'd tell him how much he'd grown and how sweet he'd been when he was little, who'd be offended when he forgot their birthdays? *Sixteen years*; in this timeline, at any rate. Whatever kind of havoc must he have been responsible for, feeding off emotions for sixteen years?

'You're upset, I can tell,' the Fey said. 'Is anything the matter?'

Chris had no idea why he told her, apart from the fact that she'd asked; and because this was just a dream, so he was just thinking aloud in his sleep. When he'd finished, she made a garage mechanic's tooth-sucking noise and said, 'I see.'

'Well?'

'You're screwed,' said the Fey. 'I really don't see how you're going to get out of that.' She sighed, a deep and genuine expression of compassion and regret. 'God, I'm glad I'm not you.'

Nice of her to care, but she really wasn't helping. 'Oh,' Chris said. 'I was hoping you'd be able to suggest something.'

'Not really. I mean, I'd like nothing more than to be able to say, do this, do that, follow the instructions to the letter and you'll be home free. Not possible, unfortunately. Terribly sorry to be so useless, but that's a real collector's item of a mess you've got yourself into there.' She paused, and frowned. 'And you're telling me it was a Fey who did this to you? One of our lot?'

He nodded; then said: 'Hold on. Did this to me?'

'Well, yes. Stitched you up. I don't think that's overstating it, do you? I mean, there you are, caught up on the sidelines of this demon civil-war thing but not really involved to any significant extent; and this Fey of yours suckers you into changing history just so she doesn't get killed and stuck in a box for sixteen years. Now that really wasn't a very nice thing to do. Not the sort of behaviour we expect.'

'Right,' Chris said, nodding enthusiastically. 'So, does that mean you'll help me? Your lot, I mean, the Fey. As a point of honour,' he added hopefully.

'Wouldn't have thought so,' the Fey replied. 'Think about it for a moment, will you? The only way you'd be able to undo all the damage and reset to zero would be to go back to the critical moment, not kill your friend, allow your friend to kill the Fey, and then get someone to take you back to your proper time. And that's not possible.'

'Yes, it is. Must be. After all, she did it, SatNav. She took me there—'

'Illegally,' the Fey replied gravely. 'Completely against the law, mucking about with time. Technically, yes, it can be done, but none of us'd ever do a thing like that, not even to help out someone like yourself. A demon wouldn't have those kinds of scruples, but a demon wouldn't be able to do it, wrong kind of dimensional focus. The Acme Portable Door could shift you through time, but they've all been hidden or destroyed, so you can forget that as a possibility. No,' she concluded sadly, 'I don't want to depress you or anything, but there's nothing anybody can do. You're stuck like it. Sucks, I know, but who said life was fair?'

Somehow, that wasn't what Chris had been expecting. 'You mean I've got to spend the rest of my life in this timeline, with a demon stuck inside me? I can't do that. That's just not me, I'm sorry.'

She smiled at him. 'Cheer up,' she said. 'Maybe you'll die young. Although,' she added, 'there's not very much chance of that, seeing how hard demons are to kill. I mean, you can forget about all your human diseases and old age and all that. A pantacopt'd do it, or a direct strike from a bolt of lightning; I gather there's some poisons, though they're incredibly rare, and I've heard it said that twenty-four hours in the core of a nuclear reactor's been known to work. Apart from that, though, it's not good. Which is why,' she added, 'if you read the small print of nearly all pension schemes, demons are specifically excluded, because they live too long. You can see their point, can't you?'

Chris didn't reply. He was replaying what she'd just told him: *it was a Fey who did this to you.* Not that he was prepared to take her word for it, or anybody's word for anything any more, not even if a United Nations delegation headed by God were to come to him and tell him his name. But belief wasn't required, just a calm analysis of the facts. For the reasons given or some other motive, SatNav had induced him to change history, and that was why he was here. Her fault. And, almost certainly, deliberate. Well, he thought, nice to know finally who the enemy was.

'Cheer up,' the Fey said. 'After all, it could be worse. That Angela seems like a nice enough kid, and so long as you're with her, you'll never go hungry. Absolute genius when it comes to stirring up stress and angst. Stick with her, you'll be all right.'

He groaned out loud. Hardly something to look forward to. 'Look,' he said desperately, 'do you think you could find SatNav for me? The Fey who did this to me? Maybe you could talk to her, get her to send me back, if she's the only one who could do it.'

He'd said the wrong thing. 'I don't think so,' she replied
icily. 'I don't associate with entities like that. Oh, I'll find her all
right, and then I'll report her to the authorities, and they'll
really make her wish she'd stayed in your plastic box giving you
directions. She's in for a really nasty time, if that's any consolation.'

No, not really, Chris wanted to say; but he woke up instead.
Angela was standing over him, scowling and shaking his shoulder.

'What're you doing out here?' she said. 'I've been waiting for
you.'

Hell, he thought. 'Sorry,' he said, 'I thought you were asleep.
Didn't want to disturb you.'

'Since when were you so considerate?' Her scowl shifted
into a grin. He couldn't make up his mind which was scarier.
No, belay that, he could. 'Anyway,' Angela said, 'I'm awake.
Come along, on your feet.'

'I'm very tired,' Chris said. It had always worked a charm
when Karen said it, but maybe he didn't quite have her delivery, because Angela said, 'Tough,' grabbed the lobe of his ear
between thumb and forefinger and hauled him out of the chair.
'You're not still on about that bang on the head, are you?'

He'd forgotten about that. 'Yes,' he said immediately.
'Actually, I've started feeling dizzy and sick, so it could be con-
cussion after all. I really think I should sit down again.'

She wasn't happy about it, he could tell; probably suspected
he was lying, but knew she couldn't prove it. 'Oh,' she said.
'Pity. Never mind.' She let go her grip on his ear, and he
flopped back into the chair. He had a strange feeling of having
just narrowly escaped, like a fish pulling itself free from a hook.
'Sorry,' she said, in a slightly softer voice, 'it's just that, well,
there's few enough perks to being stuck in these monkey suits.
Seems a shame to let an opportunity slip, as it were.'

Chris looked up at her, at the faint gleam in her eyes. No
way, he thought, not if you were the only girl in the world and
I was the only boy. Not even if it'd solve global warming. 'Oh

well,' he croaked. 'There'll be plenty of time later, when I'm better.'

He'd said the wrong thing again. She shrugged, see-if-I-care, went back into the bedroom and slammed the door. He wondered if he was still human enough for his emotions to be nutritious, or whether they were like alcohol-free lager, nothing like the real thing.

No way back, the Fey had told him; stuck here and now for the rest of his life, like a convict transported to Australia. Worse still, there was a huge gap in his understanding of the plot. It was like being back at school, being set some God-awful boring novel to read for English, trying to bluff his way in class on the basis of the blurb on the back cover.

Being back at school. Quite.

Chris tried to figure it out, though he didn't dare write anything down or draw helpful diagrams, for fear of leaving written evidence lying about that might provoke further suspicion. So, he thought: if Ellie who got killed in the girls' toilets was really SatNav all along, then why did Jill want to kill her in the first place? Now, of course, he'd killed Jill instead, and as a result here he was, shacked up with Angela the trainee, now apparently not dead after all; cheating with her on Karen, let's not forget that small detail. Not only a demon, but a love rat into the bargain. It just keeps on getting better.

Forget that aspect just for a moment; concentrate on the mechanics of the thing. Jill came here to find the dissident ringleader, thought she'd found her and killed her, only to discover that she'd slaughtered the wrong victim. Well, fine; that checked out, since Ellie, or SatNav or whoever, wasn't a demon at all. Then he'd intervened, suckered into it by SatNav, who had a selfish desire not to get killed and stuck in a plastic box; Jill had died instead, but that wasn't all that'd happened. At some point during the encounter, Chris Popham (human) had turned into a demon . . .

The practicalities of it he could account for. Demons can piggyback onto humans, dig down inside their heads and bum a lift, like a hobo on a freight train. You didn't have to be a demonology postgraduate to figure out what must've happened. Just before the pantacopt sliced her in two, Jill's demon must've hopped out of her and into him.

Chris laughed out loud, but it wasn't a happy laugh. What are friends for? he asked himself; but there's a limit. Not quite the same as looking after someone's cat for the weekend, the commitment was just that bit deeper and further-reaching. Also, with Jill dead, there was no possibility of ever handing it back. A demon is for life, not just for Christmas.

And then there was Karen – he kept forgetting about her, and he felt really bad about that, but he couldn't seem to stop doing it. Karen, also a demon, and who'd just happened to be in the Toilet of Destiny at the time the key event took place. Something odd about that, he thought. We've got Jill, who's a demon, Ellie, who's a Fey, and Karen, also a demon, all in the same toilet at the same time. Coincidence, Chris told himself, but he was wasting his mental breath. Not a coincidence, it just couldn't be.

Jill was hunting a demon, the dissident ringleader, someone at the school. Karen was at the school. Karen was a demon.

Karen?

Yes, but think about it for a moment. Jill had told him that the dissident ringleader had started at the school not long before the unpleasantness in the girls' bogs. Karen – Christ, he thought, that's right, that's when she came, the start of the spring term, the same time as Ellie.

KH4CP, written on a cubicle wall in biro.

Did demons do that? Well, it counted as antisocial behaviour, according to the government, so it was wicked and bad and you weren't allowed to do it, but even so, Chris couldn't quite square KH4CP with what he'd learned about demonkind. A demon crosses the line – a demon with a mission, to preserve her race by changing their patterns of behaviour at the most fundamental level possible – and practically the first thing she does is develop a crush on a human boy. No, he thought, does not compute. And besides, Karen and Jill were best friends, and Jill was a top-notch demon assassin; if Karen really was the one who is to come, surely Jill would have noticed, at some point.

Coincidence, then. Yeah, right.

Not that Chris cared particularly; not about whether Karen's demon was the dissident ringleader, at any rate. That whole aspect of the business seemed to have gone away, which was just as well. He had plenty of other things to think about. For instance: Angela in the unbuggered-up timeline died, presumably killed by demons. On this side, she was still very much alive. So, he'd changed something. What? A big something, or was it one of those butterflies-in-the-rainforest connections, so apparently trivial you didn't notice it at the time. What exactly had he changed?

Well, he thought, I killed Jill.

That made him shiver. Had Jill killed Angela? Bloody melodrama, the thing he hated most in the whole world. If so, why? Jill wouldn't scrag an innocent bystander – well, not twice, at any rate – so Angela must've been involved. He remembered the marks of his nails, still visible on the canvas of her jeep's passenger seat belt twenty-four hours later. If the demon who kidnapped him and drove him to the Ettingate Retail Park hadn't been in disguise after all, if it really was Angela (demons can't change their shape; who was it who'd told him that?) then she must've been after the one who is to come, and Jill killed her because she was getting too close—

In that timeline, yes. In this one— In this one, she was in the next room, having tried and failed to lure him in there with her. No reason to suppose she wasn't a fundamentalist demon assassin in this timeline, same as in the other. In which case, there was probably a case to be made out for assuming that her interest in him probably wasn't true love.

In that case, he wondered, why was he still alive?

Answer: because she must reckon that he knew where to find the one who is to come, which in a sense he did – it had been Jill, by her own admission, who'd taken over the job when the real dissident ringleader had lost her nerve after the toilet massacre. But Jill was dead, of course; dead, and her demon plausibly located inside poor bloody Chris Popham. Yes, but at the time he'd killed Jill, she hadn't changed sides.

Ibuprofen, Chris thought, I need ibuprofen, to stop my head exploding. Don't suppose we've got any, since Karen always reckoned it made her throw up. He massaged his temples with his fingertips instead. Didn't do a blind bit of good.

So Angela's a demon assassin who thinks I might know, consciously or not, how to find the fugitive dissident ring-leader. Because I'm still alive, I can probably infer that I'm not in immediate – as in at-some-point-in-the-next-ten-min-utes – danger. Jill's dead, Karen's gone, SatNav got me into this mess but now she's out of it. Also, I'm in an alternative timeline where I don't know what's happened, I'm only assuming I'm a sales rep working for JWW Retail, and if I am, chances are I'm not in line for promotion to area sales man-ager any more. Oh sod, Chris thought, I was looking forward to that.

So: what to do? Run away; it was the obvious, sensible course of action, as it had been all along, and he hadn't done it. Now, though, there wouldn't be much point. The trouble with running away is that no matter where or how far you go, whether you flee to the remote mountains or the impenetrable rainforest (neither of which, incidentally, appealed to him ter-ribly much), you always end up taking yourself with you, which in nine cases out of ten utterly defeats the object of the exercise. Wherever he went, probably even Switzerland, the demon would come too; in which case, he might as well stay home and spare himself the jabs and the cost of the ticket.

This is silly, Chris thought. I don't feel the slightest bit dif-ferent. Surely, if I'm one of them now, I should be brimming over with evil, bloodthirsty impulses, and I'm not. Not that he was complaining; the last thing he needed in his hopelessly overcomplicated life was an insatiable craving for blood and terror. Even so, it was an inconsistency, and it nagged at him like a raspberry pip lodged between his teeth.

He was too stressed-out to stay still, so he stood up and walked round the room, trying to spot the differences. There weren't many: a few things missing, stuff Karen must've taken when she left; her stuff, therefore by definition not the kind of thing he'd be likely to miss. The drawer where she kept her CDs was empty, but in it was a packet of photos which she either hadn't wanted or had overlooked. Chris opened it, and sat down on the sofa.

Karen was a person of many talents, of which photography wasn't one. She had the knack of cutting off people's feet and the tops of their heads, and all the buildings in her pictures looked like they were slowly toppling backwards. Lack of ability had never inhibited her enthusiasm, however; whenever they went anywhere, day trips or the rare, begrudged holidays, she blazed away like a paparazzo at a Hollywood wedding. Maybe that explained why she hadn't wanted the photos. They were mostly of him, standing in front of things, next to things, always looking grumpy, impatient and, of course, unnaturally abbreviated. Probably just as well they'd never had kids. Future generations turning the pages of the treasured family album would've gained the distinct impression that great-grandad was a miserable bugger with a flat-topped head who sort of faded away at the ankles.

Chris frowned. To a demon, of course, a packet like this was presumably as good as a Mars Bar, a compact feast of nostalgia, embarrassment and general guilt. He turned one over, remembering that Karen always wrote on the backs: *Chris & me in London, Chris & me in Birmingham, Chris & me summer holiday in Lanzarote.* The odd part of it was, she took pictures by the hundred, but he couldn't remember ever seeing her looking at them once they'd been developed and printed.

Well; he wasn't particularly interested in foreshortened images of himself. He started to put them back in the envelope, then paused.

Chris remembered that one. It had been their anniversary, or what she called their anniversary; he couldn't recall offhand what it was the anniversary of, but he always forgot it, except this once. On this occasion he'd managed to remember, and had booked a table for them both at the Indian restaurant just across the road. From a brownie-point perspective, one of the best things he ever did, though it was ultimately cancelled out when he forgot her birthday; still, for a short while, he'd been promoted from insensitive pig to closet romantic, and to commemorate the occasion, Karen had battened onto a harmless bystander in the street outside and made him take a picture of the two of them. Whoever he was, the stranger had been a better photographer than Karen. All four feet were in the frame with millimetres to spare, and neither of them looked like a boiled egg about to be invaded by toast soldiers. Chris was wearing his usual have-I-got-to expression. Karen was beaming, happiness shining out of her like light from a torch. He noticed that he was wearing a tie. Said it all, really.

Chris put the photos back in the drawer and closed it firmly. It was dawning on him that demonhood wasn't the only thing about Karen that he hadn't bothered to notice until it was too late. Also worth bearing in mind that you didn't have to be a demon to make a real mess of somebody's emotions. Humans can do it too.

He thought about that. A large part of it, he knew only too well, was that he'd never really believed that anybody who didn't have to could ever really love him. Sure, Karen had said she did, in so many words, but he'd always assumed that she must be exaggerating or trying to be nice, and that her reasons for choosing him were something like his own: rebound, compromise, making do so as to get the whole tiresome pairing-off business over and done with. He'd been wrong about that – natural enough mistake to make, but a mistake nonetheless, and look at the damage it had done. Yes, he told himself, but she wasn't *human*, you can't beat yourself up over being a complete bastard to a malevolent transdimensional entity. They don't count.

Chris thought about that, too; he thought, demons feed on emotion, so what better habitat could they ask for than true love, the genuine article, accept no substitutes? No different from humans under those circumstances, no different from the way human lovers nourish each other, needing no external sources of supply. If you were a demon and someone loved you, there'd be no point in going hunting and scavenging, when there was someone whose greatest pleasure in life was feeding you. The perfect arrangement, in fact; he could see that now, it was painfully obvious (but so were gravity and the displacement of water, for a million years, until someone had the wit to notice them). It had to be that: the key discovery made by the demon dissident ringleader – he could picture the eureka moment, the sudden switching on of a blinding bright light – that for a healthy, balanced, organic, sustainable, additive-free, calorie-controlled diet, all you need is love.

The door opened. Angela was standing in the doorway, looking at him. She had the most extraordinary expression on her face.

'It's you,' she said.

Chris looked round at her. 'You what?'

'It's *you*.' Wipe her voice on a microscope slide and analyse it scientifically, and you'd find substantial traces of shock, stunned bewilderment, anger and resentment, with just a hint of residual disbelief. 'You're *it*. How the hell can you be *it*? That's just not possible.'

'Angela? What the hell are you talking—?'

'You're the one who is to come.' She stabbed the words at him. 'Don't even think of denying it, I could smell it from in there, it stinks the place out. You're the one I was sent here to find. But that's crazy, it's *stupid*. You can't be, you just can't.'

Mixed signals, he couldn't help feeling. 'Make your bloody mind up, can't you?' he said.

She looked at him again. 'It's you,' she said. 'Definitely.'

'Bollocks.' Chris took a step back. 'No, really, it can't be me, I'm not even a demon. Well, I wasn't one until very recently, and that's a very long story, but I promise you, I'm not. Honest.'

'It's you,' Angela repeated, her voice as cold as ice. 'Sorry about this, but I'm going to have to ask you to come with me.'

Another three steps back; and then the wall, with which he'd never had any quarrel, had to interfere and block him. 'Angela, I swear to God, I'm not a real demon. It got into me in a toilet, but it's Jill's really, only you'll never have met her, of course, she died before you were born.' He was gabbling, but he couldn't stop, and she was getting closer. 'What do you mean,' he said desperately, 'you can smell it? I can't smell anything.'

'Demon 8845223,' Angela said hoarsely, 'I'm arresting you on seventeen counts of disruptive, deviant and antisocial behaviour. You have the right to remain silent—'

'This is silly, I'm not a demon,' Chris yelled; and, as the words left his mouth, he knew that he was lying. Maybe it had been asleep and she'd woken it up, or maybe it had been watching all the time and realised that this time it was going to have to make a fight of it. He felt it grow inside him, like one of those foldaway umbrellas where you press a button and suddenly it erupts to fill all the available space. He could feel his skin turning into scale armour, his teeth and nails evolving into weapons; like the Incredible Hulk, he guessed, only not so hard on the wardrobe. He tried to say, 'Now let's be reasonable about this,' but it came out as a long, rattling hiss. He felt his ears go back, which was extremely disconcerting. Oh well, he thought, so I really am one after all, in spite of everything. Shucks. If you can't beat 'em, eat 'em.

He was grinning. Fun, he thought. Haven't had a good scrap in such a long time. Angela had changed too; just a little bit. Her eyes were round red saucers staring out of a crazy-paved grey face, her small, thin fingers were meat hooks and her open mouth was full of needles. Curiously, she was far less scary now than she'd been an hour ago. No bother, Chris told himself, I can take her as easy as pie, even if I am a bit out of practice. He crouched, digging his toe-claws into the carpet for better purchase, waiting for her to spring.

When it came, he sidestepped easily, letting her sail past him into the wall. There was a crunch and a brief flurry of plaster dust (Karen would be so pissed off, he thought), but Angela recovered quickly and lunged again, and once again Chris took an easy couple of paces, left and back, and let her pass him, only this time he reached out his right arm and raked her neck with his claws. She squealed as the blood spurted, and slashed at him backhand, so fast he barely had time to get clear. She missed, and demolished a small table that Karen had bought in Homebase. Where her blood flecked the carpet, it sizzled.

Chris was thinking, it's good to be back, good to be normal again; and when my teeth meet in her neck, will there be enough human in her still to taste of anything? Also, he couldn't help thinking, this is so much better than love: that pale, watery substitute, nouvelle cuisine to a hamburger, all served up fancy with a scalloped carrot but nothing you can get your teeth into. So much for love, then. As Crocodile Dundee so memorably said: you can live on it, but it tastes like shit.

He was almost minded to attack, but he remembered that he was still quite rusty after his long hibernation. Better to let her come to him. He took a step back and opened his guard invitingly. Angela accepted the invitation, and sprang. This time, as Chris twitched his feet out of the way, he hammered the side of her head with his balled fist. She hadn't been expecting that. The blow dropped her to her knees, but she just about managed to recover into a semblance of a guard. Not to worry, plenty of time; though his mother wouldn't have approved, he knew. Don't play with your food, she used to say. Oh, but this was so much better than being human; he was alive again, for the first time in sixteen years, so why the hell shouldn't he indulge himself, just a bit?

'You realise you're resisting arrest,' Angela panted, through a mouthful of loosened fangs. 'That's a *crime*. You're going to be in so much trouble.'

Chris reached in and punched her again; she was so slow she hardly moved at all before the punch went home and knocked her down. Enough of this, he thought, it's getting boring. He shot out a hand, grabbed her by one ear, dragged her to her feet and started to strangle her—

He paused. There was a human in the room.

Several humans, in fact. They must've come in while his attention was elsewhere. Most of them he didn't know, but the face of the one nearest to him was familiar. In that horrible other life of his, he'd borrowed this human's polo shirt—

'Derek,' he said. 'You're Derek, from Jill's work. Piss off, I'm busy.'

The human didn't answer – of course not, because Chris had spoken in Pandemonian, the language of his own people, which humans couldn't understand. Like it mattered. He knew without needing to ask what the humans were doing here: they were Delendi Sunt, the demon-hunters, the enemy of his kind. That changed things. He let go of Angela's neck and muttered, 'You know who this lot are?'

She nodded. 'You're still under arrest, though.'

'Fine,' he replied. 'Later.' She grinned.

The humans were trying to surround them, which wasn't good; they might be mere mortals, but they weren't stupid. 'Back to back,' Chris grunted, and thankfully Angela had the sense to do as she was told. He tried roaring, but although they were plainly scared – yum! – they kept their positions. He tried a couple of trial swipes, but collected nothing more than a few nailfuls of scalp.

'Cover the female,' Derek was saying, 'I'll take the male.' Courage – a rich, slightly salty taste; not sweet, like terror. Odd, though. What did a stupid human have to feel courageous about?

Then he saw something in Derek's hand: a square yellow box, from which the human drew a long, thin steel tape. Oh, Chris thought. One of those.

But so what? He was a demon, faster, stronger, infinitely better motivated, and still starving hungry. His eyes fixed on the yellow tape, Chris took a step forward, balanced his weight and went for the lunge—

The pantacopt blade caught him on the neck, just above the collarbone, and carried on going until it came out through the thigh bone on the opposite side. He had just enough time to taste his opponent's joyous relief and to mutter 'Shit' under his breath, and then he died.

CHAPTER FIFTEEN

Chris's life flashed in front of his eyes.

The process can't have taken more than a millionth of a second in real time, because that's roughly how long it takes for the neural energy to drain out of the synapses as the brain starves of oxygen and dies, but it seemed ever so much longer. The first ten years were mostly embarrassing, like looking at photographs of yourself in your pram with chocolate all round your mouth. School was just dull, and by the time he hit puberty he was starting to fidget. Maths with Miss Whitworth was about as enthralling as it had been the first time round; ditto hanging round the Co-op car park with Danny and Neil. There were a couple of incidents, like his maiden hangover and the first time he got a ride home in a police car, that he'd much rather have fast-forwarded through, but no such luck. He was being treated to the director's cut, with all the bits that should've been edited out pasted lovingly back in. Come to think of it, his life was little more than a bloopers compilation in any case. All that was missing was Denis Norden to do the commentary. Year ten. Danny bets him he wouldn't sneak into the girls' toilets, he accepts. Suddenly, he had his own undivided attention.

I'm sitting in the cubicle. Someone's written KH4CP on

the wall in biro, just above the toilet-roll holder. I can hear voices. I can hear someone moving about in the adjoining cubicle. What do I do now?

SatNav? he thought.

'What?'

Her voice in his head. *I'm lost, SatNav. Which way do I turn?*

'Well,' she said, 'that depends. Oh, sod it, stop time.' Time obligingly stopped; he checked his watch, and the second hand was frozen. 'You do pick your moments, don't you?'

Thanks, SatNav. He stared at the door in front of him, the bolt he'd have to pull back in order to leave the cubicle. *Well, here we are again.*

'You're going to have to stop doing this before it becomes a habit,' SatNav said. 'Right, what's the matter?'

I'm dead, aren't I?

'Yes,' SatNav replied. 'You have, to coin a phrase, arrived at your destination.'

Shit.

'Yes.'

He frowned. *That's because I changed history,* he thought. *I came back here – you brought me back here – I stopped Jill from killing you, I killed Jill, you survived, so did Angela, but not me. Is that it, more or less?*

'Basically. You took the road less travelled by, and it has made all the difference. That's a quotation,' she pointed out. 'Wasted on you, presumably.'

If you say so, he thought. *But, SatNav, if I don't interfere, if I let Jill kill you—*

'Too late,' SatNav interrupted. 'It's already happened. This is just your life flashing in front of your eyes. Well-attested neurobiological phenomenon. It's not real, you can't change anything.'

You're lying.

'When have I ever lied to you?'

He shifted a little and sat firmly on his hands. *Thanks, you can start time again now.*

'You wouldn't.' Just a hint of panic, maybe? 'You wouldn't just sit there and let me die.'

Want to bet?

'You couldn't. You're not capable of it. Your inherent decency and sense of fair play—'

Whenever you're ready.

'Oh come on,' SatNav said nervously, 'be reasonable. I mean, what the hell have you possibly got to live for?'

He smiled. *About fifty years*, he replied, *assuming I lay off the carbohydrates and always look twice before crossing the road. That's enough. You've got to be in the game if you want to stand a chance of winning.*

'Someone's been reading the *Reader's Digest* again,' SatNav said. 'Face it, your life's a mess. You'll be better off without it, trust me.'

No. And besides, there's stuff I've got to do.

'Too late for that now,' SatNav said. 'Besides, wouldn't you rather leave it to someone else, let it be their problem? Think of all the aggravation.'

Restart time, SatNav. Now.

'I don't think you quite grasp the dynamics of the situation,' SatNav said desperately. 'All right, you can change things back, but it won't solve anything. You'll still be dead. You got cut in two, remember. Sorry, but that's not negotiable.'

Tick tock, SatNav. Now.

The second hand of Chris's watch jerked forward one division. He heard the door of the neighbouring cubicle open. I hope I'm right about this, he thought. He stayed where he was.

'Bastard,' said Honest John.

Chris opened his eyes. 'Hello,' he said.

'Selfish, inconsiderate bastard,' John said, reaching out a hand to pull him out of the toilet. 'You chickened out, then.'

'Yes.' He frowned. 'How did you—?'

'That was the deal,' John's head said. It was propped up in

the sink. 'You'd go back and change history, and in the altered timeline you wouldn't cut my head off.'

'You knew, didn't you? You knew if I changed history, I'd die.'

John's body hauled him out, and Chris stood on the bathroom floor, shaking a little. 'Not noticeably dead, though, are you?'

So, he'd been right after all. 'That's because it wasn't me that got cut in two,' he said. 'It was the demon.'

John's head grunted. 'You figured it out,' he said, with grudging respect. 'Pity. I never thought you'd be smart enough.'

Chris put the toilet seat down and sat on it. 'The demon got killed,' he said, 'not me. I got set free. I'm alive and I'm human again, and I'm back where I belong. That wasn't just my life flashing in front of my eyes, that was me getting my life back again.'

'Quite,' said John's head. 'You get to survive, and the hell with everybody else.' His body picked up his head. 'You got any parcel tape, anything like that?'

Chris thought. 'Sorry,' he said. 'We used to have some, but I think Karen used it all.'

'Bugger. All right,' John said wearily. 'In that case, I'll get you to cut two holes in a carrier bag for me. To see through,' he explained.

Once John had left the flat, Chris made himself a nice cup of tea, then got the superglue out and glued the toilet seat firmly shut, just in case. Then he flumped down on the bed and started to shake all over.

Music, if you could call it that. 'Shake It Loose', by the Lizard Headed Women.

'You fell asleep,' the nice Fey explained. 'Hardly surprising, after the day you've had.'

Chris sat up, looked down at the body lying on the bed. 'I'm still alive, aren't I?' he said anxiously. 'I mean, I'm not—'

The nice Fey laughed. 'Calm down,' she said, 'it's all right. You're alive, this is just a perfectly ordinary dream. And yes, you're back. It worked. It was the demon who got killed, not you.'

He sighed with relief. 'That's all right, then,' he said.

'Quite,' the nice Fey said. She looked at Chris for a moment or so, then said, 'Did you really figure it all out by yourself? I'm impressed.'

At any other time he'd have relished the flattery. 'Depends,' he said cautiously. 'Exactly what did I figure out?'

'That once the demon surfaced and took you over, it'd be killed and not you. Because that's A-level-grade demonology – not bad if you worked it out from first principles.'

'It was luck,' Chris admitted. 'And intuition as well, I suppose.'

She nodded. 'I suppose so,' she said. 'After all, it was pure chance that the demon-hunters happened to raid your flat at exactly the right moment.'

He grinned weakly. 'Not quite,' he said. 'I phoned them.'

'Oh.' She sounded impressed. 'So you had got it all worked out.'

Shrug. 'It was something you said, actually,' he replied. 'You kept telling me that I was stuck with being a demon for the rest of my life.' Chris looked away; he was trying to remember what had made him so certain it'd work, but he couldn't. Scary thought, that. 'I came to the conclusion that it was worth a try and I didn't have a hell of a lot to lose. But what I was expecting to happen was that the Delendi Sunt boys would kill the demon and I'd be left over, so to speak, but still marooned in the other timeline. This—' He waved vaguely at the universe. 'It's a bonus I really wasn't expecting. Which means there's got to be more to it than just having the demon killed.' He shook his head. 'I don't suppose you're going to tell me, are you?'

The Fey smiled sadly. 'Sorry, can't. You're on the right lines, but you're going to have to work it out for yourself. Otherwise it'd be cheating.'

'What's wrong with cheating?'

She gave him a cold look. 'I'll pretend I didn't hear that,' she said.

'Fine. What happened to Angela, by the way?'

'Dead. Oh, don't look all sad about it. Just means she's back on her side of the line, explaining to her bosses how she came to cock up the mission. But I don't suppose they'll be too hard on her. After all, she more or less succeeded.'

Chris wasn't expecting that. 'No, she didn't,' he objected. 'She was supposed to find the dissident ringleader.'

The nice Fey smiled at him, the reassuring smile you use when talking to an amiable idiot. 'Yes, she did,' she said. 'And maybe she didn't bring it back, but that hardly mattered, since it came back of its own accord at more or less the same time as she did. Think about it,' she added, as she vanished in a cloud of blinding light and deafening noise.

Which turned out to be the phone, ringing in the hall. Chris swore, extended his cricked neck and cramped legs, and hobbled out to answer it.

He recognised the voice, though it gave him a nasty jolt when he heard it. 'Hi, Jill,' he said. 'Talk of the—'

'What the *hell* do you think you're playing at?' Jill yelled at him.

'Nice to hear your voice too, Jill. What can I do for—?'

'I've just got off the phone with the permanent secretary,' Jill snarled at him. 'I've been trying to explain to him why the demon high commissioner in London's just thanked him officially for extraditing the dissident ringleader back across the line. But we haven't, I said. Yes, we bloody well have, he said, and your name was expressly mentioned, you and some old school friend of yours. I have no idea who you could possibly mean, I lied, let me look into it and get back to you. You bastard,' she added, with enough pressure of feeling to power a steam turbine. 'What've you been up to?'

Chris sighed. He'd always liked Jill, a lot, but this time he wasn't in the mood. He put the phone down, counted to three and then lifted the receiver off the cradle and laid it gently on the table. 'I just saved your life, you ungrateful cow,' he said aloud. Then he tottered into the kitchen and cut himself a sandwich.

Amazing what two slices of processed bread and a thin layer of stale cheese can do. Unfed, the most he could say for himself was that he'd somehow managed to survive the past. With a cheese sandwich inside him, he was very nearly ready to face the future. Whichever future it turned out to be.

So: the demon had left him, gone back to its side of the line. All well and good, and he was delighted to be rid of it. (He munched a mouthful of sandwich.) But there were still far too many questions hanging over him. Where had the demon come from in the first place? And which one was it?

Chris chewed steadily until he'd finished the sandwich to the last crumb. Then he took out his wallet, found a business card and dialled a number.

While he was waiting for the visitor he'd summoned to arrive, he hoovered and dusted the flat, washed up, cleaned the kitchen floor and did two loads of washing. He was surprised how much it helped; to the point where, when Derek from the department arrived, Chris was much calmer than he had any right to be.

'Thanks for the loan of them,' Derek said, handing over Frank Slade's special sunglasses. 'I wouldn't mind borrowing them again some time, if you're not using them.' Derek didn't look nearly so terrifying in this timeline. In fact, he wasn't scary at all.

'My pleasure,' Chris said. 'Oh, and I wonder if you'd mind getting rid of this for me. I've only just found out what it is, and I don't like having it in the house.'

Derek recognised the tapemeasure instantly, just as he'd recognised the sunglasses. 'Where the hell did you get—?'

'Little old lady found it in her attic,' Chris replied.

'You do know what this is?'

'Yes, and so do you. Just take it away and put it somewhere safe.'

(Somewhere I'll never be able to get hold of it again, he didn't say.)

As soon as Derek had gone, Chris went into the bathroom, stood in front of the mirror and put the sunglasses on.

'Shit,' he said aloud.

They all looked alike to him, of course, so he couldn't be sure, but if he had to express an opinion he'd have to say he was sure it was the same demon face he'd seen in this very mirror in the other timeline. Wonderful, he said to himself, I'm a demon.

But now at least he understood why.

So.

Typical bloody Karen, he thought, she buggers off in a huff and doesn't think to let me know where she's gone. Grand gesture, but utterly inconsiderate.

There was, of course, one person who could be relied on to know where she'd got to. Information central, the social hub. Chris took a deep breath and phoned Jill's number.

'If you've called to apologise, you can—'

'No,' he said. 'I need to talk to Karen.'

'I don't know where she—'

'Yes, you do.'

(In spite of everything, the stress, the aggravation, the threats of death and serious injury, a tiny bit of him was smirking.)

'All right,' Jill conceded, 'maybe I do, but she told me that she doesn't want to see you. She was absolutely clear about it. Look, I'm really sorry, but—'

'This isn't true love,' Chris interrupted harshly. 'This is business.'

She reacted as though she'd never heard the word before. 'I don't understand,' she said. 'How can it be—?'

'I've found the one who is to come,' he said. 'You know, the dissident ringleader. The real one,' he added, a trifle spitefully. 'You want it, you fetch Karen over right now. No,' he added quickly, as a tiny cog slid into place in the gear-train of his mind, 'this evening, here, the flat. Let's all three of us go out to dinner.'

'What? Chris, are you feeling all right?'

He grinned. 'Never better.'

He rang off, then phoned the Indian restaurant across the road and booked a table.

Lots of things to do before then. First, Chris nipped down to the car and rummaged about among the boxes of samples until he found what he was looking for. Just the one packet; he hoped it'd be enough. He took it through into the kitchen, read the directions on the back of the packet (they were delightfully simple: just add water) and emptied the contents into the biggest bowl he could find. Then he filled the measuring jug with water and slopped it in. It didn't say you had to stir it, but he thought it couldn't do any harm. Wrong. Two seconds, and it dissolved the head off the wooden spoon.

And to think (he thought) it's taken me all this time to figure out what it's for. How thick can you get?

Add dried water to pure distilled water and you get pure distilled water. JWW Retail DW6 powder is *essence of nothing* – because if it was anything at all, when you added it to pure water you'd get pure water plus something: impure water.

Conventional science recognises matter and anti-matter; DW6 is neutral matter. Make it into something, and that something won't exist, definitively; but it's still matter, and has 1001 handy applications around the home, workshop and office. Mix with turpentine to create an easily moulded putty which sets hard to the consistency and with the properties of brick, and you can build a solid, useful structure that *isn't actually there*. Make a saturated solution of DW6, pour it into an ordinary household ice-cube tray and pop it into the freezer, and you end up with the philosopher's stone of applied demonology, null ice. Ten cubes of null ice (roughly the amount you get out of one standard-size sachet of DW6) is sufficient to embody one average adult male demon.

(No wonder, Chris thought, as he verified his assumptions by looking up DW6 in the FAQ section of the JWW Retail website – where he'd never thought of looking. Why? he asked himself; because I'm stupid, obviously – we sell so much of the stuff. After all, ninety per cent of the people I know have turned out to be bloody demons, so clearly there's a lot of them about.)

Chris had a bath. He shaved. He put on his best suit. And (because it's not every day your future life flashes in front of your eyes) a tie.

While Chris was polishing his shoes he got a call from Mr Burnoz, confirming his appointment as area sales manager. He made a point of sounding laid-back and cool about it, but when he put the phone down afterwards he was grinning like an idiot. Not that he'd be any good at it, not after tonight, but from what he'd seen of previous incumbents of the job nobody was ever going to notice. He'd miss the road, of course, being stuck in an office a lot of the time, but there would be compensations; not least of them being that he'd no longer have any need of a satellite navigation system. Wonderful gadgets, if responsibly used, but if you're not careful they can lead you astray.

Chris had forgotten what she looked like.

Incredible but true. When he answered the door, he saw Jill and someone else, a nice-looking girl about his own age, with straight chemical-red hair and very dark blue eyes and a nervous expression that made him want to smile. It took him maybe as long as three seconds to realise it was Karen.

Jill nudged past him into the hall. 'Well?' she said. 'Where is it?'

He closed the front door and stood with his back to it. 'Here,' he said.

'Where?'

'Right here.' He smiled. 'But let's have dinner. I booked a table for us over the road.'

Jill frowned. 'Oh, not curry,' she moaned. 'I never did like curry.'

'You never liked human food, period,' he said to her, looking at Karen. 'But that's OK. There's other stuff on the menu that'll suit us all.'

Karen hadn't said a word. That was disconcerting, like dry rain or the sun rising in the west. 'I like how you've done your hair,' he said.

'It's horrible,' Karen replied. 'I hate it.'

Which confirmed she was who she appeared to be better than any retina scan could ever manage. 'I missed you,' Chris said.

'I'm not back,' she said quickly. 'I'm just here.'

'That'll do,' he replied. 'Like I told Jill, this is business.'

(He'd forgotten the elegant curve of Karen's neck, the length of her hands and fingers, the exquisite ratio of mouth to chin. Correction: you can't forget what you never really noticed before. Who was it, he tried to recall, who said that the best place to hide something is in plain sight?)

'Right,' Chris said, 'let's make a move.'

What could be more natural, he thought as they filed out into the street, what could be more pleasantly normal than this: three old school friends going out for a meal? Well, four, if you counted the demon.

'I never liked this place,' Karen said. 'We came here once and the food took half an hour to arrive and then it was cold, and I wanted to complain and you were afraid to make a scene.'

'Yes,' Chris said. 'But it's got to be here.'

'Why?'

'Something I read in a book.'

Karen wanted to argue, but Chris pretended he hadn't noticed. They crossed the road and he led the way in though the door, over which, on a basic plastic fascia board, was the name:

GANDHI
Indian Restaurant & Take Away

(Now he came to think of it, everything had been staring him in the face all along.)

'Hi,' he said cheerfully, as a waiter came up. 'Table for four – Popham.'

The waiter gave Chris a long look. 'Ah yes,' he said. 'We've been expecting you.'

On previous occasions when they'd gone there, Chris had wondered why it was that they had a back room, larger than the front area, filled with tables set out with tablecloths and cutlery, which they never used. He'd abandoned it as one of those mysteries that probably has a perfectly simple explanation, if only he could be bothered to find it out. Always a mistake, that.

'Have you really been keeping this room for us—?'

The waiter nodded. 'Sixteen years,' he said. 'But you're here now, so not to worry.'

They sat down; and immediately, all the other tables vanished and the door faded away into the wall, like a ridiculously fast-healing wound. The waiter smiled, handed them each a menu, and faded into a spinning column of smoke, which blew away in the gentle breeze from an electric fan.

'I think I'll start with an onion bhaji,' Chris said.

Karen and Jill weren't even looking at their menus. 'Chris,' Jill said, 'any particular reason why this table's set for four?'

He looked up and smiled. 'It's all right,' he said, to neither of them. 'You can come out now.'

And out the demon came.

It started as a faint grey wisp of vapour, rising from each of them like steam off wet clothes. As it rose, the three strands twisted together, weaving a shape that gradually became recognisable, then familiar. As it pulled a third of itself out of him, Chris felt a great surge of emotion deep inside: first anger, then panic, then the unbearable sorrow of parting and loss. Then there was a faint noise, a sort of pop, and the demon dropped out of the air into the chair that the waiter had pulled out for it. They all looked the same to Chris, needless to say, but it did remind him ever so much of what he'd seen in mirrors.

'Nice of you to join us,' Chris said.

Hard to tell, because of all the fangs and distorted features, but Chris fancied it was looking distinctly sheepish. 'Thanks,' it said.

'No worries. Now then,' Chris continued briskly, 'introductions. Jill, meet the one who is to come. Karen, this is the demon who's been stowing away inside all of our heads ever since that day in the girls' toilets at school.'

Jill jumped so violently that she knocked over a wineglass. '*All* of—'

So nice to be able to justify a really patronising grin. 'All of our heads, that's right. Actually, I honestly can't believe it took me so long to figure it out. So obvious, really. I'm right, aren't I?'

The demon nodded its grotesque potato-shaped head. 'We apologise,' it said, 'for any inconvenience.'

Chris poured himself a glass of water from the jug and was pleased to see how steady his hand was. 'Just to set my mind at rest,' he said. 'That day, in the toilet. You were inside Karen, right?'

The demon nodded. 'She was to be our host,' it said.

'Quite.' Chris nodded. 'And what about me?'

The demon broke eye contact. It might even have turned a slightly deeper shade of grey. 'Our larder,' it said.

Chris nodded again. 'Which is why – sorry about this, Karen, but I'm assuming you didn't know – which is why Karen fancied me, ever since we were both fifteen. That was the whole point of the exercise, wasn't it? Your grand plan for weaning demonkind off killing humans and preventing an all-out war between you and us.'

'Quite so. We could see no other way.'

'Just a minute,' Karen interrupted, and Chris recognised

the tone of voice as the first puff of smoke from the volcano. He held up his hand for silence and, amazingly, it worked.

'Again,' he said, 'it only goes to show how truly stupid I am, because I only just worked it out. Your lot need emotion to live. You figured that instead of killing us for it you'd be better off making us into a sustainable resource, milking us for your emotional needs. The main problem was how to get enough emotion out of your human host to live on, and how to do it so as not to wear us out or drive us crazy. You needed a way that we wouldn't notice or object to. Like the birds who pick the teeth of crocodiles. What's the word—?'

'Symbiotic,' Jill muttered.

'That's right, thanks. A symbiotic relationship; something in it for you, something in it for us. Now, which human emotion fits the bill perfectly? Anyone?'

Jill was frowning. Karen just looked stuffed. So: 'Love,' Chris said, 'of course. When you designed your human host – Karen – she was pre-programmed to love someone; as it turned out, me. Good choice; because, obviously, when a charmless, unprepossessing specimen like me finds out that a beautiful, intelligent girl like Karen fancies him, the last thing he's going to do is ask questions or mess about, he'll say yes please and thank you, and that'll be that. True love, happy ever after, and a lifetime supply of gourmet eating for you. Well thought out, and no harm to anyone, so long as Karen and me never learned the truth. Unfortunately,' he added, 'it didn't work out.'

The demon dipped its head. 'Alas,' it said.

'Because,' Chris went on, 'instead of falling head over heels for Karen like I was supposed to, I fell in love with Jill instead. Typical awkward human; and what made it ten times worse, Jill wasn't even a human being, she was a demon; a demon, what's more, who'd been sent here to arrest you and bring you back. Must've been a nasty blow for you. I'm sorry.'

'Not your fault,' the demon replied. 'Ours. Inadequate preliminary research, based on false assumptions and bad science. It is we who should apologise to you.'

'Yes,' said Chris. 'But anyway. There you were, pretty comprehensively screwed. And then you had a brainwave. And this,' he added, 'is where I start to get quietly angry with you, OK? Just so you're aware of it – it's only fair. You thought, what I need is something or someone to make the human fall in love with my carrier. Presumably you considered a love potion, something like the JWW love philtre—'

The demon shook its head. 'Poison to us,' it said. 'Highly toxic. May contain traces of nuts. Not a viable option.'

'I see, fine.' Chris shrugged. 'So instead, you called in a fey, because they're supposed to be able to get into humans' heads through their dreams and change all the settings. But you can't trust them, can you? Once they're across the line and in our reality, they're like kids with a bottle of whisky and the keys to their dad's car. As soon as she got here, your fey bolted; got inside the head of that other girl, Ellie, took her over, forgot all about what you wanted. Fat lot of good it did her, though, because along comes Jill, looking for you, sees the fey in Ellie's head, assumes it must be you, and the next thing anybody knows about it, there's blood on the toilet floor and everything's completely fucked. Well?'

The demon nodded sadly. 'Tragedy,' it said.

Maybe not the word Chris would have chosen. 'You were in a real fix,' he said. 'Jill was on the rampage; she'd made a mistake the first time and killed Ellie instead, but you knew she'd try again as soon as she realised her mistake; she'd almost certainly succeed the next time around, which'd mean you going back to your side of the line and getting beaten up by the authorities; also the failure of your great and noble experiment, before you'd had a chance to give it a fair go. So, on the spur of the moment, you improvised. You baled out of Karen, tore yourself in three, jumped straight into our heads and made yourself at home.' He sighed. 'And there you've been ever since. You converted Jill into a secret sympathiser, you made poor Karen here keep on loving me, even though – well, anyway. I don't know what you wanted me for, unless it was just as a backup. You know, in triplicate, like a parking-permit application. Or maybe you just wanted me for all the rotten bloody miserable emotions I've been feeling this past sixteen years. Really, I'm surprised you're not as fat as a pig by now.'

For a relatively long time – between ten and twelve seconds – nobody moved or spoke. Then Karen slowly pushed back her chair, stood up, grabbed the water jug and emptied it over the demon's head. Then she sat down again.

'I know,' she said. 'Empty gesture. But so what?'

The water, which had fallen through the demon as through a colander, was pooling on the floor under its chair; liable to give entirely the wrong impression, Chris couldn't help thinking, to someone coming unexpectedly into the room. The demon just looked faintly puzzled, as if wondering what the polite response would be.

'So why now?' Jill said. 'After sixteen years, why choose now to come back out again?'

The demon opened its mouth, but Chris got in first. 'Two things, I guess. One, your lot – sorry, you ex-lot, the authorities back home, sent another – what was the word you used? Avenger? – anyway, another one of them, to do the job that Jill should've done before she changed sides. That was my late lamented colleague Angela, who presumably is back in the office right now explaining to her boss why she cocked it up. The other reason, I imagine, was that the Fey who cheated you just happened to show up again, trapped in my SatNav, and she had the bright idea of making me go back in time and change history so that she never got separated from her hijacked body back in the girls' toilets.' He turned to the demon, who was looking surprisingly small and meek. 'Is that about the shape of it, more or less?'

'Precisely so,' the demon said, with a funny little bow. 'As you correctly deduced, the subject of our research was the human emotion that you call love. We had heard of it, but found it impossible to believe that such a thing could exist. Therefore we came here to prove it by controlled experiment.

We infiltrated the female human' (Karen pulled a truly horrible face, but stayed put) 'and used the good offices of the Fey you call SatNav to induce her to fall in love with a male human, chosen at random. To begin with, the results were most satisfactory. The female human's emotions, which we believe fell into the category of unrequited love, were highly nutritious and contained the full recommended daily intake of vitamins A, B, C, E and G2. However, we recognised that unrequited love cannot be expected to last any appreciable length of time, and we were disappointed and frankly surprised to find that the male human entirely failed to reciprocate the female's emotions, being already enamoured of the second female, the avenger. When the avenger detected our presence in the first female, we quickly enlisted the Fey to run interference, not anticipating the extent to which the avenger would be confused. Naturally, we regret the Fey's unfortunate fate. Our primary concern, however, was for our own safety and the future of the mission. As the male human has just explained, we subdivided and occupied all three of them – a manoeuvre, we might add, hitherto believed impossible, and we intend to write a paper on the subject as soon as we return to our own side. Since then, we have lived quite comfortably on the emotions of all three of you: the unrequited love of the male and our original female host, and the second-hand emotions collected so assiduously by the other female in her capacity as confidante and confessor to a close circle of friends. In passing, we note that we entirely underestimated the enduring power of unrequited love. In both cases, it lasted sixteen years; indeed, it might be said to have matured, with corresponding improvements in both nutritional qualities and flavour.'

The demon stopped talking, then beamed suddenly and licked its lips. 'Thank you,' it said. 'We greatly appreciate the waves of hatred and revulsion emanating from all three of you. After sixteen years of subsisting almost entirely on various forms of love, the change is both welcome and refreshing. And anger too,' it added, closing its eyes in pure bliss. 'Really, this is too much. We doubt whether our digestion can stand it.'

Me too, Chris thought. From his pocket he took a fold of kitchen towel, in which were wrapped six ice cubes. They'd hardly thawed at all since he'd pocketed them, shortly before Jill and Karen arrived. He tumbled them into a glass, topped it up with water from the jug and growled, 'Here, drink this.'

The demon frowned, sniffed the glass, grinned broadly and gulped, swallowing the ice cubes whole. 'Thank you,' it croaked, as first steam and then smoke began to stream out of its ears and nose. 'We believe we are indeed ready to go home. Our researches are complete. Once again, we apologise for any—'

Then it burst into flame. For about five seconds, it burned keenly with a clear green flame, and then there was nothing, not even a sprinkle of ash.

There was a long silence. Then Karen said, 'I don't know about you two, but I'm starving. Pass me that menu, will you?'

Something in her tone of voice; Chris fished the sunglasses out of his pocket and put them on.

Human. A hundred per cent.

Still, he had to ask.

'Karen,' he said.

'Mmm?' She didn't look up from the menu.

'The hummingbird. Was that—?'

Still without taking her face out of the menu, Karen brushed her hair back over her ear, to reveal the hummingbird earrings. 'They're magic,' she said, 'belonged to my aunt Jessica. I tell them what to do, and they do it.' She shook her head a little; one earring detached itself, flew across the room and came back with a wine list clutched in its tiny beak. 'Years ago, when we first got together, I told them to look after you, if you got into trouble and I wasn't there. Bit of a nuisance lately – it means I've been going round half the time with only one ear-ring.'

'I see,' Chris said. 'Thanks.'

''Salright.'

'Fine,' Jill said, and there was a brittle quality to her voice that put Chris on notice that something was about to happen. 'Well, apparently that's that sorted. Well done, Chris. I don't know, it's been staring me in the face all these years – literally, for crying out loud – and I never saw it. About time I packed in this undercover stuff. Never was my cup of tea.'

Of course, it could mean she was considering leaving her job with the department, but he didn't think so. 'You're going back,' he said.

Jill looked at him, straight in the eye. 'I think so,' she said. 'I came here to do a job and I screwed that up. In fact, I screwed it up so badly that I allowed myself to get taken over by the enemy. Worse still, even now it's cleared off out of my head I still feel the same way.' She shook her head sadly. 'Sort of puts me in my place, doesn't it? What's it called – Stockholm syndrome, is it, where after a bit the hostage starts agreeing with the kidnapper? Never knew it could affect demons, but there you are, learn something new every day. Anyhow, as far as I can tell, things really have changed back home. In fact, I wouldn't be surprised if that pompous little turd gets elected president. In which case,' she added, with a sad smile, 'it owes me, and I intend to collect. I think I'll insist on being Head of Security. We may be no great shakes at love, but we do have a finely developed sense of irony.'

'You're going,' Chris repeated.

'Yes. Besides,' Jill added, reaching for the glass that the demon had drunk from, which still held about half an inch of liquid, 'there are times when three's a crowd, and I think this is one of them.' She sniffed, then licked her lips and spat elegantly into a napkin. 'That's one taste I won't miss,' she said. 'If the grand design's ever going to work, we're going to have to do something about the way the stuff tastes.' She drained the glass and grinned at them. 'So long,' she said. 'I'd like to say how much I've enjoyed being your friends,' she went on, as the steam turned quickly into smoke, 'but unfortunately I have too much regard for the truth. Try not to mangle each other too much. Bye.'

Then the flames took her, and she vanished.

Karen and Chris looked at each other for a long time. Then Karen said, 'I think I'll go for the chicken korma, with pilau rice and some of that runny lentil stuff. What about you?'

'Hang on,' Chris replied, and he opened his menu, and folded inside it he found a copy of *The Book of All Human Knowledge*, guaranteed to tell you what you really need to know or your money back; and since JWW Retail were really, really unhappy with the concept of refunds, he was pretty sure he could trust it, now, when it mattered. He opened it at random, and read:

Yes.
*(Obviously, not as much as she did while she was under the influence of the **glamour** placed on her by the **Fey**, but there's still something there, quite definitely, should you wish to pursue it. And if not, you're a bigger **fool** than you look.)*

Chris closed the book and the menu, put them down on the table and reached out his hand. 'I'll have the same,' he said. 'And a chapati.'